DAVID WHALE

OCTOSQUID

www.WhaleWriter.com

Book Layout © 2017 BookDesignTemplates.com

Out of the Black / David Whale. -- 1st ed.
ISBN 978-0-9958100-3-7

Also by David Whale:

Radko's War

For Crazy:

What I said the first time around is still true: I couldn't have done this without your support.

For Allie:

This book is proof that if you put in the time and the effort, you can achieve your dreams. Never forget that.

He who fights with monsters should look to it that he himself does not become a monster. And if you gaze long into an abyss, the abyss also gazes into you.

- Friedrich Wilhelm Nietzsche

A lot could happen in eighteen months. A year and a half. About five hundred and forty days.

Staring at himself in the bathroom mirror, Finn Radko sighed.

A lot could happen, but very little actually had happened – at least, very little that would move the Commonwealth toward its ultimate goal of liberating Earth from the ril-galas occupation. They still held Thor's Hammer, the space station which had become the base of operations for the fight against the invaders. While the Commonwealth had also reclaimed a handful of colonies and installations, no attempt had been made to launch any kind of large-scale assault on the ril-galas defences surrounding humanity's birthplace. The so-called "Hornet's Nest" -- the fortified deployment station in Earth orbit -- remained untouched and unchallenged.

Splashing some cool water onto his face, Radko simply stood for a moment, head hung low over the sink, letting the droplets roll down his skin and drop into the stainless steel bowl. After a moment of stillness, he reached out for a towel, wiping away the remaining dampness before hanging the towel once more and scowling at his reflection.

He looked tired.

He had two days' worth of stubble.

Too many late nights, too many meetings. Too many plans and too many angles to consider. Sooner or later, he knew, it was all going to catch up to him and he was going to crash.

Flexing his fingers twice, Radko slowly did up each of the six brass buttons on his crimson uniform jacket.

Briefly, the scowl turned to an almost-smile.

When he did finally crash, he was going to make damn sure he'd sown some chaos in his wake -- chaos for the ril-galas invaders and, as his father would have said, "God willin' and the creek don't rise," a wake-up call to humanity.

Chuckling to himself, Radko headed into the main part of his quarters.

Had Radko set up quarters on Thor's Hammer, like many senior officers in the Commonwealth Navy, he would have lived in much greater comfort and with much more personal space. Several people had tried to convince him that he should do so, that a senior officer should be seen to be living at a higher level – literally and figuratively – than the general masses, but Radko had, with increasingly lower levels of politeness, refused the offers. To begin with, the fact that they would all include him in the category of senior Commonwealth Naval officer just served to illustrate how desperate their situation had become. When the ril-galas invasion had hit, he'd been a Lieutenant Commander and had served as the executive officer of the HMCS Vimy Ridge for less than a year. Though he'd been promoted to full Commander immediately after spearheading the liberation of Thor's Hammer, he would never have been called senior in the days before the ril-galas. In the days before the world ended. And while that reason alone would have been enough for him to refuse, Radko was also uncomfortable living off-ship for more practical reasons: living on-ship, in an emergency he could be on the command deck of the Vimy Ridge in thirty seconds. The airlocks on the docking pylons alone took twenty seconds to complete their cycle, and above that there was the time it would take him to traverse the station itself. If the ril-galas decided to launch an assault on Thor's Hammer...

Radko carried enough guilt about his various decisions without adding the possibility of more deaths due to his decision to sleep in a softer bed.

A knock at the door derailed his train of thought – a train carrying precious little cargo, he could admit – and tapping the door controls, he forced a smile as Anna Cortez stepped into the room carrying a simple manila folder.

"Anna."

"Morning, Finn."

Like most of the Vimy Ridge crew, Cortez had grown older since the destruction of Echo Station. Radko himself was starting to see little streaks of grey at his temples and though Cortez had only just turned twenty-one, she bore the weight of her experiences as much as he.

"Are you ready?" she said.

He chuckled without a hint of humour.

"Yeah, not really," he said, then paused for a moment. "How are you feeling?"

"I'm good."

Radko didn't believe her and evidently, it showed in his face. With a smile, Cortez reached out and gave him a big hug.

"Really, Finn, I'm good. The new meds are easier on me than the last – I'm not having any problems eating now."

"Okay," said Radko, sounding anything but okay. "Anything I should be aware of before I walk into this thing?"

Releasing him from the embrace, Cortez flipped open the folder. It was stamped with the crest of Commonwealth Naval

Intelligence. Once upon a time, it had been Radko's area of specialization – one of several reasons why a nineteen year old Cadet named Cortez had been assigned as his assistant during her field placement. But now, as the official Intel liason between all branches of the Commonwealth Armed Forces, Cortez was far exceeding what anyone had expected of her.

Radko was absurdly proud of her for it and made sure she knew.

Once upon a time, he'd been the kind of person who would keep a lot of what he was feeling tucked away, but he'd left that kind of approach behind. He'd left it back in the debris field that was once Echo Station, back where he'd left any expectation that he would ever again have anything resembling a normal life.

"Well," said Cortez, flipping through some pages. "We've confirmed that Mahoney will be there this time, so that's probably a good thing? Unfortunately, Bianca Upshaw will also be attending."

Radko swore under his breath as the pair exited his quarters and began heading through the corridors of the Vimy Ridge toward the airlock.

Upshaw. Ever since the ril-galas took Earth, the Commonwealth's reliance upon ATC Castle had been increasing exponentially and, much to the displeasure of many, their political influence had grown proportionally. And it had done so in the person of Bianca Upshaw, former director of training with the private contractor, but now acting as their primary representative in all dealings with the Commonwealth.

To say she was not a fan of Finn Radko would be an understatement.

"This could be interesting."

"When is it not?" said Cortez.

2

In the years before the ril-galas, New Madawaska had been considered a backwater, a small, resource-based colony that had
been populated by the same dozen family groups for genera-
tions. It was the butt of so many jokes that the term
"Madawaskan Cousin-Fucker" was regularly employed due to
its universality by drill sergeants in the Commonwealth Army.

However, the resource upon which the tiny colony was
based was food. Food crops and livestock. Before the ril-galas,
the colony's production had paled in comparison to that of St.
Andrew's Landing and Flamborough, but Flamborough was
now behind enemy lines and St. Andrew's Landing was nothing
more than a smoldering ruin.

As fate would have it, the cousin-fuckers had become one of
the most strategically important colonies in what was left of the
Commonwealth.

And so Regimental Sergeant-Major Freyja Sigurdsson of the
Royal Vaxjo Light Infantry found herself engaging a group of ril-
galas foot soldiers in a cornfield, within sight of a one-hundred-
strong herd of bison. And a chicken occasionally darting in and
out of the cornstalks around her feet.

"How much further?" she said, neither lowering her 33A1 assault rifle, nor wavering in her straight-ahead gaze. At her side,
the German Shepherd named Jaeger slowed his pace slightly,
but kept his ears perked and his head low in a stalking stance.
The two had been inseparable since Von Daniken's Landing.

"Fifteen metres," said Tangaroa, after a quick consultation with his wrist-mounted tracker.

"Moving?"

"Negative."

Sigurdsson swore and lowered her rifle slightly, a grinding whirr coming from both mechanical arms as she did so. The pinkie finger on her left hand began to twitch.

"Shit."

"You okay, Sarge?"

"I'm fine," she said, raising her rifle again. A popping noise accompanied the movement, but she wasn't sure where from.

Of course, she wasn't fine, not by a long shot. After her arms had been severed – by a physician and out of necessity – they'd been replaced by cybernetic limbs. The cybernetics lab connected to the medical facilities on Erindale Station were second to none – they had the most skilled physicians and technicians, the most advanced prosthetics, everything one could possibly need to get back up to one hundred percent. In fact, it had been on Erindale Station that Sigurdsson had had her right eye replaced with a multi-function piece of cybernetics several years prior.

Erindale Station was the perfect spot for her to land after losing both arms in the climactic battle on Von Daniken's Landing.

Unfortunately, Erindale had been turned into an orbital slag heap by the ril galas long before Sigurdsson had lost her arms.

Smelling smoke, Sigurdsson couldn't tell whether it was coming from somewhere up ahead or coming from one or both of her cut-rate cyborg arms. The fight on New Madawaska had gone on longer than expected and the new arms had proven to be significantly less durable than Sigurdsson had been promised.

Shoving the thought aside, she pressed on, slowly pushing her way through the dying stalks of corn, doing her best to be silent as Tangaroa maintained his position behind her. The rest of their team had already been at the rendezvous site of Fort Deering several kilometres to the south when word came in that their commanding officer, Major Benjamin Ingram, was missing. Thankfully, he'd been carrying a tracking device like Tangaroa's and so they could pinpoint his location with reasonable accuracy.

Suddenly, Jaeger stopped, a short, low growl rumbling in his throat. Sigurdsson quickly held up a closed fist signalling Tangaroa to stop. He did, even before seeing Sigurdsson's signal. They had both learned to trust Jaeger's instincts.

A further signal showed that Sigurdsson would move forward on her own to check things out. She could see, as she moved forward, that a sort of cleaning opened up ahead, though it was less an actual clearing and more a section of the cornfield that had been trampled enough to have a certain range of visibility. And at the centre lay Major Ingram, face-down in the broken stalks.

"I need cover," she said, the collar-mounted comm microphone automatically piping it through to Tangaroa's earpiece.

There was a soft rustle behind her.

"Go."

One of the things she really liked about working with Tangaroa was the total lack of any unnecessary communication.

Slinging her rifle over her shoulder, she dropped down on one knee beside Ingram and gently rolled him over onto his back.

"Goddammit."

The lower half of his face and part of his upper chest were missing.

"Bait," said Tangaroa.

Sigurdsson nodded and stood, but as she was unslinging her rifle, something large burst from the cornstalks to her left. Too close to use her rifle, she simply lashed out with her left arm, catching the ril-galas soldier heavily in its manta-shaped head with her forearm. Sigurdsson felt nothing, but the ril-galas reeled and a piece of Sigurdsson's arm broke off, exposing the wires and hydraulics beneath. A jet of liquid squirted from somewhere around her elbow as Tangaroa double-tapped the ril-galas soldier in the chest.

"Go, go, go!" she yelled as she raised her own rifle and began scanning the stalks for other enemies. She could hear them moving around, but none were visible. Firing random shots into the stalks, Sigurdsson had to simply rest the barrel of her rifle on the wrist of her left arm – evidently, the impact had damaged the arm to the point that only her thumb was still functional. "This is Sigurdsson to all ground units. Major Ingram is KIA. We are returning to base camp with hostiles in pursuit – repeat, *hostiles in pursuit.*"

"This is Hartwood," came the crackling reply. "We're setting up snipers for support – lead them in, Sir, we'll take care of it."

Rather than responding, Sigurdsson and Tangaroa fired a final barrage into the cornstalks then turned and ran, Jaeger leading the way. They could all hear the crashing of the enemy in pursuit, but none looked back.

Jaeger was the first out of the cornfield, taking off like a rocket over the open swath of grassland that separated the cornfield from the walls of Fort Deering. Tangaroa and Sigurdsson came next and immediately after them, a trio of ril-galas soldiers.

Moments were all it took. The booming of the ril-galas canons, dirt and plant matter exploding all around. Spitting out a mouthful of soil, Sigurdsson didn't dare look back. And then the sharpshooters from the walls of Fort Deering engaged. The comforting pop of their rifles brought hope, and with each pop, the barrage from behind lessened.

As soon as Sigurdsson and her group were inside the walls of the fort and the doors had closed and been secured behind them, a medic ran up to Sigurdsson.

"Sergeant, I can-."

"Later," she said, pushing him aside and making a direct line to the communications bunker. Her left arm hanging limply at her side, still leaking what she assumed was hydraulic fluid, she used her good hand to activate the connection to the Commonwealth Navy carrier in orbit. "Captain Himura, this is RSM Sigurdsson, do you copy."

"Yes, Regimental Sergeant-Major. Go ahead."

"Your bombers are clear to start their run, Sir."

"Understood. Good work, RSM Sigurdson."

"Thank you, Sir."

Closing the connection, Sigurdsson left the bunker and, like many of the soldiers in Fort Deering, headed to the top of the walls to watch dozens of Commonwealth bombs fall on the one ril-galas outpost on New Madawaska that the Army had been unable to crack.

"After many setbacks, I'm pleased to say that the HMCS Royal Sovereign is ready for launch," said Rear Admiral Philip Mahoney, leaning back in his chair with a satisfied smile.

Watching the man – the man now in charge of the entire Commonwealth Navy – Radko bit his tongue. The Royal Sovereign, the largest and most complex warship ever built by human hands, had become something of a legend since it was first rumoured to be in development at Cagliari Aerospace, but its legendary status had become something of a joke lately. Mahoney had in three previous meetings announced the ship's readiness for launch only to have to backtrack on that statement when the ATC Castle engineering teams ran into yet another snag. Blame was frequently placed at the feet of the Cagliari designers by Upshaw and her people, but rumours had been swirling for months that it was more a case of the ATC Castle staff having trouble following and integrating the advanced concepts put forth by the late Anton Cagliari and his design team.

"We are preparing her for a shakedown cruise as we speak," continued the Admiral. "And barring any last-minute adjustments required by said shakedown cruise, the Royal Sovereign will be entered into active service within the month."

"Good to hear," said Prime Minister Rocco deFreitas, slapping his palm on the table. "Damn good to hear – we could certainly use another ship on the front line."

And again, Radko bit his tongue and took a sip of water while very deliberately not meeting the glance thrown his way by another member of this haphazard advisory committee thrown together by deFreitas. For months, Radko had been beating the same drum, arguing to increase both offensive and defensive strength by forging formal alliances with the Soviets and the icarans, and all to no avail. Despite the informal alliance between Radko, Kovalenko and Locaris that had enabled them to strike back at the ril-galas, nothing had been formalized. The Commonwealth government had declined the assistance of the icarans – who had returned to their homeworld to protect their own people – and the old animosities of the Commonwealth/Soviet dynamic had proven too great to overcome for many, despite the threat of extinction facing the human race. The Soviets who were present on Thor's Hammer kept to the "Soviet Block" and none were ever invited to be involved in the Prime Minister's planning sessions.

The thought process that led them to this point was a mystery to Radko, but he supposed that was simply the effect of his thinking tactically rather than thinking politically. Many in the Commonwealth trusted neither the Soviets nor the icarans. DeFreitas was still concerned about public opinion.

"Adding the Soviet fleet to ours would help our front line as well," said Nasrin Khaifa. "Has that option been explored further?"

Radko coughed into his water.

Though *his* name was relatively well-known, Khaifa was quite possibly the most famous human in the universe given the wide distribution of her ril-galas autopsy video. She had also been named Director of the Ministry of Health a matter of weeks after her return from Von Daniken's Landing.

"Miss Khaifa-."

"*Doctor* Khaifa."

"Doctor Khaifa," said Mahoney. "Given our history with the Soviets, an alliance with them would be fruitless. We simply cannot trust them. I realise that your experience on Von Daniken's Landing has deeply affected you. Believe me, I, as anyone fighting the front lines of this war, fully understand. But we cannot grasp at straws to be victorious, and an alliance with the Soviets would be just that – grasping at straws. I believe even your friend Commander Radko would agree with that statement."

Radko sat up straighter, opened his mouth to reply then closed it again. Learning to be more restrained with his commentary was more alien to him than the icarans, but he would try...

"I beg your pardon?" he said.

"We are all on the front lines of this war, Commander," said deFreitas. "And just because we have a new threat to face doesn't mean old threats simply go away."

He waved his hands as he said it, like he was swatting away a cloud of mosquitos.

"I understand that there are deep ideological rifts between us and the Soviets," said Khaifa, with a level of diplomacy Radko knew he'd never achieve. "But I still feel that holding to old ideologies, in our current situation, is dangerous. They could help us. We could help each other."

The Prime Minister offered the doctor one of the most condescending smiles Radko had ever seen, but it was Mahoney -- perhaps seeing how the discussion was developing -- who spoke.

"We appreciate your input, Doctor, but these... are difficult situations. Difficult times, of course. Those of us fighting on the front lines, how can we focus on the war if we're not certain whether we can trust those at our side?"

Closing his eyes, Radko tried to concentrate on his breathing, tried to find his inner calm.

"Are you fucking kidding me?" he said.

Everyone sat up straighter and all eyes turned to the Commander.

"Commander Radko, do you have something to add?" said the Prime Minister.

"Yes, I do. I absolutely do. First off, stop talking down to the doctor like she's a ten year old. You have no idea what she faced on Von Daniken's Landing any more than you have any idea what I've faced with the Vimy Ridge out on the front lines, because *you are not on the front lines.* You have never left this station, Admiral. Not once since the Vimy Ridge – in an alliance with the Soviets and the icarans, I might add – broke the ril-galas blockade have you *ever* left Thor's Hammer," said Radko, amazing even himself with his even, matter-of-fact tone.

"Commander Radko, I would remind you that you are only part of this meeting as a courtesy, given your past service to the Commonwealth," said Mahoney.

"And this will be my last time attending, Admiral, because I'm tired of listening to all of you talk in circles, accomplish nothing and plan nothing but more meetings, then pat yourselves on the back for it and act like you're saving mankind."

"Commander-."

"I'm not done yet, Admiral," he said sharply, looking at Mahoney, Upshaw and deFreitas in turn. "You want to save mankind? Pull your collective heads out of your asses and realize that we can't do it alone. We cannot do this alone. Even the

Soviets know this. They're willing to talk, but apparently I'm the only one listening."

DeFreitas glared at Radko.

"Are you saying, Commander, that you are currently in contact with an enemy of the Commonwealth?"

"Really? That whole speech and *that's* what you take out of it?"

"I think what the Commander is trying to say," said Khaifa, leaning forward, elbows on the conference table. "Is that we shouldn't completely discount the possibility. If, heaven forbid, we were to lose one of our warships, we have neither the resources nor the personnel to build new ones. I think we can all agree that the continued delays on the Royal Sovereign taught us that lesson very clearly. An alliance – whether the Soviets or the icarans or anyone else – would strengthen our capabilities immensely."

Back in the beginning, Radko himself would have worded the argument in that manner, more as a possibility to consider than something that absolutely had to be done. But that was then. A lot could happen in eighteen months. A year and a half. About five hundred and fifty days.

"It simply is not a course of action this government is comfortable exploring," said deFreitas.

A lot could happen, or nothing could happen. And Radko had run out of patience with people who could not see the bigger picture. Without another word, he stood and exited the room.

"Well that was certainly overdramatic," said Bianca Upshaw, turning to the Prime Minister. "I believe I warned you about including him in these meetings. He's a loose cannon."

"But he knows what he's doing," said Mahoney, almost choking on the words. "I don't like him, but if I had to hand-pick someone to lead our fleet into battle..."

"Then your fleet would be destroyed. He's an idealist, not a realist. He doesn't understand that sometimes you have to make strategic decisions, that you have to think with your head, not just bluster in leading with your heart."

"You must be thinking of someone else," said Cortez, speaking up for the first time in the meeting. "Because Finn Radko made the decision to save you guys from a ril-galas blockade rather than launch an assault on the ril-galas force occupying Earth. He felt that was the best *strategic decision*. It meant that probably millions of humans would die on Earth, but that it would give us our best chance at saving millions more. And so far, none of you have given him any reason to believe he made the right call."

And she stood and followed Radko's lead, leaving the room.

After several moments of silence, Khaifa spoke up.

"The sad truth is that they're right."

"When the Royal Sovereign launches, we will make progress," said Mahoney, tapping his index finger on the table. "We will make progress."

It sounded as if he were trying to convince himself as much as anyone else.

"I will talk to Radko," said Khaifa. "Try to smooth things over."

"What's the point?" said Upshaw. "Prime Minister, I'd like to once again table my suggestion that we relieve Radko of command and place the Vimy Ridge under the command of-."

"We are not putting a Commonwealth Navy vessel under the command of a deserter," said Mahoney.

"Edward Vossek is not-."

"Edward Vossek was a sergeant in the Commonwealth Army who quit in the middle of the greatest crisis to hit mankind for a higher paycheque with ATC Castle and is in no way qualified to command a space ship. Full stop," said the Admiral. "Radko is... unpleasant. Most times I speak with him, I'd like to wring his neck, but anyone who tries to take him off the command deck of the Vimy Ridge will have to go through me first."

"I will talk to him" Khaifa said again. "I'll talk to him."

4

The trip back to Thor's Hammer from New Madawaska had been mercifully short and Sigurdsson, her useless left arm held against her body in a makeshift sling, had spent the entire trip pacing the cargo hold – converted into barracks – aboard their troop transport, the HMS Battersea Park. Though Sigurdsson was glad to be back aboard the massive space station, she was not pleased with the wait list to see one of the handful of doctors aboard Thor's Hammer with any expertise in cybernetics. She was even less pleased with the way the consultation had gone when she'd finally been called.

"These are industrial prosthetics," the elderly doctor had said with a resigned sigh.

The scuttlebutt around the station was that he'd retired several years ago, but come out of retirement to help after the rilgalas had shown up. Sigurdsson had to respect a man who would do something like that in his late seventies – maybe even early eighties – but that didn't mean she had to like what he had to say.

"They were designed as limb replacements for factory workers, mill personnel, miners – industrial applications, you see, not military," he said. "While these cybernetics are certainly hardier than civilian-grade replacement limbs, they are a far cry from military-grade."

The question of why she wasn't given military grade prosthetics was on the tip of Sigurdsson's tongue, but she already knew the answer. Erindale Station.

"So, what do we do? Where do we go from here?" she asked instead.

"I can authorize repairs on both limbs to allow you to at least be functional for the time being. I can also requisition another set of prosthetics and, once they arrive, we can perform another replacement surgery."

"Shit. Fine," she said. That would be her second replacement set. Sooner or later, the Commonwealth Armed Forces were going to decide it was more cost-effective to bring in someone new to fill her role than to keep paying for new arms for Freyja Sigurdsson. "How long?"

"We have a waiting list," he said, with the way he said it implying an apology. "I would expect thirty days as our best-case scenario."

Sigurdsson closed her eyes.

"And I can't be cleared for active duty," she said, holding up her one functional hand. "Until I get these replaced."

The doctor nodded and Sigurdsson swore.

"Thanks, Doc. Just... just let me know if that timeline changes. Okay?"

Without waiting for an acknowledgement, Sigurdsson left the medical centre and began wandering more or less aimlessly through the station. Passing areas designed for military purposes that had been repurposed into shopping areas by the civilians, passing the guarded doors that lead to the Soviet Block, she unsurprisingly found herself standing outside the doors of The Pub. Despite its owner's lack of creativity in the naming department, The Pub had become a favourite haunt of many off-duty members of the military, officer and non-com alike. Its design allowed for plenty of social interaction for those who wanted it, but also a number of secluded booths for those who didn't.

As she entered the bar, Sigurdsson headed directly to a booth, sliding into the far side where she was least likely to be noticed by the other patrons. Tapping the call button for the waitress, she ordered a bottle of the terrible whiskey they distilled somewhere in the stations bowels.

"Here you are," said the waitress as she returned, setting the bottle and a passably clean metal cup on the table. "Enjoy."

"Could you pour? Please?"

Shrugging, the waitress poured some whiskey into the cup before heading off again to serve another table.

Sigurdsson was staring into the bottom of her empty cup when she felt a pair of eyes on her and looked up with a scowl. And then smiled.

"Heard a rumour you were back on-station," said Radko, sliding in across from her.

"Only been back a few hours."

They both just smiled at each other for a few moments. Though Sigurdsson looked tired – understandably so – Radko was glad to see her. It had been too long. The hair on the sides of her head was starting to grow back, but she'd no doubt shave it again when she had the chance. It was an affectation all the survivours of the Von Daniken's Landing garrison had taken on after their exfiltration, shaving the side of their heads. Radko didn't know the specific significance of it and he had never asked. Some things were meant to be for a select group of people and if Sigurdsson ever felt like he should know, he was sure she'd tell him.

"New Madawaska was a success," he said. "Though it looks like you took a bit of a beating."

Sigurdsson snorted.

"Yeah. I'm on medical leave."

With a sigh, Radko nodded.

"Heard that too."

After glancing around unsuccessfully for the waitress, he stepped out of the booth and grabbed an empty glass from a nearby table that had yet to be cleared. Sniffing it, he shrugged, sat back in the booth and poured himself some whiskey.

"Didn't you say this stuff was the shittiest whiskey you've ever had?" said Sigurdsson, the ghost of a grin twitching the corners of her mouth.

"Yeah, but it's what's here right now."

"Can I get a refill, too?" asked Sigurdsson, pushing her metal cup forward.

As Radko complied, Sigurdsson shifted in her seat a little uncomfortably.

"Also," she said. "Can I ask you... what might be kind of a weird favour?"

"Okay," he said after a moment's hesitation.

"Can you... can you rub my eyes?"

"Your eyes...?"

Holding up her right hand, she waggled her fingers.

"These things. They're in such a fucked up state right now that I'm not sure I can even hold a bottle without shattering it. My eyes have been bugging the hell out of me, but I don't want to end up accidentally crushing them. So..."

Radko chuckled.

"Sure. Lean forward."

As she did, he reached out, placing his fingertips on either side of Sigurdsson's head and gently placing his thumbs over her closed eyelids. He wasn't sure how much pressure to apply, since it was hard to judge how hard to press into someone else's eyeballs – which in itself was not something he ever thought he'd have to take into consideration -- but he began rubbing in a circular motion.

"Harder."

He complied, increasing pressure.

"That's great. Thank you."

"No problem," he said as they both sat back in their benches.

"Jesus. You have no idea how good that felt," she said.

Sigurdsson held up her cup and Radko held up his glass and they both downed their drinks.

There was silence as he poured them each another, but then Sigurdsson cleared her throat lightly.

"How's Cortez?"

"She's okay," said Radko, swirling the liquid in his glass. "Good days and bad days, but mostly good right now. At least, that what she keeps telling me."

Sigurdsson nodded and sipped her drink. Radko knew that *she* knew the subject of Anna's health was a difficult one for him and he appreciated that she didn't press for more details. The fact was that regardless of what Cortez was telling him, she was still facing a terminal diagnosis. Exposure to the radiation within the Ishtar Gate – the gas cloud within which Radko had ordered the Vimy Ridge concealed while they planned their attack on the ril galas blockade – had exacerbated a previously undiagnosed brain tumour. By the time it had been discovered, it had been deemed inoperable.

Just one more death he could chalk up to his decisions. But unlike the people still dying on Earth, this death he was watching happen, bit by bit, every day.

"I know what you're thinking," said Sigurdsson. "And you need to stop it."

"Not sure what you mean."

She scowled at him.

"Fuck off. You know exactly what I mean."

She waved her cup around in the general direction of the ever-increasing number of patron in The Pub.

"These people? Most of them have no idea. About any of it. They don't know what it was like fighting in those first days of the invasion," she said. "Fighting an enemy you knew not one goddamned thing about. Fighting and watching people die all around you – people you didn't know, people you'd known for years. Friends, colleagues, strangers, even people you didn't like. Soviets, Commonwealth, icarans – I watched an icaran's fucking face melt off – they all died. We didn't. We survived. And no matter what we may say to ourselves when we look in the mirror – don't give me that look Radko, I know you do it, too."

He stayed silent but nodded.

"Just because we survived doesn't mean it's our fault that they didn't."

"I'm sorry to interrupt."

They both looked up, surprised to see Khaifa standing beside their booth.

"Doctor Khaifa," said Radko.

"Doesn't really seem like your kind of place, Nasrin," said Sigurdsson. "I take it this is business."

"Yes. Yes, it is," she said, glancing quickly at Sigurdsson, then back to Radko. "Commander, may we speak... privately?"

"No."

"Umm..."

"I'm sorry Doctor, I'm really not trying to be rude, but I've had my fill of politics for the day."

"Believe me, I understand that feeling more than you know," she said, running a hand through her hair. "But I really do need to speak with you."

"So have a seat," said Sigurdsson.

The Doctor hesitated for a moment, then slid into the booth next to Radko. He knew from past discussions that while Sigurdsson held no animosity toward Khaifa for the doctor's amputation of her arms, Doctor Khaifa had been uncomfortable around Sigurdsson ever since.

"First off," she said. "I agree with most of what you said in the conference room, just as I've agreed with you all along. But I can't fight these boardroom battles on my own. We both know that this advisory committee the Prime Minister has assembled is mostly for show. I may be Director of the Ministry of Health, but I don't have any *real* power in there, other than what support I can give someone who actually does have some sway."

"And you think that's me?"

"You're Finn Radko," said Sigurdsson, shrugging. "Like it or not, you're the guy people will listen to."

"More than that," added Khaifa. "You're someone – the only one in that room, honestly – who has actually accomplished anything in this war. Like it or not, this has very much been your war from the start – you were there as it began and you fought your way through it to this place. Without you, we'd all be dead right now."

"I wouldn't go that far. If I hadn't done it, someone else-."

"That's irrelevant," said Khaifa. "No one else *did*. You did. When something needs to be accomplished, you do it."

She paused, fidgeting with the bracelet she wore.

"Even if... the means of doing so are not entirely legal."

Radko exchanged a look with Sigurdsson before he spoke.

"Doctor..."

"Just... I've been in contact with someone. This individual has... let's say *resources* that could help our cause."

"But?"

"But we can't access them right now due to certain political roadblocks," she said, then met Radko's gaze for the first time. "So I need the help of someone who doesn't care about political roadblocks."

"I don't know what you're asking of me, Doctor."

"For now, all I'm asking is that you meet my contact. Speak with them. That's it. Hear their story straight from them and then decide what – if anything – you want to do about it."

Silence prevailed for a moment as Radko stared at his glass, knowing both the doctor and Sigurdsson were watching him. The Commonwealth, or what remained of the Commonwealth, was struggling to bring assets to the war. It wasn't any great secret that the military was stretched thin, and that was the primary reason for the newly and uncomfortably close relationship between the government and a private military contractor like ATC Castle. That Khaifa was coming to him directly rather than through the official channels of the Commonwealth Navy was a tell, and a very clear one: whoever her contact was and whatever they had to offer, getting their assets into play was going to be neither easy nor was it likely to be strictly legal.

Looking Khaifa in the eye, Radko nodded once.

She thanked him, then turned her attention to Sigurdsson.

"I heard that New Madawaska has been secured?"

"Yeah. Took us a while, but we got it locked down. Probably still a few hostiles running around, but the clean-up crew will deal with them."

"I'm surprised you're not in the cybernetics lab right now," said Khafia, nodding toward the damaged arm.

"Yeah," said Sigurdsson, then went on to explain about the wait list for replacement limbs. "And even when I do finally get them, there's no guarantee the same fucking thing won't happen to the new ones."

A long silence followed, during which it appeared to Radko that Khaifa was engaged in some kind of internal debate.

"Do you remember the brill doctor? From Von Daniken's Landing?" she said finally.

"He's kind of hard to forget," said Sigurdsson.

Khaifa nodded and pulled a small writing pad and pen from her jacket pocket.

"Go speak with him," she said, jotting down an address in the lower decks of Thor's Hammer, tearing off the page and, folding it in half, sliding it across the table to Sigurdsson. "He has some experience with... alternative medicine."

Sigurdsson took the paper, but looked skeptical.

"How exactly is medicine going to repair damaged cybernetics?"

"The brill have been advancing medical science since before humans had our first off-planet colony. Just trust me," she said as she slid out of the booth. "Radko, I'll set up that meeting. Today, if possible. I'll let you know."

She said hasty goodbyes then disappeared into the crowd.

"What do you make of all that?"

"I've known Nasrin for a while," said Sigurdsson. "If she's doing this kind of secret meeting, cloak and dagger bullshit? She must really believe it will make a difference."

5

Dusk was settling in over the United Kingdom and for the first time in a very long time, the city of Edinburgh was quiet. Fires still burned in the rubble, casting their eerie glow on the smoke-blackened facades of the few buildings that remained standing, but it was quiet.

And with the quiet came the implied threat of what may come next.

From her vantage point on the Half-Moon Battery, the woman looked beyond the gates of Edinburgh Castle and down the Esplanade and its rows of wooden stakes, a severed ril-galas head mounted on each. A message to the occupying force that Edinburgh Castle remained free.

"How long are you going to stand there, Mister Hutchings?" she said, not turning from her vigil.

A man stepped out of the shadows, shaking his head.

"No one can ever catch you by surprise, can they?" he said. Like the woman, Hutchings was dressed in civilian clothing under military grade body armour and tactical vest, with an X6 sidearm strapped across his chest and a Caliburn submachine gun in his hand.

"That's why I'm still alive."

No one knew the woman's real name. She'd never told anyone who she was. It was irrelevant, she'd said – it didn't matter who she'd been before the world had ended, it mattered who she'd been in the year and a half since. When she had first become prominent in the resistance, they had taken to calling hear Headhunter due to her tendency to decapitate dead ril-galas and leave the heads out in the open as very clear warnings to the enemy. That name had very quickly been shortened to Hunter, which had stuck ever since. But beyond the fact that she was Asian, no one knew a thing about her.

"Have the boys light the bonfires and start up the music," said Hunter, tugging at her shemagh as her long hair whipped in the cold Scottish wind. "And I want the sniper teams and their spotters on the walls tonight. Two hour shifts, continuously."

"Expecting trouble?"

"Listen to the city."

He frowned, listening to nothing but the sound of crackling fires.

"Shit."

"The ril-galas are up to something," she said.

And as far as they could ascertain, with the fall two weeks ago of Stirling Castle to the north, Edinburgh Castle represented the final bastion of human resistance in Scotland. If something were brewing, there was little doubt as to what the target would be.

"Sound a full lockdown as well. I don't want the civilians milling about."

Nodding, Hutchings hurried away to relay the orders.

Shaking her head slightly, Hunter took another long look out over what remained of the city. She had never been to Edinburgh prior to the ril-galas invasion, but from what she could glean from its rubble, it had once been a beautiful city. Maybe one day it would be again, but Hunter doubted it, just as she doubted many of Earth's cities would ever be the same – or even be rebuilt at all. When she'd first arrived, she'd been told that before the ril-galas had set up a forward operating base in Holy-rood Park, the population of Edinburgh had been just over five hundred and fifty thousand. The current population of Edinburgh Castle hovered around nine hundred, some military and some civilian – a line that was becoming more blurred every day – and while the foraging parties they sent out daily were still encountering other pockets of survivors, they were becoming fewer and fewer. Assuming that other population centres were suffering a similar fate, there would neither be enough manpower left to rebuild Earth's cities, nor enough of a population base to make it necessary.

Though she never admitted it to anyone, Hunter knew that they weren't fighting the ril-galas to save Earth – they were fighting to keep themselves alive long enough for an evacuation. Because even though she had no religious faith whatsoever, no belief in any god or higher power, there was one thing – one person – she did believe in.

"Finn Radko," said the tiny woman. "It's a pleasure to meet you. My name is Kestrel Cagliari."

Shaking her hand was like shaking the hand of a child. Cagliari, who couldn't have been more than a few years older than Anna Cortez, was short and thin and seemed perfectly suited to be cast in the role of a pixie in a fantasy movie, right down to her short and spiky bright blue hair. What she did not look like was the owner and president of one of the most advanced aeronautical engineering and design firms in the Commonwealth.

Cagliari Aerospace, despite its undeniable innovations in spacecraft design, had fallen out of favour with the Commonwealth for political reasons that were in reality more racist that they were political. Kestrel Cagliari's mother had been Chinese and a card-carrying member of the Communist Party prior to her love affair and marriage to Anton Cagliari. Their marriage had been a major scandal as certain members of the Commonwealth government began questioning – at first in whispers and then in chest-thumping speeches – the wisdom of having the development of the Naval fleet in the hands of someone with such close ties to the Soviets. Only with their successful design bid for the HMS Royal Sovereign had Cagliari Aerospace resumed doing work for the Commonwealth.

"Likewise, Miss Cagliari. And thank you for designing the Isaac Brock class to withstand so much punishment," he said.

"With everything the Vimy Ridge has gone through, she's still in remarkably good shape."

Cagliari smiled and it made her look even younger.

"I appreciate that. And please, call me Kestrel."

"All right, Kestrel," he said, then pausing for a moment. "I don't mean to be rude Kestrel, but..."

"Yes. Yes, sorry – you're probably very busy," she said. "Please."

She waved toward a two-seat table nearby. Though given how small the coffee shop was, nearly everything could be classified as nearby. As Radko took a seat opposite Cagliari, he noticed for the first time that there was no one else in the shop... and, in fact, a 'sorry, we're closed' sign hung in the window.

"I rented the whole place for an hour," said Cagliari, following his gaze. "It seemed like the best way to do this. And it's not like money has much meaning anymore."

"Can't argue with that."

"Okay. So. I'll get right to the point," she said, laying a manila folder out between them. "Have you ever heard of Project Argentavis?"

Radko shook his head.

"It was a project we were working on entirely on spec. We weren't getting any funding from anyone, it was just something we were doing to try to break back in with you guys in a big way. Try to stop you from sucking at the teat of ATC Castle, to put it bluntly," she said. "We designed a multipurpose fighter – interceptor, bomber, superiority fighter, capable of both atmospheric and space flight. I'm not throwing out a sales pitch when I tell you the Argentavis is the most advanced fighter ever designed by humans."

Having seen the designs used for the Royal Sovereign, Radko had little reason to doubt the statement.

"Okay," he said, taking a look at a schematic she handed him. "It certainly looks impressive."

He wasn't just speaking figuratively about its capabilities – the fighter *looked* impressive. Named after an enormous extinct bird of prey from Earth's past, the Argentavis fighter looked the part: beak-like nose cone, powerful and aerodynamic body, massive articulated wings.

"Maneuverability is second to none," she continued. "I've seen video of the way the ril-galas fighters move and I'm one hundred and ten percent certain that the Argentavis can outperform them. As for weaponry, we have what is essentially a pair of integrated, up-scaled icaran *aoran* assault rifles in addition to a full rack of conventional warhead missiles and the capability of carrying several different types of bomb for-."

She stopped as Radko held up a hand. One thing he hadn't wanted from this meeting was for it turn into a request for him to lend his fame to support another military contractor. ATC Castle was already one PMC too many, as far as he was concerned.

"All very impressive, but this is sounding very much like a sales pitch."

"I'm sorry," she said, sitting back in her chair. "The Argentavis was my pet project – I get rather... animated when discussing it. And I guess, in a way, it *is* a sales pitch."

"I guess what I'm wondering, Miss Cag... Kestrel... is why are you telling me all of this? I don't have any say in what projects the Commonwealth Armed Forces choose to fund," he said, shrugging apologetically as he handed back the schematics. "They're barely listening to me now on topics I do have some experience with."

"Commander, I'm not looking for funding. The project was completed," she said. "We finished production on thirty Argentavis fighters – with our own money because of how much we believed in this project. I can bring thirty highly advanced, heavily armed and armoured starfighters to the front lines on this war. I know from hearing the stories how much the fighter wing from the Leonid Gorshkov helped your initial efforts – imagine having a fighter wing based on the Vimy Ridge. But not just any fighter wing."

She held up the schematics and smiled, her eyes bright with excitement.

"A wing of *these* fighters."

Her body language made it clear that Cagliari believed in her fighters. And the Gorshkov's fighters had been instrumental in several engagements with the ril-galas and having a fighter wing at his disposal was something he'd been advocating for ever since the alliance with the Soviets was allowed to wither on the vine.

"If these fighters are finished and ready for action," he said. "Why are we only hearing about it now? We've been fighting this war for well over a year."

"Yes, I know it looks bad from a timing perspective," she said. "But honestly, Commander... we only recently found them."

"Excuse me?"

"Our production facilities are located outside the Commonwealth, in neutral space," she said, sounding mildly embarrassed. "Tax reasons, I'm told. I've never been involved in those kind of discussions – I've not been head of the company very long."

Clearing her throat, she leaned forward again and, despite the fact that they were still alone in the café, she lowered her voice.

"We were shipping the fighters in a pair of our large cargo haulers from our production facility on Muriel's Moon to our main hangar on Mars. Both ships went missing about a week before the ril-galas attack. At first, the company just assumed we had communications issues, which can happen. It's actually not that unusual to lose contact with cargo haulers for brief periods. And then the ril-galas swept into town. We thought maybe the transports had changed course to try to avoid the swarm and either been destroyed or had somehow made it to safety and gone into hiding. Then three weeks ago, I received a message from someone with whom I'd gone to university," she said. "He's a software engineer now, working at the ATC Castle R&D centre on Duster's Range."

"I think I know where this is going..."

"Turns out, ATC Castle landed a contract to design new fighters for the Commonwealth," she said, nodding. "But couldn't offer enough improvement on current designs to justify what they wanted to charge. The bottom line is that those sons of bitches have my fighters and I want them back."

"You're certain they have them?"

"My contact sent me photos," she said, bringing out a tablet and tapping a few commands before handing it over to Radko. "They're in a secure hangar beneath the Duster's Range installation. It looks like they tore two of them apart to try to reverse-engineer our work, but the other twenty-eight are intact."

Scrolling through the photos, Radko just nodded. It was possible the photos had been doctored, but he didn't see what the point would have been in that.

"I want you to help me get them back and get them into the fight," said Cagliari.

"And I take it you haven't been able to get anywhere with the government?"

"No. I don't have any connections, I don't have any pull with anyone. I was never supposed to be in a position to run the company – up until eight months ago, I was just a test pilot with pretty solid job security. Well. Maybe not *just* a test pilot, but you get my point."

There was a long silence as Radko stared at the photos and thought about what the young woman was asking.

"Please, I'm begging you," she said. "Not even because of what it could mean for Cagliari Aerospace – I think that ship has sailed – and as much as I'd like to hurt ATC Castle, forget that too. Just think about how these fighters can help humanity. Not just humanity, everyone – all of us."

"Who would be cleared to fly them? They're pretty much experimental, aren't they?"

"Me. I've flown every prototype through the entire development phase. And I have ten others who have flown this latest version. Five human and five icaran."

Radko looked up sharply.

"You've been working with the icarans?"

Cagliari shrugged.

"How do you think we've been able to be so innovative with our designs over the last few years? We started looking outside the human sphere and started studying what other species were doing."

"And the icarans just loaned you pilots?"

"Hardly. The icaran government didn't know anything about this, but do you think humanity is the only species with freelancers?"

"All right," said Radko, steepling his fingers in front of him. "Assuming I were open to the idea, what's your plan for getting them back?"

"Well... if I ask for them to be returned, ATC Castle will just deny and stall until they can move them somewhere else."

"So you're hoping the Commonwealth will park a dreadnaught on their doorstep and demand the fighters be turned over?"

"Do I have your word that this discussion is off the record?"

Radko nodded.

"I have my pilots on standby and have a ship ready to take us to Duster's Range as soon as I give the order," she said. "But I've never launched a military operation and I know that facility will be heavily defended."

"I can't be directly involved in an assault against ATC Castle. Another assault against ATC Castle," he said. "I'm still feeling heat over the other one. However, I agree that those fighters would represent a significant war asset. Give me a couple days and give me the details of this ship you have waiting for you and I'll see what I can come up with. Okay?"

"Yes. Great. Thank you," she said, shaking his hand vigorously.

7

Finding the location address Khaifa had given her had proven more difficult than Sigurdsson had been expecting. Originally, the lower levels of Thor's Hammer had been designed as storage bays for parts and supplies and so were not laid out as cleanly as the upper levels. Only after a half hour of taking one passage then doubling back to take another had Sigurdsson found the door to which a fabric MediCorps patch had been glued.

Pausing for a moment, she took a deep breath and released it slowly. She was trying very hard not get her hopes up about this meeting – after all, it was hard to see any benefit coming from seeing a medical doctor when it was her cybernetics that were the issue – but she could feel little butterflies of hope flitting around in her belly regardless. She pushed the door open and was immediately hit by the smell of disinfectant.

Despite the rather industrial exterior, the interior of the MediCorps lab was clean and bright. It appeared to Sigurdsson as if the entire setup had been rebuilt piece by piece from the remains of a MediCorps vessel. Probably one of the several that had returned to Thor's Hammer after the blockade had been broken and that were, while largely intact, no longer spaceworthy.

"Good afternoon. I will be with you in a moment, please."

The voice was bright and metallic and entirely familiar and Sigurdsson waited patiently for its owner to emerge from a secondary room. When Brill had first been assigned to Duster's

Range, its presence was one to which everyone had taken some time to adjust. The brill species was unique in many ways, but the three most prominent were that they did not have given names – each simply referred to itself as brill, which was a difficult concept for humans in particular – the second was that brill did not have different sexes and so "him" and "her" were irrelevant, and the third was that brill were one metre long isopods that survived in a liquid soup of chemicals that would kill any other known sentient species. For interactions with other species, most brill travelled in crab-like mechanized exoskeletons with manipulator arms, but a few – including the brill for which Sigurdsson waited – chose to use a humanoid shaped exo-suit.

"Ah. Freyja Sigurdsson," said Brill happily as it entered the room, the single large eye on its exo-suit head pulsating blue as it spoke. "I am pleased to see you remain living."

Sigurdsson had forgotten that it said just about everything happily. Brill had modified its vocal emulator from the standard monotone to something more cheerful in the hopes it would help humans see it as less of a mechanical monstrosity.

"I'm pleased to be living," she said. "Sorry to see that they've stuck you down here in the storage section, though"

Brill managed a very convincing version of a shrug. Though every time it had such a human-like reaction – a shrug, a nod, a wave of the hand – Sigurdsson couldn't help but wonder just how much effort it took the little isopod inside the suit to execute the move and how long it had taken the brill to perfect it.

"In fact the storage area is the perfect location for this lab, providing me with ample cryogenic units," it said.

"Oh. I guess that's good then."

"It is indeed," it said cheerfully. "Your left upper appendage appears in very poor repair – would you like it removed?"

"No. Thanks. But, uh, Doctor Khaifa suggested I come down and see you."

"Doctor Khaifa is a very intelligent and skilled physician. Are you and she still engaging in sexual activity?"

Sigurdsson just stood in stunned silence.

"Apologies. That was an inappropriate question, perhaps? I am still learning the intricacies of human social interaction and am not always aware of what would be considered an acceptable line of questioning. Your sexual activities are largely irrelevant to this visit, perhaps?"

"Very."

"In that case, how does Doctor Khaifa feel I can assist you, Freyja?"

"I'm not entirely sure," she said, leaning against a lab table and glancing around uncomfortably. "I've been having serious issues with my arms and she said you might be able to help. I think 'alternative medicine' was the term she used."

"Ah. I see. And she did not further explain?"

"No, she didn't," said Sigurdsson, eyes narrowing.

"Are you aware of a branch of medical science called xenocuriatology?" it said, waiting for Sigurdsson to shake her head before continuing. "It is, essentially, the science of using genetic material from one species to treat ailment in another. Humans have a general aversion to this particular branch and so I am unsurprised you were not aware of its existence."

"Doc... let's pretend I have a concussion and that I'm not following where you're going with this..."

"Come."

It waved for her to follow into the back room, where the walls were lined with cryogenic cases, some the size of a briefcase, some as large as an industrial freezer. Sliding one of the smaller cases out of its rack, Brill set it on the lab table and opened it. Inside was a human hand. Or a partial human hand – the thumb and index finger of the hand had been replaced with the thumb and finger of an icaran. If not for the difference in flesh tone and skin texture, Sigurdsson would never have known they were parts of a different species – there was no seam, no scar. The parts meshed together perfectly.

"That is some serious Frankenstein bullshit," said Sigurdsson. "But I still don't get it. How does this help repair my cybernetics?"

Brill glanced up at her, then back to the hand, then back up at Sigurdsson.

"Not repair. Replace."

It was her turn to stare.

"What?"

"Icaran genetic material has very strong regenerative properties," said Brill. "In addition to a very high level of cross-species compatibility, making it ideal for xenocuriatological applications."

Sigurdsson just stared at the brill's unblinking mechanical eye for several moments. It was clearly waiting for her to clue in to what it was saying, but for whatever reason, that just was not happening.

"Remember that part where I said pretend that I have a concussion...?"

"Apologies," it said, picking up a pair of forceps. Gently, Brill prodded at the near-invisible line where the icaran fingers were joined to the human hand. "As you see, the skin has merged almost perfectly, leaving no scar. The underlying musculature had bonded in a similarly seamless fashion, as has the bone. This operation was a resounding success, though results are tempered by the fact that it was performed on a severed appendage rather than a living specimen. And of course a simpler procedure than replacing a pair of arms, but the principles and processes would be similar."

Sigurdsson looked up sharply. Brill appeared not to notice, instead moving to the larger containers, checking the labels. He passed on three before stopping.

"Ah. Yes. This one would appear to be the correct size. Icaran female."

It slid the container open, revealing the cryogenically preserved body of an icaran female. At least part of a body – there was nothing below the pelvis, but the torso, arms and head were perfectly intact.

"You will of course have an adjustment period as you become accustomed to having three fingers per hand rather than five."

"Are you...? What the actual fuck? Are you suggesting to replace these," she said, indicating her damaged arms. "With icaran arms? Actual living icaran arms? Is that even legal? Is it ethical?"

"Ethics vary depending on the species. My conception of what is ethical is different than yours, perhaps?"

"And what about legal?"

Brill shrugged.

"The procedure is too new a concept to have been regulated as of yet."

It paused and then shrugged again.

"No doubt it will be outlawed in the Commonwealth once the lawmakers fully understand xenocuriatology and its many possible applications. Humans are very averse to change."

"And what about the icarans?" she said, feeling a sweat break out on her forehead. She wasn't sure if it was a reaction to the strangeness of what was being proposed or her nervousness at how seriously she was considering it. "Do they feel it's ethical?"

"Do you wish to discuss it with them?"

"I can't. If I tried, the transmission would be flagged and killed before it reached them."

"Brill communication networks. Due to our position within the universe as healers, we maintain contact with most sentient species – exchanges of knowledge and supplies would be very difficult otherwise – and as such, we maintain our own, unregulated communications networks. The Commonwealth does not have control over those networks," it said. "I would be pleased to allow you access."

Sigurdsson pulled over a stool and sat down slowly. This was all a little too much to process. She'd come to grips very quickly with the fact that she'd lost her arms and had just taken it as a given that she'd adjust to life with two cyborg limbs. Of course she'd known there would be problems now and then – even the best of Commonwealth cybernetics were not immune to wear and tear and all required maintenance from time to time – but the problems she'd faced and the prospect of continuing to face those same problems indefinitely weighed on her. So Sigurdsson found herself – to her own shock and even mild horror – seriously considering the brill's offer of turning her into a monster.

A monster. She almost smiled as she recalled the exchange with Khaifa back in the observation tower on the walls of Fort Hathaway what seemed like a lifetime ago.

"Do you think I'm a monster Nasrin?"

"No," said Khaifa without hesitation. "I think you're a woman under enormous pressure, doing what you feel needs to be done. I think you've done the wrong thing, but for the right reason. I think that it's more important whether you think you're a monster, Freyja."

Sigurdsson forced a smile.

"I think we're going to find that out soon enough."

In retrospect, the discussion seemed prophetic.

Sigurdsson had seen many broken soldiers in her life. The walking wounded, the wounded who could no longer walk. Some adjusted well to their handicaps, but some hadn't. She'd seen them panhandling on the streets, lining up for their veterans' benefits cheques at the VA offices. Drinking away their pain, reliving old adventures with no expectation of new ones to come. They'd drink away their pittance or gamble it away or whore it away and then they'd die leaving nothing behind but their medals – assuming they hadn't already been pawned.

Freya Sigurdsson was a fighter, always had been. Even before joining the military, she had fought, sometimes for the right reasons, sometimes for the wrong reasons, sometimes for no reason at all. From the streets of Johannesburg to the training grounds of Fort Baggett to the walls of Fort Hathaway. And now to the bowels of Thor's Hammer.

Broken. Sidelined. Out of the fight.

She looked down at her broken left arm and her failing right.

"Fuck that."

"Fuck what?" asked the brill, his voice still cheerful, making the epithet sound like something out of a children's book.

"How long would the surgery take and how long would I be out of commission?"

8

The ril-galas had certainly been up to something, but it wasn't the attack on Edinburgh Castle that everyone had been expecting.

Hunter was in the governor's house, which had been converted into the mess hall for the new castle garrison, when she received word of one of their scouts returning. The news was of particular interest because they had not sent out scouting parties in nearly a week.

"It's MacDowall," she said, her brow furrowed, as she strode across the grounds, Hutchings at her side.

"How do you...? It can't be. He's been missing for weeks."

And yet, as they rounded Foog's Gate to St. Margaret's Chapel, they found MacDowall inside – battered and bloodied and very much the worse for wear – sitting uncomfortably and sipping water. As soon as he saw Hunter, he tried to stand, but she waved him back down.

"MacDowall, where have you-."

"The King!"

"I'm sorry?"

"He just keeps saying that," said one of the medics patching MacDowall's wounds.

"What King, MacDowall?" said Hunter.

Odds were that the man had simply lost his mind wandering through the city. It had happened before to scouts who had gone missing for weeks – they'd finally turn up, ranting and raving about the most random things, sometimes even insisting that they'd dreamed the entire ril-galas occupation and that it was safe for everyone to go home.

"Arthur! At Balmoral!"

"King Arthur," she said dryly. "Of course. Did he have Excalibur with him?"

"Uh, Hunter...," said Hutchings, motioning for her to join him out of earshot. "I know you aren't from Britain, so just wanted you to know that Arthur wasn't just a fairy tale."

"Hutchings-."

"No, no, I don't mean *that* Arthur wasn't a fairy tale. I mean Arthur was also the name of the youngest son of the reigning Queen of England, Elizabeth III. And Balmoral Castle has been a vacation home of the Royal Family for centuries."

She glanced over to MacDowall, then back to Hutchings.

"You think he means this Prince Arthur is holed up in Balmoral Castle?"

"Possibly. And since we know for a fact that the Queen, her consort and their other son were killed when the ril-galas destroyed Buckingham Palace-."

"If Arthur is alive, that would make him King, I suppose?"

"Yeah, it would."

Leaning against the cold brick of the chapel, Hunter chewed her lower lip in thought.

"How far is it from here to Balmoral?"

"If we can take the chopper, probably two hours? Why?" he said, then ran a hand through his hair and sighed. "You're not thinking to go after him, are you? We haven't heard a peep out of Balmoral – we don't even know if the castle is still standing!"

"No, we don't. But if there's a chance that the King of England is alive..."

"He's a kid! He's sixteen years old and one person – one single, solitary person. How can you possibly think about wasting resources to-."

"Mister Hutchings, are you aware of the mindset of most people in this castle? Are you aware of how most of them feel that defeat is inevitable? They see no light at the end of this tunnel. They see no hope," she said, jabbing an index finger into his chest. "How do you think those same people would feel if the King of England walked out of the rubble of their city, a survivor, just like them?"

She laughed then.

"His name is Arthur, for god's sake. Even I know the legend – the once and future King who will return from the mists of Avalon to lead his people in their hour of greatest need! Tell me you don't think these people," she said, waving back toward the barracks where the majority of the civilians slept. "Need something like that."

Hutchings sighed.

"He's still just one person. We'd be risking a lot of lives for this."

"And if he were anyone else, I wouldn't be doing it. I'm not interested in him as a person, I'm interested in him as a symbol. Just like we put out ril-galas heads on pikes, we could have the King of England in our castle – the continuation of a centuries-old Royal bloodline that the ril-galas could not terminate."

"You're not going to change your mind."

"No."

"Volunteers?"

"No. I will lead the team and I will pick them myself. I don't want word of this mission to get out – if we fail, I'd rather people not know what we failed in doing."

"Failing to rescue the King could be as great a blow to morale as saving him would be a boost."

"If not moreso."

"All right," said Hutchings after a lengthy pause. "When do we head out?"

"First light, if the chopper can be ready."

"I'll make sure it is."

"Azrael's Tear," said Radko.

Cortez at his side, he stood on the second level of the Vimy Ridge command deck looking out of the observation dome at the ship docked beside them. It was small – a quarter of the size of the Vimy Ridge – and its hull, cobbled together from several different types of vessel, was covered with angular plates of flat black armour.

"A pirate ship," she said, taking a sip of her water.

"Yeah."

With the Vimy Ridge on a down-cycle – not being on standby for the time being – Radko and Cortez were alone on the command deck. She had insisted on joining him, despite his insistence that she needed to rest. Though she was no longer part of his crew, having been re-assigned permanently to Commonwealth Naval Intelligence, he didn't expect he'd ever stop feeling responsible for her and her well-being.

"That armour," she said. "Is that the LiDAR-masking plating developed by Cagliari Aerospace?"

"Could be. That would explain how easily the Azrael's Tear came into Cagliari's employ," he said. "And from a strictly objective point of view, she couldn't have made a better choice, either ship or captain."

The Azrael's Tear was a notoriously fast and agile ship and her captain, Jagat Sohal Singh, was just as well known for his

shrewdness and skill in planning and executing his pirate operations. He was without a doubt the most famous of the pirates
to accept the Commonwealth's offer of amnesty in return for assistance with the war effort. With him on board with Cagliari's
plans, Radko estimated, their odds of success were increased by
a fair margin. That didn't make Radko's own part in the operation any easier. Or what he'd have to ask of others. Putting his
own career on the line was one thing – he had a tendency to do
that every time he met with the Navy brass, though not always
intentionally – but asking others to do the same was another
matter.

"Duster's Range has some pretty advanced security features,"
said Cortez, referring to a small notebook she carried, filled with
tight, crisp handwriting. "A compliment of full-time security
personnel – essentially ATC Castle soldiers – as well as some
drones. Launching a direct assault like we did on the other ATC
Castle facility would cost a lot of lives. However, I had another
idea."

As she flipped the page, Radko smiled slightly. They had all
changed, everyone who had been on the Vimy Ridge through
the first stage of the war, but none more than Cortez. She'd been
a nervous cadet then, thrown into the role of communications
and intelligence officer because Radko didn't have anyone else
and she'd performed better than anyone could have expected.
And now the field promotion he had given her to Sub Lieutenant had been made official, as had her assignment as an
intelligence officer. The only part of it that Radko wasn't happy
about was that she'd been assigned to Thor's Hammer itself and
not the Vimy Ridge.

"The facility contains a medical research lab," she continued.
"One dealing with all kinds of medical-related stuff, including

infectious diseases. And probably biological weapons, though ATC Castle has never admitted to it. Here, have a look."

She handed him the notebook and Radko read through the plan, a slow smile spreading across his face.

"You can actually do this?"

"Yep. Cagliari's inside man gave her the access codes. Once I'm inside the system, it's easy."

"All right," he said, handing back the notebook. "I think we can pull this off. But I'm still not comfortable leaving it in the hands of pirates, amnesty or not. I want people I can trust."

"If we send Commonwealth soldiers, ATC Castle is bound to find out, maybe even before the operation starts."

Turning his back to the observation dome and the Azrael's Tear, Radko looked down into the empty command deck, the heart of the Isaac Brock class frigate.

"Those untraceable comm channels you set up for me when I was still trying to bring the Soviets back into the fold... can you set them up from here?"

"Yeah, I can do that," said Cortez, nodding. "Do you want Kovalenko or someone else?"

"Actually, I don't want the Soviets at all. I want a line to Icar Prime."

Cortez's brows shot up, but she simply nodded and the pair headed down into the main part of the command deck.

Setting up the requested comm line took far less time than Radko had been expecting, but Cortez certainly knew what she was doing. Those transmissions used an encryption code of her own design and were bounced off so many relays – Commonwealth and Soviet – that not only would no one be able to tell what the transmission contained, but it would take them months just to determine its point of origin.

With the transmission active, it took only moments for an icaran face to pop up on the screen. His eyes immediately narrowed.

"What does the human want?" said the icaran, its voice transformed into the bland sound of the Commonwealth translation software in Radko's earpiece.

"The human is Commander Finn Radko of the HMCS Vimy Ridge," he said, taking more than a little pleasure in watching the icaran's expression change at the mention of his name. "And I need to speak with Brigadier General Locaris of the Venator ICA Commandos on a matter of great importance."

The icaran on the other end of the line hesitated for a moment.

"Standby, Commander."

Radko nodded as the standby screen popped up.

"I saw that," said Cortez, smirking.

"Saw what?"

"The little twitch of a smile when he reacted to your name. Enjoying the notoriety, are we?"

He chuckled.

"It has its uses."

Their attention returned to the monitor as the standby screen disappeared and in its place was a familiar face, if not the one they were expecting.

"Captain Elgrapharr," said Radko.

"Commander Radko, I am pleased you are well. It appears today is my day for speaking with humans."

It wasn't clear to Radko what the icaran soldier meant, but he pressed on.

"Likewise, Captain. I, uh, don't mean to be rude, but I was hoping to speak with Locaris."

Elgrapharr bobbed his head in the icaran equivalent of a nod.

"I understand," he said. "I regret that communication between our peoples has been... lacking. Brigadier General Locaris was killed in action three months ago, defending an icaran colony from a ril-galas attack."

For just a moment, the news didn't register with Radko. But only a moment, and then it hit him, like a physical blow, as if he'd been punched in the stomach. He felt Cortez's hand on his arm as she gently pushed him down into the chair and then simply stood beside him.

Locaris was dead. Locaris, who had agreed to put aside all the years of animosity between humans and icarans to help Radko along the entire turbulent journey to Thor's Hammer, who had advocated to his own government the necessity of working with the humans to defeat the ril-galas. Somewhat egotistically, Radko had always seen four pillars in the beginning of the war with the ril-galas – himself, Alexei Kovalenko, Freyja Sigurdsson and Locaris. Kovelenko had been so mired in political backlash that he had been able to accomplish even less than Radko. Sigurdsson was injured and sidelined for who knew how long. And Locaris was dead.

"I'm sorry," was all he could manage.

"As am I. Icaran familial relations are... somewhat more complex than those of humans," said Elgrapharr. "But he often referred to you as *aveyorn Radko*."

When the translation failed to come through, Radko opened his mouth to speak, but Elgrapharr held up a three-fingered hand.

"Your translator will not find an appropriate substitute for the word in your language. The closest equivalent would perhaps be 'brother in arms.' He held you in great esteem, Commander."

"And I him," said Radko, blinking back tears.

There was a moment's pause before Radko cleared his throat.

"I'm sorry, Elgrapharr, but I've come asking for help."

At the icaran's head-bob of acknowledgement, Radko explained the problem presented by Cagliari, the benefit that could be gained by reacquiring the Argentavis fighters and the problems that he faced in trying to achieve the goal of getting a wing of advanced fighters into the war. And then Cortez stepped in and outlined her plan.

"What I am requesting," said Radko after everything had been laid on the table. "Is for a small number of icaran commandos to assist in the operation."

"You do not trust these... pirates that your acquaintance has retained."

"No. And believe me, Elgrapharr, I understand that given the situation right now between our governments that I am asking a lot of-."

"Of course."

"Sorry?"

"Of course I will help, Commander. Our governments may bicker like younglings, but we are not... *shitheads*, I believe is the word?"

"That's definitely the word," said Cortez, grinning.

"I will lead the team myself," said the Captain. "Arrangements will need to be made here, in addition to details of transportation. I will also have specific requirements of personnel I will need to establish."

"Understood. We can send you schematics of the facility so your team isn't going in blind."

"Excellent. Am I able to contact you directly once this transmission terminates?"

"No," said Cortez. "That would be difficult – government paranoia and all. I can arrange another encrypted transmission in two days?"

She glanced from Elgrapharr to Radko and both nodded their agreement.

"We shall speak in two days' time, then," said the icaran.

"In two days," said Radko, then hesitatedg slightly before continuing. "Captain... does Locaris have family?"

"Yes. He is survived by a wife and four offspring, as well as a brother."

"Please, if you could, pass along my condolences. Locaris was... he was there for me when I badly needed a friend and an ally. His support... you know, we humans have an old, old saying that you don't know what you've got until you lose it. I took a lot of shit from my government for standing alongside Locaris in this fight and I know he took shit for it when he got home, too. But I'd do it again in a heartbeat, because unlike those politicians and their yes-men, Locaris knew just like I do – just like you do, Elgrapharr – that sometimes you need to just swallow your pride and get down to the business of protecting people. It's a trait I wish more of my own people shared."

Elgrapharr bowed his head. It wasn't a motion Radko had seen before and was unsure at first how to interpret it.

"I served with Locaris for thirty-seven years," he said. "And he would very much appreciate your words. I shall convey them to his family. And I shall speak with you again in two days' time."

Radko nodded as the transmission closed and Cortez's encryption protocol automatically transformed itself into a targeted virus, wiping all trace of the call from the ship's computer systems.

"That was really nice, what you said about Locaris," said Cortez, breaking the lengthy silence. "I didn't know how much he meant to you."

"I'm not sure I did either."

Another long silence followed before Radko stood, placing a hand on Cortez's shoulder. He hadn't realised just how tired she looked – dark circles were beginning to form under her eyes.

"You should go get some rest."

"I need to work on some logistics of how I'm going to pull this off," she said, shaking her head.

"Please, Anna. That can wait a few hours. I need to confirm everything with Cagliari first, anyway – just take some time. Get some rest. The plan isn't going anywhere without you."

"Okay. Okay, you're right, I really could use some sleep," she said, rubbing her eyes and sighing. "I don't have the energy I used to anymore. I think it's the new medication. The side effects are a whole lot better than the last stuff, but I'm wearing out a lot quicker."

"Is there anything else they can try?"

She shook her head.

"The doctors said this was the only other stuff they had that would still do what they needed it to. It's this or go back to the ones that made me nauseous all the time."

Radko sighed and it occurred to him that he spent a great deal of time these days sighing and he wondered what that said about his mental state. No doubt some psychiatrist would say it spoke to his feelings of helplessness in the face of circumstances out of his control, be it the immovability of the Prime Minister and his advisory committee or the cancer slowly killing Anna Cortez. A psychiatrist might even have prescribed him an antidepressant. However, he hadn't spoken to a psychiatrist, so instead he'd have to self-medicate.

"You can use my quarters on the ship if you don't want to go all the way back to the station," he said. "I'm going to get a drink."

Cortez nodded, understanding, and he walked her to his quarters before heading back through the ship and onto the station, making his way to The Pub. It was a blessedly quiet night, only a dozen or so people in the place, which suited Radko just fine. Taking a booth near the back – the same booth where he'd sat with Sigurdsson the night before – he ordered a gin and tonic. Probably the first of many.

The alliance he'd built out of the ruins of the ril-galas attack had itself fallen to ruins.

Nodding his thanks to the waitress as she dropped off his drink, Radko took a long sip, thankful that despite all the problems mankind faced, they had managed to continue producing alcohol.

He silently toasted Locaris, the friend and ally he valued as both but didn't know nearly as well as either as he would have liked. Tapping his glass on the table for all those who couldn't be there, he thought about all the lives lost, but also about the splintering of his little group. Quon Li-Chen had, as promised and as Radko himself had recommended, vanished without a trace. And as much as her psychic abilities had helped and would have continued to help, they had both known that having been a part of Operation Nightwatch, at the very least she'd have been arrested on sight by the Commonwealth, if not simply shot.

He even mourned Harlan Gray. Though the man had tried to forcibly take command of the Vimy Ridge – resulting in his own death – he'd done it for the right reasons. Even when Radko had been staring down the barrel of the Colonel's sidearm, he hadn't been able to see the man as an enemy, not really. The war effort needed more men like Colonel Gray, not fewer. That had been the first thing he'd told Nasrin Khaifa upon meeting her. Certainly she'd heard from someone at some point the truth of what her estranged husband had attempted aboard the Vimy Ridge, but she had not and would not hear it directly from Radko. No purpose would be served by tarnishing the man's reputation when he and Radko were just two sides of the same coin – both going to extreme measures to do what they felt right.

Though he hadn't realised it, the waitress had already taken away his empty glass and brought it back refilled.

He was taking his first sip when Cagliari slid in across from him. In a bar where ninety percent of the clientele wore uniform, the owner of Cagliari Aerospace would have stood out even had her hair – now slicked back rather than spiky – not been vibrant blue. She wore a form-fitting sleeveless black dress and several gold bangles around each wrist that jangled with every movement.

"A reception," she said, explaining away her attire. "Hosted by the Prime Minister."

Radko grunted and sipped his drink.

"I miss lime."

Cagliari stared at him and blinked twice.

"Excuse me?"

"Lime," he said, swirling his drink. "I always liked a slice of lime in my G&T. We always had a hard time growing citrus offworld. Kind of makes you wonder if we'll ever have limes again."

He took another sip, then downed the rest of the drink in one gulp, holding up the empty glass to get the waitress's attention.

"A lot of things we won't have again, I suspect," he said as the waitress whisked away the glass. "For all we know, this here is the new normal for humanity."

"Are... you all right, Commander?" said Cagliari, her left brow cocked slightly.

"No, not really."

Sitting back, she waited for the waitress to deliver Radko's drink.

"I'll have one of those as well, please."

Once the waitress brought the second drink and disappeared again, Cagliari leaned forward.

"Do you need to talk about it?"

"Not really," he said, swirling the ice in his glass. "Just spending a little time with some dead friends."

"Ah."

With a nod, Cagliari lifted her own glass and clinked it gently against his.

"I'll drink to that."

They both sipped their drinks silently for a few minutes before Cagliari broke the silence.

"I was passed out after a three-day party."

Radko looked up at her and frowned.

"That's why I'm alive and the rest of my family isn't," she said. "I was passed out on a hotel bathroom floor, so I missed our flight back to Earth. Rich kid syndrome, I suppose, not growing out of the party lifestyle. Rich kid *and* a test pilot."

"Dangerous combination."

"Yeah. So I was saved by a hangover."

She stared at her drink for a moment and Radko saw a cloud pass over her expression. Gone was the bright-eyed young multi-billionaire, and in her place was someone a little darker, a little more driven, a little more dangerous.

"My entire family was killed," she said, her voice steady, but flat. "But I survived by virtue of being a self-absorbed shit. Now I'm left here alone, trying to make that worth something. Trying to make my survival mean more than just another cosmic toss of the dice."

She ran a hand through her hair, the gold around her wrist jangling.

"That's why I wanted to talk to you about...," she paused, glancing around as if having forgotten where they were. "About what we talked about. It's not about the company, it's about doing something to make a difference."

First impressions, Radko had learned, were frequently garbage. He, Gray, Locaris, Kovalenko, Quon, they'd all misjudged each other based on first impressions and if they hadn't been willing to let go of those first impressions, the Vimy Ridge might not have survived her ordeal. And so Radko felt no hesitation in admitting his first impression of Kestrel Cagliari – the sheltered little rich girl trying to turn Cagliari Aerospace into another ATC Castle – had been completely wrong. He let it go. He didn't care enough anymore about his own ego to even feel chagrinned, he just admitted he was wrong and moved forward from the point where he saw into the real Kestrel Cagliari.

"One of my greatest allies is dead," he said slowly. "A man who could have been one of the most prominent officers in the war effort was killed trying to remove me from command of my ship; one of my strongest allies within the Commonwealth is essentially crippled and one of my best and most loyal friends through all of this shit is dying of cancer."

Setting down his glass, he rubbed at his face with both hands.

"And with the exception of the first one, they can all be laid at my feet to some extent or other."

"How can you say that cancer is-."

"Because it is," he said sharply. "A year and a half ago we broke the blockade and made this station the single most important strategic installation in human history and we have done fuck all with it. I have watched our fleet slowly grow as vessels that had gone into hiding make their way home and as we salvage others and get them back into fighting shape. I've seen enlistment in all branches go up as people become more willing to put their lives on the line to protect their fellow man. I've seen people sacrifice and go without in order to help their neighbour. But I've also seen politics drive a wedge between us at a time when we should be pulling together as an entire species. I've seen unrepentant xenophobia isolate us in the galaxy at a time when we desperately need friends. And we've all watched as we make smaller and smaller gains in outlying colonies while Earth burns. And I am tired of it, Cagliari. Fucking tired of it. We as a species are already being pushed toward extinction and every day we remain holed up here in our little fortress in the stars, we get even closer. Nobody seems to understand why the ril-galas haven't launched a major offensive against Thor's Hammer. They're not afraid of us, they *want* us to feel secure – they want us to stay put, all warm and cozy, while they finish entrenching themselves in our star system."

He slammed a fist down on the table and Cagliari, who had been leaning ever farther forward, jumped slightly. Noticing a handful of strange looks he garnered from other patrons, Radko forced himself to lay his hands flat on the table, palms down, as he continued.

"We can't go on like this and expect to survive. I refuse to allow Locaris and Harlan Gray and...," he trailed off, not wanting to say the next name as a foregone conclusion. "And others. I refuse to have those deaths be meaningless. Your family. My friends. Every sentient being who has died in this war. I intend to make sure the ril-galas remember us when they've been driven back to whatever shithole that spawned them. And your... your *corporate assets* are going to help make that happen. So yeah, I'm on board."

When he'd finished, Cagliari swallowed heavily and simply stared at him for what seemed like a very long time before speaking.

"We need to go to my place. Right now."

10

"I just want to say one more time that I don't think this is a good idea," said Hutchings, his voice barely audible over the rotors of the antiquated helicopter.

Sliding her heavy backpack and the gear that wasn't already strapped to her body behind the cargo netting, Hunter climbed in beside him.

"I know, Hutch. That doesn't change the fact that we're doing it anyway."

She strapped in as the rest of her team followed suit. There was Hunter and Hutchings, as well as Davey Williams and Alvin Morgan – pilot and co-pilot, respectively – Harley Ransom, the tracker, Douglas Grieve, the sniper, and two former members of the Lothian & Borders Police, Jamie Fairbairn and Jasbir "Jazz" Pradesh. All were decked out in a random assortment of military and civilian garb, some camouflage and some not, but all muted colours, and all wore military-grade body armour and tactical vests. Grieve cradled an older-model Trondheim Arms 32A OSR sniper rifle in his arms while Ransom tested the action on her compound bow. The two were a study in opposites. A veteran of military service with the Commonwealth, Grieve had retired from the army nearly ten years prior at the age of fifty-five, keeping up his skill as a sniper through various shooting competitions. On the polar opposite end of the spectrum was sixteen year old Ransom, the daughter of two Canadian wilderness guides who had passed along the craft to her. When the ril-galas had struck, Ransom had been in Glasgow for the Commonwealth Games, competing in archery. She was the only one of the group Hunter hadn't known -- she was just the tracker with the wild red hair -- but Ransom had been included at Grieve's insistence as his spotter.

They were an unconventional pair, but had apparently developed an almost father/daughter bond.

"How long we up for?" asked Ransom, trying to hide her nerves.

"Hutch says about two hours," said Hunter. "But it depends on how many ril-galas patrols we have to avoid."

The young girl nodded and went back to studying her bow.

As the helicopter gently lifted into the air, Hunter motioned for everyone to put on their headsets. It was time for the briefing.

"Before I explain our mission, I want to apologize for both the secrecy and the last-minute assignment," she said. "It was all very necessary."

All members of the team were watching and listening intently.

"You can consider this a search and rescue operation. You all know that Graham MacDowall came home last night," she said. "But what he brought with him was information about the Royal Family – that the youngest son of the Queen, Arthur, is not only alive, but is in Scotland, hiding out at Balmoral."

"Is this credible information?" said Grieve.

"MacDowall saw the boy with his own eyes."

"Graham was a football commentator before the invasion," said Pradesh. "He's got good eyes."

"I'm sure some of you will think this is a fool's errand," said Hunter. "But our people need a symbol to inspire them in this fight. I don't expect this kid to be carrying Excalibur, but the heir to the throne of Britain not just surviving, but standing tall on the battlements of Edinburgh Castle? Consider what that could mean to our people. And then consider what it could mean if we were able to broadcast that image to other cities – maybe even around the world."

She let the image sink in for a moment before continuing.

"So we go to Balmoral, we find King Arthur and we evac him back to the castle."

To their credit, not one member of the team – not even Hutchings – pointed out how insane the plan was and how the odds were stacked against a favourable outcome. But then, everyone knew that they were desperate, grasping at straws. How much longer they could realistically hold out against the ril-galas forces was anyone's guess, but at the rate the human strongholds were falling, Hunter herself gave the Edinburgh Castle garrison four to six months. And that was being generous.

However...

As she'd seen with her own eyes and felt within her own heart and mind when all this had begun, a little inspiration and a little hope instilled at the right moment could drive people to greatness.

It could even inspire a jaded woman with no faith left in humanity, a woman who wanted nothing more than to disappear to the edges of the galaxy, to put her life on the line to protect others. To turn her ship around and not only rejoin the fight, but drive straight into the heart of the ril-galas occupation and reinvent herself as a freedom fighter.

If Radko could see her now, she wasn't sure if he'd be surprised or if he'd just give her that wry smile and tell her he was glad she'd finally decided what kind of person she wanted to be.

She hoped both she and Radko lived long enough to see each other again. As the first one to treat her as an actual person rather than an asset, she would like to show him the kind of person she'd become.

Though it felt strange to admit it to herself, she hoped he would be proud of her.

The two-hour flight seemed to pass quicker than expected, with the entire team remaining silent but for a few brief whispered conversations. Even their minds were relatively quiet, focusing on their preparation. It was a nice change for Hunter, to be away from all the noisy thoughts of the several hundred people holed up in Edinburgh Castle.

"Hunter," said Morgan, the co-pilot. "Looks like a fire-fight at Balmoral Castle."

Unstrapping herself, Hunter moved forward into the cockpit and followed Morgan's gaze to the distant castle courtyard. Bursts of light were erupting from two clear lines – the familiar muzzle flash of Commonwealth weapons from the castle itself and the now all-too-familiar bright blooms of ril-galas cannons. There were more humans in the castle than she would have thought, which gave her hope that MacDowall had been right about Arthur.

"Is there a safe place to land?"

"I'm surprised we even made it here without being shot down," said Williams. "The only landing spot I'd call safe is the one we took off from."

"There," said Morgan. "Behind the ril-galas line. They're not holding any ground, just driving forward to the castle."

"Yeah we can make that work. Better gear up quick and strap in again, Hunter – this landing isn't going to be a patient one."

"Once we're off, you guys get airborne again. Keep moving," she said. "We'll signal when we need you back."

Both pilot and co-pilot nodded and Hunter stepped back to the cargo netting and began handing out the gear.

"Prepare for a hard landing," she said, strapping on her own gear, then taking her seat once more. "We bring back Arthur at any cost. Clear?"

They all nodded.

Suddenly a jolt went through the entire helicopter, accompanied by the sound of shattering glass and tearing metal and a spray of red arced through the cockpit access way. The chopper was a mere six feet off the ground and it dropped like a stone the rest of the distance, hitting the earth with a heavy thud.

Hunter could hear someone screaming and the confused yelling of others and overlaid on top of all that was a cacophony of panicked and terrified thoughts and even worse mental screams of pain and suddenly the chopper lurched onto its side, rotors biting into the ground, kicking up clods of grass and soil. And then the mechanism, stressed beyond all reason, snapped, bursting into flames and Hunter was finally able to focus again. There was something wet dripping down the side of her face as she cut through her restraints with a utility knife, but she had no idea whether it was her blood, someone else's blood or some kind of fluid from the helicopter itself.

The rest of the team was already climbing out of the side cargo door – which was now facing straight up to the sky – and Hunter joined them, hauling herself out of the wreck and dropping to the ground. She winced at the pain in her ankle as she landed, but she could still put weight on it with only mild pain. It couldn't be that bad.

Williams was climbing out of the cockpit, covered in blood, but uninjured based on his mobility. Morgan, however, was dead. The image of the co-pilot she saw in Williams's mind was horrific, his chest blown open to the sternum, his head nothing more than a splattered mass across the back of his chair.

"Morgan...," stuttered Williams. "He's... Morgan's dead."

Hunter simply nodded and raised her Caliburn submachine gun to her shoulder. The weapons carried by the squad were an odd amalgam of military, paramilitary and civilian, scavenged from whatever sources they could. The members of the garrison who had been police officers or soldiers had brought in many of the weapons they still used, and Hunter had brought a crate of ATC Castle weapons and ammunition with her. She dropped to one knee and stared down the Caliburn's iron sights.

"Incoming."

The rest of the team raised their firearms – even Ransom, who had slung her bow over her shoulder in favour of a pistol – as a portion of the ril-galas line turned and began marching toward their downed chopper, manta-like heads bobbing side-to-side.

There was the sudden report of a rifle and one of the ril-galas foot soldiers dropped, unmoving.

Grieve, the sniper, had notched his first kill of the day.

Crouching low and jamming the stock of her Caliburn against her shoulder, Hunter advanced, Hutch to her left and Ransom to her right. Heart pounding in her chest as it always did in such situations, Hunter forced herself to breath steadily, evenly, and forced her mind into sharp focus. What she may have lacked in military training, she made up for in mental discipline -- no matter the situation, Hunter could sharpen her focus with pinpoint accuracy, one of the few aspects of her past she could point to and reasonably call a benefit.

Squeezing off a burst from her submachine gun, Hunter caught one of the ril-galas foot soldiers in the arm, its gun pod dropping uselessly to its side. It wasn't what she had been intending -- her aim was not the greatest, and their ammunition stores were such that she couldn't justify hours at a shooting range -- but as the foot soldier raised its remaining gun pod, swinging it toward Hunter, a trio of shots rang out from her right and slammed into the creature's chest. It dropped heavily to the ground, the ril-galas pilot within dead.

"Hutch," said Hunter, quickly nodding a thanks to Ransom. "Some grenades would be welcome right now."

She didn't need to look at him to tell he was grinning. She could hear it in his voice.

"I think I can make that happen."

11

The bed was the most comfortable Radko had been on in close to two years and he really did not want to leave it.

Cagliari's rooms aboard Thor's Hammer were spacious by space station standards, all furniture of the highest quality still available. It was, in fact, the kind of lodging that most of the Commonwealth senior officers had taken and the same kind that Radko himself had been offered and refused. For someone like Cagliari, it made sense – this was home for the foreseeable future – but Radko's home would be, now and for as far into the future as he could look, the HMCS Vimy Ridge.

A fresh mug of tea in each hand and wearing nothing but her underwear and a t-shirt advising 'your mom won't like me,' Cagliari came back into the bedroom and, handing Radko one of the mugs, sat cross-legged on the bed. She sported one of the most impressively abstract examples of bed-head Radko had ever seen.

"All I have is Earl Grey – I hope that's all right," she said.

"Perfect," he said with a small smile. "I'll take what I can get. I don't think we have any colonies under Commonwealth control still producing tea."

"No limes and no tea," she said, trying to hide a lopsided grin behind her mug. "War is truly hell."

They sipped their tea in silence for a moment before Cagliari spoke up again.

"Okay," she said, sitting up a little straighter. "I can have Captain Singh ready to leave within a few hours, if that works?"

Radko chuckled. He was more relaxed than he had been in weeks. Perhaps it was having someone new to talk to, to confide in, or perhaps it was finally -- finally -- having a course of action before him. A clear goal.

"Slow down. We're not just rushing in and I'm not leaving it to Singh's people – I want people I know I can trust and I want to make this as covert an operation as we possibly can."

"Yes, you're right. I'm sorry, I'm just... I'm eager to get into the fight."

"And we will get you into the fight, but we need to make sure we launch an operation that has the highest possible odds of success," he said. "Cortez has found a way to get a team inside Duster's Range with little to no resistance and give you exactly four hours to get your planes out."

She nodded, sipping her tea.

"Who are you planning to send in with us? We can't take Commonwealth soldiers – that would create some huge problems, wouldn't it?"

"Icaran commandos."

"What?" she said, choking a little. "Icaran commandos? Seriously?"

"Much to the displeasure of the Prime Minister and his cronies, my friends come in many shapes and sizes and political affiliations. Including icaran. With them agreeing to help, it keeps this thing from looking too much like what it really is – an inside job."

"I'm impressed, Commander. You might be more of a devious little shit than I am."

"Quite possibly the strangest compliment I've ever been given."

"I believe it. The question is, though – sorry, getting back to the icarans, I mean – how do we get them to Duster's Range? An icaran ship would be picked up on their LiDAR and raise the alarm."

"Muriel's Moon," he said. "You have a facility there, and while it isn't under Commonwealth control, the ril-galas haven't shown any interest in it either. The icarans will be waiting for you on the dark side, where they will transfer all personnel and equipment to the Azrael's Tear."

Her smile slowly spreading, Cagliari nodded.

"Which is invisible to LiDAR and so ATC Castle won't see us coming. That is brilliant. Absolutely brilliant."

"I have my moments. But if you think that part is good, wait until you see what Cortez has cooked up to get you onto Duster's Range."

12

Waking was a very slow and difficult process. To Sigurdsson, it felt like surfacing – slowly – after having been underwater a few seconds longer than she should have been, lungs burning and a weakness burning itself through her entire body. And a dull ache everywhere. Her head hurt, her chest hurt, her legs, her arms – everything.

Holy shit.

Her eyes snapped open and she immediately winced and coughed up a curse. It was very, very bright wherever she was and it didn't help her headache.

But her arms hurt.

But she didn't have arms. She had cybernetic arms that didn't work right and didn't hold up to the strain of her job and didn't give her any ability to feel them. But her arms hurt. Her mind raced in several directions at once, a confused jumble of memories stitching themselves together to make sense of where she was and why she could feel limbs she didn't have. And the answer was that she did in fact have them.

The surgery. The experimental surgery that was only legal because the Commonwealth government hadn't gotten around to understanding the principles well enough to write a law forbidding its application. The surgery that had made her part icaran.

Slowly opening her eyes, Sigurdsson glanced down to her right and for the first time in a year and a half was not greeted with the sight of the articulated metallic shoulder plate designed to hide the horrible scarring where her flesh ended and the machinery began. Instead, there were bandages and beyond that, there was an arm. Its skin was a rich, deep blue, broken by a dozen or so horizontal white lines on the outer side, their ends tapering like the stripes on a tiger.

A glance to her other side showed a matching limb.

She felt a tingling in her fingers, all six of them. Two fingers and one thumb on each hand and they were all tingling.

Swallowing heavily, Sigurdsson closed her eyes and took several deep, hopeful breaths.

"Don't get ahead of yourself. Don't get ahead of yourself," she said quietly.

And then she slowly clenched her hands into fists and relaxed them again.

"It worked…"

"Indeed it did," said Brill.

Sigurdsson jumped.

"Apologies, I did not mean to startle you," it said, stepping up to the bed and poking and prodding various points on Sigurdsson's new arms. "Surgery went exceedingly well and healing is progressing at a faster rate than I had hoped. Icaran physiology truly is marvelous. Please, you may stand if you wish."

After a moment's hesitation, she did so, using her arms – *her arms* – to push herself off the bed.

"How do you feel?"

Slowly raising her new hands in front of her face, Sigurdsson flexed her fingers once more, turning her hands over and back, taking a good close look at them. And she had no idea how to answer the question. She didn't quite know how she felt. Certainly it seemed the surgery had been a complete success, but when it came right down to the facts, she was currently wearing a dead woman's arms – and not just a dead woman, but a dead woman who wasn't even the same species. There would be many on Thor's Hammer, possibly including her superiors in the army, who wouldn't be able to come to grips with the change. Could she even be considered human anymore? Cybernetics had gained wide acceptance in the Commonwealth, but she wasn't sure many people would...

"Cybernetics," she said. "My eye. I had a contact node in my right index finger to activate my optics."

The brill doctor nodded and took her right hand in his. She felt the smoothness of the metal exo-suit and the rough edges of the finger joints and it sent a shiver down her spine. She could *feel things*.

"I took the liberty of transplanting the contact node as well," it said, gently turning her hand over and showing her the barely-visible implantation scar on her fingertip.

"Thank you. Thank you. How long have I been out?"

"Sixteen hours."

She looked down at the brill in surprise.

"That's it?"

It nodded. Sixteen hours. Sixteen hours and a batshit crazy brill surgeon was all it had taken for her to regain control of her life. It seemed an easy price.

"As I said, remarkable physiology, the icarans – impressive tissue regeneration. Once I bridged the gap between your extant skeletal structure and that of the donor arms with synthetic bone and completed the basic connections between cardiovascular and nervous systems, and of course injected a steroid and tissue-growth enhancer, the icaran biology began to complete the procedure almost on its own. Very fascinating to observe."

"I'm sure it was," she said. "So, uh... how long do I need to rest?"

"You mean to ask when you may return to active duty."

"Yeah, that's what I mean."

The brill shrugged.

"I would recommend not over-taxing your shoulders for the next few days while the icaran tissue finishes melding with your own, but I am comfortable saying you may return to duty once you are comfortable using your new limbs," it said. "However, I would strongly recommend practicing a multitude of tasks to help in adapting to having two fewer fingers on each hand."

The brill picked up a tablet from a nearby table and brought up the Commonwealth Armed Forces messaging system.

"Please log in to your account and send me a message."

Taking the offered tablet, Sigurdsson frowned as it took her several minutes to manipulate the interface properly to log in and even longer to send the actual message.

She handed the tablet back to the brill.

"There. It took longer than usual, but-."

"And your spelling is atrocious."

It turned the tablet so Sigurdsson could see the message as he'd received it.

OKay doc snedingyou messge. See no problwm.

"Typing was never my strong point anyway," she said with a small chuckle. "In fact, pretty sure I never used more than two fingers to type at the best of times. I'm more worried about whether I'll be able to use a firearm."

"Understandable. As your physician, I should recommend against any strenuous activity, including any participation in combat. However, as I am not mentally deficient, I know you would ignore said recommendation – in which case I will simply advise against the use of weapons such as assault rifles that require you to brace them against your shoulder, or any weapon with significant recoil. And, it should go without saying, any hand-to-hand combat."

"Okay. That I can probably handle. For how long?"

"Two weeks, at least. I would like to re-examine and re-evaluate in twenty-four hour intervals for the first week and, assuming no issues, forty-eight hour intervals for the second. Is this acceptable?"

"Yes, absolutely."

Under normal circumstances, she would have been annoyed or even downright hostile at the suggestion she would need to check in with medical so frequently, but this monster-maker of a brill had given her a shot at being a soldier again. At being Freya Sigurdsson again. As stubborn as she was, Sigurdsson did not want to jeopardize the opportunity by pushing off her assessments.

"In that case, you may consider yourself discharged. We speak again at this time tomorrow?"

Nodding her agreement, Sigurdsson pulled on her coat, revelling in the feeling of the coarse fabric on her arms, stuffed her hands in her pockets and headed back into the guts of Thor's Hammer with a single thought on her mind: getting back into the fight.

13

For appearance's sake, Radko had not met with Captain Singh nor set foot aboard the Azrael's Tear, despite his curiosity regarding both. Cagliari served as an intermediary for coordinating anything that need to be coordinated between Singh's people and the Vimy Ridge, which, as it turned out, was serving them all in good stead.

"Just a standard patrol, Admiral," said Radko.

On the command deck of the Vimy Ridge, Radko stood by the sand table. In a floating holographic window was Admiral Mahoney, while above the sand table hovered a three-dimensional star map. Thor's Hammer was marked with a pulsating orange diamond, and a thin dashed line – pulsating in the same orange – traced a long, elliptical route through several sectors of space before looping back to the diamond.

"The Ridge has been docked here for nearly a month," he continued. "I don't want the crew getting complacent. And to be perfectly blunt, I think we've all gotten a little comfortable here. The number of patrols we send out has been dropping off quite a bit lately."

The admiral looked exhausted as he took off his glasses and rubbed his eyes.

"Agreed, Commander. But I don't want you going out there looking for a fight."

"Of course, Sir."

Inside, Radko sighed. Sooner or later, the Commonwealth was going to *have* to go out looking for a fight or nothing about this war would ever be resolved. But for the time being, he'd play the good officer and follow orders.

"It looks like your route will take you not far from Muriel's Moon?"

Radko made a show of double-checking his proposed patrol route.

"That would be correct, Admiral. I'm not really familiar with the location – is there something in the area we should be alert for?"

"No, nothing like that. There's an old manufacturing plant there – the Azrael's Tear is planning a salvage operation."

"The pirates," said Radko, throwing a small amount of distaste into the words.

"I know, I know, but they have their uses, Commander. It might be advisable for the Vimy Ridge to escort the pirates to Muriel's Moon. Safety in numbers and all that."

"We can do that, Sir. Does the Azreal's Tear have a scheduled departure yet?"

"Tomorrow, oh-eight-hundred hours. Can you be ready by then?"

"Won't be a problem, Admiral."

Mahoney nodded and terminated the link and Radko sent the holographic window spiralling off into oblivion.

Cagliari would already be aware of the timeline, since she was more or less in control of the pirates for the time being. At least, as in control as one could ever be with pirates. However, Cortez would need to be brought up to speed. She had said that her part in this wouldn't require more than a couple of hours advance notice, but where hacking of computer systems was involved, the more advance notice that could be given the better. Radko knew little about the actual process, but he'd heard enough stories about encounters with unexpected security software to make him nervous about it.

He made his way to his office, which Cortez had a standing offer to use whenever she happened to be aboard the Vimy Ridge, and was surprised to find not only Cortez there, but also Freyja Sigurdsson. Sigurdsson was for some reason wearing mitts.

"Cold?"

"Something like that," she said with a smile.

She certainly seemed to be in better spirits than she had been the last time they'd spoken and Radko was glad of it. As strong a bond as he'd formed with Anna Cortez over the course of their experiences, he felt a unique kinship with Sigurdsson. The two had faced similar circumstances, each ending up by pure happenstance as the head of a small group of survivors, fighting against the ril-galas and responsible for the lives of those who looked to them for leadership. While she fought on Von Daniken's Landing and he in space aboard the Vimy Ridge, they'd maintained contact as much as possible, each knowing that the other was perhaps the only human left alive to know – to really know – what they were going through emotionally. When they had finally met in person it had been several weeks after the breaking of the blockade at Thor's Hammer. Sigurdsson and her group had been evacuated from Fort Hathaway, a new garrison left behind to hold the fort. She'd been in the hospital recovering from the first of her surgeries and only had one cybernetic arm at that point, the other arm still ending in a bandaged stump halfway down her deltoid.

Meeting and speaking together in person had been a surreal experience.

Since that time, the two had kept in touch as much as their respective assignments would allow.

"How are the arms?"

She hesitated slightly.

"Good. They're good. The doctor that Nasrin recommended... I think everything will be fine now."

"Glad to hear it," he said, then turning to Cortez. "We are scheduled for launch at o-eight-hundred tomorrow for our patrol mission."

The young officer nodded.

"Okay. I was just explaining the situation to Freyja."

The look on Radko's face clearly conveyed his dismay, because Cortez held up her hands and Sigurdsson shook her head.

"Don't worry," said Sigurdsson. "I'm not going to tell anyone. I'm... actually not a member of the Commonwealth Armed Forces anymore."

"And since you said you wanted to have people on this mission you knew you could trust," said Cortez. "I've asked Freyja to be involved."

"Okay, hold on. Let's backtrack for a second," he said, frowning in confusion. "Why aren't you in the armed forces anymore? I thought you were on temporary medical leave."

"I was. Then I got better and the army decided they didn't like it. So I was given an immediate honourable discharge. About an hour and a half ago," said Sigurdsson. "Pretty good, huh? From Regimental Sergeant-Major winning a key colony to unemployed in under a week."

"How... You got better and...? I feel like I have a concussion – why the hell would the army be upset that one of their best soldiers was getting closer to returning to duty?"

"Because they're racist," said Cortez.

Radko looked at Cortez, then back to Sigurdsson, the tall, blond-haired and blue-eyed Freyja Sigurdsson. She was the epitome of the old Earth concept of the Aryan Ideal.

With a small, almost resigned smile, Sigurdsson pulled off her mitts, first left then right.

And she waggled her slender blue fingers.

Frowning, Radko opened his mouth, closed it again. Raised a brow and opened his mouth again to speak. Then just shrugged.

"Okay."

"Okay?" repeated Sigurdsson. "That's it?"

"Yeah, I can't think of anything else."

"Maybe," said Cortez, trying very hard not to laugh. "You should explain the discharge?"

"Apparently, back when the Commonwealth thought that AI was going to develop differently than it did, the armed forces wrote in some additional rules about members having to be human," said Sigurdsson. "Seems the brass doesn't feel I meet that requirement anymore."

"Are you fucking kidding me?" sad Radko.

He seemed to be saying that far more frequently than made him comfortable.

"It really shouldn't surprise you that much, Finn," said Cortez. "We had the icarans interested in an alliance and the government shot it down because, in their minds, the icarans couldn't be trusted. Why would they trust a human-icaran hybrid?"

"I don't know whether I need a pot of tea or a bottle of Scotch."

"We're out of both," said Cortez.

"I hate everything," he said, rubbing his hands over his face. "Okay, so first question: you now have icaran arms?"

"Yeah."

Taking off her coat and tossing it onto a chair, Sigurdsson rolled up her sleeves to the elbow – which seemed a little more awkward with her new three-fingered hands – to show off her new arms.

"Not that this matters," said Cortez. "But they're a really pretty colour."

"Thanks, I thought so too," said Sigurdsson, chuckling.

Radko cleared his throat pointedly and Sigurdsson looked back at him with a huff.

"Yes, I have icaran arms. The brill have this branch of medical science called xeno... xeno-something-ology. It's using genetic material to heal injuries, treat diseases and all that across different species. From what the brill told me, its people have been using icaran tissue for years because they heal so fast. It said it could give me new arms."

"And it worked," said Radko, shaking his head. "I don't know what's crazier – that it worked or that you agreed to it in the first place."

"Me either, really."

Silence, longer and more awkward than when Radko and Sigurdsson had first met face to face, and Sigurdsson finally cleared her throat.

"So yeah, icaran arms."

"Sorry, I'm sorry," said Radko, rubbing his face again. "I don't care."

He watched Sigurdsson's eyes narrow and her jaw muscles twitch -- a sure sign she was preparing for a fight -- and he quickly held up a hand to ward it off.

"I mean that I don't care if you have icaran arms. Or robot arms or human arms. I care that you're back and whole and happy."

Her expression immediately softened, more than he'd ever seen.

"Thank you."

"However, about you joining this mission -- if we put you on the Azrael's Tear with the icarans, will *they* have an issue?"

"No," said Sigurdsson, shaking her head. "I spoke with Elgrapharr before making my decision."

So that was why Elgrapharr had made the comment about speaking to humans a lot – Sigurdsson had asked for his blessing on her surgery.

"Then a more practical question. Are you medically able to participate in this thing?"

"Doc says stay away from weapons I need to brace against my shoulders or anything with major recoil. Means I can't use my sniper rifles, but I don't see that happening in the hallways of an underground research place anyway," she said with a shrug, looking somewhat pleased at the action -- probably, Radko figured, glad that she could do it without hearing and feeling the whir of gears in her shoulders. "I'm a good shot with a pistol, too, so I can still help."

"I have no doubt," said Radko. "We've been asked to escort the Azrael's Tear to Muriel's Moon. You can stay with us and transfer to the pirate ship when we rendezvous with the icarans."

There were nods all around and Cortez excused herself to pass along the revised plan to Cagliari while Radko dropped heavily into one of the two chairs facing his desk and pointed Sigurdsson toward the old-style globe of Earth bolted to the floor.

"It opens."

Frowning, she stepped over and examined it, then flipped it open on its Equator to reveal four glasses and two bottles of amber-coloured liquid nestled in high-density foam. One had been opened, but one remained sealed and Sigurdsson plucked them both from their protective foam recesses with a grin. The grin quickly disappeared when she saw the label on the unopened one.

"Shit, Radko, how can you afford this?"

It was a twenty-five-year-old single malt and would have been painfully expensive even back when Scotch was still being produced.

"That was a gift. Saving it for a special occasion – pour us a couple glasses of the other stuff."

She nodded and gently put the unopened bottle back in its foam, then poured two glasses from the other bottle. She handed one to Radko then settled into the chair next to the Commander. Almost at the same time, they each put their feet up on his desk.

"To your health," he said as they clinked their glasses, then tapped them on the arm of their chairs.

"And my loss of humanity."

Radko winced slightly.

"Yeah," he said. "Are you... okay with that?"

She sighed heavily, then took a sip before answering.

"I'm okay with it in the sense that I don't give a shit what people think of me. I assumed people would be all shifty or downright disgusted – I knew that shit would happen if I went through with this. What I'm not okay with is them using it as an excuse to take away my job. I'm a soldier, it's what I am. It's pretty much all I am."

"That's not true."

"It is, though. I've been in the army since I was seventeen. It's like waking up one day and having your dad tell you to get out of the house and never come back," she said, taking a very long sip, and staring into her glass for a long moment. "I've just been kicked out of a second family."

"Is that why you enlisted? To find a new family?" he said. She'd never spoken much about her past and, Radko realized, he'd never asked her about it.

To his surprise, Sigurdsson laughed.

"I enlisted to avoid prison."

Radko's glass paused at his lips.

"What?"

"My mom died when I was really, really young. Don't even really remember her that much. And my father was a raging alcoholic. Spent so many days just in a black-out drunk stupor. Couldn't hold down a job either – as you can imagine – so we weren't financially stable by any stretch," she said. "I spent a lot of time just out on my own, doing whatever the hell I wanted. Fell in with the wrong people, blah, blah, blah. A little shoplifting led to a little pickpocketing. I was a tough kid, too, so I got some work as a... let's say a debt collector. Kick some heads, collect overdue drug money, that kind of thing."

She paused, blowing out a breath as she ran a hand through her hair.

"Long story short, I got caught at it red-handed. Literally – guy's blood on my knuckles. Aggravated assault, assault with a deadly weapon, because I was wearing brass knuckles. I think they even tacked on extortion and living off the proceeds of crime. I was looking at a substantial prison term. But then I ended up in front of a judge who believed in rehabilitation. Said I needed structure in my life and it was my choice whether I got that structure in prison or in the army. So here I am," she said, holding up her glass in a mock toast. "Or here I was."

"You know why I joined the navy?"

She looked over at him and shook her head.

"Chicks dig the uniform," he said.

Sigurdsson burst out laughing and swatted his shoulder.

"You're such a prick."

"What? I'm not kidding," he said. "I went into the Royal Military College because of a girl."

"Are you fucking with me?"

"Why would I fuck with you? You probably still carry brass knuckles."

"Ass."

"There was this girl named Candy-."

"Her name was *Candy*?"

"Well, no, her name was Candace, but everyone called her Candy. Anyway, I had a huge, huge crush on her. I thought she was the most beautiful thing in the galaxy – flaming red hair, these cute little freckles," he said, shaking his head at the memory. "I tried so hard to impress that girl. I tried out for the high school hockey team, but I was a horrible skater. I wrote a song for her – no seriously, stop laughing – but never got up the guts to actually sing it. And then she gave this speech for the school at one of our Remembrance Day events and she was talking about the honour of serving the Commonwealth."

"So you joined the Commonwealth Navy to get laid."

"Essentially."

"And did you?"

"Not with her," he said, taking a sip of Scotch. "Turns out she was a lesbian."

The laughter burst forth from Sigurdsson with the force of a minor explosion, so hard there were tears streaming down her face. She wiped them away with the back of her hand.

"I tell you this very personal story of the struggles that led me to where I am today and in return you tell me about trying to get a chick in bed."

"Essentially."

"You're such a bastard," she said, laughing again. "I'm betting now all you'd have to do is introduce yourself and you could get any woman you want."

"It's possible," he said, taking a drink. "But it's not a theory I'm going to test."

"Not interested in getting laid?"

"Not interested in getting laid simply because I'm *that guy*. As great as that story about Candy is, it was another life. What it means to be human has changed, and I don't mean you and your arms, I mean everyone. Things that used to matter don't anymore and things that I used to always push aside are becoming more important to me. There are plenty of people on that station – even people who are part of my crew – who spend all their free time drinking and fucking and getting stoned because they figure why the hell not? I just keep thinking about that."

Sigurdsson nodded. She'd done her fair share of all three of those things during her life, but the frequency of all three had dropped dramatically after that first transmission from the Vimy Ridge had made its way to her at Fort Hathaway.

"Drinking and fucking and getting stoned isn't enough to fight for," said Sigurdsson. "There needs to be something more, or what's the point?"

"Exactly," said Radko, downing the last of his Scotch.

Sigurdsson did the same, then stared into her glass for a moment.

"So. You and Cortez...?

"No. Pretty sure everyone thinks we are, but we're not. We're just... I was going to say that we're just good friends, but we're not *just* good friends. We're family now."

"Many other men would have tried to take advantage of that."

"I'm not many other men."

"Does this creep you out?"

"What? Does what creep me out?"

She held up a hand and waggled her three fingers.

"Oh," said Radko. "No. It certainly caught me by surprise, but no, it doesn't bother me. Like I said: human arms, robot arms, icaran arms – doesn't change who you are."

"Thank you," she said. "That means a lot."

14

The ril-galas attack had been disorganized and consisted of only a small number of foot soldiers, which concerned Hunter. Odds were that it was a simple scouting party, but if that were the case, she worried that a larger attack force was nearby and would come looking once the absence of the scouting party was noticed.

The crossfire from those still alive within Balmoral Castle had allowed Hunter and her team to move into the shelter of the castle's broken front wall, but several ril-galas remained.

Without being directed to do so, Grieve set up a sniper position low to the ground, where a hole in the wall's brickwork allowed him a reasonable line of sight. Ransom knelt beside him as his spotter, provider of cover fire and, Hunter knew, bait if need be. The two former police officers took turns breaking cover, while Williams the pilot simply stayed behind the wall. Though he was armed with a standard sidearm, the pilot seemed to be useless outside the cockpit. She hoped she'd be proven wrong, but it was looking like Williams would become a liability.

There was a loud, cracking boom as Hutch fired his high-powered shotgun.

Hutch was a wildcard, Hunter knew. He'd come north from Sheffield after the fall of London and while his knowledge of weapons and improvised explosive devices had been of great help to the resistance, everyone knew he had not served in the military and no one wanted to ask, then, how he came by his skills. Hunter had seen small glimpses in his thoughts as they flickered by – police, prisons, even an anarchist rally or two – but she had never asked him about his past and never delved into his mind for details. Considering where she herself had come from, literally and figuratively, she understood the role a major crisis could play in reinventing oneself. The last thing she would want for herself was for someone to judge her based on her pre-invasion life as opposed to the person she'd been in the months since. She had decided long ago that she would not pry into the lives of those with whom she fought, either by asking them questions or by probing into their minds.

But she didn't need to enter his mind to know that Hutch was an incredibly angry man. Hostility came off him in waves and she was thankful that for now he could pour it out into the ril-galas.

If they ever drove the aliens off Earth, Hunter worried where and how Hutch would channel his anger.

"One left," she heard Ransom say, shortly after Grieve's rifle barked and then, after a heavy fusillade from the as-yet-unseen defenders of Balmoral, she shrugged and spoke again. "And done. Hold for confirmation."

Pulling out a small pair of binoculars, Ransom climbed atop a pile of rubble and scanned the battlefield. As she lowered the binoculars, the girl made a whistling noise that sounded identical to the calls made by one of the many types of bird that now nested at Edinburgh Castle. One of Ransom's talents, she recalled Grieve saying before the mission: if she could hear it, she could mimic it.

Ransom caught Hunter's eye and nodded.

"All clear, boss."

With a nod, Hunter signalled her team to regroup and began to lead them toward an opening in the castle wall. It may have been where a door once stood, but it was hard to tell.

The small group hadn't made it ten feet before a shot was fired into the ground in front of them, stopping them short.

"Halt! Identify yourself and state your intentions!"

A middle-aged man stood in the doorway, armed with a Trondheim Arms 33A1 assault rifle. He wore a military uniform of some sort, his coat a bright red with a black collar and a white belt. He was surprisingly neat and clean for someone holed up in a half-demolished castle.

Hutch tensed to attack, but Hunter held out a hand, stopping him. No one could see into the castle, but she could tell there were other shooters drawing aim on her group.

"My name is Hunter," she said. "We're from the garrison holding Edinburgh Castle."

"You don't sound Scottish."

"Neither do you, yet we seem to both find ourselves in Scotland regardless," she said, spreading her arms dramatically and looking at their surroundings.

"Coldstream Guards, yeah? Number Seven Company," said Grieve.

The man in the uniform hesitated, then nodded.

"Aye. Corporal Walter Hobson, Coldstream Guards."

"Sergeant Douglas Grieve, retired. Third Battalion, Royal Regiment of Scotland."

"The Black Watch," said Hobson, straightening slightly. "I'm honoured, Sergeant. And glad to see a fellow soldier still in the fight."

Even with her ability to sense thoughts, the sudden change in Hobson's demeanour left Hunter confused. Obviously sensing it, Hutch leaned in and spoke quietly.

"The Black Watch and the Coldstream Guards are the two oldest regiments in Commonwealth history," he said. "They actually pre-date the Commonwealth."

Hunter nodded, thankful for the information.

"Corporal Hobson, we're here to help," she said. "I'd greatly appreciate it if you'd ask your shooters to stand down."

"I don't know what you mean, Ms. Hunter."

"It's just Hunter. And yes you do. You have a man with a hunting rifle in the second story window to my right – targeting me right now, as a matter of fact – and four others armed with various weapons currently redeploying to get better shooting position against us."

"She's always right about this stuff," said Hutch. "Creeps the shit out of me, but she's always right."

"I'm going to ask you again to state your intentions," said Hobson, clearly uncomfortable.

"The Restoration," said Grieve.

"Beg pardon?"

"After the bastard Cromwell," said Grieve, spitting onto the fallen bricks at the mention of the name. "When his bullshit Protectorate failed and Charles II was restored to the throne, we called it The Restoration."

"That was in the seventeenth century, Sergeant," said Hobson.

"And now, with everything having fallen apart, we aim to do it again. Restore the monarchy."

Frequently, Hunter didn't need to use her abilities to know what people were thinking or feeling. The slight hesitation and the millimetre drop in the barrel of Hobson's rifle told her that MacDowall had been right – the heir to the throne was inside Balmoral Castle. And he was being guarded by one or more highly trained members of the Coldstream Guards.

"I don't know what you're talking about," the Sergeant said stubbornly, making it even more obvious he knew exactly what they were talking about.

"Let's pretend for a moment that any of us believes that," said Hunter. "And let's think practically. Your castle is crumbling. The ril-galas will be back and be back in force. You have, what, seven men? How many of them as well-trained as you? I'll say three."

He just stared, clenching his jaw, so she continued.

"We have Edinburgh Castle. Its walls are intact, its cliffs too steep for the ril-galas to scale. We are well-defended, well supplied and of our active combatants, over half have either military or police training."

It was an exaggeration, but Hobson couldn't know that.

"What does that have to do with us?"

"Seriously?" said Hutch, with an exasperated sigh. "Are you fucking daft, man? She's offering you a safe place where there will be a whole lot of other people to help you protect your little boy-king."

Though it may have been better delivered without the heaping dose of scorn, the message was received.

"Which sounds lovely in theory," said Hobson. "But how do we know we can trust you?"

Hutch turned back to Hunter.

"This was a waste of time and resources. Just let them-."

"Shush!" said Ransom, suddenly alert and looking out toward the treeline.

A sharp look from Hunter killed the retort forming on Hutch's lips and in the resulting silence, they all heard what had caught Ransom's attention: the unmistakable droning of the large ril-galas airships, the ones that would deploy the deadly flying creatures identified by the Fort Hathaway garrison as 'bats.' All spikes and blades and wings, a bat could tear a human – even a human in body armour – to shreds in an instant.

The reaction of the Coldstream Guard was instant and decisive.

"Everyone inside," he said, lowering his weapon and waving for Hunter and her group to follow.

With a nod, Hunter took up position on one side of the door and Hobson on the other, both keeping watch on the skies while everyone entered the castle. They could just make out the airship in the distance when they ducked inside.

"That's Wiggins," said Hobson, pointing to a much younger man wearing a similar but far dirtier uniform. "Follow him."

Wiggins led them to a spiral staircase and down into a basement that even in its damaged state was impressive. To her left, Hunter saw what looked like a movie theatre and to her right...

"Is that a pool?"

"Yeah," said Wiggins, not pausing, heading straight into the room with the long rectangular pool.

At one end of the pool, another Coldstream Guard stood, rifle in her hands, watching over a despondent-looking teenage boy who sat cross-legged at the edge of the pool, tossing bits of rubble and watching the splashes and ripples.

"What's going on?" she demanded.

"Flying things coming in for another go," said Wiggins. "Don't worry Tombs, these are friends."

Tombs grunted but didn't relax her stance in the least.

It was at that moment that Hobson entered the pool area, three others behind him. His left arm was soaked in blood.

"Henderson is dead," he said, and all of his team swore softly. "They're giving us quite a beating up there. It looks like we may have no choice but to take you up on your offer, Hunter."

"It's a sound tactical decision, Corporal," she said.

"Of course, we need to actually *reach* Edinburgh for it to matter," he said. "Your helicopter is down and we'd be far too conspicuous on the open road."

"We have a couple lorries," added Wiggins. "But not enough space for all of us to go."

Hutch shook his head.

"Trucks aren't fast enough, agile enough, or quiet enough."

"The river," said Ransom, squatting beside the pool, swishing her hand in the cool water. "We can follow the river. River Dee to Clunie Water. We'd need to follow Old Military Road for a little bit, but then we can pick up more rivers. Get to the River Tay and it'll take us to the coast. Follow the coastline around St. Andrews and Kirkcaldy and we'll reach Forth Road Bridge. March straight in to Edinburgh."

"Once we get across that bridge it's only about a four hour walk to the castle," said Grieve.

"But how long a walk to follow all those rivers and coastlines and actually reach the bridge?" asked Pradesh.

Ransom puffed out her cheeks as she blew out a breath.

"Probably four days? Assuming we don't need to hole up anywhere for any length of time."

"Wait, walking for *four days*?" said Williams. "Four days trying to avoid ril-galas patrols? What do we eat? Where do we sleep?"

"We have plenty of supplies here," said Hobson. "We can each fill a pack."

"And we sleep under the stars," said Grieve, with a surprisingly cheerful smile.

"You're right, Hunter – our walls here won't hold out much longer and we don't have the manpower to keep this up," said Hobson, slinging his rifle over his shoulder. "Once the ril-galas airship moves on, so do we. We stick to the rivers like..."

"Ransom."

"Like Ransom suggests. Does anyone disagree?"

There were one or two skeptical looks, but no one spoke up.

"Good," he said. "Now, I believe I should introduce you to the person we're all here for."

He turned toward the boy sitting at the edge of the pool and saluted. The rest of the Coldstream Guards followed suit.

"His Royal Highness King Arthur II, King of Britain, Co-Regent of the Commonwealth. Your Majesty, I'm pleased to present Hunter, a new ally."

The boy looked up sullenly from beneath an untidy mop of blonde hair.

"Fuck off."

15

With the Vimy Ridge preparing for patrol, the crew had been recalled and Radko had done his best to greet them each as they'd returned to duty. Most of the crew were the same people who had been with him since Echo Station, with some additions and some replacements for those who had been unable or unwilling to return to the front lines. He couldn't blame the unwilling. There were times when he wondered how he managed to continue and to not let himself become overwhelmed by the idea that the human race was facing extinction.

Maybe there was something wrong with him. But if there was, it had chosen the perfect time to manifest itself.

"Commander Radko."

Standing at the sand table reviewing the patrol route they'd be taking, Radko turned and smiled.

"Lieutenant Commander Owens."

The two men shook hands heartily. Owens, who had been the logistics officer aboard the Vimy Ridge, had been forced into the role of Radko's XO against his own protests. The man had since been promoted to Lieutenant Commander and been given command of his own ship, a gunboat called the HMCS Haida Gwaii. With the Haida Gwaii undergoing major maintenance work and scheduled to be in dry dock for several weeks, Owens had volunteered to fill in for the patrol mission in his old role as logistics officer, a spot left vacant by an alcohol-fueled head injury to Owens's original replacement.

"You're looking well, Sir," said Owens. "A little grey around the temples, though?"

"Yeah, maybe a little. Good to have you back."

"Good to be back, though I met your new XO on the way in. I think she might be feeling a little territorial."

Radko sighed.

"No, she's really just... kind of like that. Excellent at her job, but a stick so far up her ass I don't think she can sit down."

"Understandable, given the circumstances," said Owens.

Lieutenant Commander Amira el Bahari had come highly recommended and in fact directly assigned by Admiral Mahoney, but she had once commanded a ship of her own – the command and communications boat HMS Lord Wellington. Her experience would no doubt be a great asset, but it also made for some awkwardness, with el Bahari being demoted in responsibility if not rank. The Lord Wellington had been badly damaged as el Bahari guided it back to Thor's Hammer and by the time she arrived, every space-worthy ship already had a commanding officer. When the music stopped, she'd found herself without a chair and so, after commanding a CCB for nearly two years, she'd found herself assigned as executive officer aboard the Vimy Ridge. Given the ship's reputation, it was an assignment many officers would have been excited to receive. El Bahari was clearly not one of them.

"I know," said Radko. "And don't get me wrong, she really knows her stuff, we just have very different ideas of how to run a ship."

Owens nodding his understanding.

"It's always good to have different perspectives," said Owens, shrugging.

"Commander," said the young communications technician, raising her hand like a schoolgirl to get his attention. "Azrael's

Tear is signalling that they're ready for departure whenever we are."

"Thank you, Specialist Traynor. Advise Captain Singh we will be ready to disengage from Thor's Hammer within thirty minutes."

She nodded and relayed the message. A moment later she came back to Radko, clearing her throat uncomfortably.

"Captain Singh has asked why it's taking us so long, Sir."

"Advise Captain Singh that if my ship was as small as his, I'd be ready too."

"Um. Really? You want me to say that?"

"Yes. Those exact words," said Radko.

As the young woman scurried off to relay the message – no doubt worried about how it would be received – el Bahari stepped onto the command deck.

"Lieutenant Commander el Bahari," said Radko. "Have we passed your visual inspection?"

Standing as rigidly as ever, her uniform immaculate, el Bahari glared at Radko.

"A provisional passing grade," she said.

"Sounds like my time at the Royal Military College," said Radko. "Commander, get us ready for departure in..."

He trailed off, turning to Owens.

"I told Singh thirty minutes, right?"

"Yes."

Nodding, Radko turned back to el Bahari.

"Commander, get us ready to depart Thor's Hammer in exactly forty-five minutes."

There were a few chuckles around the command deck and for a split second, Radko thought he saw the normally immovable facial muscles of Amira el Bahari twitch slightly.

The Vimy Ridge got underway right on schedule – Radko's schedule – and not without two further complaints from the pirates. He'd put on a bit of a show in making the Azrael's Tear wait, but the truth was he was just as anxious to get underway as they were, he just couldn't show it. What they were about to do was not exactly above-board, and Radko had to insulate as many people as he could from the inevitable fallout.

The ships travelled along side by side and they were just past the halfway point of the journey to Muriel's Moon when Sigurdsson joined Radko in the command deck observation dome.

"So. Heard a rumour about you," she said.

Radko, who had been watching the Azrael's Tear, glanced at Sigurdsson for a moment before turning back to the dome. He wasn't certain what rumour she was referring to, but he had a hunch. After all, it's not like he'd made any attempts to hide his multiple visits to Cagliari's lodgings.

"Don't believe everything you hear."

"No shit," she said, leaning up against the dome beside him. "But it was a good call. You can certainly pick the right people, that's for sure."

"Um. Thanks, I guess."

"Weird as it sounds, it'll be good to fight alongside them again."

Frowning, he looked up at her.

"What?"

"The icarans. It'll be good to fight alongside them again. You made a good call bringing them in," she said, her brow also creasing in a frown. "The hell did you think I was talking about?"

"Cagliari," he said after a moment's hesitation.

"Oh. Yeah," she said. "Well, I heard that one too."

She looked uncomfortable, but was trying hard to hide it.

"Wasn't going to ask about it."

"Nothing happened," he said, lowering his tablet and trying to meet her gaze.

Sigurdsson continued to look out into space.

"Finn, it's none of my business who you sleep with."

"We didn't sleep together. I mean, I guess we did -- we fell asleep in the same bed -- but I mean we didn't *sleep together*. It was a cover."

Turning to face him finally, Sigurdsson cocked a brow.

"We needed to plan this thing, so we needed a reason why she and I would spend that much time together," said Radko. "A reason that wouldn't make anyone suspicious. I guess she had a reputation before the invasion, so she suggested we make it look like we were..."

"That's actually pretty good," said Sigurdsson. "But I'm kind of pissed you didn't even tell *me* what was going on."

"Well..."

Radko fell silent as el Bahari approached and cleared her throat.

"Sir, the MediCorps doctor is looking for Miss Sigurdsson," she said.

"Yeah, I guess it's about that time," said Sigurdsson, slapping Radko on the shoulder. "We'll chat more about this later, yeah?"

"Can't wait."

She headed off down the ladder to the main command deck, then out, Radko and el Bahari watching her go.

"I don't like having civilians on the command deck, Sir," said el Bahari, her brow furrowed as usual.

"It's a temporary situation – she'll be disembarking at Muriel's Moon."

El Bahari nodded, still staring down into the command deck. Owens was busy at the sand table and several crew members were milling about, tablets in hand.

"Have you met the doctor?" she said. "The brill?"

He shook his head. He hadn't had the opportunity – the brill's addition to the crew had been very last minute. It had apparently invoked some rarely-used sub-clause in the MediCorps Act invoking its right to remain with a patient requiring ongoing care while on a Commonwealth Naval vessel. Radko had never heard of it, and in fact had a feeling the brill made it up, but he wasn't going to argue if the doctor's presence was going to help Sigurdsson.

"I did," said el Bahari. "It's unsettling. Speaking with it, knowing that the 'it' you're speaking to is actually a small creature nestled inside the chest cavity of the bipedal robot."

Radko nodded. He knew exactly what she was thinking, but he allowed her to continue – partly because it was the first time she'd ever spoken to him about something that wasn't strictly business.

"Ever since I first saw that autopsy video, I've been uncomfortable around brill," she said. "Even the brill doctor assisting Doctor Khaifa said it – there are a lot of similarities."

"The icarans and the udukiin walk around on two legs like us. Doesn't make us the same."

"I know. It's just a hard image to shake."

"It's the same brill, by the way."

She turned to him, her frown deepening.

"From the autopsy video," he said. "It's the same doctor we have aboard the Vimy Ridge."

"Our universe has become very small, hasn't it?"

"It has."

They stood in silence for a moment before Radko, rubbing his eyes, spoke again.

"I have some intel reports to review. You're in command -- I'll be in my office if anything comes up."

After a nod from el Bahari, Radko headed down to his office, set an alarm for forty-five minutes, put his head down on his desk and fell asleep almost immediately.

When Radko returned to the command deck, el Bahari was up in the dome, standing ramrod straight, hands clasped behind her back. When he stepped up beside her, she glanced briefly at him before returning her gaze to the shadowed side of Muriel's Moon.

"Sir," she said. "LiDAR has detected another vessel on the dark side of the moon. They believe it is icaran."

"They're not sure yet?"

"I've ordered a heavy LiDAR scan – we should have the results momentarily."

Explaining the rendezvous with Elgrapharr and his commandos had always been expected to be tricky. Between he, Cagliari and Cortez, they'd come up with a plausible story and it was now time to see if it would pass muster.

"LiDAR scan ready, Commander," said the LiDAR operator.

Radko snapped his fingers and pointed to the secondary sand table in the observation dome and a second later a holographic ship appeared, slowly rotating. It was clearly an icaran vessel, but Radko and a select few aboard the Vimy Ridge had known it would be.

"Owens, get me Captain Singh," he said.

"Should we not be broadcasting to the icarans, demanding to know their purpose for being here?" said el Bahari.

Radko shook his head.

"First, we're outside Commonwealth space. We don't have any claim here to start making demands," he said. "Second, we know some pirates have done trade with the icarans. Singh didn't really want us as an escort and I'm wondering if this is why."

She nodded, but her frown remained fixed.

"This is Captain Singh," came the hollow-sounding voice, piped through the command deck speakers.

Being an older model ship, the Vimy Ridge didn't have the same universal video feed capabilities as other ships in the Commonwealth fleet, meaning that in many instances Radko had to rely on voice-only transmission when not in the immediate vicinity of larger comm networks. Many had complained about it, including Owens, but Radko actually preferred it. He could focus solely on what was being said and how it was being said without being distracted by visuals.

"Captain, this is Commander Radko," he said. "I trust you've noticed that we're not alone here."

"Yes," said Singh, his voice much, much deeper than Radko had expected. "We have detected the icaran transport. You need not be alarmed, Commander, this was arranged."

"Captain, this is Lieutenant Commander Amira el Bahari. Do you mean to say that you have set up a meeting with this icaran vessel? If so, for what purpose?"

"Artefacts, Lieutenant Commander el Bahari. My crew had salvaged some icaran artefacts from a derelict vessel some weeks ago. They had no value to us, but cultural significance to the icarans and so we have arranged to return them. Does this satisfy your curiosity?"

The pirate captain injected some hostility into the last sentence. The man was a decent actor. El Bahari stiffened slightly.

"I suppose it does."

"Captain," said Radko. "Can I make a request?"

"I make no guarantees that I will grant it, but yes."

"I'd like to be involved in this," he said. "It's no secret that we need allies. If a Commonwealth officer were to be involved in returning cultural artefacts, it could help our cause if the Prime Minister ever asks for icaran support."

There was a long silence as Singh pretended to consider the request.

"That could be dangerous, Commander," whispered el Bahari. "We don't know the disposition of the icarans toward the Commonwealth right now."

"Risk is part of what we do, Amira," he said, pretending not to notice her twitch at being addressed by her first name. "We put our lives on the line for the good of the Commonwealth."

Whatever response she had was silenced by that of Singh.

"I will allow it," he said. "You will come aboard the Azrael's Tear and we will meet with the icarans here. We will open our shuttle bay. The icarans will be here in fifteen minutes."

With that, the connection was terminated.

"All right," said Radko. "It looks like I'm playing ambassador for a bit. The ship is yours, Commander."

El Bahari nodded and Radko was fairly certain he saw a twinkle in her eye, an excitement at being placed in command of the Vimy Ridge and in that moment, Radko knew without a doubt that she was gunning for his job.

"Good luck," he said with a smile. "Owens, have Sigurdsson and the brill meet me in hangar one for immediate departure."

By the time Radko reached the hangar, Sigurdsson and the brill doctor were already there, their gear loaded onto the Flamingo shuttle. Back on Thor's Hammer, Cortez would have received her code from Owens – a specific turn of phrase in an otherwise mundane report – to begin setting in motion her part of the plan.

The trip over to the Azrael's Tear was short, but to Radko it still felt like an eternity. They were so close to getting their two plans underway -- his and Cagliari's -- that he was beginning to get antsy. Sitting in the shuttle, he had to force himself to stop bouncing his knee and then after that, to stop drumming his fingers on his armrest.

Looking down at Muriel's Moon, an ugly little pock-marked planetoid, didn't help and he only regained some measure of calm once the shuttle rose into the belly of the Azreal's Tear.

"Well," muttered Sigurdsson. "Let's get this started."

Disembarking, the group from the Vimy Ridge was greeted by Cagliari and two pirates – one of whom was very clearly Singh. While not overly tall, Singh cut an impressive and imposing figure. Beneath his white turban, a pair of bushy eyebrows shadowed dark eyes. His long, full beard was shot through with grey and his long coat was a rich purple, embroidered with gold. Around his middle, over the impressive coat, was a wide leather belt, his Kirpan strapped on his left.

"Welcome aboard the Azrael's Tear," he said in his deep voice. "I am Captain Jagat Sohal Singh."

"A pleasure, Captain, and thank you again for taking part in this," said Radko as they shook hands. "Finn Radko."

Though Radko would have loved to speak with Singh at length about his ship, particularly about the anti-LiDAR shielding, the small icaran shuttle entered the Azrael's Tear and settled into its landing zone. A troop of six figures exited, all wearing the traditional and somewhat unsettling faceless battle helmets of the icaran commandos.

As they marched up to the gathering of humans, the lead icaran removed his helmet. Like most icarans, his skin was brightly patterned, fading from a deep forest green to almost white, and speckled with spots of orange and stripes of bright yellow.

"Captain Elgrapharr," said Radko, smiling.

"Commander Radko," said the icaran, extending his hand in a traditional human handshake. "It is good to see you once again."

"And you. This is Kestrel Cagliari, the woman behind this little adventure, and Captain Jagat Sohal Singh, the man who'll be getting you there."

"Captain Singh. Miss Cagliari."

"And, I think you already know this one," said Radko as Sigurdsson stepped up beside him.

"Indeed I do," said Elgrapharr, surprising Radko by giving Sigurdsson a hug.

"Oh, and this," said Sigurdsson, waving the brill forward. "Is Doctor Frankenstein."

"I am pleased to meet you, Doctor Frankenstein."

Both the brill and Radko looked back and forth between Sigurdsson and Elgrapharr multiple times. It was the brill who spoke first.

"The pleasure is mine, Captain. I have the utmost respect for the icaran people."

"And we for the brill. I understand it was you, Doctor Frankenstein, who performed the operation on Sigurdsson that dramatically improved her appearance."

Radko did a double-take. Icarans were not known for their humour. The brill – who was now, thanks to Sigurdsson's joke, apparently answering to the name Frankenstein – didn't miss a beat.

"Yes, it was a very interesting procedure to perform and I am pleased with its results so far."

"So," said Radko. "The icarans are okay with it? Using parts of your deceased this way?"

He was fairly certain Sigurdsson shot him a dirty look, but he ignored it. He had to be in leader mode and not friend mode – he had to know that Sigurdsson's presence wouldn't upset the other icarans and possibly jeopardize the mission.

"We do not treat death as humans do," said Elgrapharr. "There is no ceremony around the carcass of the deceased, no putting the remains on public display. That is... somewhat unsettling to us. Morbidly staring at a carcass."

When put that way, Radko was inclined to agree with the icaran.

"For icarans, when the body dies it ceases to be anything useful. It is refuse to be discarded," continued Elgrapharr. "Once the body dies, the individual lives on in their song. The body is nothing. We do not have fields where we bury remains and mark their location with stones – we simply incinerate them. Or, should the carcass be in a condition that allows it, we place it in stasis and have it sent to the brill for use in their medical research. So it has been for centuries and so it will continue. For any icaran, it would be an honour to know that after death, their physical remains were used to help heal another. So no, Sigurdsson's surgery will be an issue for none of us. Had it been possible at the time, I would have gladly allowed Aeltheer's remains to have been so used."

Radko nodded respectfully. He knew from his many long talks with Sigurdsson while she recovered after returning from Von Daniken's Landing that Aeltheer had been the other icaran commando Locaris had sent with Elgrapharr and the rest of the reinforcements to assist Fort Hathaway. She had died a fairly gruesome death at the hands of the ril-galas horde. And she had been Elgrapharr's wife.

"Understood Captain. Understood and greatly appreciated," said Radko. "Though I'm not supposed to say things like this, I really wish my government would get its head out of its ass and reach out to your people. I think you'd be a good influence on us."

Not for the first time and probably not for the last, Radko wished Locaris had been there.

Feeling a hand on his shoulder, Radko turned to see Sigurdsson looking at him intently, frowning slightly.

"You okay?"

"I'm fine," he said. "But I should go."

After wishing everyone luck in their mission, he turned back to Sigurdsson before stepping back onto the shuttle.

"You be careful," he said.

"Don't worry about me," she said with a grin.

"Freyja, I've been worrying about you ever since I got that first call from Fort Hathaway."

"Yeah," she said, the grin fading. "Yeah, ditto."

As they embraced, Radko spoke again, quietly.

"Seriously, take care of yourself."

"You too," she said, giving him a last squeeze before they released each other.

She stayed in the hangar until Radko's shuttle had departed for the Vimy Ridge.

"He's a good man," said Caligari.

"Yeah. No one I'd rather have in my corner, that's for sure," she said.

"That's not what I meant," said Cagliari with a small chuckle. "But okay."

By Hunter's estimation, the ril-galas airship had hung around Balmoral Castle for just over six hours before heading off. Ransom said it had headed north and Hunter had learned to trust the girl's sense of direction. Several of the two groups – Hunter's own team and the Coldstream Guards – speculated that the airship was heading to Inverness, but all that mattered was that it was leaving.

In what used to be the wine room, Hunter checked through the supplies Hobson and his team had hoarded. It was an impressive stash that included a generous supply of canned food and military rations, plenty of first aid kits, antibiotics and painkillers, and an entire rack of spare weapons – from the advanced 33A1 assault rifles and Trondheim Arms T19 semiautomatic pistols to antique bolt-action rifles and even swords. Beside the weapons rack sat three buckets filled to the brim with spare magazines.

Picking up a T19, Hunter held the pistol at arm's length, testing the weight and balance.

"We had just received those at the barracks," said Hobson. "They're brand new – the latest and greatest from Trondheim."

Hunter popped out the mag, then slid it back in. It was the first pistol design by Trondheim Arms in which the magazine was located in front of the trigger as opposed to within the grip. Its name came from the fact that its standard magazine carried a total of nineteen rounds.

"Reliable?"

"So far I've been impressed," said Hobson, patting the T19 slung on his hip. "I haven't had a misfire yet."

"Would you mind if I kept one?"

"Help yourself. You might want to think about leaving your Caliburn behind," he said, nodding to the submachine gun slung across her chest. "Unless you have more spare magazines. We don't have any that would be compatible."

Nodding, she set aside the Caliburn and selected a 33A1 – like the ones the Coldstream Guards carried and like the ones she'd seen carried by the Rangers aboard the Vimy Ridge.

As the rest of the team members, hers and Hobson's alike, began filtering in, Hunter stood aside while Hobson and Ransom offered suggestions to everyone as to what supplies they should be adding to their large backpacks. The pair were trying to ensure that every member of the amalgamated team was carrying a balance of supplies. A practical aim, to be sure. If one member were to be lost, the remaining team would still have a balanced reserve.

After packing was complete, Ransom and Grieve were sent above and returned thirty minutes later with the all-clear. The ril-galas were nowhere to be seen.

A light rain began to fall shortly after the group left Balmoral Castle, all but the scouting team of Ransom and Grieve laden down with their heavy supply packs. And of course, the King. He carried nothing but the chip on his shoulder. Before departing the castle, Hunter had selected a sword for him - an old sword, but in excellent condition. Though she knew nothing about swords, she'd chosen one that she felt looked passably regal without looking ostentatious. An attempt to further connect this boy-king with his legendary namesake, she'd set the weapon aside almost immediately. A grand idea, perhaps, that would have carried some impressive symbolism once they reached Edinburgh, but hardly practical. The sword was heavy and of questionable efficacy against the ril-galas. A grand idea, but deadweight. And, she thought as she watched the young Royal sulk through the rain, an idea that would very likely have failed.

Pradesh and Fairbairn were chatting amongst themselves, as usual. One of Hobson's men – Wiggins – had taken point and Hutch had fallen in just behind him. Hobson, Tombs and the two remaining Coldstream Guards, Kaur and Ellis, stuck close to Arthur while Williams brought up the rear, grumbling the whole time.

Keeping the River Dee to their right, they made slow, but steady progress, despite the worsening rain. They'd been walking for just over three hours when Hunter saw Ransom crouched under a tree and the girl waved her over.

"Problem?"

"Not of the shooting variety, but yeah," said Random, pulling her wool hat – her toque as she called it – lower over her ears and pointing to the Western sky. "Check out those clouds."

It was mid-afternoon, but to the West, the sky was as black as night. As Hunter watched, a bolt of lightning snaked through the clouds.

"We should find shelter," said Ransom. "I don't think we want to be walking in that."

"I agree."

"There's a castle up ahead, a small one. Braemar. It looks to be mostly intact, but Grieve has gone for a closer look. We could hunker down there until the storm blows through?"

"Assuming Grieve is comfortable with it as well, I see no reason to disagree. I'll speak with Hobson."

"I'll go up ahead with Grieve," said Ransom, standing and pulling her jacket a little tighter.

As she headed off, Hunter turned back to the group. They were moving even slower than before, with Hobson having to cajole both Arthur and Williams into keeping their feet moving. As she caught his eye, he moved and fell into step beside her.

"There appears to be a storm front moving in," he said.

"That's what I wanted to speak with you about. Ransom and Grieve have found a small castle up ahead. They're checking now to make sure it's safe, but assuming it is we're going to take shelter there until the storm passes."

He nodded.

"I think His Majesty would endorse that course of action."

Hunter glanced at the King. He was, again, scowling and stomping through the grass, shoulders slumped miserably.

Clenching her jaw, Hunter forced herself to look away.

"I think your King would endorse any course of action that would allow him to sit and sulk."

Hobson stiffened slightly, but said nothing.

"Or stare at Ransom's ass," said Hunter, shaking her head. "He spends a surprising amount of time thinking... looking at it."

"Royal or not, he's a teenaged boy," said Hobson. "Crowns and crises cannot destroy the hormones of the teenage boy."

Waving everyone in, Hunter and Hobson had the group huddle under tree cover while they waited for Grieve and Ransom to report back. It was a great relief to all when they did, and announced that everything was clear. Within twenty minutes, the entire group was through the castle's curtain wall and into the main structure and very happily dropping their heavy packs onto the floor of the stone-vaulted kitchen.

"I will pay all kinds of money I don't have," said Tombs, pointing to the big stone fireplace. "If someone can start a fire."

"Won't the aliens see the smoke?" said Williams, looking worried.

Hutch looked at the pilot and rolled his eyes.

"The entire world is on fire, shithead."

"Enough," said Hunter. "Ransom, a small fire would be nice."

The girl nodded and set to work. Hunter didn't know what Braemar Castle had been used for in recent years, but the kitchen was stocked with enough iron pots and utensils that soon after Ransom got the fire going, others were warming up beans and Hobson even had a pot of tea steeping.

"A very British thing, that," he said, nodding to the teapot. "Wars come and wars go, but there is always time for a cup of tea."

"What are we fighting for if not our freedom to drink tea in peace?" said Ransom with a small giggle.

"To not be eaten," said Hutch.

There was an understandably awkward silence. Everyone knew now what the ril-galas were doing with their human captives. Everyone knew that the 'processing plants' set up in various locations across the globe were really slaughterhouses and rendering plants, turning humanity into a food source and anyone who doubted the stories need only look at the piles of discarded bones outside the plants. The ril-galas had made no effort to disguise what they were doing, but somehow, even on Earth, many people had been able to simply forget it. To forget what would happen to them if they were captured by the enemy.

"Hutch, you're a ray of fucking sunshine, you know that?" said Ransom.

Leaving them to their hopefully good-natured bickering, Hunter poured tea into two chipped ceramic mugs and sat down cross-legged on the floor across from Arthur. The King of Britain had selected the corner farthest from everyone else in which to sit.

As she joined him, Hunter caught an image of Ransom that was floating through his mind.

"Stop it," she said.

He looked up at her, giving her a look that someone might give the sticky substance they've just scraped of their boot. A look that says they aren't sure what it is, but that it's caused them some annoyance regardless.

"Stop what?"

"Those thoughts you're having about Ransom."

"I don't know what you're talking about. Leave me alone."

"No," she said, handing him a mug of tea and being surprised when he accepted it.

"Why not?"

"Because you're the King of Britain, which means you don't have the luxury of being left alone."

"I don't want to be the King. My brother was supposed to be King."

"The way I understand it, no one particularly wants you to be King," said Hunter, sipping her tea. "But your brother is dead and so we're left with you. Lucky us."

A very graphic image of her flitted across his mind.

"There are some men I would be more than willing to do that with," she said. "But you are not one of them."

The King of Britain stared at her, eyes wide, mouth agape.

"There's something you should know about me, Your Highness," she said quietly, leaning forward. "I can read minds. I can see that every single thought in your head revolves around the concept of 'me.' And I am telling you right now that that will change. You will start thinking of the greater implications of what's happening with Planet Earth."

"Why should I? It's not like any of it is going to matter. The aliens are just going to get us eventually."

"You are a shitty King."

"Fuck off."

"Grow up, you selfish little shit. Good people are putting themselves in harm's way to keep you alive," she said, standing. "Look at them."

She pointed over to where the rest of their little group sat around the fire. Grieve was singing, Hobson playing an over-turned cooking pot like a snare drum.

Hark now the drums beat up again
For all true soldiers gentlemen
Who stand and fight both night and day
Over the hills and far away
Over the hills and o'er the main,
To Flanders, Portugal and Spain,
The King commands and we'll obey
Over the hills and far away.

"If any of these people die because of your apathy, it will not end well for you," she said. "Your people need you to stand up and be visible. They need a symbol."

"Then you do it."

"What do you think I've been doing while you've been cowering in a basement for the last year and a half?"

`Gainst ril-galas on hill and field,
The Black Watch men shall never yield,
Fight until the end will they,
Over the hills and far away
Over the hills and o'er the main,

> *To Flanders, Portugal and Spain,*
> *The King commands and we'll obey*
> *Over the hills and far away.*

"These lives we're leading may be short," she said. "But that gives us all the more reason to make them actually mean something."

That very realisation had hit her quite hard some eighteen months prior and had led her to turn her shuttle around, to rather than make a run for freedom, drive straight into the belly of the beast. She was, she discovered quite suddenly, very proud of it.

> *The Coldstream at our side will be,*
> *To march with us to victory,*
> *And peaceful in our beds we'll lay,*
> *Over the hills and far away.*
> *Over the hills and o'er the main,*
> *To Flanders, Portugal and Spain,*
> *The King commands and we'll obey*
> *Over the hills and far away.*

"Think about it, Your Highness."

Without waiting for a response – and not really expecting one – Hunter walked away and rejoined the group. There was a mild cheer as she sat down and was handed the communal pot of beans that was being passed around. She noticed a strange grin on Grieve's face as he continued singing.

> *Now Hunter there is no silly lass,*
> *I tell ya boys, she'll kick your ass,*
> *From here until enterni-tay,*

Over the hills and far away!

Everyone laughed. It felt good to laugh, to forget the serious-ness of their situation, if only for a few minutes. The moments of levity were always too brief.

At first, Hunter had mistaken the quiet buzzing of thoughts she felt at the edge of her awareness as those of petulant royalty and paid them no mind. They weren't the alien touch of ril-galas minds, which were always enough to make a chill run down her spine and grab her full attention. It was only when she caught an image of armed humans creeping slowly through the curtain wall and toward the castle entrance that she realized something was amiss.

Standing, she drew her sidearm.

Without a word, Hobson was at her side, assault rifle in hand, giving her a questioning look.

But it was too late. Two men burst through the door, one armed with a hunting rifle and the other with the bulky TA204 – the assault rifle that had been the Commonwealth Army standard issue until the 33A1 had been developed.

"Nobody moves!" yelled the one with the hunting rifle.

Two more people came in behind them, a man and a woman, both armed with pistols. Hunter could sense there were two more still outside standing as a rear guard.

"We're all human," said Hunter. "There's no need-."

"Shut up! Tell me what you're doing here!"

"Shall I shut up or shall I tell you what we're doing here?"

"Don't fucking test me, lady."

"We're just here for shelter until the storm passes."

"Not anymore you're not," said the rifleman. "Leave all your supplies and get out."

"We should take them prisoner," said the man with the assault rifle.

The rifleman thought about it for a second and nodded and in his simple mind, Hunter saw clearly what they had in mind for her and Ransom, but also what they had in mind for the rest of the group. She saw flashes, a jumble of images. Other captives. Forced marches at gunpoint. Ril-galas processing plants. Some kind of sleek ril-galas she had never seen before handing the rifleman some kind of device -- a bracelet? And the rifleman and his people *walking away unharmed*. A deal had been struck for the group's own continued survival.

"Leave now and you leave in peace," she said quietly.

The rifleman just laughed and Hunter decided then that she would kill him, one way or another.

"Now listen," said Williams, standing. "This is ridiculous – we have plenty of supplies to share, we can-."

His offer of assistance was cut off as two bullets hammered into his chest and he dropped to the stone floor. The woman with the pistol who had fired the shots kept her gun raised and pointed it toward Tombs, who happened to be sitting beside Williams.

"Anyone else?"

"These people are selling out their own kind to the ril-galas," said Hunter. "That's what they do with most of their captives. They trade them in so they can get some kind of protection from the enemy."

She noticed that all three wore some kind of band around their wrist, the same as she had seen in the flashes of memory – probably a way for the ril-galas to identify them.

The attackers at least had the decency to look uncomfortable that their secret had been revealed.

And then the woman with the pistol put a bullet in Tombs's head.

"Shut up and follow fucking orders," she said.

Hunter stared coldly into the woman's eyes and began concentrating very hard. The process was an incredibly difficult one and the effort it required was enormous. She could already feel the headache starting and wouldn't have been at all surprised if she ended up with a nose bleed at the end of it, but she forced her mind into that of the pistol-wielding woman – whose name she now understood to be Mary Sheehan, an Irishwoman who had been a school teacher before the world ended – and drove deep like a dagger into the very centre of the woman's mind.

Mary simply stared back, her eyes widening with each passing nanosecond as Hunter fed images into her mind. Images of things Hunter had seen while with Radko, images she'd seen piped through from Sigurdsson on Von Daniken's Landing, things she'd seen while on Earth and, most importantly, forcing in both her pride at how the survivors at Edinburgh Castle had banded together to help each other and her absolute revulsion at what Mary and her group had been doing to survive.

And then she began to twist and pull.

The human mind could be a fragile thing, especially when already compromised by fear.

Mary slowly raised her pistol, face twitching slightly, and placed the muzzle against her own temple.

"Mary? The fuck are you doing?" said the rifleman.

Saying nothing, Mary pulled the trigger, splattering brain matter and skull fragments across the wall.

Hunter staggered slightly as if a massive weight had suddenly been removed from her shoulders and Ransom reached out to steady her. The feeling passed in a second, but the head-ache, as expected, remained.

Two more shots rang out in quick succession and the man with the assault rifle dropped to the ground.

"Set your weapons on the floor," said Hobson calmly, a thin wisp of smoke curling from the barrel of his rifle as he aimed it at the remaining intruders. Wiggins and Hutch were at his side in an instant, both training their weapons on the men.

In the fog that followed such an exertion of her abilities, Hunter had allowed her guard to drop. She hadn't sensed the other two men that came barging through the door, firing pistols.

The first bullet hit her square in the chest and the second in the ribs as she fell.

Before she blacked out, she saw an arrow impale the rifle-man's throat and heard the loud boom of Hutch's shotgun as half of another attacker's head disappeared in a coarse red mist.

17

Upshaw had been lounging in her office reading the latest reports from the front lines furnished her by the Commonwealth Armed Forces. She was to have a meeting with Prime Minister deFreitas and Admiral Mahoney later in the day to advise them on strategy and though she knew what she wanted, she had to ground her argument in facts. DeFreitas was on board with a lot of what Upshaw, and by extension ATC Castle, wanted to do in terms of revamping the Commonwealth Armed Forces. And no matter what face Mahoney might put forward initially, she knew that deep down he understood the necessity of giving ATC Castle more input and control over deployment. They were, after all, already in control of the majority of training and supplying the majority of equipment.

The deFreitas government had racked up quite a significant account with the private military contractor in the days since the ril-galas annexation of Earth and Upshaw intended to succeed where her predecessor had failed, in making ATC Castle not simply a capitalist force, but a political force.

Setting down her tablet, Upshaw rubbed at her eyes and stood, heading to the large window with her coffee. When she'd replaced Alvin Curran as Director of Operations, she'd also taken over his office on Thor's Hammer. One of the larger offices on the station, it had an excellent view of three of the station's docking arms. An ATC Castle battleship, the SS Freedom, was just returning from an uneventful patrol.

The more successful missions that her people could complete, the greater her leverage with the Commonwealth and the greater her influence with deFreitas in particular.

Her train of thought was suddenly derailed by an alert chime on her tablet. She swore under her breath: the icon was flashing orange.

Internal ATC Castle alerts were always colour-coded, both in the alert sent out to senior staff and in the alert lights that would be flashing – along with an audio announcement – on the facility or ship where the event was occurring. Blue was a medical emergency, red was a physical attack, green was a radiological alert. And orange meant a biological containment failure.

The doorway to her office burst open and Vossek entered, waving a tablet in his hand.

"Have you seen this?"

"The alert just came through," she said, picking up her own tablet and skimming the report. "God damn it."

Duster's Range.

"Containment has failed on one of our biological projects on Duster's Range," said Vossek.

"Yes, I can read," she said sharply.

"Jackson has already begun lockdown and evac procedures. He should have everyone out and to the safe zone within the next fifteen minutes," said Vossek. "The medical research labs have already been sealed off and the staff undergoing quarantine."

She nodded, staring angrily at her tablet. Duster's Range was the jewel in the ATC Castle crown, a multi-pronged research and development facility responsible for well over half of the products currently marketed by the company. Their medical research wing was developing some promising work, including several biological weapons that, had Duster's Range been within

Commonwealth space, they would have been legally unable to develop. She hoped against hope that it turned out to be something relatively minor, because if one of those weapons broke containment, they could be looking at a serious loss of assets and the possibility of an entire research division being unusable for an extended period of decontamination.

As it stood, standard biological emergency response was quarantine of those potentially directly exposed and the complete evacuation of the facility for a minimum of four hours before sending in recovery specialists. They would be wearing containment suits and be equipped to properly assess the extent of the contamination.

"Keep your fingers crossed that this is something minor, Mister Vossek," she said, pacing behind her desk. "The last thing we need is a major loss of assets just as we're trying to reinforce how much the Commonwealth needs us."

"Do you want me to head out there?" said Vossek.

"Not yet, but soon. Investigate from here first. You are not to set foot in that facility until the assessment team has done their job," she said. "I won't risk any more assets."

Vossek nodded.

"Any word from the Vimy Ridge?" said Upshaw.

"No, but we weren't expecting anything yet."

"I want updates on the Duster's Range situation every thirty minutes. Go."

Nodding, his hand twitching slightly – he was used to saluting superiors from his time in the Commonwealth Army – Vossek exited the office to keep watch on the Duster's Range situation.

Upshaw continued to pace behind her desk.

18

"We brought you gifts," said Elgrapharr as one of his commandos carried in a metal crate.

Sigurdsson sat in the crew lounge of the Azrael's Tear with Elgrapharr, Cagliari, Elgrapharr's commandos and Cagliari's pilots. She had been curious as to how the icaran commandos would react to the five icaran pilots Cagliari had brought, given that they were essentially mercenaries, but there had been no issues at all. In fact, they all seemed to get on splendidly.

"This should be interesting," said Cagliari, throwing a lopsided grin at Sigurdsson.

The commando set the crate down in front of Sigurdsson and stepped away.

"What, for me?" she said.

"Now that you are partly icaran, we wish to welcome you to our species," said Elgrapharr.

Somewhat hesitantly, Sigurdsson popped the seal on the crate and opened it. Inside, nestled in a bed of spongy, foam-like material, was a brand new *aoran* assault rifle and one of the boxy *vayan* sidearms carried by all of the commandos.

Sigurdsson grinned as she picked up the *vayan* and tested its weight. The pistol was heavier than the Trondheim Arms models she was used to carrying, but like the *aoran*, was designed for the icaran hand – making it a far more comfortable grip for her.

"Thank you," she said, forcing a smile while clenching her jaw. She swallowed the lump in her throat and pretended to be very carefully examining the sidearm with her increasingly blurry vision.

She considered it fortuitous when Singh entered, the distraction giving her enough time to collect herself.

"We have received confirmation that the biological alert has been triggered and evacuation is underway," he said. "We will launch our operation in thirty minutes."

"Okay then," said Cagliari, drumming her hands on the table. "Details, right?"

The assembled teams looked at her expectantly and she grinned.

"Basically, this is a smash-and-grab."

The humans all nodded, but the icarans exchanged confused glances.

"We go in, grab what we came for and get the hell out as quickly as possible," said Cagliari. "We have a friend with insider access to the computer systems on Duster's Range. She's just triggered a bogus evacuation order, which buys us about three hours working time once we get on-site."

"What happens after three hours?" asked one of the icarans. Sigurdsson wasn't sure of her name.

"The mercs start coming back and we're fucked."

With the shuttle from the Azrael's Tear already loaded, the team filed into the cramped hold. The icarans clad in their battle armour, the pilots in their flight suits with their helmets in backpacks, Sigurdsson felt underdressed in cargo pants, a t-shirt and a ballistic vest. The brill doctor, who had insisted on accompanying the team, was the lone member to go unarmed. Fully kitted out, the icaran commandos carried assault rifles and sidearms and the pilots each carried a pistol. Holstered and strapped to Sigurdsson's thigh was her *vayan*.

As the landing craft from the Azrael's Tear settled on the landing pad at Duster's Range, the atmospheric trails left by the evacuation shuttles leaving the ATC Castle facility were still visible. The facility was in full lockdown mode, as Cortez had promised. Elgrapharr and Sigurdsson led the team off the shuttle, reaching the entrance door and waving the all-clear.

Running the short distance to join them, Cagliari quickly tapped in the code she'd been given by her source on the inside, the code that would – supposedly – allow them access to the facility despite the lockdown.

The door bleeped and slid open.

"So far so good," said Sigurdsson.

Stepping inside the facility, Sigurdsson took a moment as her eyes adjusted to the orange cast of the light. It seemed she wasn't the only one, as Cagliari stumbled slightly on the doorframe. The icarans didn't miss a beat, the holographic interfaces within their faceless helmets automatically adjusting to filter the light in the most efficient manner for their wearers.

Raising his *aoran* to his shoulder, Elgrapharr took the lead, Sigurdsson and her bulky pistol at his side. Behind them were two of the icaran commandos – a male named Lorocan and a female who was called Aylarr – and then Cagliari and the brill, who everyone was now referring to as Frankenstein. The pilots were bunched in between them and the two commandos brought up the rear.

When they'd first arrived on the Azrael's Tear, Cagliari had been worried about only having six commandos. If for some reason they did run into resistance, she'd said, she'd like to think they had enough soldiers to make a difference. Sigurdsson had just chuckled and shook her head and asked the woman if she'd ever seen an icaran commando in combat. She hadn't of course. Sigurdsson had chuckled again and walked away.

"Cortez has set their security cameras on an infinite loop," said Cagliari, glancing at her tablet as they walked. "But she says there are some ASD units that she can't control from where she is."

"ASD units? What does this mean?" said Elgrapharr.

"It stands for Automated Security Drone," said Cagliari. "Robots with rudimentary artificial intelligence designed to be part of a facility's standard security deployment. They can't broadcast alerts outside the facility with Cortez's lockdown, but they can still function and communicate with one another."

"How well-armed are they?" said Sigurdsson.

"I don't know. They're designed to replace security guards, not soldiers – we shouldn't be looking at military-grade weapons."

"Shouldn't."

"I can't make any promises, Freyja."

The facility was eerily quiet aside from the soft hum of the ventilation systems. The hangar where the Argentavis fighters were supposedly held was three floors below their entry point, its large doors opening from the side of a cliff. With the elevators shut down as a result of the biological contaminant alert that had allowed them to gain access in the first place, traveling through the facility and down to the hangar would take the better part of an hour, cutting their total available time down to just over two hours. After that, the ATC Castle teams would start returning and escape would become all the more difficult.

Once it became clear that this had been an intrusion and not a containment failure, the gloves would come off and the PMC would put considerable resources into making sure Sigurdsson and her group never left Duster's Range.

"The medical research facility is that way," said Cagliari, pointing down a corridor that branched off to the left.

As a consideration for all he had done for her, Sigurdsson had agreed to escort Frankenstein to the research lab and let him have a look around while the others made their way down to the hangar. Nodding, she turned to Elgrapharr.

"Good luck the rest of the way. We'll rendezvous back at the shuttle."

"Good luck to you as well," he said, the words coming out strangely as there was no actual icaran word for 'luck.' "Aylarr, go with them."

Without a word, the female commando stepped in line beside Sigurdsson and Sigurdsson was struck again by the command structure of the group. Unlike the Commonwealth Army, with its ream of officers and non-commissioned officers of varying ranks, within the icaran commandos, there were only two ranks – you were the captain, like Elgrapharr, or you were a commando. Once in a while there would be a higher rank involved who commanded more than one unit, and thus had two Captains under his or her command – Locaris, for example, had been a Brigadier General – but this simplified rank structure appealed greatly to Sigurdsson. There were no pissing matches and there were no arguments about who was responsible for certain duties. The job just got done.

The two groups split off to reach their respective goals and Sigurdsson activated her link with the Azrael's Tear.

"This is Sigurdsson. You copy up there?"

"Affirmative," came Singh's no-nonsense reply.

"Elgrapharr and Cagliari have taken their group and headed toward the hangar," she said. "I'm with Aylarr and Frankenstein heading to the medical labs."

"Very well. I have spoken with our medic. He has transmitted a list of medicines to Doctor Frankenstein's tablet he would like for you to acquire."

Sigurdsson watched as Frankenstein checked his tablet and nodded.

"All right, we'll see what we can do," she said and closed the connection without waiting for a reply. While she understood the rationale behind amassing supplies when one could, she wasn't thrilled about this becoming an actual pirate raid. The mission was supposed to be about taking back assets that ATC Castle had stolen from Cagliari Aerospace and, as a favour very much owed, allowing Frankenstein a sneak peek at whatever was being developed in the medical labs. But Singh had managed to tack on to the mission some actual thievery.

Not that she could blame the man. He and his crew had survived for a very long time both before and after the ril-galas attack by scavenging and plundering what they could when they could, and passing up the opportunity to restock the shelves of their small medical bay would have been a horrendous mistake.

And so Sigurdsson planned to humour the captain.

Following the map on Frankenstein's tablet, they reached the medical labs quickly and began looking around.

"Fucking hell," said Sigurdsson.

In a long alcove on one side of the lab were six glass-fronted chambers, each containing a naked icaran – three male and three female. The steady beep of life support mechanisms could be heard emanating from each pod. A small touch screen was mounted on the front of each pod and Sigurdsson stepped up to the first in the line.

ICARAN SPECIMEN "A" – MALE. SMALLPOX.

Beneath it was an infection date and status updates regarding infection, symptoms and damage caused by the infection going back nearly three years.

The next pod in line was an icaran female who had been infected with necrotizing fasciitis seven months prior. Then a male infected with hemorrhagic fever. A female with bubonic plague. A male with some form of coronavirus. A female with cholera.

ATC Castle was researching biological weapons to use against the icarans. And worse, with the exception of the female with plague and the male with smallpox, all the infection dates were within the prior twelve months. The research was continuing despite the assistance the icarans had given the Commonwealth in the early days of the ril-galas war.

"They have not been allowed to die," said Aylarr, removing her helmet. Her skin was a pale orange broken by vibrant blue stripes and small white speckles.

"No. No, they haven't."

"I don't understand. Why is this being done?"

"It appears ATC Castle is trying to determine which human-originating diseases can have the greatest effect on icaran physiology," said Frankenstein, stepping up to the disturbing display and scrolling through the infection notes. Tapping a few commands into the small display, a larger, more easily readable version of the data began scrolling across his tablet. "Life support is being maintained in order to observe long-term effects of these pathogens."

"If we were to turn off the machines, they would die?"

"Yes," said Frankenstein.

"Please do so."

"You... do not wish us to attempt to treat them?"

"No. I wish us to let them go."

"But-."

"Frankenstein, just let them go," said Sigurdsson. "They've suffered enough."

"Of course, I understand," he said, moving unit to unit, entering a few commands into each. Slowly, the machines began to cycle down and within a few minutes, the steady sound of life support was no more.

Looking up toward the ceiling, Aylarr began to sing a low song about the loss of unknown lives.

"Let her mourn," she said quietly to Frankenstein. "Find those drugs Singh wants. I'm going to check out the rest of the lab."

Heading further down the corridor, Sigurdsson saw stasis chambers like those Frankenstein had in his own lab, from which he'd brought her new arms, and she decided against checking what they held. She had a hunch she wouldn't like it. But it also made her wonder if ATC Castle employed any brill. As much as she liked Frankenstein – the name was appropriate – he sometimes seemed more interested in what was *possible* with medical science over what *should be done* with medical science.

Sigurdsson flexed her fingers, feeling the tendons tighten and release.

She wouldn't be judging him too harshly.

Continuing on her way, Sigurdsson hadn't proceeded more than ten steps when she stopped dead in her tracks.

There was a glass... cage, for lack of a better term. Completely walled in, floor-to-ceiling with what she could tell at a glance was ballistic-grade glass, easily a foot thick. The cage itself was probably four metres square and at its centre, slumped over and unmoving, was a ril-galas foot soldier.

It twitched.

"It's alive," she said to no one but herself, then activated the comm channel that would go to everyone on the team as well as the Azrael's Tear. "They have a live ril-galas foot soldier in here."

"Unrestrained?" said Elgrapharr, a hint of static in his signal due to what they now understood was a degree of low-level radiation given off by the ril-galas themselves.

"Negative. It's in a containment cell and it seems... I don't know," she said, leaning in closer to the glass. "Drugged, maybe."

"I should very much like to see this," said Frankenstein. "I will join you momentarily."

"Yeah. Okay."

It surprised her, as she waited for Frankenstein, how fascinated she was by the creature and how different it looked now, trapped in a cage, versus how it looked on the battlefield. The manta-like head of its biomechanical 'power armour' as Commonwealth Naval Intelligence called it, in constant motion in the battlefield, now sagged to the left, motionless but for the occasional twitch or the blinking of one of its six eyes.

Suddenly, Sigurdsson staggered backward, an overwhelming feeling passing through her that someone or something was crying for help.

"Are you well, Freyja?" asked Frankenstein, suddenly by her side.

"Did... did you hear anything?"

"I'm afraid I did not."

She shook her head, trying to clear it, but the feeling came again, washing over her like a wave.

"Doc, could that thing be trying to communicate? With its mind, I mean?"

Frankenstein looked up at her, then back to the ril-galas.

"I do not believe so. Based on the medical readings displayed here," he said, pointing to the monitoring station set up in front of the cell. "This creature is essentially comatose."

The feeling was still there. Sigurdsson glanced down the corridor and saw another monitoring station set up about six metres away, presumably in front of another glass-fronted cell. As she cautiously approached the station, there was a feeling of hope and then, as she stepped in front of the cell, an image appeared in her head of ATC Castle scientists and a memory of intense pain. So vivid was the image that Sigurdsson had to brace herself on the console to make sure she remained upright.

Shaking her head to clear it again, she stared into the cell.

Like the cell holding the ril-galas, this one was a simple box crafted of ballistic glass and possessing the same dimensions. At the centre of this cell sat a largely shapeless mass of mottled black and dark brown. It wasn't much bigger than a basketball.

"What the hell are you?" said Sigurdsson. The words were muttered to herself more than any attempt at gaining an answer from anyone, but almost immediately, an image forced its way into her head, an image of an udukiin soldier.

Brows knitting together in a deep frown, Sigurdsson stabbed a finger at the console, activating the touch-screen display.

There was no way that thing could be an udukiin, not unless the ATC Castle scientists had performed some horrific experiments upon it. Udukiin may have been odd-looking, with their almost Y-shaped heads and their four arms, but they had heads, they had arms, they had legs. The thing in the cage appeared to have none of those features.

Bringing up the details of the cell's contents took her a moment, but when it finally rolled onto the screen, Sigurdsson was unable to stop the gasp that escaped her lips.

PAIN THRESHOLD RESULTS FOR SUBJECT 33...

TELEPATHIC AND EMPATHIC STRESS RESULTS FOR SUBJECT 33...

DETAILED MORPHOLOGICAL ANALYSIS FOR SUBJECT 33: UDUKIIN MATRIARCH...

An udukiin Matriarch.

She looked up from the screen and back at the shapeless mass. ATC Castle had captured an udukiin Matriarch.

Feared by most other species for their ferocity in battle, the udukiin were intentionally avoided by even the icarans. The entire race was considered mentally unstable by many, with their entire culture based upon prophecies tens of thousands of years old. Even a grunt like Sigurdsson knew bits and pieces of their prophecies, about a great Matriarch coming out of the black – 'the black' being the traditional udukiin term for space – and leading their people to their rightful place in the galaxy. But in all the years since humanity first encountered the udukiin, none had ever seen a Matriarch. At least, not that had ever been officially reported. She wasn't even sure the icarans had encountered a Matriarch since the last icaran-udukiin war – and that had ended several hundred years ago.

The udukiin, according to the sparse intel reports she'd read, were a species unlike any other that humanity had encountered. Though they had two sexes, the female sex had a rare subgroup – the Matriarchs. Though sharing many genetic markers with 'regular' udukiin, Matriarchs were symbiotic creatures, merging their bodies with that of an udukiin female. Through this union, the ruling class of the Udukiin Priex was formed, with a triad of Matriarchs governing the Priex. It was rumoured that when required, a different type of Matriarch – a War Matriarch – was born and at her joining, the udukiin would march to war. It sounded a little too far-fetched to Sigurdsson that a species would base its wars on the birth of one particular subset of their population... but the udukiin were a strange society.

And ATC Castle had a Matriarch.

She'd have had an easier time believing that they'd been breeding trolls. And yet here it was. Asking for help. She wasn't sure what to do and found herself asking what Radko would do in her place. The answer was simple: he'd help the Matriarch. He'd help the Matriarch in the hopes that doing so would generate enough good will that the udukiin would agree to join forces with the humans and icarans against the ril-galas.

Likely a slim chance, but one she had no doubt Radko would take.

It took her a few minutes to figure it out, but Sigurdsson found the right controls to open the cell. Before hitting the final command, she hesitated. Opening the cell could also be an enormous mistake.

She hit the command and cell door hissed, sliding straight out and then to the side.

Taking a deep breath, Sigurdsson stepped into the doorway.

"Can you hear me?"

There was no verbal response, but somehow Sigurdsson knew the Matriach understood.

"I don't know much about your people," said Sigurdsson, approaching the Matriarch in extreme slow motion. "I don't know if it's bad that I'm talking to you or what, but I want to help. Okay?"

Again, she felt something akin to agreement, or at least understanding, wash over her.

As she stepped up beside the Matriarch, the creature quivered slightly and Sigurdsson knelt beside it.

"Are you still in pain?"

It wasn't. But it had been very recently.

"How long have you been here?"

There was nothing by which the creature could gauge time while in its cell.

"Would your people help mine in battle if I could get you home?"

At the word 'home,' a flood of images poured into Sigurdsson's mind, images of a planet she'd never seen. Lush vegetation. Streaming banners. A shining city that seemed to float in the air. The deluge of imagery was so sudden, so massive, so forceful that she lost her balance, reaching out a hand to steady herself.

The moment her flesh touched that of the Matriarch, the shapeless mass reared up and launched itself at Sigurdsson, wrapping itself around her. She tried to yell for help, but the Matriarch stretched its rubbery skin over her mouth and then then over her nose and she felt tiny filaments crawling across her face and sliding under her eyelids and into her eye sockets.

Unable to breath, Sigurdsson keeled forward, trying desperately to claw her way to the door and hopefully to assistance.

Surely Frankenstein had heard her thrashing?

As she reached forward, her vision dimming from lack of oxygen, she saw the Matriarch's flesh flowing down her arm like an oil slick, enveloping her wrist and palm and squeezing between her fingers and then suddenly the blockage over her mouth and nose was gone and she gulped in several mouthfuls of air. Her eyes stung and her arms and neck felt like they were on fire.

Scuttling away to the far side of the cell on her hands and knees, Sigurdsson tore her *vayan* out of its holster and frantically aimed at each square metre of the cell in turn, but the Matriarch was gone.

But it wasn't. She could sense the damn thing.

"Freyja?"

Doctor Frankenstein raised his hands calmly when she spun to point the pistol in his direction.

"Please allow me to examine you."

"I'm fine," she said, her voice barely a croak. "Where is the Matriarch? Did you see it?"

The brill paused momentarily before answering.

"I have seen it, yes. Please allow me to examine you."

"Where did it... son of a bitch," she said, struggling to her feet, then squeezing her eyes shut and massaging her forehead. She had a headache more intense than she'd ever experienced with her cybernetic optics. "Where did it go? It attacked me and then just vanished."

"It... did not."

"I'm not playing this game, Doc – where the fuck did it go?"

"It is still here," he said, reaching out and taking Sigurdsson's left forearm in his hand, raising it into her line of sight.

"Shit."

She spun to face the glass wall of the cell, taking in her reflection. Her arms, shoulders and neck were covered in a dark, chitinous armour and a pair of small, angular lines – tendrils – snaked out from the armour on her neck up across her cheek and into her organic left eye.

The Matriarch hadn't attacked her and escaped.

"The udukiin Matriarch can by its nature only gain agency through symbiosis," said Frankenstein. "Without symbiosis, it is extremely vulnerable and at the mercy of those around it."

"It fucking bonded. To me."

"Indeed."

"Scan me. Now. What the fuck is it doing to me, Doc?"

A feeling of calm washed over her, but she pushed it away, knowing exactly where it was coming from.

"No, don't you try to calm me down, you fucker," she said. "I offer help and you do this?"

A complete absence of feeling followed, which Sigurdsson understood to mean her point had been taken.

Frankenstein led her to a full-body medical scanner and had her lay down inside it. It seemed to Sigurdsson to take forever for the scan to complete, during which time the Matriarch remained blissfully silent.

"You are in excellent health," said Frankenstein finally. "And in fact the points where your human and icaran physiologies merge are healing at a greater rate now than they were before."

"This thing is making me better?"

"An overly simplistic view of it, but yes. It is promoting healing."

"And what's it taking in return? It's a parasite, right, so what's it doing to me?"

"This is not a parasitic relationship," said Frankenstein. "More accurate to call it a conjunctive symbiosis. In parasitic relationships, the parasitic entity reaps all benefit. In symbiosis, the relationship benefits both component species. In this instance, you are being healed and have, one would presume based on your armoured appearance, gained some measure of protection, while the Matriarch has gained the ability to act and communicate through you."

"Well, that's just fucking great for her, isn't it?"

"Absolutely," said Frankenstein, the sarcasm blowing by him at high speed.

"Is this permanent?"

"I am unsure-."

"Not you, Doc. The Matriarch. Is this permanent?"

It wasn't. The symbiosis could be reversed. And again she saw images of what she now knew for certain was the udukiin homeworld.

"We need to find the others," said Sigurdsson, swinging her legs over the side of the scanner bed and hopping off. Wobbling on her feet slightly, she steadied herself on the scanner and rubbed a hand over her face. "And once we get Cagliari's fighters out of here, I need to take a trip to the Udukiin Priex."

Very little had been accomplished in the last meeting of the Prime Minister's advisory committee, but that didn't stop him from calling meetings. That was one thing for which the PM could always be counted on, thought Khaifa – calling meetings that served no apparent purpose.

As she'd entered the meeting room, Khaifa had noticed Upshaw and her right hand man Vossek engaged in a quiet but very tense discussion and Vossek had hurried off shortly after. Finding out the cause of the discussion didn't take long, as Upshaw demanded the floor as soon as the meeting was brought to order.

"A biological containment failure was reported at our Duster's Range facility earlier today," she said.

Like everyone else at the table, Khaifa knew what Duster's Range was, but unlike everyone else at the table – with the exception of Upshaw – she also knew what was being secretly housed in its hangars.

"Your personnel have been safely evacuated?" asked de-Freitas.

"They have," said Upshaw, nodding. "But we have reason to believe the alert was triggered intentionally."

"I'm not sure I follow," said Mahoney, frowning. "Why would someone intentionally violate containment procedures?"

"Admiral, I mean that someone intentionally triggered the alert as a ruse, not that there was an actual breach," she said, her tone providing the insult that her words did not. "While safely housed in our emergency facility, some of our medical research specialists continued to remotely monitor their projects. Six were physically shut down from within the complex and one simply vanished."

"Why would someone go to all that trouble to shut down some science experiments?" said Mahoney.

Upshaw continued as if he hadn't spoken.

"System logs clearly show that the six were powered down from the monitoring terminals physically connected to the projects. The one that vanished shows a continued stream on monitoring data, then a second set of data intrudes – indicating the presence of an entity foreign to the experiment – and then both streams disappear. This appears, according to both the scientists involved and to our head of security Mister Vossek, as if the project has been stolen."

"What's the nature of the project," said Khaifa, knowing she'd never get an answer. "That someone would break into your facility to steal it?"

"The nature of the project is classified."

"Classified by ATC Castle or by the Commonwealth?"

"Classified by ATC Castle, Doctor Khaifa. Not every project we undertake is in conjunction with our Commonwealth contract."

"I see," said Khaifa, nodding.

She watched as Mahoney's eyes narrowed slightly and he also nodded, understanding her thought process.

"In that case, Ms. Upshaw," said Khaifa. "I'm not sure your missing project is a matter for this group. It seems a more internal security issue for ATC Castle."

"Agreed," said Mahoney.

"Though it's apparently escaped your notice," said Upshaw, her face flushing. "ATC Castle is a large part of the reason there still is a Commonwealth. So if something concerns us, it should be of concern to you as well."

"Or you'll withdraw your support of the war against the alien invaders turning us into a food source?" said Khaifa, raising a brow. "You certainly haven't risen from the ranks of ATC Castle public relations, have you?"

Upshaw shot to her feet, slapping a palm down on the table.

"We have just been the victims of a clear attack on one of our facilities and you're making jokes? You should be rushing to our assistance!"

"Perhaps we're simply waiting for you to offer us a contract," said Khaifa.

The room went deathly quiet. Every single person present knew exactly what she meant. In the early stages of the war, ATC Castle had steadfastly refused to be drawn into the conflict, going so far as to refuse to provide supplies to the HMCS Vimy Ridge when she was desperately in need of them. That stance – one that had been taken by Upshaw's mentor, a man named Phelps – was one that had resulted in Radko leading an assault on one of their facilities, taking the supplies by force. And, much to the eternal anger of ATC Castle, convincing an entire section of well-trained operators to abandon ATC Castle and join him in defending the Commonwealth.

The private military contractor had maintained its stance of neutrality until a contract had been negotiated with the Commonwealth outlining what support they would provide and what remuneration they would receive in return.

After the moment of shock wore off, Upshaw's eyes narrowed, a vein pulsating in her forehead.

"How dare you-."

"I think maybe we should all take a moment," said Prime Minister deFreitas. "And remember that we're on the same side."

Reluctantly, Upshaw took her seat.

"Now, I believe Bianca is right – we should be assisting them to find and prosecute the culprits. ATC Castle interests and Commonwealth interests are one and the same these days."

"I'm sorry," said Khaifa. "But when did that happen? Was it before or after they refused to give us supplies? Before or after they declined to send troops to Von Daniken's Landing unless we gave them complete control over the mines?"

"Doctor Khaifa," said deFreitas. "You're here as my advisor on medical issues. This is clearly a military-level decision."

Mahoney cleared his throat.

"Then I would like to voice my support," he said, then paused for dramatic effect. "For Doctor Khaifa's position."

"We are building you your goddamned warship," said Upshaw.

"And doing such a poor job of it that we're nearly a year behind schedule," said Mahoney. "Cagliari Aerospace was *on schedule*, but when the construction contract was handed to you people – for no apparent reason – everything ground to a halt."

"Perhaps it should stop completely? And you," said Upshaw, pointing at Khaifa. "Mister Vossek has traced the command that triggered the lockdown at Duster's Range. It was sent from outside the facility. It was sent from Thor's Hammer. Perhaps it was you who sent it?"

"Perhaps it was," said Khaifa with a weary shrug. "Go ahead and find some evidence to back up that claim."

Standing, she slid her chair back into place at the table and smiled at Upshaw.

"But until that time, please feel free to go fuck yourself."

"I want that woman investigated," said Upshaw, after Khaifa had walked out of the room.

"I'm sure you have ample resources to do that," said Mahoney.

"And I want a Commonwealth Navy gunboat to escort one of our vessels – the Adirondack – to Duster's Range for a complete investigation and pursuit of the perpetrators."

Mahoney sat back in his chair and sipped his coffee.

"Again, this is more of an internal matter for ATC Castle to handle," he said. "I'm not willing to commit Navy resources that would be better utilized in the war effort."

"Well, let's not be too hasty in our decisions," said deFreitas. "I would like us to assist in this matter and I think giving ATC Castle a gunboat is reasonable."

"With all due respect Prime Minister, our fleet is stretched very thin as it is. With the Haida Gwaii still undergoing repairs, I'd have to pull a gunboat from active patrol. I can't justify compromising our perimeter for the sake of some ATC Castle property that *may* have been stolen."

The Prime Minister nodded, but didn't look Mahoney in the eye.

"I understand, Admiral. I understand," he said. "I will expect you to provide Ms. Upshaw with the details of which gunboat you'll be assigning to the Adirondack within the hour, please."

"Mister Prime Minster," said Mahoney slowly. "As I said, I don't see how we can justify-."

"I'm making this an executive order, Admiral. Get it done."

Mahoney stiffened slightly, but nodded none the less.

"Understood. An executive order relating to military action must be made in writing-."

"You'll have it as soon as it's typed and printed for me to sign," said deFreitas.

20

The hangar.

At last, the hangar.

Cagliari was practically twitching with excitement as she worked to override the security codes and gain access to the large area where her fighters were being kept. At least, where she hoped they were being kept. Her contact had sent photos showing that the Argentavis fighters were there, but Cagliari had no way to know if they'd been relocated in the time between the photos being taken and Cortez triggering the evacuation of Duster's Range.

She had to believe they were there. If they weren't, she would have just wasted a substantial amount of time, resources and money on a fool's errand. But more importantly, she would remain sidelined in the war, and that she simply could not accept. With a degree in aerospace engineering and experience as a test pilot, she should have been at the forefront of the Commonwealth's attempts to rebuild their fleet and get trained pilots into play. She should have been, but she wasn't. ATC Castle had become too entrenched in the Commonwealth military machine to involve any but their own people in development or training – and they would certainly not be open to the involvement of a Cagliari. It was Cagliari Aerospace and Trondheim Arms that had prevented them from becoming the sole provider to the Commonwealth Armed Forces.

The control panel for the door hissed and the locking mechanism clanked as it disengaged.

Cagliari grinned.

"We're in."

"I will lead with my commandos," said Elgrapharr.

There was a protest forming on her lips, but Cagliari managed to swallow it. The icaran troops were better trained to deal with anything that might be waiting for them. She already had few enough pilots, so losing even one would be a huge blow. So instead of arguing, she nodded, and waved over her pilots while the icaran commandos prepared to enter the hanger.

"Stay behind the commandos," she said, drawing her pistol. "But be ready to defend yourself, just in case."

There were nods all around as the other nine pilots drew their weapons as well.

As the door slid open, Cagliari heard a whirring sound that didn't seem to be coming from the door mechanism, and then Elgraphaar fired two rapid shots from his assault rifle into something just inside. The remains of an ASD, still smoking and sparking, dropped across the hatchway and one of the icarans kicked it aside.

"If these automatons are able to communicate with each other," said Elgraphaar. "We can assume others are on their way."

The commandos filed in, weapons ready, and Cagliari gripped her sidearm a little tighter as she followed.

She heard the gunshots before she saw anything. Heard the ping of a projectile ricochet off icaran armour. Then she saw three more ASD units sprinting across the hangar to join the two that had already taken up firing position.

Elgraphaar dropped to one knee, one of his commandos following suit as two others took up standing positions behind them. They fired in pairs and in perfect sequence, one high and one low, taking out the two nearest opponents before the other three could join the fight.

Raising her pistol in unsteady hands, Cagliari fired a shot toward the remaining three robots, who were now close enough to fire back. Her shot went wide -- horribly wide -- but gained the attention of one of the ASDs. It raised its weapon and fired at her, but suddenly there was an armoured commando between them and a split second after she heard the bullet ping off the icaran's chest plate, she heard the boom of an *aoran*, followed by several others.

And then everyone seemed to relax.

"Clear," said one of the icarans.

It had all happened very quickly and Cagliari, wiping the sweat off her brow with the back of her hand, couldn't have been happier to holster her weapon.

"Okay," she said, taking a deep, shaky breath. "Okay... that was interesting."

"These drones have cameras," said Elgrapharr, nudging the remains of an ASD unit with his toe. "Destroy all of them."

He fired three times into the unit's head, turning it into a smoldering pile of scrap. The rest of his commandos followed suit as Cagliari turned away. And caught sight of her goal.

Sitting in the hangar, bathed in light from the overhead floods, was a line of Argentavis fighters: black hulls gleaming, wings folded at their sides as if they were the great birds after which they'd been named, their flock at rest.

She stepped up to the nearest of the fighters and, pulling off her gloves, gently stroked its nose. A smile spread across her face as she felt the cool composite beneath her fingertips.

"Oh, you pretty bird... you pretty, pretty bird..."

Wiping away the tears forming in her eyes, Cagliari forced herself to turn away from the fighter and address her pilots.

"Check on the status of the other fighters and see how many are still loaded in those cargo haulers," she said. "Gregson and Wade will pilot the haulers, the remaining eight of us will pilot individual fighters."

As the others ran off to follow the order, Cagliari tethered the Argentavis to her tablet and activated the cockpit access. In the fighter's underside, a hatch hissed open, an armature lowering a reclined chair to the hangar bay floor. The armature had barely stopped moving before Cagliari had dropped into the seat and, after donning her helmet, had begun tapping a new sequence of commands into her tablet. The armature retracted, lifting Cagliari into the belly of the Argentavis and plunging her into total blackness.

A second later, the fighter's holographic screens blinked to life, revealing the view directly in front of it in complete clarity. The armature slid Cagliari forward to the optimum position for her height and weight.

"Well done, pretty bird," she murmured. "Now let's get a full view."

Hard-docking her tablet to the mount directly above her, Cagliari activated what the design team had officially named the UHUD – short for Universal Heads-Up Display – but which Cagliari had always called world-view. Using advanced camera technology based on a type of icaran sensor array and tying it to the holographic sandbox technology already employed in most Commonwealth Navy ships, the designers had created the UHUD, allowing them to cast aside the old notion of a 'cockpit' and thus eliminate a clear weak point in every Starfighter. Instead of seeing space through a clear canopy, the pilot of an Argentavis was completely enveloped by a holographic display of their surroundings. Anywhere they looked, they could see what was happening.

Inside the Argentavis, Cagliari laughed as the entire hangar popped into existence around her.

Before she could request check-in with the rest of the pilots, her external comms crackled to life, the tethering of her tablet automatically routing all communications to the headset in her helmet.

"This is Captain Singh. What is that status of the operation?"

"Captain Singh, this is Cagliari. We have the fighters in our possession – we're just running tests and getting everything ready."

"We are running out of time," said Singh. "Information has just been passed along that the Adirondack and the HMAS Newcastle left Thor's Hammer on a direct course for Duster's Range one hour ago."

"Shit."

"ATC Castle is apparently aware the alert was a ruse," said Elgrapharr.

"All right everyone," said Cagliari. "We need to be airborne ASAP. Elgrapharr, get your team back to the shuttle and make sure you pick up Sigurdsson on the way – we can take this from here."

"Understood."

She watched as Elgrapharr rounded up his commandos and they headed out of the hangar. This was it. This was the moment she'd been living for for the last... well, she supposed she'd been living for this moment since the ril-galas destroyed her concept of a life, but this moment specifically – sitting in the cockpit of an Argentavis – since she'd learned about the treachery of Bianca Upshaw and her cronies.

"Okay Cags, this is it," she said to no one but herself.

"Please repeat," said Daxma, one of the better icaran pilots Cagliari had hired.

"Uh, nothing, just...," she said, stumbling for a moment, and then slowly grinning. "Outlaw Squadron check in."

She almost giggled. That line had been repeating in her head non-stop for months, though it had taken her some time to settle on the simple name of Outlaw Squadron. At times it had been Argentavis Squadron, but that had seemed too cumbersome. Same with Blackguard Squadron – though it was wholly appropriate. Once she'd even considered Salt Squadron, given how downright pissy she'd been about being sidelined. But in the end, Cagliari had settled on Outlaw, because she felt like if they could manage to pull this off, they'd be a little like Robin Hood -- robbing from the rich ATC Castle and giving to the poor war effort.

As the remaining nine pilots in Outlaw Squadron, including the two powering up the haulers, checked in, Cagliari took a deep breath.

"Outlaw Squadron, power up engines," she said. "And prepare to take flight."

As her engines cycled up, the wings of Cagliari's fighter unfolded, stretching out to their full fourteen metre span, and the fighter lifted off the ground.

"Weapons free as soon as we break atmo," she said, maneuvering the fighter toward the now-open hangar doors, her seat armature keeping her seat gyroscopically stabilized. "We have ATC Castle incoming and I want those haulers defended."

Despite how she felt inside, she didn't smile as her ship slowly glided out of the hangar, the clean lines and metallic edges of the facility giving way to yellowish crags of Duster's Range. The joy of once again flying an Argentavis – of having Outlaw Squadron a reality rather than a pipe dream – was still there, but it had been pushed down a layer, beneath the knowledge that she was now responsible for not only keeping her squadron alive, but for leading them into battle. For ensuring they could make a difference, just as she'd promised Radko.

"Azrael's Tear, this is Cags," she said, automatically reverting to the nickname she'd earned as a test pilot. "Outlaw Squadron is taking wing."

And she hammered her thrusters full power, swooping up toward the stars in a double barrel roll, the rest of Outlaw Squadron close behind.

21

"Where are you right now?" said Vossek the second the audio-only link was established and unscrambled.

The man had a tendency toward intentionally and immediately getting people on the defensive. It was his way of trying to control a situation. El Bahari didn't know if he'd always been like this, but he'd certainly been the same in the year that she'd known him. She had also always completely failed to stop herself from reacting to it.

"We're on patrol. I told you I would check in when I could."

"That doesn't answer my question."

Sitting on the floor against her bunk, el Bahari leaned her head back and sighed. A bottle of water at her side and a tablet in her lap, she'd been reviewing status reports from the various ship department when the encrypted call from Vossek had come through.

"We are approximately one hour out from Outrider," she said wearily. "From there, we head-."

"You're not at Duster's Range?"

She leaned forward, staring at the tablet as if Vossek's face would be there. That face, with its chiseled features, had caused no end of trouble for many women, el Bahari included.

"No. Why would we be at Duster's Range? And besides, I told you and your Dragon Lady that I'd keep you informed as to our movements," she said. "If we'd deviated that far from our course, I would have told you."

"There's been a security breach at Duster's Range," he said, as if she hadn't spoken at all. "My gut tells me Radko had something to do with it."

"Your gut also told me I'd be getting my own ship."

He had no response to that. Even at the time she'd known it was just pillow-talk, but she'd allowed herself to believe it anyway.

"You will," he said. "We have the Ranger fixed up and ready to launch as soon as you complete this mission for us."

Of course, they had never actually specified how long this 'mission' of theirs would last. How long would ATC Castle need her to watch Finn Radko, record and report his every move? El Bahari knew the man was a loose cannon and she felt it was only a matter of time before he did something foolish, but she wished he would do it quickly. As proud as she was of her Commonwealth Navy uniform, if the Navy wouldn't recognize her skills and abilities and place her where she could do the most good, then she would take up with an organization that would.

"I'll keep a closer eye on Radko," she said. "But we're nearer icaran space than we are Duster's Range."

The Vimy Ridge's internal comms crackled to life.

"Lieutenant Commander el Bahari to the command deck please."

"I have to go," she said to Vossek, but he'd already killed the connection.

"Look at this," said Radko as el Bahari stepped onto the command deck.

He stood at the sand table, the LiDAR technician Staubitz at his side. Staubitz tapped a command in to his tablet and the LiDAR monitoring screen popped up over the sand table, hovering above the full holographic schematic of the Vimy Ridge that had already been floating there. Radko reached out and swapped the two images, the LiDAR screen taking up the bulk of the sand table projection and the Vimy Ridge being relegated to a smaller, inactive selection.

"Is there a problem?" said el Bahari, buttoning her uniform jacket.

"We don't know yet," said Radko.

Frowning, el Bahari stepped up to the sand table and looked over the LiDAR images. The results Staubitz had generated were being overlaid onto a detailed starmap laying out the nearby contours of icaran border space. Just beginning to cross that border out of icaran space and into the no-mans-land between the Icaran Colonial Empire and the Commonwealth was a large icaran warship.

"Have they tried to contact us?"

Exchanging a glance with Owens, Radko shook his head.

"No," said Radko. "They're not broadcasting at all. Not even the usual low-level chatter we can usually pick up."

"If they're running silent...," she said slowly. "Do you think they're planning an attack?"

"No."

Running a hand through his hair, Radko sighed.

"I mean, I'd like to think not – we have a common enemy after all," he said, then shrugged. "But I can't even convince our own government of that, so who the hell am I to say?"

Before she could reply, a ping sounded from the sand table. The LiDAR had detected a second icaran warship entering the sector.

"This has to be an attack," said el Bahari, pulling out her tablet and quickly issuing orders. "All gun crews to your stations. Missile batteries on standby."

"Sir," said a comm tech, raising her hand as if she were in school. Which she probably should have been, given her age, thought Radko. "Sir, I have an incoming transmission from the icarans."

He nodded and the girl put the call on speakers.

"Attention Commonwealth vessel, this is Admiral Rhekarr of the Icaran Colonial Navy vessel Venn Shakara."

"Admiral, this is Commander Finn Radko of the HMCS Vimy Ridge. Do you require assistance?"

Radko and el Bahari exchanged a look. The answer from the icarans would of course be no, whether they were planning an attack or not. It was the way in which they declined the offer that would – hopefully – tell the humans whether an attack was imminent.

They waited for a few moments for the icaran officer to respond.

"It is possible, Commander," said Rhekarr.

"I'm sorry," said Radko, exchanging a concerned look with el Bahari. "I don't understand."

"Nor do we at present, Commander Radko. You have no doubt detected two icaran vessels leaving our established territory."

"We have."

"The Venn Shakara is the second of those vessels. The first is the Vor Tokar," said Rhekarr. "The Vor Tokar has been missing for three months. We have thus far been unable to communicate with the vessel."

"So it's a ghost ship," said Radko.

"No. It has been making course adjustments. Even now, you will see it beginning to alter its course."

El Bahari nodded toward the sand table where Radko clearly saw the vessel beginning to turn.

OUT OF THE BLACK

"Admiral, this is Lieutenant Commander Amira el Bahari, executive officer of the Vimy Ridge. How long have you been tracking the Vor Tokar?"

"Our sensor relay stations have been tracking her for eleven days. The Venn Shakara was only dispatched to intercept three days ago."

"What can we do to help, Admiral?" said Radko.

"At this juncture, nothing. We just wish you to be aware that we are launching a shuttle to board the Vor Tokar and that we have no intention of taking hostile action against the Commonwealth."

The icaran paused briefly before continuing.

"Once we have regained control of the Vor Tokar, we will resume our prior mission, Commander Radko."

"Understood, Admiral. The Vimy Ridge will stand by until you regain control of the ship," said Radko. "Just in case our assistance is required."

"That is acceptable."

Radko quickly climbed the ladder into the observation dome, el Bahari right on his heels. They watched as the icaran shuttle fired its thrusters and exited the Venn Shakara and headed toward the ghost ship.

El Bahari frowned.

"That ship is firing maneuvering thrusters."

She was right, Radko realized. The Vor Tokar was indeed repositioning itself. But for what? And who was at the controls?

He reactivated the transmission line between the Vimy Ridge and the Venn Shakara.

"Admiral Rhekarr, there's something not right here."

"I agree, Commander Radko," said Rhekarr, the uneasiness in his voice conveyed easily despite the blandness of the voice used by the translation matrix.

"Look," said el Bahari suddenly, pointing toward the Vor Tokar. "It's breaking apart."

As she and Radko watched, large sections of the icaran battlecruiser began to separate, like pieces of a three dimensional puzzle.

"No it's not," said Radko, gripping the observation dome railing a little tighter. "It's opening."

"It's a trap!" said Rhekarr, just as loud alert klaxons began to blare throughout the Vimy Ridge.

The automated detection systems had found traces of the distinctive radiation signatures of ril-galas vessels.

Out of the empty shell that had once been the Vor Tokar, two ril-galas battleships and several wings of fighters emerged. The icaran shuttle was vaporized before it had finished turning back toward the Venn Shakara.

22

Hunter came to suddenly, jerking into a sitting position and immediately feeling a sharp pain in her chest.

"Take it easy," said Hobson, placing a hand on each of her shoulders and gently but firmly pushing her back to a reclining position.

She sat on the floor of the kitchen, propped against the wall using someone's backpack to allow her to lay back. Off in the corner opposite, two bodies lay under a tarp. Hunter assumed they were the bodies of Williams and Tombs. The bodies of the people who attacked them were nowhere to be found, but she could vaguely sense the minds of two survivors who had been tied up and were left outside in the rain.

"How long," she said and stopped, pain shooting through her chest as she took a breath. "How long was I out and how bad is it?"

"Almost two hours," said Hobson. "And not as bad as we'd thought. Your vest took the brunt of it, but at such close range, you still have two broken ribs."

Hunter nodded. She could feel that her ribs had been wrapped tightly and was glad that even before she'd shown up, everyone who took shelter in Edinburgh Castle had mandatory training in basic first aid. She accepted the bottle of water Hobson handed to her, but as she drank, she noticed several of her compatriots giving her odd looks.

"What is it?" she said after swallowing.

"The King," said Hobson, hesitantly. "Doesn't think that woman committed suicide."

Hunter glanced over to where the King sat, off by himself, as usual, then back to Hobson.

"She put a gun to her head and pulled the trigger. How would His Royal Highness like to classify that?"

"He says... that you forced her to do it. With your mind."

Taking another swig of water, Hunter carefully closed the bottle and set it down before slowly and with great difficulty – not to mention shooting pains through her entire torso – got to her feet. Bracing herself against the cool stone wall, she looked to each surviving member of the team. And intentionally not Arthur.

"I see. So this is where the paranoia starts."

"No one ever catches you off guard," said Hutch, the only one actually looking her in the eye. "And you always seem to know when the ril-galas are attacking."

"I saw her face when she was about to pull the trigger," said Grieve. "It weren't the face of someone doing something they wanted to."

"I saw your eyes," said Ransom, staring down at some kind of insect as it crawled across the toe of her filthy hiking boots.

Moving gingerly over to the fire, Hunter served herself a cup of beans. They were still warm, but they were overcooked. She didn't care – she was hungry and angry and in pain.

"I didn't know if it would work," she said.

Even though no one had been speaking, the room seemed to find a higher grade of silence. Hunter ate a spoonful of beans while she tried to figure out how to word things so that people – regular people – would understand.

"It... wasn't a simple process. I first had to make her feel shame at what she was doing. Disgust, even. And once I made her understand that-."

"Bloody hell," said Wiggins. "Listen to you, talking like this shite is normal!"

"Look around you and then, please, tell me what 'normal' is," said Hunter.

"It isn't fucking with people's minds until they kill themselves," said Hutch, his hand – consciously or not – settling on his holstered sidearm. "We don't even know who you really are or where you came from. You just showed up one day."

"I am exactly who I've been for the last year and a half that we've been fighting this occupation, Mister Hutchings," she said. "And I am also a weapon. A weapon designed by and discarded by the Union of Soviet Socialist Republics."

There was dead silence as she finished her beans and then tossed her mug aside.

"I was born in Lijiang, China to a very, very poor family. When I was four, I began to show signs of extrasensory perception. When I was five, my parents heard that the government was looking for children who had shown such signs, so they sold me to a government division called Project Nightwatch. I spent the next twenty years of my life in a lab, being forced to undergo testing and experimentation and endless hours of training to become a psychic assassin and when the project was deemed a failure, I was scheduled to be *liquidated*."

Picking up the water bottle again, she opened it and drank.

"So I escaped. I killed nine men in the process, if you were wondering – all by conventional means, if you were also wondering about that. I was on the run for a year before the Commonwealth caught me and imprisoned me and made a deal to hand me over to ATC Castle for research purposes. But I was

159

fortunate in that the ship that was to transport me to ATC Castle happened to be the HMCS Vimy Ridge, commanded by Finn Radko."

She noted a few people straighten a little. Most survivors had seen the ril-galas autopsy broadcast before the ril-galas had killed all off-world communication and so knew who Radko was.

"He freed me in exchange for my help as a means of early detection. And then, of my own free will, I came to Earth, despite the fact that the Commonwealth, the Soviets *and* ATC Castle have all put a price on my head," she said. "I came here to help fight the occupying force."

"You should have told us all of this," said Hutch.

"Why?"

"Because we deserve to know who we're sharing space with!"

"Do we indeed? Do the rest of you agree?"

There were murmurs of agreement.

"I see. In that case," she said. "Hutch, perhaps you'd like to share with everyone why a man with no military training is such a skilled bomb-maker? Ransom, maybe you'd like to explain the four tally marks you have cut into your left forearm? I'm sure the rest of you have secrets in your past you'd all like to share? Despite being a psychic, I have never gone into your minds looking for your secrets or digging into your pasts. We are now who we have become since the ril-galas invasion. At least, that's how I see it. I don't *care* how you came to be an expert at explosives. I don't care if someone was a priest, a porn star or a contract killer before the world changed – all I care about is who they are today and whether they're helping keep the human race alive."

She ran a hand through her hair, surprising even herself at how emotional she was becoming. It was a strange feeling after having spent so much time devoid of any emotion but anger.

"I had no choice in what I was trained to be. What I was brought up to be from the age of five. And I didn't think I would ever have a choice... but then Radko opened my cell door and gave me the chance to choose the kind of person I wanted to be," she said, then spread her arms wide. "And this is what I chose. A life lived on the razor's edge, fighting to protect those who need protection."

Dropping her arms, she winced slightly. The action caused a ripple of pain through her ribs.

"If that isn't good enough for you, then you are a bunch of hypocrites who aren't worth my efforts."

When no reply was forthcoming, Hunter shook her head and stepped outside, sheltering from the rain under an overhang. She could hear murmured conversation inside the kitchen, but couldn't make out individual words. If she'd reached out with her mind, she had no doubt she could pick out what each person was thinking, but she found she didn't care.

A chill was just starting to set in when Ransom appeared at her side, carrying Hunter's jacket. The girl helped her put it on without a word and then just stood for a moment, staring out at the torrential rain battering the castle's grounds and curtain wall.

"Kills," she said finally.

Hunter turned to look at her.

"The cuts I made on my arm," said Ransom. "I'm counting kills."

"I would have thought you'd killed more than four ril-galas," said Hunter, already knowing, or at least strongly suspecting, what Ransom's response would be.

"Human kills."

Hunter just nodded.

"You don't look surprised," said Ransom.

"When I saw you take out that traitor and then saw a fresh cut on your arm, it was easy to put two and two together," she said. "Without resorting to mind-raping you."

Ransom had the good sense to wince at that.

"I'm sorry I didn't stick up for you in there. I should have."

"It's fine. I don't expect anyone to understand me or my past or how I feel about any of it."

To Hunter's surprise, Random chuckled humourlessly.

"Yeah, knowing the kind of horrible things you're capable of and being more than a little afraid of it? Who could ever understand that," she said, her voice dripping with sarcasm.

Pushing up her sleeve, the young redhead held out her left arm to Hunter. There were four short scars visible, plus the fresh one Hunter had noticed earlier, making five and not four as Hunter had thought.

"The first one was a guy I saw back home hunting moose," said Ransom. "They're endangered. I guess most things are endangered now, though. He didn't see me – I was always really good at stealth. I was surprised at how easy it was, just an arrow through the throat."

She pulled down her sleeve and crossed her arms over her chest. The temperature was really starting to drop.

"And it felt good," said Ransom. "Three of the five were before the ril-galas came. The fourth was right after the shit hit the fan and everyone was all panicky. I didn't even need to worry about being caught."

"Harley..."

"No, I just want you to know that I get it. Why you didn't want to talk about your past. I get it. When I think about what

I was before all of this, it scares the shit out of me," she said. "I think maybe you and me are the only people in the universe whose lives were *saved* by the invasion. For me anyway, it gave me a place to focus these... I dunno, these tendencies? Urges? I don't even know what to call them. But whatever. I don't care. Psychic assassin or not, I still consider you a friend."

She looked up at Hunter with a sad, lopsided grin.

"Think a psychic assassin and a teenaged serial killer can still be friends?"

"I can't think of a better pairing."

"Hunter!"

She and Ransom turned quickly at the shout from the doorway. Hobson stood there, looking excited.

"Grieve was going to set up on overwatch upstairs," he said. "And... you have to see this."

Hobson immediately turned and headed back inside, Ransom and Hunter following close behind. He led them upstairs to a small room, in which the furniture had all been pushed to one side. Standing in the centre of the room was Grieve, and beside him sat a piece of machinery, large, but not overly so. Straps had been attached that indicated it was designed to be transported like a backpack.

"It's a transmitter," said Hobson. "A long-distance transmitter."

"The same kind we used to use in the Black Watch," added Grieve. "When we were deployed and need to call out into orbit for evac."

A transmitter that could launch a transmission into space. Hunter tried her best not to get her hopes up. But if it worked, they might be able to reach someone, anyone who could help them, not to mention find out how the war was unfolding off-planet.

"Is it functional?" she asked.

"It appears to be."

"And you can operate it?"

Grieve nodded.

"We take it with us," she said. "I'd offer to carry it, but..."

"Not with your ribs in the state they're in," said Hobson. "I'll carry it."

"As soon as the storm breaks, we send out a transmission with as much power and as wide a dispersal as we can manage," said Hunter. "And then we get on the move immediately."

23

Bracing a hand against the corridor wall, Sigurdsson closed her eyes for a moment. When she opened them again, the corridor was still spinning and she took several slow breaths to prevent herself from vomiting. The low-level buzz in the back of her skull, which she had to assume was the psychic presence of the Matriarch intruding on her own consciousness, came and went in waves. Sigurdsson didn't understand why that was – she assumed it was just the usual comings and goings of thought – but she knew that whatever it actually was, it was alien enough that her brain was having a hard time adapting to it.

"It won't do either of us any good if I'm too fucked up to get off this planet," she said to herself and, by extension, the Matriarch.

Almost immediately, the buzz lessened considerably.

"Thank you."

"Sigurdsson," said Elgrapharr as he and his commandos stepped into view. "Are you injured...?"

She looked up, forced herself upright and faked a smile.

"No, I'm fine."

"She is lying," said Aylarr and Sigurdsson shot her a dirty look.

"You are wearing armour," said Elgrapharr, all four of his eyes narrowing as he examined her arms and neck.

"Yeah, it's-."

"An udukiin Matriarch has bonded with her," said Aylarr, earning another dirty look from Sigurdsson.

"Yeah, fine. Matriarch. Bonded. Whatever. Can we get the fuck out of here please? As if ATC Castle didn't have reason enough to shoot me, I'm now playing host to an escapee from their little torture lab."

"Is it safe to bring her back aboard the ship?" asked one of Elgrapharr's commandos. Sigurdsson couldn't remember his name, but wanted to slap him regardless.

"Safer than staying here," she said.

"She has a point," said Elgrapharr. "Doctor Frankenstein?"

"From what we know, bonding with an udukiin Matriarch does not replace the host personality nor does the Matriarch control the host's actions. In the early stages of bonding, very little change occurs," said the brill. "Once the bonding process is complete – which takes several days – the Matriarch serves as an enhancement to the host. It does not control."

"I accept the brill's explanation," said Elgrapharr. "And knowing Sigurdsson's stubborn nature, I don't believe an udukiin Matriarch would easily overcome her personality."

Sigurdsson smiled and showed him her middle finger. Or tried to, before realizing that her icaran hands did not have a middle finger.

The rest of the icarans accepted Elgrapharr's judgement call and everyone fell into step back to the shuttle.

When Sigurdsson, Frankenstein and Elgrapharr arrived on the command deck of the Azrael's Tear, Singh was waiting for them.

"We are breaking orbit now," he said, scratching at his bushy beard. "The haulers are with us and Cagliari is flying escort with her fighter wing. We will be moderately late to the rendezvous point, but not unreasonably so."

"We may require... a detour," said Elgrapharr.

"To the Udukiin Priex," added Sigurdsson.

For the first time since their arrival, Singh turned away from the observation windows and looked directly at them.

"What reason would we have for travelling to the Udukiin Priex?"

"We freed an udukiin Matriarch from Duster's Range," she said, quickly continuing before Singh could ask any questions. "We need to take her home."

"The udukiin attack any ship entering their space," said Singh. "I have no intention of taking the Azrael's Tear into the Priex."

"Actually, Captain, the udukiin are very attuned to one another psychically," said Frankenstein. "Not a hive mind, per se, but more aware of their fellows than humans or icarans."

Singh simply frowned his well-practised frown.

"Given the high level telepathic abilities generally attributed to the Matriarchs, it stands to reason that our entry into the Udukiin Priex would be noted and the udukiin would be well aware of the presence of the Matriarch on board the Azrael's Tear."

Sigurdsson looked from Frankenstein back to Singh.

"They'd know she's on board," she said. "The udukiin revere their Matriarchs. They won't attack."

"My contract with Miss Cagliari was for the retrieval of the Starfighters and their safe delivery to the rendezvous point," said Singh, turning his back to them. "Now if you please, the command deck is becoming crowded and we will have two very capable military vessels joining us in this system momentarily."

The two haulers were starting to pick up speed and though they would never have the same thrust power as the fighters,

Cagliari was glad to see they wouldn't be a hindrance. She watched as they moved into formation beneath her fighter and then looked back up as the AI in the Argentavis picked up the incoming vessels. A second layer of holographics popped up over the area from which the ships came, a magnification layer, and even though they were still too far away to identify by name, it was clear that the larger ship was an ATC Castle vessel while the smaller one appeared to be Commonwealth Navy.

"They're not even pretending to be separate anymore," she said to no one in particular. "Outlaw Squadron, heads up on the incoming. Your UHUD should already be picking them up."

"Hauler One ready for system-exit burn on your order, Cags."

"Ditto Hauler Two."

"Hey Cagliari, you there?" said Sigurdsson, coming through on a private linkup to Cagliari's fighter.

"Hold steady, Outlaw Squadron," she said, before switching to Sigurdsson's feed. "Yeah, what's up?"

"I need you to convince Singh to take me to the Udukiin Priex."

"The fuck for?"

"There was a Matriarch down there, Kestrel. An udukiin Matriarch. They were torturing her, testing her."

"Are you serious? And she was still alive?"

"Yeah. And I have her aboard the Azrael's Tear. I have to take her home."

Cagliari thought for a moment, watching the other ships getting larger on her screens. The udukiin were notoriously vicious fighters. And if Radko could pull off even half of what he'd talked about while they'd pretended to sleep together, earning some goodwill from the udukiin could be a massive coup.

"Put Singh on the line."

A few moments of silence followed before Singh's gravelly voice came on.

"She's asked you to talk me into going to the Priex," he said. It wasn't a question.

"I'm already paying you a lot of money," said Cagliari.

"Not enough for that."

"Don't forget, Captain, that if not for me, you wouldn't have your fancy LiDAR scrambling armour."

"The answer is still no."

"You have two pursuit craft in your docking clamps," she said. "Malkova Industries model 971. They were shit brand new and that was twenty years ago."

She could hear his sigh even over the comm line.

"What is your point?"

"If you take Freyja to the Udukiin Priex to return that Matriarch, you can replace your shitty 971s with two Argentavis starfighters."

Silence followed.

A long silence, and the ATC Castle ships – she considered them both ATC Castle ships now – continued to close the gap.

Cagliari was about to prompt Singh for a response when he spoke again.

"You have a deal. I will collect the fighters from the rendezvous point upon my return from the Priex."

The connection closed and Cagliari smiled. Two fighters was a small price to pay if everything worked out the way she hoped.

"All right, Outlaws," she said, switching back to the squadron-wide channel. "We're going to be on our own for a bit – the Azrael's Tear is leaving on a different heading. Cover their escape, but more important, protect those haulers."

She watched as the Azrael's Tear began its burn, heading out deeper into the black. The enemy ships were closing, but she had no worries about Singh getting away. The armour plating on his ship had been the prototype version of what covered the sleek hulls of the Argentavis fighters – not as advanced or refined to be sure, but he, like them, should be all but invisible to LiDAR. The haulers, though, were another story. They were simple civilian-grade heavy cargo carriers, albeit with upgraded engines to cut down travel time.

Only a moment later the external communications lines crackled to life.

"Attention cargo haulers leaving orbit of Duster's Range. This is Edward Vossek, Assistant Director of Operations for ATC Castle. You will power down your engines immediately and submit to inspection. We have reason to believe you have stolen property aboard."

"Mister Vossek, this is Kestrel Cagliari, President and CEO of Cagliari Aerospace, and I'm just taking back what you stole from us. So fuck you."

"If you do not power down and submit to inspection, we will use force," he said. "Be smart about this, Kestrel. Two gunboats against two cargo haulers are not good odds."

"Agreed," she said, a smile creeping into her voice. "But I feel pretty good about two gunboats against eight Argentavis fighters."

Dead silence followed from the radio for nearly three full minutes. Cagliari got some satisfaction out of that, as it told her Vossek knew just how advanced her fighters were and how they were beyond anything ATC Castle could manage. And that eight of them versus a pair of gunboats tipped the odds in her favour.

"This is Commander Ty Tagakara of the HMAS Newcastle. I have no idea what an Argentavis fighter is, but acts of piracy against-."

"Shut the fuck up, you corporate shill."

"I am an officer in Commonw-."

"Yeah, I'm sure you may even still believe that, but it's a lie. You are now an officer in the corporate clusterfuck that is ATC Castle - it just hasn't been made official yet," she said. "These haulers contain property - two squadrons of starfighters, specifically - belonging to Cagliari Aerospace and stolen by ATC Castle. I'm taking it back. Stay the hell out of my way or I will declare you a hostile and we *will* attack."

Once again, silence followed, and Cagliari knew the discussion that was taking place across closed comm lines. The Commonwealth ship would be wanting to know if she was telling the truth and pointing out that they would have a hard time fighting Starfighters that their LiDAR couldn't even detect, while Vossek would be trying to push them into holding firm.

Cagliari chewed her lower lip as she waited for a response. Her fighters were fully capable of engaging, but butterflies had appeared in her gut at the thought that she might have to order an engagement against a Commonwealth Navy vessel.

"Haulers, this is Cags," she said, the fighter's AI automatically switching her back to the squadron's closed channel. "Hard burn and get the hell out of here."

"What about those ships?"

"We'll worry about the ships, you worry about getting to the rendezvous."

"Understood."

The entire mission and all the planning and setup would be for nothing if Vossek got his hands on those haulers.

A soft beep came from her UHUD and Cagliari saw that both the Adirondack and the Newcastle were altering course.

"God damn it."

The Newcastle was setting an intercept course for the haulers while the Adirondack was...

She immediately opened a link to the Azrael's Tear.

"Captain Singh, this is Cagliari. I don't know how, but it seems like the Adirondack is tracking you. They've just started on a course that plots right along yours."

Whether he responded or not she didn't know – at that moment, the Newcastle opened fire. The bursts were random and unfocused, with the fighters still being too far away and with their black hulls being too difficult to see against the blackness of space. The closer the ship came, the easier it would be for their gunners to visually aim, but Cagliari knew that the Newcastle would disengage once the Adirondack was out of system.

At least, that's what she was hoping.

"Evasive maneuvers and warning shots only, Outlaw Squadron," she said.

"They are the aggressors," said Daxma. "We should be defending ourselves."

"The point of this operation was to bring more assets to the war effort, not subtract any. Just occupy them long enough for the haulers to go and then we follow. Understood?"

"Understood," came the response from each of the other pilots.

"Checkers and Dee," said Cagliari. "On my wings. Prepare for close-range flyby of the Newcastle observation dome."

Both pilots acknowledged. Checkers, a middle-aged Frenchman, had been a test pilot at Cagliari Aerospace when Cagliari was still in high school, and Dee – whose real name was Theodora Damianopolous and thus very early on had been given a much easier nickname – had been a certified Ace with the Commonwealth Starfighter Corps before it had been absorbed into the Commonwealth Navy five years prior. The three of them had been the first pilots to ever fly the Argentavis and had logged many hours together.

As Checkers appeared on her right and Dee slid into place on her left, Cagliari couldn't help but smile. Maybe it was weird and maybe it spoke ill of her mental state, but she was really enjoying this.

"On my mark," she said, then paused for a few moments. "Mark."

In unison, the three fighters dove toward the Newcastle, their wings folded back like attacking birds of prey.

24

Admiral Mahoney had only just entered Naval Command when Cortez quickly approached him. She was pale and tired and she felt awful, but there was nothing to be done about it so she simply carried on. Even if she'd wanted to go back to her quarters and rest, she couldn't. Not now.

"Admiral, I need to see you," she said.

"Can it wait, Lieutenant? I haven't even had my coffee yet."

"No sir, it can't."

He sighed.

"Look, Lieutenant, I know you're used to having a certain amount of leeway with Commander Radko, but you're-."

"We've received a transmission from the Earth's surface, Admiral," she said quickly.

He stopped dead in his tracks and stared at her, mouth open slightly.

"What?"

"It came in about three minutes ago. I'm having it run through every piece of software we have to see if we can authenticate it, but...," she paused for a second, feeling lightheaded.

"Are you all right, Cortez?"

"I just need to eat something, I'll be fine."

"Okay," he said, snapping his fingers at a nearby enlisted crewman. "Get the Lieutenant a protein bar ASAP."

Turning back to Cortez, he stroked his mustache.

"How do we know this isn't a ril-galas trick? We haven't heard a peep from Earth in nearly a year."

"We're trying to authenticate now, but Admiral, the person making the broadcast identified herself by name," said Cortez. "And I know her. I've met her."

She handed him a tablet and her tapped a command to play the file. It was audio only of course, so to avoid distraction Mahoney closed his eyes as he listened.

"This message is going out to any humans who can hear it. Or icarans, for that matter," said a woman's voice. She spoke English with a slight accent, but with the low quality of the broadcast, it was hard to pinpoint exactly what kind of accent. "There is a resistance movement on Earth, fighting the ril-galas occupying force. We are small in number, but have fortified defenses. We are surviving, but supplies – food and ammunition – will eventually run out. We need assistance. Earth has fallen, but its population... some of its population can still be saved. We have garrisoned Edinburgh Castle in Scotland and for the time being we are safe behind its walls, but we need help."

There was a pause in the broadcast and some other voices could be faintly heard in the background.

"The ril-galas have set up processing plants," the woman said. "They're rendering plants, turning humans into meat. We save as many as we can, but we don't have the people or equipment to fight a war."

Another pause.

"And we have the heir to the British throne. I repeat, Prince... King Arthur is with us. He is alive and he is with us."

The woman paused again and when she continued her voice was quieter, almost intimate.

"Once upon a time, I was called Quon Li Chen. I was part of the Soviet program called Project Nightwatch."

Cortez watched as Mahoney twitched at the mention of Nightwatch.

"Radko... you let me choose my path and this is it. Now my name is Hunter and I am fighting for the survival of the human race."

The transmission ceased and slowly opening his eyes, Mahoney stared at the tablet in silence for a moment before speaking.

"Nightwatch," he said. "Do you know what Nightwatch was, Lieutenant?"

"Yes. She told me about it, Sir."

As far as she was aware, no one had ever asked Radko what had happened to the 'package' the Vimy Ridge had been tasked with delivering to Duster's Range prior to the attack on Echo Station. Certainly no one had asked Cortez and there had been no follow-ups in the intelligence file – she'd checked several times, just to see if Quon had been recaptured.

"She said Radko let her choose her path?"

"Yes," said Cortez. "He offered her freedom in exchange for her help. Her abilities – her ESP – allowed her to sense the rilgalas at a time when we hadn't figured out how to calibrate our LiDAR to do the job."

The admiral nodded.

"Even Radko's biggest detractors would have to admit that the man knows how to improvise," said Mahoney, seemingly more to himself than Cortez. "I assume you've already forwarded a copy of this to the Vimy Ridge?"

"I did, Admiral."

There was no sense in denying it.

"Response?"

"Not yet. I just sent it off a moment before you came in."

"All right. I want you to..."

He trailed off, his frown deepening as Bianca Upshaw strode into the command centre with a quartet of armed and armoured ATC Castle security guards at her side.

"Ms. Upshaw, the command centre is off-limits to civilians."

"Except as it pertains to ATC Castle's duties as provider of security to this facility," she said, a thin, humourless smile on her lips. "And, sadly, that's the capacity in which I'm here now."

With a sigh, Mahoney set aside his tablet.

"Please explain yourself, Upshaw, before I have you removed."

"We were unable to trace who sent the lockdown command to Duster's Range. The person responsible is very good at encryption and using multiple relays to cover their tracks. However, it seems that with one of their subsequent transmissions – the one warning the pirate vessel that we'd dispatched the Adirondack – the culprit slipped up and forgot to add all the usual layers of encryption."

She snapped her fingers and pointed at Cortez. Immediately, two of the armed guards were at her side, grabbing her roughly by the arms.

"Anna Cortez, you are under arrest," said Upshaw, her smile becoming more genuine.

"On what charge?" said Cortez, feeling remarkably calm. She supposed that the knowledge she was already dying had removed a great deal of her fear.

"Treason."

"*Treason?*" said Mahoney, stepping between Upshaw and Cortez. "Even if she did assist the pirates, acting against a corporate entity is in no way treason."

"The charge is treason," said Upshaw. "If you disagree, you may feel free to speak at her court martial. It starts tomorrow."

25

The deckplates shook under Radko's boots as another volley from the ril-galas battleship struck the Vimy Ridge. Beside him at the secondary sand table in the observation dome, el Bahari tried to keep track of the ril-galas fighters and direct the gunnery crews, but the little ships were moving too fast and maneuvered too quickly. He watched the XO wipe the sweat from her brow as she kept trying.

At the main sand table below, Owens worked feverishly, walking a constant circle around the table which displayed a three-dimensional schematic of the ship, damage points flashing red. Like el Bahari, he was doing his best to keep on top of his work – assigning teams to deal with damages – but like el Bahari, he was becoming overwhelmed.

It was time for a new tactic.

"Lieutenant Commander el Bahari."

"Sir?" she said, looking up from the holographic display.

"Prepare for deployment of nuclear warheads. I want two, both to target the nearest of the battleships."

After a moment's pause, she nodded and, relaying the order to the missile batteries best positioned for the shot, el Bahari undid the top button of her uniform coat and pulled out her launch key, hanging on a chain around her neck. Radko did the same and together they plugged the small rectangular code keys into the sand table ports. Their retinas were immediately scanned, unlocking the ship's nuclear arsenal.

The Vimy Ridge had carried nuclear warheads all along, but after the destruction of Echo Station, the weapons had been unavailable. They had sat in their racks, just so much dead weight after the ship's commanding officer, Commodore Edwards, was lost along with the entire station. With only the XO's activation key, the nuclear arsenal could not be armed.

"Missile batteries two and three report ready with nuclear warheads, Commander," said el Bahari.

"They can fire at their discretion."

Again she relayed the order and Radko didn't have to wait long to see the missiles lance outward.

The first impacted the ril-galas battleship on the top half of its front section, the explosion gouging an enormous channel through the ship. The second warhead stuck moments later and, the ship already heavily listing, its explosion tore the battleship in half.

There was no cheering on command deck.

"Admiral Rhekarr, what's the status of the Venn Shakara?" said Radko. From the moment the battle began, he'd insisted on keeping an open line between the two ships.

"We are taking damage, but it is not excessive at this point," said Rhekarr. "I commend your gunners."

"I'll pass that along."

He instinctively ducked as two ril-galas fighters streaked by within a few meters of the dome.

"Commander," said Owens from below. "We need to deal with those fighters! The damage they're causing is starting to add up – I've just had to take an engine offline."

"Understood, Mister Owens. Commander?" he said, looking back to el Bahari.

She rubbed at her face and blew out a breath. Then she shook her head.

"Our turrets can only rotate so fast. We're trying to bring the automated point defense cannons back online, but..."

"I don't remember them moving this fast before."

Suddenly several dark shapes rocketed past the dome, firing salvoes at the alien fighters.

"Outlaw Squadron to HMCS Vimy Ridge," said Cagliari. "We are engaging the fighters, please check your fire."

Grinning, Radko slapped the console.

"Glad to have you with us, Cagliari," he said, then turned back to el Bahari. "Refocus fire on the remaining battleship. Rhekarr, we now have starfighters in play."

"Understood, Commander."

"Where did they come from?" said el Bahari.

"Long story. I'll explain after this is over."

As it turned out, it was over very quickly. The Venn Shakara had already severely damaged the other battleship and the Argentavis fighters lived up to every promise Cagliari had made – they wheeled and dove and flew circles around the ril-galas fighters. A handful of enemy fighters escaped, but most were reduced to small bits of flotsam.

The main hangar of the Vimy Ridge, usually empty save for a pair of landing shuttles, was soon filled with the birdlike Starfighters, their wings folded as if at rest, along with an icaran transport shuttle.

Radko leaned against a wall in the maintenance crew lounge, which had been temporarily taken over for the impromptu meeting.

"We received this from Cortez at some point during the battle. We were too occupied to notice it arrive," he said, and then played the assembled group the recording from Quon – or Hunter as she was calling herself.

Standing together in the small room were Radko and Owens, el Bahari off to one side, Cagliari still in her flightsuit and Admiral Rhekarr standing a head above all of them.

"So she didn't leave Commonwealth space after all," said Owens.

"Doesn't appear that way."

A message from Earth had caught Radko by surprise and the fact that it had been Quon sending the message had set his mind spinning. Her plan had been to leave Commonwealth space, yet she was on Earth, apparently leading a resistance movement. A resistance movement that was in dire straits.

"Admiral," said Radko. "We may have to consider moving our timeline forward."

"I understand," said Rhekarr. "The Venn Shakara suffered some weapons systems damage, but that will be repaired within the day. We can be ready at any point after that."

"Outlaw Squadron can be ready at any time," said Cagliari.

Rhekarr bobbed his head in the icaran equivalent of a nod.

"Our pilots are aboard the Venn Shakara and stand ready to join you."

"Wait. Stop," said el Bahari, holding up both hands. "Can someone please tell me what is going on here?"

"I'm planning a strike against the Hornets' Nest," said Radko.

The large structure in Earth orbit was a staging ground not just for the continued occupation of Earth and the battles against the human remnant, but for strikes outward, into icaran space and even beyond. It was one of the key bases of operation for the ril-galas armada.

"This incident with the Vor Tokar was accidental," said Radko. "But encountering the Venn Shakara wasn't. The icarans know as well as we do that the Hornets' Nest is the key to the ril-galas presence here. Take it out and they become stretched too thin with too few bases. We weaken their entire grip in one action."

"And the Commonwealth has only assigned us to this mission?"

"The Commonwealth doesn't know about this mission," said Radko. "I've been advocating this for a year and they always found reasons why we can't do it. So I started assembling the resources I'd need to do it myself. The Venn Shakara was one resource and Cagliari's fighters turned out to be another, though I didn't even know about them until recently."

Cagliari took over and briefly explained the situation with the fighters and the act of piracy – or perceived act of piracy – that led to their liberation.

"The rest of the fighters are waiting at a rendezvous point," she said.

"Admiral Rhekarr has brought some pilots to fly them, and we'll also be meeting up with the Leonid Groshkov-."

"The Gorshkov? That's a Soviet carrier!"

"As you may have noticed, Commander, our hangar is pretty full with just eight fighters," said Radko. "If we're going to launch thirty, we need somewhere to launch them *from*."

"There has to be another way to do this," said el Bahari. "You... you just broke I don't know how many laws by helping those pirates and now your just *giving* super-advanced starfighters to the icarans and the Soviets? This... I just... who do you think you are, Radko?"

"I think I'm a human who doesn't give a damn about politics or corporate espionage or toeing the party line while our species is *fucking dying*."

"And your crew doesn't get a say as to whether they want to take part in this? Disobeying direct orders from Naval Command?"

"You said it yourself when I came aboard," said Owens, staring at his shoes. "There are a lot of old Vimy Ridge crew who came back for this patrol run."

El Bahari stared at him for moment before it clicked.

"You stacked the roster with people you knew would follow you no matter what."

"People we knew would be on board with doing the right thing," said Radko. "And given this transmission from Earth, I'm more convinced than ever that what we're doing is the right thing."

"The Icaran Colonial Navy agrees," said Rhekarr, looking down at a wrist-mounted screen. "I have just confirmed that the Venn Vaar and the Vor Rokhar are both on their way to the rendezvous point."

"I can't believe I'm hearing this," said el Bahari. "You can't just start making military alliances on behalf of the Commonwealth! The Prime Minister-."

"The Prime Minister has his head so far up his ass he can't see that we're barely holding on to what we have, Amira. You know that as well as I do," said Radko. "Because you're not stupid. You're intelligent and observant and that's why I didn't fight the orders when Naval Command assigned you here."

"Well maybe you should have," she said, storming out of the room.

"Uh, should someone go after her?" said Cagliari after an uncomfortable silence.

"Let her have some time to digest it all," said Owens. "Then I'll speak with her."

As she stalked through the corridors of the Vimy Ridge, her scowl driving anyone and everyone out of her way, el Bahari pulled out her tablet and tapped in the activation key for her encrypted link to Vossek. As always, it took a few minutes for the transmission to go through, and she was already pacing in her office when he answered.

"Yes?"

"You were right about Radko being up to something," she said. "He's working with the icarans and possibly even the Soviets."

"To do what?"

She hesitated for a moment.

"Cagliari is here as well. She claims to have been behind a pirate attack on Duster's Range."

"Yes," said Vossek. "I'm in pursuit of the pirate vessel now, but Cagliari escaped. It doesn't surprise me she fled to Radko – Upshaw just found evidence that one of Radko's associates has been helping the pirates all along."

"Cagliari claims the fighters she stole actually belonged-."

"She broke into an ATC Castle facility, destroyed several projects that were underway and I am now pursuing a pirate vessel that has escaped with stolen ATC Castle property. She and Radko and everyone helping them are criminals. There is no grey area here."

The fact that he avoided the question didn't escape her, but she found herself nodding regardless.

"What do you want me to do? I'm not sure I can take any direct action – Radko managed to fill the ship with his supporters," she said. "I'd probably be tossed out an airlock if I tried anything."

"It shouldn't come to that. We have an ace up our sleeve that Radko should be finding out about very soon."

"What does that mean?" said el Bahari, her frown deepening.

"Just watch Radko. Report regularly on what he's doing and who he's speaking with," he said, once again avoiding her question. "Make it look like you're reluctantly on board with his plan."

"And then what? I'm one person out here, Edward, I'm not sure..."

She trailed off. The transmission had been terminated on Vossek's end. With a snarl of frustration, she threw her tablet across the small room.

"I hope you get shot out of the sky, you bastard."

26

The first salvoes from the Adirondack had exploded around the Azrael's Tear twenty minutes before they'd reached the perimeter of the Udukiin Priex. By the time it crossed into udukiin territory, the HMAS Newcastle had caught up and Singh's pilot – a cadaverous blond man named, of all things, Crash – was sweating profusely as he dove and banked and performed evasive maneuvers with old-style control sticks.

"They're getting really fucking close, Singh," said Sigurdsson, bracing herself against a bulkhead as an explosion rocked the small ship.

"Please keep your calm," said Singh.

"We've crossed into the Priex!" someone yelled.

"LiDAR on full alert. Visual spotters to your stations," said Singh, his deep, gravelly voice cutting through everything.

Whatever else she may have thought of the man, Sigurdsson couldn't deny his aura of authority. As one of the designated visual spotters, she'd unquestioningly taken her spot at one of the observation ports – a circular window about as wide as her arm-span.

"No sign of intercept," she said as she looked at the empty starfield.

Not quite empty, she corrected herself. The Udukiin Priex was rich in planetoids and asteroid belts and, though she couldn't see it yet, the infamous udukiin homeworld. If anyone knew its native name, it hadn't become common knowledge, but its odd composition was well known. It was right there in what everyone but the udukiin called it – The Shattered World. Millions of years ago, the planet had fractured into two separate pieces, but those pieces had remained close enough together that they had retained the same orbit and even the same atmosphere. The udukiin had reportedly even built bridges between the halves of The Shattered World.

The Azrael's Tear banked sharply again, dodging some weapons fire that Sigurdsson couldn't see, and Jaeger huffed as he stumbled against her calf. Reaching down with her left hand, Sigurdsson rubbed his head reassuringly. At least she hoped it was reassuring.

Then one of the other spotters shouted and moments later Sigurdsson saw it: a large almost x-shaped vessel appearing and disappearing within the Priex asteroid field.

An udukiin warship bearing down on them.

The external comms crackled to life and for a moment, Sigurdsson expected to hear the blandly translated voice of an udukiin. Instead, she heard Vossek.

"Captain Singh, the udukiin have seen you and are moving into position. If you surrender now, we will help you escape."

Though Singh replied, Sigurdsson missed what he'd said. The buzzing in her head had exploded, flooding her mind with images and sounds and even smells and she somehow understood what was happening: the Matriarch was communicating with the alien warship. As she watched, the ship changed course sharply, heading to intercept the Adirondack and the Newcastle.

"Captain Sing," said Sigurdsson. "You need to get your ship and crew out of here while our pursuers are occupied. I'll take the icaran shuttle to The Shattered World."

Singh turned and looked at her for a moment, then simply nodded before turning back to his screens.

Hurrying off the command deck, Sigurdsson stopped only briefly to grab her duffle bag – her duffle bag that represented all of her belongings – and her *vayan* pistol on her way to the small shuttle bay of the Azrael's Tear. When she arrived, Elgrapharr and his commandos were already loading their gear onto the gleaming blue shuttle.

As she and Jaeger approached, the dog ran up to Elgrapharr and the tall icaran knelt to scratch him behind the ears.

"We can depart at your command," he said, looking up at Sigurdsson.

"You don't have to come," she said. "I don't know what to expect down there and you've more than covered your agreement with Radko."

"I would like to see The Shattered World," he said, standing. "And I would not like for you to die there."

At the mention of the planet, a feeling surged through Sigurdsson via the Matriarch that told her without a doubt she was doing the right thing.

Without another word she tossed her bag onto the shuttle and climbed in, Jaeger on her heels and Elgrapharr not far behind.

With Aylarr at the controls – strange, entirely holographic controls that Sigurdsson didn't understand in the slightest – the icaran shuttle launched at a far faster speed than would otherwise have been advisable, just barely dodging rail gun fire from the Adirondack.

As they arced outwards and toward the planet, Sigurdsson felt another burst of emotion and images.

"You better be telling your people to leave Singh's ship alone, too," she said quietly.

Glancing around, she was caught by a momentary wave of dizziness unrelated to the Matriarch. Somehow, the shuttle had become almost skeletal, the space and stars and asteroids around them becoming visible. Elgrapharr reached out a hand to steady her.

"It is holographic," he said. "To allow the pilot full field of vision."

Nodding, Sigurdsson took a deep breath and watched the asteroid field streak by. Looking aft, she saw the udukiin vessel engage the Adirondack, but saw the Newcastle in pursuit of the shuttle. At the edge of her vision, a second udukiin ship appeared.

"Don't destroy the Commonwealth ship," she said to the Matriarch. "Scare them off, do whatever, but don't do any serious damage. We're already low on resources."

And again, she knew the Matriarch understood. It was amazing to Sigurdsson how quickly she'd begun to understand the Matriarch and it her.

She glanced down at Jaeger, sitting happily at her feet, watching space fly by, his tail wagging slowly. The dog's calm calmed her... to a certain extent.

"The Shattered World," said Aylarr.

Almost in unison, the icarans and Sigurdsson all turned toward the front of the shuttle.

And all of them stared.

Hearing the name 'The Shattered World,' one thought one knew what to expect. It would be a broken place, fractured into shards, where the hardy udukiin eked out their existence in an unforgiving landscape.

But it was none of that.

"It's beautiful," said Sigurdsson, her voice barely a whisper. She felt a surge of agreement from the Matriarch.

The Shattered World. The place with a native name unpronounceable to any but the udukiin, looked like a paradise. Lush greens and reds and yellows covered nearly the entire surface, broken only by sparkling purple mountain ranges and deep blue oceans and rivers. And, of course, the jagged bisection of the planet, through which shone the light of its sun. The Shattered World was not what any of the shuttle's occupants had expected. And, in that moment, with her connection to the Matriarch, Sigurdsson understood that the protection of their beautiful homeworld was one reason for the extreme territorial nature of the udukiin.

Having seen what many other species – humans especially – had done to their own homeworlds and to their colonies Sigurdsson couldn't begrudge them their stance.

Just as suddenly as it had been cast, the spell was broken. The small shuttle bucked wildly from impact of weapons fire.

The Adirondack had managed to outmaneuver the larger udukiin ships and was again in pursuit of the shuttle.

"I'm taking us down," said Aylarr. "This will be a more rapid descent than preferable. I'd recommend securing yourselves."

The icarans immediately donned their battle helmets and Sigurdsson watched as they withdrew devices about the size of her head from the walls and secured them to the deck. Each icaran, save Elgrapharr and Ventaris, sat in front of a device and activated it, their bodies immediately being enveloped in an opaque force field. Elgrapharr clamped one to the deck in front of Sigurdsson and motioned for her to sit, while Ventaris did the same for Frankenstein. Sitting as instructed, Sigurdsson clutched Jaeger to her chest.

"I shall see you once we make planetfall," said Elgrapharr, then he activated her device and everything went dark.

Though she could see nothing, she could feel impacts striking the shuttle's hull at regular intervals and then she felt the shuttle vibrating and then she could *hear* the shuttle vibrating. Sounds meant atmosphere. Which meant they'd-.

And then the shuttle slammed into the surface of The Shattered World.

27

"Any word from the Azrael's Tear?" said Radko.

Back on the command deck, he was going over the plans once more with Rhekarr. The icaran was shorter than average for his species, but still stood taller than Radko. His skin was such a deep green it appeared almost black in most lighting, broken only by an uneven pattern of pale yellow striping.

"Nothing yet, Commander," said a communications technician.

Radko sighed and rubbed at his eyes. He knew Sigurdsson was more than capable of taking care of herself, but that didn't mean he wouldn't worry about her, and the desire to simply redirect the Vimy Ridge and go find her was strong.

"Are you all right, Commander?" said Rhekarr.

"Just worried about a friend."

"As are we all, to some extent, I believe," said the icaran. "And that is why we do what we do. Is it not?"

"Yes. Yes it is, Admiral."

He looked up as el Bahari joined them at the sand table. She looked uncomfortable, but the fact she was there gave Radko hope.

"Commander," she said.

"El Bahari. How are you feeling?"

"I still have reservations," she said carefully. "But – and not to sound egotistical – your plan stands a greater chance of success if I'm part of it than it does otherwise."

Rhekarr made a chuffing sound that Radko had long ago, during the time he'd spent with Brigadier General Locaris, discovered was the icaran equivalent of a chuckle.

"I enjoy your bluntness, Commander el Bahari," said Rhekarr.

"I'm glad someone does."

"I'm glad you're with us," said Radko. "We're en route to the rendezvous now and should be arriving in about twelve hours."

She nodded, but before she could otherwise respond, a communications technician spoke up.

"Commander Radko, incoming transmission from Thor's Hammer. Admiral Mahoney, sir."

Immediately, Rhekarr withdrew, so as not to intrude upon Commonwealth military discussion.

"Put him through."

A second later, a floating window appeared over the sand table, framing the Commonwealth Naval seal. Too far from any sizeable communications hub, the Vimy Ridge was on audio-only long distance transmissions once more.

Radko already knew what he'd be telling the Admiral if any questions were asked about progress or what they'd seen on patrol. Some would even be true, like the encounter with the 'ghost ship.'

"Admiral. I just finished compiling a report for you," said Radko. "It will be on its way shortly, but you need to be aware that the ril-galas are using the empty hulks of lost vessels to conceal attack forces."

The only response from Mahoney was a small grunt. It concerned Radko, given how sharp he usually found the old man.

"Trojan Horses, sir. We encountered an icaran warship that had been converted that way."

"Understood," said the Admiral, sounding surprisingly disinterested. "I'll pass along the details of your report to the rest of the fleet."

"This won't be popular Admiral, but it should go to everyone. Commonwealth, Soviet, icaran, krellin, udukiin..."

"Yes, yes, agreed," said Mahoney, causing Radko even more concern. The old man was being unusually agreeable.

"Radko, I have information you need to hear about an associate of yours."

"The transmission from Earth?"

"It's not that," said Mahoney. "It's about Cortez."

Owens and the handful of others who knew about Cortez's illness fell completely silent, looking to Radko. And Radko simply stared at the sigil that represented Mahoney, feeling his heart sinking into his stomach.

"Sir?" he managed to say.

"She's... she's been taken into custody. Arrested," said the Admiral.

For a moment, Radko simply stared, waiting for his mind to process the statement. He'd been prepared -- almost prepared -- to hear that Cortez's health had taken a serious turn, but...

"*Arrested?*"

"It seems ATC Castle found evidence she helped a group of pirates raid one of their facilities."

"I see," said Radko, clenching his jaw and feeling immense satisfaction in imagining himself punching Bianca Upshaw right in her perfectly made-up face. "What's the charge, sir? Or do we just arrest people on ATC Castle whims these days?"

"I don't like this either, Commander," snapped Mahoney. "She was charged with treason."

"*Treason?!* How the living fuck does an act of piracy against a PMC constitute treason?"

Mahoney cleared his throat and, based on his very precise and clipped diction, Radko assumed he was reading from the official arrest report.

"Given the current status of the Commonwealth Armed Forces and the new symbiotic relationship between the Commonwealth and ATC Castle, it is determined that an attack on one constitutes an attack on the other," he said.

A brief silence was followed with a disgusted sigh.

"Radko, you've known me long enough to know that I don't swear. But even I will admit that this is utter horseshit," said Mahoney, sounding more weary than Radko had ever heard him. "I'm sorry, Radko, I really am. I spoke on her behalf at the court martial, but it was less court martial than witch trial."

Radko staggered slightly and el Bahari quickly stepped to his side to support him.

"The court martial has already happened?" she said. "What about due process? What about time for her advocate to examine the evidence against her?"

"The evidence was considered iron-clad and she was not appointed an advocate."

A rage was building in his chest, and taking a deep breath, Radko forced it down.

"The sentence," said Radko. "When is it to be carried out?"

"Twenty-four hours. Upshaw can be very persuasive."

Radko bowed his head and smashed his tablet over the sand table console. El Bahari's eyes went wide.

"Admiral," she said. "That charge carries the death penalty."

"Yes, it does."

She stared, open-mouthed for a moment. Owens had stepped up beside Radko and had a comforting hand on the man's shoulder as he slumped against the bulkhead, staring at the deckplates.

"By firing squad," said Mahoney, sounding entirely drained. "In twenty-four hours."

"And this... this arrest and court martial," said el Bahari. "This was pushed through by ATC Castle?"

"Yes."

"Why didn't you tell me earlier," said Radko. "I could have testified, I could have been her advocate."

"No, Radko. That was the game, you see? Upshaw knows you and Cortez are close. It's all games now, here. All games."

"Explain, Admiral," said el Bahari.

Despite using the man's rank as a form of address, the phrasing and tone made clear that el Bahari had given her superior office an order. Mahoney didn't show any signs of noticing, answering as if she'd asked nicely.

"ATC Castle wants Radko. They know he protects his own, so they're using Cortez."

"Prosecute Cortez because they can't reach Radko," said Owens.

"Cortez is bait, Commander Radko," said Mahoney.

"What if I agree to surrender myself for prosecution once the war is over?" said Radko.

"When do you think that will be, Commander?" said Mahoney with a sigh. "Upshaw is trumpeting this treason nonsense like a zealot. I argued several different ways, proposed punishment ranging from a suspended sentence to a prison term. DeFreitas and Upshaw would have none of it."

"They want to make a point," said el Bahari, nodding to Radko. "To you, and to everyone else."

Standing again, Radko approached the sand table. His jaw was clenched, his eyes burning.

"Admiral. Would you be so kind as to relay a message to Ms. Upshaw?"

"Of course, Commander."

"Please tell her that I would strongly recommend that the death sentence of Anna Cortez be commuted."

"I don't think she'll-."

"Advise Ms. Upshaw that if Cortez is executed, once I'm finished with the ril-galas I will be coming after ATC Castle."

The command deck, already having seen a significant reduction in noise during the call, became deathly silent.

"I'll relay the message," said Mahoney after a long silence.

The connection closed.

It was Rhekarr who broke the silence.

"My condolences, Commander."

"Thank you, Rhekarr," said Radko. "El Bahari, you're in charge. I'll be in my quarters."

El Bahari nodded and watched Radko go. She'd disagreed with a great many of his decisions, but it was still difficult to see him as he was, facing the death of a close friend with no power to do anything about it. At the same time, both Radko and Cortez were authors of their fate. Both had circumvented the chain of command and circumvented laws and even engaged in outright piracy.

Still, executing a girl of twenty-one for treason?

"Lieutenant Commander Owens, would you please take over command for a few minutes?" said el Bahari. "I... have contacts on Thor's Hammer. It's a long shot, but they may be able to help the Cortez situation."

As expected, Owens nodded and el Bahari headed into the XO's office, just off the command deck.

Pulling out her tablet, she keyed in her ATC Castle encryption passcode. It took much longer than usual to connect and when it finally did, el Bahari was somewhat surprised to hear a voice other than Vossek's.

"Yes?" said Bianca Upshaw.

"Uh... I'm sorry Ms. Upshaw, I was expecting Edward Vossek."

"He's currently on assignment and unreachable. Do you have information?"

"Nothing beyond my last report to-."

"Then why are you contacting us?"

El Bahari stared at the tablet for a moment.

"Radko just received word that one of his former crewmates, a woman named Cortez, has been brought up on charges," she said.

"Yes."

"And that she's been convicted. Of treason."

"Yes."

"That must have been difficult to arrange. I can't imagine the legal footwork that must have gone into getting a conviction for treason given the target of her actions was ATC Castle and not the Commonwealth," said el Bahari. "Quite a master stroke."

"Yes, it was a beautifully executed move – if you'll pardon the pun. But is there a point to this, Amira?"

"Yes there is, *Bianca*. Radko may be many things, but stupid is not among them. You need to tread very carefully right now – he will be out for blood."

"I appreciate your concern, but we can handle Radko."

"If that were true, Bianca," said el Bahari. "He'd have already been dealt with."

There was silence on the other end of the line, but the connection was still open.

"The rendezvous is taking place at the same location where the stolen fighters are being kept," said el Bahari. "I will have the exact location for you shortly."

Tapping the tablet, she closed the transmission without waiting for a reply.

28

Mahoney sat in one of the moderately comfortable armchairs in the nominal office of the director of Thor's Hammer medical while the owner of the office paced – or more accurately stalked – the breadth of the room.

In her younger days, Khaifa had earned a reputation as a hot-head. Her temper had gotten her into trouble more than once in her teens and early twenties, but with age and experience, the temper had cooled. Even as her relationship with her late husband, Colonel Harlan Grey, began to deteriorate, any anger that had come had been a mild burn.

But as she stalked her office, she felt positively nuclear.

"How can you commit treason against a corporation?" she said, probably for the hundredth time.

Mahoney just listened, nodding.

"Her trial was a sham and you know it," she said. "This whole situation throws away the entire concept of human rights. The Commonwealth is becoming a privatized dictatorship, Admiral."

"I don't disagree," said Mahoney.

"And you warned Radko?"

"Yes," he said, answering the question for the fourth time since he'd arrived.

After another moment or two of pacing, Khaifa dropped into her chair, her expression a mix of bewilderment and resignation.

"This is insane," she said. "How did we end up here? How does something like this happen?"

"There's no accountability, because the electorate is more concerned with survival than the state of their democracy," said Mahoney, shrugging. "And you have a paranoid leader who had trust issues with the Soviets and the icarans even before civilization as we know it came to an end."

"So is this it, then? Is this what humanity is? We just keep our heads down, let this whole thing devolve into a dictatorship and just be happy we're alive? I can't buy that, I'm sorry. We can't just hand over power to ATC Castle. No corporation should have any say in the functioning of our courts of law."

"Perhaps someone should stand up and say so publically."

She looked up sharply.

"You mean me?" she said. "Believe me, I'd like to, but what good would it do? I'd more than likely just find myself standing beside poor Anna Cortez in front of the firing squad."

"If someone were to speak out, they may find they have support. Support that could offer protection from ATC Castle."

"What are you suggesting, Admiral?" she said, her eyes narrowing.

Stroking his mustache, Mahoney smiled thinly.

"I'm not suggesting anything, Doctor."

"Good. Neither am I. But while we're not suggesting anything, I wonder if a senior military leader were to stand up-."

"It would be portrayed as a military coup," he said. "Which would accomplish nothing."

She sighed and nodded. Given that the path they were on seemed to be leading toward a dictatorship propped up by the military muscle of ATC Castle, a military coup – whether real or perceived – was not a viable alternative. If an alternative was to be found, it would have to be a civilian-led initiative. It would have to be someone seen as trustworthy, someone who people knew or at the very least knew of.

One of the most famous people in the extant Commonwealth, for instance.

Khaifa rested her face in her hands and swore softly.

"I need some time to think," she said.

Nodding, Mahoney left without another word.

She was back on Von Daniken's Landing, standing atop the massive wall that surrounded Fort Hathaway. Winter was closing in -- a light dusting of snow covered everything, but it was a far cry from the incredible volume of snow and ice that forced full evacuation of the colony every winter.

There was no wind at all, which was Sigurdsson's first clue that she was dreaming. Even in the warm summer months, the winds up on the walls of Fort Hathaway could be fierce, but as she looked out across the colony, not a single snowflake stirred.

Her second clue was the dead man standing to her left.

"Was it worth it?" said the corpse of Chanz. Blood oozed from the blackened hole in his forehead.

"Fuck you," said Sigurdsson.

"You shot me to make a point," said the corpse.

"I shot you because you got a lot of people killed for absolutely no reason."

"And you don't even regret it."

"No. I'd do it again in a heartbeat."

"Maybe when Khaifa asked if you were a monster you should have said yes."

"Maybe I should have," she said.

She felt the presence behind her before she heard the voice.

"You're not a monster," said Radko.

He was wearing his uniform as he always seemed to be when she saw him. As she looked up into his eyes, Sigurdsson had her third clue that she was dreaming – in real life, she was taller than Radko, but here he seemed to almost tower over her.

The corpse of Chanz barked out a laugh.

"They're all dead because of you," he said, pointing out beyond the wall.

Looking out onto the snowy landscape, Sigurdsson realised that what she had taken for rocks and snow drifts were in fact dozens of human corpses.

Placing a hand on her shoulder, Radko turned her around to face the inner compound of Fort Hathaway.

"They're all alive because of you," he said.

In the compound, dozens of people milled about, doing the kind of everyday tasks they'd have done in the days before the ril-galas attack. Danner was there, giving orders to the garrison. The diminutive sniper Ustorf was carrying a bag of supplies. The old drunk miner who always caused her so many problems was there, drunk as always, but seeming in a better mood than ever. And then she smiled as she saw Jaeger weave his way through the crowd, sit down in the open space and look up at her, head cocked to the right.

Before Sigurdsson could say anything, she felt a sharp jolt and the world went black.

"Sigurdsson?"

She opened her eyes. Everything was still black and she felt something coarse and warm and wet slap against her face. And fur. She felt fur.

"Jaeger."

The pod. The icaran escape pod.

The jolt came again.

"Sigurdsson, are you conscious?"

"Yeah. Yeah, I'm here," she said, just as the pod's force field disintegrated and sunlight flooded her vision, broken by the silhouette of Elgrapharr.

"We need to move," he said, reaching in and roughly yanking her out of the pod. "There are ril-galas ground forces converging."

"Shit."

An image suddenly flashed into her mind of the race back to Fort Hathaway after first sighting the ril-galas horde on Von Daniken's Landing. Shaking her head, she drew her sidearm and checked its charge.

"Okay. Did we lose anyone?"

"Unfortunately yes," said Elgrapharr, nodding toward a twisted icaran corpse that lay not far away. "Otapharr's pod failed him."

Everyone looked sharply skyward as the distant screams of the ril-galas bats echoed across the narrow valley in which they'd landed.

Elgrapharr again stated the necessity for them to clear the area as quickly as possible.

"Yeah, agreed," said Sigurdsson.

Stepping over to what remained of Otapharr, she picked up his *aoran* assault rifle and, finding it in working condition, slung it over her shoulder. She may have been under medical instructions to avoid the use of assault rifles while her shoulders fully healed, but these were exceptional circumstances. If Doctor Frankenstein had a problem...

The line of thought died out as she looked around quickly.

"Fuck. Where's Frankenstein?"

"Scouting ahead," said Elgrapharr, tossing aside a damaged *vayan* pistol. "With Aylarr and Ventaris."

Keeping a close watch behind them for enemy contacts, Sigurdsson, Elgrapharr and the rest of the group headed out along the valley floor. Though the foliage was dense on either side, the centre of the valley remained fairly easily traversable, covered only with a thick yellow and green striped grass that rarely reached above the knee. Regardless, a heavy canopy of leaves and branches blocked out large swatches of the sky as they extended outward and upward from the twisted and gnarled trunks of what Sigurdsson decided to call trees, but appeared more akin to massive vines. Their root systems spread across large areas of ground and even up along and into the rocky crags of the valley walls. As she looked at their pattern and spread and layout, Sigurdsson thought it even possible that they were all part of a single, enormous organism.

The cries of some kind of native bird – or bird equivalent – echoed through the valley.

An overwhelming sense of home surged through Sigurdsson, and such a strong feeling of love and joy at returning that she felt her eyes welling up with tears.

"Welcome home," she said softly.

Again she felt the wave of gratitude she'd felt upon embarking on this quest, but then, just as suddenly, she felt something else. Alertness. Awareness that something was amiss, but it didn't seem to be coming from the Matriarch.

In the sun-dappled grass, Jaeger stood stock still, ears pricked up, nose in the air.

"Something's wrong," she said.

"How do you mean?" said Elgrapharr, raising his rifle and scanning the nearby brush.

Danger. A smell of danger on the wind.

She had no idea how the thought came into her head, but it was there and the feeling was unmistakable.

Waving heads.

Again the thought came from nowhere, but it only took her a moment to interpret it. Waving heads. The descriptor immediately brought back that terrifying first glimpse she'd had through the blowing snow of the advancing ril-galas horde, their manta-shaped heads weaving back and forth in constant motion.

"Ril-galas. They're here. They're somewhere here."

"All units report in," said Elgrapharr, the communications gear built into his armour automatically routing it through to the surviving members of his commando squad.

One by one they reported in. All but two.

"Thelcaris and Rehendarr, report," said Elgrapharr.

No response was forthcoming. The two commandos unaccounted for had been their rear guard, the ones who were to warn the rest about any ril-galas coming up from behind.

"We need to move faster," said Sigurdsson.

"Agreed."

They broke into a run and caught up with Aylarr, Ventaris and Frankenstein in moments. Sigurdsson noticed that Jaeger kept throwing glances behind them, the fur along his spine standing on end. It was the same thing he'd done when they had first run from the ril-galas to get back behind the walls of Fort Hathaway.

"We have a problem ahead," said Aylarr.

"We have a problem behind us, too," said Sigurdsson.

"Our rear guard has vanished," said Elgrapharr.

Jaeger was facing back the way they had come, growling. Reaching up and tapping the activation node embedded in her temple, Sigurdsson brought her cybernetic optics to life, immediately switching to infrared. The image jumped slightly as it was prone to do when first activated, but it was a momentary glitch and within a second, Sigurdsson was scanning the trail, looking for any sign of the enemy.

"Three of them," she said. "One about thirty meters back, the other two farther down the trail. Definitely ril-galas... but different."

They had the same manta-like heads, but they were smaller creatures than the usual solidly-built ril-galas foot soldiers. They were sleeker, lighter looking, and they moved with a quickness the foot soldiers could not match.

"Then the problem ahead has become a greater issue than before," said Frankenstein.

"The Gateway of Ur," said Aylarr.

Switching off her optics, Sigurdsson turned back to Aylarr. The icaran woman was pointing ahead of them, where the valley opened up slightly, its walls widening and becoming less choked with vegetation. Embedded in the valley was a massive stone archway – a perfect circle of stone nearly ten metres thick – its top half towering above and portions of its lower half protruding from the valley's rocky walls and grass-covered floor. The top of the arch, or the Gateway of Ur as Aylarr had called it, reached so high into the sky that its highest point faded into the cloud cover.

The sense of awe Sigurdsson felt at the sight of the structure wasn't only her own.

"There might be a city or something beyond the arch," said Sigurdsson. "Somewhere to take cover."

"There is nothing beyond," said Aylarr.

"Just more valley?"

"No. Nothing. Ur is a figure from udukiin folklore, a prophet who stepped across the Great Divide. The Gateway of Ur marks the edge of this hemisphere of The Shattered World."

There was literally nothing beyond the Gateway.

Clenching her teeth, Sigurdsson checked the charge on her *vayan* again and figured that if they had nowhere to run, nowhere to take cover, the pistol would probably last longer than she would. Holstering the pistol, she unslung the *aoran* assault rifle and checked its charge. It would still outlast her, but she'd make a lot more noise before she went.

The first of the ril-galas stalkers emerged from the long grass moments later. It was just as sleek as Sigurdsson's optics had shown her and like the ril-galas foot soldier, it had two sets of arms – one set ending in gun pods smaller than those of the foot soldier, and the other ending in a trio of razor sharp talons. Unlike the foot soldiers', these gun pod arms were the secondary arms, kept tucked in close to the chest, while the talons appeared to be the stalker's primary weapon.

This one's talons were slick with icaran blood and another substance Sigurdsson couldn't readily identify.

But she didn't have to. The surge of emotion she felt from the Matriarch told her all she needed to know. The other substance was udukiin blood.

Sigurdsson brought her *aoran* to her shoulder and the cylinder spun up, generating the kinetic force the icaran weapon required to fire its powerful projectiles.

Pounding two rounds into its chest, Sigurdsson hoped that through the misty cloud of yellowish blood she'd destroyed not just the stalker, but the pilot she knew resided in its chest cavity.

"We can't stay here," said Sigurdsson, keeping her rifle up and ready. "There are two more nearby and who knows how many more on the way."

"If the gate has so much cultural significance," said Elgrapharr. "Perhaps there will be some sort of population centre nearby. If not beyond it, perhaps adjacent."

Sigurdsson switched her optics back on, looked back down the valley and swore.

"Fucking hell. I got two closing in and four... shit, *five* more inbound. We need to find a way out of this."

With Elgrapharr and Aylarr hanging back as a rear guard, the group moved out with Sigurdsson taking point, Jaeger at her side. When they began to hear the rustling of foliage and undergrowth behind them, they all broke into a run, with the rear guard firing random shots into the grass in the hopes of slowing down the stalkers.

Passing through the Gateway of Ur, Sigurdsson skidded to stop just before the world dropped away into nothingness. Staring at the endless crevasse, she swallowed heavily,

She could see stars.

It was like looking over a cliff into an ocean, but the ocean was space. She could look straight down through the centre of this planet and see the stars on the other side.

The phrase 'the edge of the world' used to be thrown around a great deal back on planet Earth, but it had always been a stupid phrase, since no one of consequence in any modern society had believed the Earth actually had edges. But here on The Shattered World, the phrase wasn't hyperbole, it was fact: Freyja Sigurdsson was standing on the edge of the world.

She took a step closer, feeling a hot lump forming in her chest as the toe of her boot extended out into the nothingness. Jaeger, seemingly making smarter decisions than she was, took a step backward.

It was with great effort that Sigurdsson peeled her eyes away from the nothingness to look first left and then right in the hopes of seeing some sign of habitation. There was none. But somehow, likely due to her increasingly smooth psychic link with the Matriarch, she had always known they would not find what they'd hoped.

Her eyes drifted back to the nothingness.

And then they drifted upward, looking across the nothingness to the other half of The Shattered World. The gap was perhaps one and a half kilometers at this point, the other half of The Shattered World perhaps half a kilometer lower, and she could see an archway similar to the Gateway of Ur emerging from the treeline on the other side. And beyond it, there was something else. Reaching up and tapping her temple, Sigurdsson activated her optics and zoomed in. It took a moment for the image to sharpen and when it did, she saw the spires of what could only be a city.

"Look," she said, pointing across the gap. "A city."

"Unfortunately," said Frankenstein. "There does not appear to be a bridge."

"We have slowed them," said Elgrapharr as he and Aylarr joined the rest of the group. "But they still come."

"And in greater numbers, we believe," added Aylarr.

Cycling up his *aoran*, Ventaris surveyed the area, underneath the Gateway of Ur.

"We have little cover and no further avenue of retreat," he said. "This appears to be where we make our final stand."

"None shall know our fate," said Aylarr softly. "None shall sing our song."

"We shall sing our own song, until the last of us falls," said Elgrapharr, placing a hand on Aylarr's shoulder, then turning to Sigurdsson. "And we shall sing yours as well, Sigurdsson. You are one of us now."

She just nodded. With the lump that had formed in her throat, she didn't trust her voice.

It wasn't that she was afraid to die. Quite the opposite, in fact. That she'd survived as long as she had in the war was somewhat surprising to her, given the situations she continued to find herself in. What she found hard was that Elgrapharr would offer to sing her song. The icarans considered their songs – of history, of lives lived and lost – to be their most sacred of treasures and to not just hear those songs but to be offered one of her very own was an honour Sigurdsson knew had never before been extended a human.

Of course, she reminded herself, she wasn't considered a human anymore.

"I'm honoured to be counted among you," she said quietly.

Drawing her *vayan* from its holster, she handed it to a surprised Frankenstein.

"Doc," she said. "I know you probably have something like the Hippocratic Oath that says you should do no harm..."

Much to her surprise, the brill accepted the weapon with a nod and double checked its power levels.

"The Hippocratic Oath is a human construct and largely irrelevant to the brill. Even in triage, medical professionals prioritize treatment and choose which patient to treat first. The process can result in greater harm or even death to those deemed low priority," he said, shrugging. "I have prioritized the lives of my current comrades over the lives of the ril-galas."

"So killing them will not be an issue for you?" said Elgrapharr.

"I believe the autopsy performed by Nasrin Khaifa and myself essentially taught everyone how to truly kill ril-galas. One could argue I have already been responsible for many ril-galas deaths."

"Then let's get this last stand underway," said Sigurdsson, raising her rifle.

If death was on its way, it would find Freyja Sigurdsson ready, armed and prepared to make a fight of it. Dying was not something she wanted to do, but it had seemed inevitable from the first day of the ril-galas invasion and so she'd resigned herself to it – but she planned to carve her name into the ril-galas cultural memory by the time they killed her. Though she would have liked to have done more, Sigurdsson thought she could be satisfied that she'd given them enough of a bloody nose to go to her grave with a smile.

The first stalker broke from the long grass and every one of the surviving party members fired. Yellowish blood spattered across the ancient stone as the creature was cut to pieces.

The difficult part for Sigurdsson was that if they all died here, at the Gateway of Ur, no one would ever know their fates. The udukiin weren't on friendly terms with human or icaran governments and with the ril-galas seeing humans as a food source, odds were that there would be nothing left of Sigurdsson's corpse anyway. Eventually it would be assumed that she had been killed somewhere, but for a long time she'd just be considered missing in action.

Her friends might never know what had happened to her. And she'd never know what happened to them. She'd never know whether they survived; she'd never know if Radko's plan had worked.

Radko.

Something uncomfortable happened in her chest when she thought about never seeing him again. At first, she thought it was regret, which made perfect sense to her, but as the stalkers launched another attack, she realised that the feeling was also partly anger. These creatures were stealing away any possibility of her finally telling Radko how much their long-distance conversations – him on the Vimy Ridge and her sheltering behind the walls of Fort Hathaway – had meant to her, how they'd kept her going.

But more importantly, they were taking away her chance to...

She cried out in pain as a stalker slammed into her from the left, its claws raking across her armoured shoulder with the scraping sound of fingernails on a blackboard. As she and her attacker tumbled heavily to the ground, Sigurdsson tried to bring her rifle to bear, only to have it knocked out of her hands. The stalker reared back and slashed down with its claws. Desperately thrusting her forearm upward, Sigurdsson barely managed to deflect the strike, claws glancing harmlessly off the Matriarch armour. She clenched her free hand into a first and drove it toward the stalker's head and as she did so, she felt the armour of the Matriarch shifting, moving forward to cover her knuckles.

The impact of the punch knocked the stalker off-balance enough that Sigurdsson could gain leverage and she rolled them both over and continued to throw punches, driving her fists into the creature with every ounce of strength her new icaran arms could provide. Yellowish blood sprayed upward in arcs as she reduced the stalker's chest cavity to a pulpy mass of shattered bone-like material and globs of internals.

Hearing a sudden cry, she shot to her feet, her arms slick with the yellow blood of the ril-galas from fingertips to halfway up her biceps and splattered across her torso. Before she could react, Sigurdsson saw Ventaris go down under the weight of three stalkers, his helmet torn from his head. Ventaris barely reacted when the first of the stalkers sunk its claws into his head and by the time the second tore away a fist-sized chunk of skull, he was already dead.

Just as they all would be within the next few minutes.

Gritting her teeth, Sigurdsson scooped up her *aoran* and double-tapped Ventaris's killer in the chest while she waited for her turn to come.

But something in the back of her mind still felt there was a way out.

Gravity.

The word kept floating through her mind, the way a song lyric sometimes would when she had been on patrol duty or overwatch for long periods – just flitting through at the edge of her awareness, like a mosquito buzzing by her ear in the night.

It was different. The gravity was different.

She cautiously glanced over the edge of the cliff and into the absolute nothingness below. She saw the stars again, the stars on the other side of The Shattered World, where night would have fallen hours ago and she saw, in the space between, rocks both large and small. Just floating there in the gap.

The gravity was different, its strength diminished somehow by the splitting of the planet millennia ago, creating a dead zone in the Great Divide.

Follow the path of Ur.

And with that, Sigurdsson had no doubt where the thought had come from.

"You have got to be shitting me," she said quietly.

But as she looked back, she activated her infrared optics and saw in addition to the four stalkers Aylarr and Elgrapharr were putting down, there were dozens more heat signatures approaching through the valley.

As Elgrapharr took down the last of the first wave, Sigurdsson walked past them, putting a fair distance between herself and the edge of the world. She slung her rifle across her back and tightened the sling as much as she could.

"What are you doing?" said Elgrapharr. He still wore his face-less helmet. Aylarr's was gone – lost or damaged Sigurdsson did not know.

"Let's call it a leap of faith," she said, staring straight through the Gateway and across the Great Divide. "If this works, follow me. If it doesn't... it's been an honour."

Both icarans stared at her for a moment, then Sigurdsson thought she saw something akin to incredulity pass across Aylarr's face.

"Sigurdsson, you can't-."

But she was already running, running toward the edge of the world with all the energy she could force into her legs. Back in her early days in boot camp, she'd always been able to run circles – literally – around the other recruits. She was tall, which meant she had long legs and a stride to go with them, but she also had some power in her muscles and now, passing under the Gateway of Ur, she used all of it.

Reaching the edge of the cliff, she launched herself outward, into the void.

For the first few seconds, she felt she'd made a fatal mistake. Nothing felt different about the gravity. Her momentum was carrying her forward, but she was also starting to fall and then, to both her surprise and elation, the tug of gravity let go and she was sailing – almost flying – over the Great Divide. Above her was the blue and yellow sky of an alien world while below was a great chasm with no end – only stars. She was flying through space wearing a tee shirt and cargo pants and the thought was equal parts hilarious and terrifying.

And then she felt it. Just as the gravity of the one side of the Great Divide had released her from its grip, she began to feel the other side take hold.

The other side, which had seemed so far away moments ago, came rushing up to meet her, but the end result of Sigurdsson's rushed lift-off was a poor landing trajectory. As she sailed toward the ground, through the other gateway, her left shoulder clipped the old stone arch, sending her into a spin. She smashed into the pathway of cut stone hard, flat on her back, the air rushing out of her lungs as her *aoran* was crushed into scrap.

Staring up into the sky, it was all Sigurdsson could do to remain conscious. Her shoulder was on fire and clearly dislocated and she thought based on the level of pain that it was entirely possible she'd torn open the seam between the human and the icaran. As she drew a shaky, painful breath – after what seemed an eternity – she heard light footsteps approaching. Her right hand instinctively slid to the drop holster on her thigh, but it was empty. She'd given her pistol to Frankenstein. Her rifle was trash. She was without a firearm and she was in so much pain she could barely move, let alone stand and fight.

Suddenly a jolt went through her whole body like a shot of adrenaline and the pain, while not disappearing, was certainly lessened and Sigurdsson rolled herself onto one knee and prepared for...

"Jaeger!"

Tail wagging, the German Shepherd trotted up and licked her face.

"Jaeger, you crazy bastard," she said, laughing – which hurt quite a bit as it turned out – and rubbing him behind the ears. "Always got my back, hey? Good boy. Good boy."

A loud crashing sound signalled the arrival of Elgrapharr, Aylarr and Frankenstein. Elgrapharr had the brill in a bear hug, using his body and his heavy armour to protect Frankenstein's exo-suit from the impact. After a few seconds' recovery, the three stood and Sigurdsson did the same, her dislocated left arm hanging limply by her side.

"Well," she said, gingerly unstrapping and tossing aside the remains of her assault rifle. "It worked."

"You may be certifiably insane, Sigurdsson," said Elgrapharr.

"Don't pretend that wasn't one of the coolest things you've ever done," she said, laughing and wincing again at the pain it caused. Her wince deepened into a grimace as she felt a grinding in her shoulder and then a tightness and then a painful pop and her dislocated shoulder was no longer dislocated.

The Matriarch.

"Doc, I need you to check out my shoulder," she said, waving over the brill.

As Frankenstein complied, Sigurdsson noticed Aylarr look her up and down, a strange look on her face. She glanced to Elgrapharr then back to Sigurdsson, still splattered with ril-galas blood, and then back to Elgrapharr.

"What?" said Sigurdsson. "What is it?"

"Following in the footsteps of Ur she shall come," said Aylarr, still looking at Elgrapharr. "The blood of her enemies falling from her like rain."

"The fuck is that supposed to mean?"

Both icarans looked back at her. Aylarr had the same strange look on her face. Elgrapharr removed his faceless helmet, revealing an expression very similar to that of his compatriot.

"The Gateway of Ur," he said. "Was erected on the path taken by Ur on his quest to establish the Udukiin Priex."

"Okay. And...?"

Again the icarans exchanged a look, but then began to move.

"We need to continue on before the ril-galas decide to follow," said Elgrapharr.

"I find no damage to your shoulder, Freyja," said Franken-stein. "And this would, perhaps, be better in your hands."

The brill handed back her heavy icaran pistol and fell into step behind the two icaran commandos, leaving Sigurdsson confused on many fronts.

Just as she began to jog to catch up, Sigurdsson saw Jaeger stop in his tracks, his ears perked, and a feeling of imminent danger washed over her. Then Elgrapharr and Ayalarr suddenly stopped and she heard a voice – a voice that maintained a level of ominousness even through the bland translation matrix in her earpiece.

"Icarans," it said.

"Icarans," echoed a half dozen other voices.

"And a brill," said the first voice.

"Brill," said the chorus.

"We do not seek hostilities," said Elgrapharr. "We were attacked and-."

"Icaran will cease its words," said the voice.

"Cease," said the chorus.

They'd made contact with the udukiin, though in less than ideal circumstances. It should have been an awe-inspiring experience, being the first human – or close enough to human – to meet the udukiin on their own world, and it should have been even more incredible given that Sigurdsson had only ever seen udukiin in pictures shown during her military training. In person, they were shorter than she had imagined. Of the five she could see from her vantage point, well back of the icarans, Sigurdsson was at least a head taller than the largest of them, though they were stocky and powerfully built with four arms. Their heads were almost Y-shaped, with a jutting lower jaw and six eyes – clustered in threes at the base of each of the two crests that extended from the main body of the skull at forty-five degrees.

All the udukiin carried large, dangerous looking pikes and each had a pair of long, curved knives strapped to its chest.

A brief wave of dizziness passed over her and then Sigurdsson felt a jolt within her body, almost but not quite like a shot of adrenaline, followed by a feeling that something was finished. But she had no idea what.

The lead udukiin raised its pike, poised to strike.

"Hey!" yelled Sigurdsson.

"Human!"

The voice was almost right beside her and out of the undergrowth an udukiin warrior lunged at her.

"Human," she heard the other udukiin repeat as the bulky body slammed into her, taking her heavily to the stones.

The suddenness of the impact prevented the udukiin from getting a grip on her and Sigurdsson rolled out from under it and managed to get to one knee before the pike came swinging in her direction. As she blocked the shaft of the pike with her armoured forearm and shot to her feet, she felt adrenaline and something else, something stronger, coursing through her veins. And when she saw a pike driven into Aylarr's midsection and the icaran commando drop to the ground, she felt the surge even stronger. Her right had shot out and clamped around the udukiin's throat and Sigurdsson lifted the shorter creature off the ground, one-handed.

"Enough," she said through gritted teeth.

Small spikes began to grow from the Matriarch armour as she spoke.

"We didn't come here to fight," she said. "But believe me, we will if we have to. And it won't end well for you."

"Release him or we will kill your compatriots," said the lead udukiin.

"Will kill," said the chorus, all taking a step forward and raising their pikes menacingly.

"You will do no such thing," she said, tossing aside the udukiin she had been choking and striding confidently toward the hostile grouping. "Because we..."

She trailed off as the udukiin gasped, all of them, and their eyes went wide.

"You have stolen a Matriarch!"

"Matriarch," repeated the chorus.

"You will die for your-."

"Shut the fuck up," she said. "We *rescued* the Matriarch! We freed her from a shitty little cell on a shitty little planet and came all the way here, through... the fuck do you guys call space? The black? We came through the black and survived a crash landing and an ambush by ril-galas and jumped across the fucking crack in your planet to bring her home. So either get out of my way or I swear I will beat you senseless and feed you your own shit."

The udukiin were silent, staring at Sigurdsson as if seeing her for the first time and she could feel *something*, almost like the buzzing in her head she'd felt when the Matriarch had first bonded with her. But this was different. It was like the buzzing was happening outside her mind, like it was being projected outward.

"From out of the black," murmured the lead udukiin.

"A great Matriarch shall arise," came a whisper from the rest.

"Following in the footsteps of Ur she shall come," said the leader.

"The blood of her enemies falling from her like rain," whispered the group.

And every single one of them dropped to one knee, laid down their pike on the ground and extended their hands, palms down.

"Kaigor Kai Rii," they said in unison.

As Elgrapharr helped the thankfully uninjured Aylarr to her feet, Sigurdsson shot them both a look that conveyed her confusion over what had happened.

"One of their prophecies," said Aylarr, wincing slightly. The pike must have caught her at a bad angle. "A new War Matriarch will come from outer space – out of the black, as they say – to lead them."

"And they think the Matriarch that we've brought here is this War Matriarch?"

Aylarr just stared at Sigurdsson for a moment before speaking.

"To a certain degree, yes."

"To a certain degree? What does that mean?"

"Kaigor Kai Rii," chanted the udukiin.

"And what does *that* mean, Kaigor Kai Rii?" said Sigurdsson. "My translator isn't translating."

"It wouldn't," said Aylarr. "It is an ancient udukiin dialect. It means 'the Matriarch of the Three.'"

Frowning, Sigurdsson nodded. She'd learned in the relatively short time since discovering The Matriarch something that had never occurred to her before: given the average life span of an icaran, they frequently had two or more careers over the course of that lifetime. In Aylarr's case, she had been what humans would call a xenoanthropologist, studying alien cultures. The krellin and the udukiin, specifically.

Suddenly, the udukiin all stood, collecting their pikes. The leader tapped the butt end of his weapon on the stone pathway six times.

"I am called Udrach Kai Togru."

Aylarr stepped forward before Sigurdsson or Elgrapharr could respond and Sigurdsson had no issue with that. If any of them were knowledgeable enough on udukiin custom to avoid getting them all killed, it was her.

"Udrach, we are honoured to know your name title," said Aylarr. "I am called Aylarr of Icar Prime and this is my leader, Elgrapharr of Icar. And this is Freyja Sigurdsson of..."

She stumbled slightly over her words and Sigurdsson couldn't blame her. After all, she'd not had a real home since she was child and even that was questionable. She hadn't even been to Earth in nearly a decade. And with her status as a human now apparently in question, there was only one place Sigurdsson felt she could honestly say she was from.

"The black."

There was a moment of silence as Aylarr stared at her, seeming to have an internal debate as to whether to repeat Sigurdsson's words. But she turned back to Udrach.

"Freyja Sigurdsson of the Black."

"Of the black. Kaigor Kai Rii," murmured the gathered udukiin, and it struck Sigurdsson that her answer may have been a poor choice.

"Yeah, okay, I don't mean to be rude, Udrach, but can we get out of here?" she said. "Clearly you guys want your Matriarch back and I don't want to be here when those ril-galas figure out they can jump over the Great Divide."

All the udukiin snarled at the same time. It was unsettling to say the least.

"Ril-galas," they said.

"Yeah... exactly."

"We shall go to the Matriarch," said Udrach, turning on his heel and marching down the stone pathway.

Sigurdsson – Jaeger at her side – Elgrapharr, Aylarr and Frankenstein quickly followed and the remaining udukiin formed up around them in a manner that was left open to interpretation as to whether they were guarding prisoners against escape or important dignitaries against attack.

Her brow furrowed in confusion, Sigurdsson turned to Aylarr.

"They're taking us to the Matriarch?"

"Yes."

"I thought this was the Matriarch," she said, holding up her arm to indicate the armour plating that had resulted from her bonding.

"That is *a* Matriarch. Though the udukiin Matriarch is far rarer than the standard udukiin, many do exist at one time," said Aylarr, keeping her voice low. "Matriarchs bond with female udukiin appropriate for their roles. It is an oversimplification, but the explanation will suffice for now. The Matriarch who will lead the Priex, for example, would bond with an udukiin of great wisdom and patience, while the one responsible for development of the udukiin space fleet would bond with one of high intellect and ingenuity. And the War Matriarch... she would choose someone of great skill in combat and the ability to inspire and lead."

"Okay. And so they think this Matriarch I'm carrying will be a War Matriarch? Once it's bonded to an udukiin?"

There was again a slight pause and Aylarr's hesitancy to answer was starting to worry Sigurdsson.

"They do appear to feel that the War Matriarch has arrived."

"The Matriarch of the Three," she said, nodding slowly. "What's the 'three' thing about, though?"

This time, Aylarr looked at her but said nothing.

"I believe," said Elgrapharr. "That we will find out shortly."

He pointed ahead, where through the last of the trees, a small city could be seen.

"Her Vibrant Colours," said Udrach and it took Sigurdsson a moment to understand that he was giving them the name of the city.

The name was, much to Sigurdsson's surprise, very apt. Given the reputation of the udukiin for their savage defense of their home system and for their historic wars with several species – icarans included – Sigurdsson had been expecting a utilitarian, militaristic society. But Her Vibrant Colours was an incredible sight to behold. It was nestled in a large depression in the ground, likely the site of an ancient asteroid impact – possibly even the one that created the Great Divide eons ago – and its towering spires, visible from the other half of the Shattered World, soared upward as high or higher than any of the tallest buildings Sigurdsson could remember from Earth. And they were much more beautiful, appearing to be sculpted as opposed to constructed, and made of green stone that shimmered with tiny flecks of silver in the sunlight.

The entire city sat on a platform, hovering above the floor of the depression through either some form of advanced technology or perhaps even a similar gravitational effect that allowed Sigurdsson to leap across the Great Divide. A single, easily defendable bridge led from the edge of the crater to the city platform.

The four udukiin standing guard at the bridge stepped aside as Udrach approached and spoke to them in a low voice. All four of them stared at Sigurdsson and the group passed and she felt a shiver go up her spine. Something was not right with their situation and she was getting the distinct impression that she was missing some crucial piece of information – and that she was the only one missing it.

Crossing the bridge and entering the udukiin city, Sigurdsson tried not to gawk. The city's name was appropriate -- aside from the shining towers, the wide streets were lined with tents of every colour Sigurdsson could name and a few that she couldn't, under which udukiin merchants transacted their business, selling bright pink fruits and brown-and-blue striped vegetables and flowering plants with purple stems and green petals, and hand-carved toys and entire boxes full of things Sigurdsson had no hope of identifying. And above the tents, even more colour. Strung in four tiers criss-crossing the streets were flags or banners of varying size, some simple solid colours, some two-toned and bearing a pair of sigils. All were the same shimmering, translucent fabric.

As Udrach led onward, passing an open-air restaurant of some sort, Sigurdsson smiled slightly. There was a patio. Outdoor tables and chairs, at which udukiin sat, drinking... whatever they drank. Having snacks. One appeared to be eating a sandwich. Two udukiin children argued over who was to eat the last of what she assumed to be some kind of sweet, based on its puffy appearance.

The whole scene was so... normal. Before the ril-galas, you could have walked down any street on any human colony -- even on Earth -- and seen the same thing. Just people going about their lives. A scene like this was something to which the old Sigurdsson wouldn't have given a second glance.

It reminded her about her conversation with Radko, about the little things feeling more important than ever. Which is why she needed to deliver the Matriarch and get back to the fight. For the first time in a very long time, Sigurdsson wanted to do the little things.

Looking up again, she saw the flags and banners were in this street too, though there appeared to be more of them bearing sigils.

"Those symbols," said Sigurdsson, slowing to match pace with Aylarr. "What do they mean?"

For a moment, the icaran stared up at the banners, her four eyes blinking as she took in the sight.

"That is not an easy question to answer," she said with a very human-like sigh. "Udukiin written language is very different than icaran."

"And from human, I assume?"

Aylarr actually laughed at that.

"From human? Do you mean English? Or Russian? Or Chinese? You are an incredibly confused species."

"No argument here."

"Udukiin written language is more concepts than written equivalents of vocalizations," she said, but her expression showed she was unhappy with her explanation. "For example, if I wanted to tell you to be strong, steadfast and to not yield to outside forces, I could say -- with symbols as those above us -- 'the walls of Fort Hathaway.' Your experience and knowledge would draw the connection and you would understand my meaning. For the udukiin, these are cultural touchstones. In most, I believe the first symbol refers to a Matriarch."

"A War Matriarch?"

"Not all, but some, yes. Some, like this one," she said, pointing out a yellow and silver banner with two dark blue glyphs. "Tell the story of a Matriarch helping rebuild a town after a natural disaster. And the orange one over here appears to be about universal health care."

30

The chime had sounded twice before Radko had bothered to open the door to his quarters and admit Owens. He knew he looked like hell, and could see it in the Lieutenant Commander's eyes.

"I know I shouldn't have threatened ATC Castle," said Radko.

"Probably not," agreed Owens. "But I would have done the same thing. All of us would have."

"This is now two death sentences I've given her."

Owens looked up at him, brows raised.

"What?"

"Her cancer," said Radko, dropping heavily into a chair as Owens gently lowered himself into the one across the table. "We stayed in the Ishtar Gate too long. My orders. The radiation exposure made it worse, turned it from operable with something like ninety percent survival rate to inoperable with a four percent survival rate. And now this -- convicted of treason for helping me."

"You couldn't have known she had that tumour, Commander."

"But I thought about it, Owens -- I thought about it. While we were in there, I thought 'some of us are probably going to develop tumours from this' and I still kept us in."

"And keeping us in as long as you did is the main reason we were able to catch the ril-galas by surprise and break the blockade at Thor's Hammer."

Radko leaned forward and rubbed his face.

"I know. I know. The tactical side of my brain says she's just one person -- on the balance sheet of the greater good, losing one person is a small price to pay. But she's not just one person, she's Anna Cortez."

"That she is," said Owens, sinking back into his own chair. "I feel like we saw her grow up."

"In a lot of ways, we did."

"Sorry, turns out I am terrible at pep talks."

"We all have our weaknesses," said Radko, chuckling. "But I appreciate you trying. I'll be okay, I just-"

"Have this insane desire to be heroic and go rescue her."

"Pretty much."

"You know that if you decided to do that, everyone on this ship with the possible exception of el Bahari would follow."

"Which is why I need to get my shit together. I can't let myself lead this crew against the very people we're trying to protect. Especially not for the sake of one life, no matter how important that life may be to me."

Sighing once more, Radko stood and smoothed out his uniform jacket.

"Assemble the crew in the mess hall. I want to speak with them face to face, not over intercom."

Under thirty minutes later, the whole crew -- minus one member from each key station to keep the ship flying -- was assembled in the mess hall. The first time Radko had done this, back when the ril-galas had first appeared, they had been able to accommodate everyone there because of how short-handed the crew had been. Now, short-handed was the new normal for Commonwealth vessels and everyone had become accustomed to it.

As Radko stepped up to the podium, he briefly locked eyes with el Bahari, who seemed far more subdued than usual. She was an excellent officer and Radko hoped she'd come to understand that he wasn't trying to grandstand with this mission, that he wasn't trying to wrest control from anyone. Just that he knew they needed to make progress.

"I'm not going to have a big preamble for you today," he said, his voice amplified through the mess hall. "I know rumour travels quickly round a ship of this size and I wanted you to hear the truth directly from me."

He paused for a moment as he considered his words.

"Anna Cortez, whom most of you know, has been convicted of treason and will be executed within twenty-four hours."

The crew erupted in roars of indignation and Radko had to hold up his hand to silence them.

Once the noise had quieted, a voice from the back yelled out that the charges were bullshit and Radko nodded.

"Of course they're bullshit. We all know that. So do the people who charged and convicted her. They're petty, terrified little people who are beneath every single person on this ship. They're beneath every icaran aboard the Venn Shakara. They're beneath the pirates of the Azrael's Tear," said Radko, his upper lip curling in disgust. "They are fucking cowards."

He looked down and saw el Bahari glancing around uncomfortably at the crew, who were also voicing their outrage. It was clear she had no idea what he was doing and probably feared he was about to advocate civil war.

Instead, he held up his hands once more for silence.

"But they're not who we serve," he said firmly. "We don't fight for a head of state. We don't fight for a government or a flag. We have to be above that. We *are* above that. We fight for humanity and we fight for the icaran people and we fight for everyone who can't fight for themselves. And what we do, we do because it gives us our best chance of helping all of them, and though I would love nothing more than to have Anna Cortez right here, right now, we have to be... I have to be... above revenge. I have to put the needs of humanity above my own, even though it will cost me the life of a dear friend."

Voice cracking slightly, Radko paused and cleared his throat.

"Just like the decision to liberate Thor's Hammer rather than try for Earth did," he said softly. "And I seem to be running out of friends."

Harlan Grey was dead.

Locaris was dead.

Anna would be dead within hours.

And Sigurdsson... he felt his gut tighten even more. There had been no reports on Sigurdsson since Singh's crew reported the dropship being shot down over the Shattered World.

Freyja could be dead, too.

He closed his eyes and took a deep breath.

"I need my friends," he said, spreading his arms wide. "But I can't put their lives ahead of all of humanity, no matter what impulse in my brain is telling me to get on my white horse and ride in to the rescue. I have to be above that and it makes me angry and frustrated that I have to be above that, but it doesn't make it any less true. The future of the human race outweighs the lives of any one of us -- myself included."

Gripping the side of the podium, Radko met as many gazes as he could while he collected himself.

"We can mourn our friends once we've driven the ril-galas from our home. But now, we have a job to do."

"You don't think much of Prime Minister DeFreitas," said el Bahari.

After the meeting, Radko had immediately returned to the upper command deck. El Bahari had joined him, both staring out past the Venn Shakara, into the black.

"He hasn't given me reason to."

"He's the Prime Minister. He should be given the respect-"

"*Given* the respect? Respect is earned, Commander, not given out like Halloween candy to any idiot who rings the doorbell," said Radko. "He's spineless. He cares more about politics than governance. He's so fixated on staying safe that he's losing sight of what a Prime Minister is supposed to be. And he can't even take a shit without Bianca fucking Upshaw giving him the okay and instructions on how to wipe."

She simply stared at him for a moment, mouth agape.

"Don't pretend I'm wrong," he said.

"I... don't have the access to the Prime Minister's inner circle that you do," she said carefully. "So I couldn't hazard an opinion."

"His inner circle is just Upshaw now. He doesn't even listen to Mahoney anymore -- the guy who runs the goddamned Navy."

"So we simply ignore the chain of command? Ignore that the Commonwealth Navy is ultimately answerable to the Prime Minister?"

"Once this mission is over, I am fully prepared to be answerable to the Prime Minister, and even to the woman pulling his strings. After the mission, not before."

"Because you know they would never approve it," she said, nodding.

"Exactly. And we would spend another year and a half talking and talking and talking and letting the ril-galas further entrench themselves on Earth," said Radko.

"And you don't care if it costs you your career?"

"My *career*? They just convicted Cortez of treason just for helping plan this. Commander, even if I survive this mission, I'm not convinced I'll survive the fallout."

El Bahari just stared at him.

"I meant what I said: I have to be above all the bullshit. I'm not worried about personal consequences, I'm worried that if I don't take this opportunity, there won't be another."

"You think we'd just sit on our hands without you leading the charge?" she snapped. "More than a bit egotistical."

Radko smiled slightly.

"Tell me, el Bahari -- what has anyone done in the last year and a half that makes you feel like the current do-nothing state of affairs will be coming to an end?"

As he expected, she didn't have an answer for that.

"This has nothing to do with my ego. I would love nothing more than to have what currently passes as Commonwealth leadership actually leading us, but how long should we wait for that to happen? Another year? Two? Ten? Do you think the Earth will last that long?"

"You're the one who prioritized Thor's Hammer over Earth."

It was a weak argument and her voice betrayed that she knew it.

"I did, and a lot of people on Earth have died because of that decision. Which I will have to live with for however long I have left," he said. "But my decision was based on adding war assets to enable us to take back Earth, not to create a little bubble around the station and go into fortress mode until this whole thing blows over."

Staring out at the Venn Shakara for several moments, el Bahari took a slow, deep breath and exhaled just as slowly. It was a technique Radko knew well from his therapy sessions, a way to steady the mind, to clear away the emotions that were about to get you in trouble. He almost smiled, seeing el Bahari do it. Not because it showed a weakness, but because it showed her awareness of and focus on dealing with a weakness.

That kind of self-awareness was missing in a lot of people.

"Commander," she said, finally turning back to him. "I want to be clear here. I agree with... certain parts of what you're trying to do. Clearly I agree we need to liberate Earth; that we need to drive them out not just for the people of the Commonwealth, but for the future of humanity as a whole."

Frowning momentarily, she glanced back to the icaran warship.

"I am even willing to concede that alliances that would, in better times, have been inadvisable at best may now be necessary."

"However...?"

"However. Your methods are beyond questionable. You have no regard for the chain of command or the oath you swore to the Commonwealth as a naval officer. You are reckless. You are answerable to no one but yourself and have surrounded yourself with people who wouldn't even think to question your actions, motives or methods."

Crossing his arms, Radko leaned back against the observation dome. When he smiled at his XO, he could tell by the twitch of her jaw muscle it wasn't the reaction for which she'd prepared herself.

"I only disagree with two of those points," he said. "First, I take my oath very seriously -- more seriously than many others, it seems. I swore to protect the Commonwealth and all of its citizens, which is not a promise I can keep with the Vimy Ridge parked at Thor's Hammer and my ass parked in a conference room chair. Second, I do have someone to question me. I have you. You're very good at it and I expect you to continue doing so."

He didn't think it possible, but her frown deepened.

"I'm not a tyrant. Do I think I'm right? I wouldn't be doing this," he said, nodding his head toward the icaran vessel. "If I didn't. But I'm also not an idiot -- I know the dangers of making decisions in an echo chamber."

"I think you're dangerous."

"So do the ril-galas."

31

For the third time in as many minutes, Khaifa smoothed out the wrinkles in her suit jacket and straightened its lapels. There was nothing wrong with the jacket, no new wrinkles had formed since her last smoothing, but it was something to do, something to occupy her mind. Not that it could fully distract her from the fact that she was about to attend a political execution.

Sighing, she looked at herself in the mirror.

"How did we come to this?"

When her reflection refused to answer, she sighed again and looked at the clock.

Ninety minutes.

Less than two hours is all that remained in the life of Anna Cortez.

She would have been turning twenty-two in less than thirty days, but instead she would be twenty-one for the rest of her life.

Not for the first time since the Cortez conviction, Khaifa was reminded of Natasha. Her daughter with Harlan Grey would have been twenty-one as well, had she survived the boating accident that took her life twelve years prior. Their daughter's death was the catalyst for the slow downfall of her marriage with Grey and for Khaifa to throw herself into her work with MediCorps as well as several ill-advised relationships. As her personal life fell apart, her professional life soared and now here she was, a highly-placed government official, arguably the second most famous person in the Commonwealth after Finn Radko. And, thanks to her alien autopsy video, the most recognizable.

But with Bianca Upshaw well-entrenched as the Prime Minister's right hand, Khaifa's role as advisor was now honourary for all intents and purposes. There appeared to be nothing she could say or do to save a young officer from a sham of a trial or an abomination of a sentence.

When her door chime sounded, Khaifa ignored it at first. She didn't want to have to deal with anyone; she didn't want to have to put on a public face. All she wanted was to go see Cortez, talk to the young woman, let her see a friendly face before she died and to be with her when that moment came. To make sure she didn't have to die alone.

After the chime sounded for a third time, the doctor reluctantly opened the door. She didn't recognize the man standing there smiling at her with a smile that seemed equal parts friendly and intentionally non-threatening. He wasn't particularly tall -- only marginally taller than Khaifa herself -- but he was powerfully built. His hair was a buzzed Mohawk and he wore a simple grey t-shirt with simple block letters spelling out 'Revelstoke.'

A REV1 pistol was strapped to his left thigh.

"Doctor Khaifa," he said, the smile widening slightly. "Captain Maximillian Ironhorse, Revelstoke Ranger Company."

Khaifa forced a smile.

"A pleasure to meet you, Captain Ironhorse," she said. "How can I help you?"

"It's the other way around, ma'am -- I've been asked to serve as security for you."

"Security... you mean a body guard?"

"More or less, ma'am."

That anyone felt it was necessary for her to have a body guard while on Thor's Hammer spoke volumes about the situation. That she was glad to have someone watching out for her spoke volumes about her own feelings on the situation.

"All right then," she said. "I have somewhere I need to be right now, Captain."

He nodded, the smile finally fading.

"Yes ma'am."

"So you've heard about the Cortez situation?"

The Captain fell into step beside her as Khaifa exited her office and began walking down the corridor.

"I'd be surprised if anyone here hadn't, ma'am."

"And your thoughts?"

There was a momentary pause before he replied.

"I wasn't at the court martial, ma'am. I wasn't privy to the case being presented."

It was a carefully neutral answer, one that she knew was designed to be non-committal.

"I was. It was a travesty of justice."

Before Ironhorse could reply -- assuming he had been planning to, which was not a given -- the pair rounded a corner and came face to face with a pair of ATC Castle security agents, each carrying a Caliburn SMG.

"Doctor Khaifa," said the taller of the two. "We're here to act as your security detail."

"On whose authority?" asked Khaifa, fairly certain she knew the answer.

"Deputy Prime Minister Upshaw."

"*Deputy Prime Minister* Upshaw?"

She didn't even try to hide the combination of incredulity and indignation in her voice.

"I am the doctor's security," said Ironhorse.

The tall security man looked down on Ironhorse, literally and figuratively.

"We have orders from-"

"I am the doctor's security."

The shorter of the agents -- shorter, though still a head taller than Ironhorse -- stepped forward, the muzzle of his submachine gun twitching ever so slightly in what Khaifa could tell was a subtle and intentional threat.

"Stand aside. Our orders come directly from-"

"I am the doctor's security," said Ironhorse, stone-faced.

The tall agent, a snarl on his lips, took a quick step toward Ironhorse, raising his weapon and before Khaifa could protest there was a blur of motion and the tall man was on the floor, clutching at his dislocated elbow, his Caliburn in Ironhorse's right hand while the Captain's pistol -- in his left -- was pointed at the second agent. Its muzzle was a hair's breadth from the man's forehead.

"ATC Castle's services are not required here," he said. "I am the doctor's security."

Red-faced, seething, the agent looked down at his injured comrade, then back to Ironhorse.

"My name is Ironhorse," said the Captain, cutting off the bluster forming on the agent's lips and handing him his comrade's weapon.

At the mention of the name, Khaifa saw the agent's eyes widen. Even the injured agent, slowly getting to his feet, stopped his cursing and fell silent. The pair exchanged a look and then, nodding to Khaifa, suddenly found they had somewhere else to be.

"What was that all about?"

"Easier to keep tabs on you if they have their own people guarding you."

"Yes, of course," she said quickly. "But I meant their sudden change of heart once they heard your name."

Ironhorse holstered his pistol and shrugged, the small smile returning.

"Names carry the weight of reputation."

He nodded down the hallway.

"Shall we, ma'am?"

"Please don't call me ma'am," she said as they resumed walking. "I didn't graduate medical school to be called ma'am."

"Sorry, Doctor. Didn't mean any offense."

She shook her head, forcing a smile once more.

"I know, I'm sorry, I'm just... this is not an easy day."

Seeming to know it wasn't something Khaifa wanted to discuss -- or perhaps not caring enough to ask -- Ironhorse just nodded and walked the rest of the way with her in silence. It left her alone with her thoughts, which while not necessarily a good thing, was nonetheless something she needed. Getting through the coming hours was going to take all of her concentration and willpower -- and even then, it could just be the beginning.

When they arrived at the detention centre, it was both too soon and not soon enough.

"Doctor Nasrin Khaifa," she said. "I'm here to see Lieutenant Cortez."

The guard nodded and wordlessly led her and Ironhorse into the cell block, where they found Cortez standing, leaning against the bulkhead and staring out her small window into space. Toward Earth. She was dressed in the putrid orange jumpsuit of a convict, one size too big for her tiny frame.

They hadn't even let her wear her uniform.

Out of the corner of her eye, she noticed Ironhorse's jaw muscle twitch as he clenched his teeth. He knew it probably better than she did -- dressing Cortez like a common criminal was all part of the game, both to humiliate her and enrage those for whom this production was really meant.

"Lieutenant Cortez."

Khaifa could already feel the tears welling up in her eyes. She didn't know Cortez well, but she'd come to know her well enough through her close association with Radko to see the girl... to see the *woman* as a friend.

And Cortez did not look well. She was gaunt, her eyes bloodshot -- though dry. She hadn't been crying. And despite her obvious frailty, she held her head high, her back straight. Her gaze, when she locked eyes with the doctor, was clear and unwavering.

"Doctor Khaifa," she said, smiling a smile so genuine one would think they'd just run into each other at a shop. "It's good to see you again."

"Likewise, Lieutenant. Oh, and this is-"

"Captain Ironhorse," said Cortez, shaking hands with the Ranger, though gently. "A pleasure."

Ironhorse nodded a greeting.

"Of course," said Khaifa. "You're in Intelligence -- you probably know who everyone is."

"*Was* intelligence. Now I'm a traitor, remember?"

"No one believes that."

"The court martial did."

"That court martial was a...," she trailed off. Her fists had clenched and she had been starting to raise her voice, but she stopped herself. What was done was done. She hadn't the power to undo it. "I'm sorry, I'm just... sorry."

The tears came. She tried to fight them, but they came anyway and she turned away from Cortez and Ironhorse to wipe her eyes.

"Captain," she heard Cortez say quietly. "Would you mind giving us a few minutes?"

The doctor didn't hear a verbal response, but she heard the cell door open and close and then felt Cortez's hand on her shoulder.

"It's okay, Doctor, really," she said. "I'm at peace with what's happening."

"How? How can you be at peace with a death sentence for something... something you didn't do? You're not a traitor, Anna."

"Oh, believe me, I know. I'm not at peace with being a pawn in someone else's game, I'm at peace with dying. I've been dying, slowly, for a long time now. Honestly, it's nice to know when it will happen, rather than wondering if it's today or tomorrow or two months from now."

"You're being made a scapegoat. And bait."

"And if my life is what it takes to wake people up to what's been going on here..."

"Radko's going to do something stupid, isn't he?"

Cortez smiled again, but there was a hint of sadness in it.

"No. He's going to do what's in the best strategic interest of mankind. He knows that's what I'd want him to do," she said. "I just wish I could have had a chance to say goodbye."

"Would you like me to try to arrange it?"

Cortez shook her head.

"You said it yourself -- I'm bait. I won't feed into that. You just pass along a message for me, okay?"

It was Khaifa's turn to nod.

"Tell him I said not to stop until he's finished. See it through. All the way," she said and then added quietly: "And tell him I have always and will always believe in him."

"I will," said Khaifa, barely choking out the words.

After a silent moment, the cell door opened and Ironhorse walked in, flanked by the same two security agents he had summarily dismissed as Khaifa's security detail earlier.

"It's time," said the taller one, still holding his right arm close to his body -- still clearly in pain. "The prisoner will proceed to maintenance airlock twenty-one."

"The prisoner has a name," said Khaifa. "Please use it."

The agent ignored her, reaching out and roughly yanking Cortez to her feet.

"She can walk under her own power," said Ironhorse, stepping directly in front of the security agent.

He then whispered something to the man, something Khaifa thought she heard, but was convinced she couldn't have heard correctly: *no one will care if I kill you.*

Whatever he actually said, the security agent unhanded Cortez, who, standing tall, led the procession to airlock twenty one. DeFreitas and Upshaw were there, looking pleased with themselves. Mahoney was there, looking like he was ready to vomit. And a four-member firing squad -- ATC Castle, every one -- stood ready as executioners.

Cortez walked past them all and stood ramrod straight in the centre of the bay. As a maintenance airlock, it was large enough in which to land a shuttle, and the echoes of her footsteps lingered. Cortez smiled at Mahoney -- a silent thanks for his efforts on her behalf -- and refused to even look at DeFreitas and Upshaw.

"Anna Nekane Cortez," said Upshaw, a note of triumph in her voice. "You have committed treason, knowingly and willingly, against the Commonwealth. Your sentence is death by firing squad, to be carried out immediately."

She paused for a moment, probably gloating and savouring her victory, thought Khaifa.

"I'm sorry, Anna," said Mahoney. "So very sorry."

"It's all right, sir. I know you tried."

"Firing squad make ready," said Upshaw.

"Wait!"

The word was out before Khaifa even realised she was speaking, and everyone turned toward her.

"This is insane," she said. "This isn't what the Commonwealth is about. This isn't what we do."

"Yes it is," said Cortez as all eyes turned to her. "This is what these two people have turned the Commonwealth into."

Finally, she turned to Upshaw and DeFreitas.

"They'd rather have us scared of our own shadows and looking for enemies within than to have to risk facing the real enemy."

One of the security agents started to reach for Cortez, to silence her.

"The prisoner will-"

But he never reached her.

It took four heavy punches to the face before the agent had the good sense to stay down.

"She's about to die," said Ironhorse, wiping the blood from his knuckles onto his pants. "I don't recommend anyone else try to interrupt her last words."

"Thanks, Captain," said Cortez, smiling again. "Yes, I'm about to die. My life doesn't matter. I was going to die anyway -- you've seen my medical records. I'm about to die because you're too afraid to make a stand; because I helped the one man who wasn't. But executing me won't change that, it will only make it worse. When I'm gone, someone else will step up to take my place."

She paused, chuckling slightly.

"You're scared to go after Radko directly because of what he symbolizes to the people here on Thor's Hammer, but you're too blinded by your fear to realise that killing me won't make a difference. It won't make him suddenly swear allegiance to you. It won't weaken his resolve. It won't even weaken his support, because he's *Finn Radko* and *he's right*. He's been right *all along*, you were just too stupid to listen. So go ahead and execute me. I will go to my death happily, knowing that one day soon, no one will remember the names DeFreitas and Upshaw, because Finn Radko will have returned -- with his friends -- and saved humanity from extinction."

"Pretty speech," said Upshaw. "But you're wrong."

"Radko will face his own charge of treason soon enough," added DeFreitas.

Upshaw smiled.

"We will bring him down. But you won't be around to see it," she said. "Firing squad make ready."

The four-man squad took their positions.

"Aim."

Weapons raised. Barrels pointed at the chest of Anna Cortez.

Khaifa clenched her fists. She could feel herself shaking, but refused to look away.

Cortez smiled and locked eyes with the doctor. She nodded slightly, as if letting Khaifa know everything would be okay -- as if forgiving her for failing to stop the execution. It hadn't been an act, her acceptance of her fate. The young Lieutenant was perfectly at peace with it and was willing to accept it, regardless of the fabricated nature of the charges and the conviction.

Cortez said she knew that someone would step into the void left by her death.

Someone.

"Fire."

Khaifa twitched as four rifles barked in unison and Cortez staggered backward two steps and then dropped heavily to the deck plates.

Rushing to her side, Khafia was both relieved and devastated that Cortez was already dead. One of the shots had gone straight through her heart, making her end mercifully quick. Reaching out with her left hand, Khaifa gently closed the young woman's eyes.

"Justice is done," said Upshaw.

The doctor had to physically bite her tongue to remain silent. The self-satisfied tone of the ATC Castle woman was enough to make her years of practice at controlling her temper feel inadequate and it was only feeling Mahoney's hand on her shoulder that really held in check the words threatening to come out.

"It wouldn't do anyone any good," he said quietly.

He was right, of course. Though the old man would probably be deeply troubled by the comparison, Mahoney reminded her a little bit of what she imaged Radko would be like in thirty years: strong, competent, but quieter and very, very tired of everyone else's bullshit.

After tucking a loose strand of hair behind Cortez's ear, Khaifa stood and turned toward DeFreitas and Upshaw.

"Earlier today I heard someone refer to you as Deputy Prime Minister," she said to Upshaw.

"Yes," said Upshaw, raising her chin slightly. "As of this morning. We'll be releasing a statement soon to make the appointment official."

"Appointment?" she said, turning her eyes to DeFreitas. "The Deputy Prime Minister is elected by the citizens of the Commonwealth. I don't recall hearing anything about an election."

Khaifa could feel Mahoney's presence behind her and wished she could see his reaction to the exchange. Out of the corner of her eye, she saw Ironhorse looking between her and Upshaw as they spoke.

"Extreme circumstances," said Upshaw.

"Mister Prime Minister, does she speak for you now?"

There was a time when DeFreitas would at least have looked chagrinned at such a question. Now he simply shrugged and smiled.

"As she said, extreme circumstances. I have also appointed her to the position of Minister of Defence. Admiral Mahoney, you will now report to Deputy Prime Minister Upshaw -- she will coordinate and direct the war effort."

There was a lengthy pause before Mahoney responded.

"Understood, Mister Prime Minister."

"Good," said the PM, clapping his hands once. "And now that this unpleasantness is behind us, I believe we should all get back to work."

Khaifa forced a smile and nodded, while touching her necklace -- and deactivating the recording device secreted therein.

32

"I think she may be as much a threat as he is."

Standing in her quarters aboard the Vimy Ridge, el Bahari wished she had a window. She'd always liked looking at the stars -- it helped her think. She glanced down at her desk, where her tablet sat, a highly encrypted audio-only link to Thor's Hammer active.

"I have no doubt about that," she said. "But most of her power is largely tied up in her connection to *him*."

"So he needs to be... removed," said Ironhorse.

"I don't see any other option. Do you?"

"No," he said after a lengthy silence. "I'm not in a position-"

"No, of course not," she said, shaking her head despite the lack of visuals. "And even if you were, we can't act yet. There are too many assets tied up in this mission now to jeopardise it."

"I thought you were against Radko's mission?"

Sighing, el Bahari rubbed a hand over her face.

"We need to be very careful here, Max. Whatever we end up doing, there will be fallout."

"Amira, I can handle fallout. But if we're going to act, we can't wait forever," he said, and she heard him sigh. "He's going to destroy the Commonwealth."

"He thinks he's going to be the one to save it."

"He's not. He's not strong enough."

There was a long silence before Ironhorse spoke again.

"Khaifa recorded everything today."

El Bahari frowned.

"She told you this?"

"She didn't. When I worked intel ops, we outfitted agents with the same kind of device -- I could tell what it was as soon as she activated it."

"Keep an even closer eye on her. She still hasn't asked who assigned you to her?"

"No. I assume she thinks it's Radko's doing."

"Let her keep thinking that."

33

The inside of the udukiin government building -- or whatever they actually called it -- was intensely creepy. Jaeger spent the entire trip from the massive front doors and through the high-arched corridor pressed against Sigurdsson's leg, a line of fur down his back standing on end. She wasn't sure if it was the same thing bothering him that was bothering her, or whether he was picking up on something else entirely, but she almost wanted to stop looking at the walls.

Almost.

But she couldn't. The entire corridor, up one wall, through the arch and down the other, was covered with finely detailed, unsettlingly realistic carvings. Of ril-galas. Foot soldiers, bats, tanks, stalkers, and several other types she had never seen in the flesh but bore enough similarities to identify as ril-galas.

It was like being surrounded by the horde she'd faced on Von Daniken's Landing.

"This is unsettling," said Elgrapharr.

"No, it's fucking creepy," said Sigurdsson.

"I am in agreement with Sigurdsson," said Frankenstein.

Udrach, who had been leading them in silence until that point, finally spoke.

"The Corridor of Mirnas, the last great War Matriarch."

At the name, Sigurdsson felt a surge of something akin to pride mixed with hope come from the Matriarch and felt a faint wave of some something else from the udukiin -- something that felt like longing.

When she looked over to Aylarr, the icaran was nodding.

"I have heard the name. This would be her Corridor of Final Passage."

Udrach nodded once, but said no more.

Lowering her voice, Aylarr explained.

"When a War Matriarch dies, her body is brought to a special resting place, where she will spend eternity with her fellow Matriarchs. Her Corridor of Final Passage takes her to that resting place and is carved with the images of those over whom she achieved victory in life, so they may never forget her name in death."

Sigurdsson stopped and ran her fingers -- her icaran fingers -- over the stone. It was amazing how easy it was to forget the surgery, despite the fact that she now only had two fingers and a thumb. Running her fingers along the carved outline of a ril-galas bat, she frowned, remembering watching one of the creatures dive out of the sky and tear Danner -- one of her soldiers at Fort Hathaway -- to ribbons. She and her soldiers had scratched out their victory, but the cost had been enormous.

Her head snapped up.

"Those she'd beaten in life -- that's what you said, right?"

"Yes, those over whom-"

"They're fucking ril-galas," said Sigurdsson, suddenly no longer creeped out. "All of them. All over the goddamned walls -- ril-galas."

They were all looking at her -- Elgraphaar, Aylarr, Frankenstein, Udrach and the rest of the udukiin. Even Jaeger, though he at least sat down and wagged his tail. He always could understand her better than most humans could.

Spreading her arms wide, Sigurdsson spoke slowly, enunciating every word as if speaking to a small child or an idiot or both.

"Her Corridor of Last Whatever. Immortalizing the enemies she kicked the shit out of," she said. *"They're fucking ril-galas."*

Elgrapharr suddenly looked up to the ceiling, then to one wall and the other, all four of his eyes widening, his mouth dropping open slightly.

"Songs of Life," he said.

She'd never heard him swear, but figured that given icaran culture and the importance of song -- and their role in remembering the lives of the dead -- Sigurdsson assumed he'd just uttered the icaran equivalent of *'goddammit'* or *'Christ on a bicycle.'*

"Wasn't one theory about the disappearance of some kind of ril-galas empire that they ran into someone they couldn't push around?"

She turned to Udrach.

"Is that what happened?"

"The War Matriarch Mirnas and the udukiin army under her drove out the ril-galas. This is true," said Udrach, speaking slowly as was the udukiin way. "More than that, you must speak with the Priex Matriarch."

"Their leader in all things non-military," said Aylarr, sparing Sigurdsson the need to ask.

Udrach began walking again and Sigurdsson fell into step between Elgraphaar and Aylarr, Jaeger trotting along behind, keeping pace with Frankenstein.

"Assuming all this is truth and not just some legendary Hercules-type bullshit, we need this to go well. We need to get this new War Matriarch on our side," said Sigurdsson. Her mind was reeling with the possibilities of what the udukiin could bring to that table -- if they could convince the... what was the term the udukiin kept using? Kaigor Kai Rii. If they could convince her to join the war against the ril-galas it could completely turn the tide. "What do you think our chances are?"

"Of convincing Kaigor Kai Rii to fight the ril-galas?" said Aylar. "I believe first, we must get her to understand who she is."

Sigurdsson frowned, trying to understand, but before she could ask any questions, Udrach rapped his staff sharply on the stone floor three times.

The group stood in front of a pair of doors, easily twice even Elgraphaar's impressive height, carved from shimmering green rock. Ornate handles and hinges of orange metal glinted in the low light.

"Beyond these doors lies the audience chamber of the Udukiin Priex," said Udrach, his voice barely a whisper. "It is said that no off-worlder has set foot in the chamber since Ur negotiated peace with the krellin a thousand years past."

Feeling she was the one to make the argument, given that she was the one physically carrying the supposed new War Matriarch, Sigurdsson stepped forward and similarly lowered her voice.

"Thank you for bringing us here, Udrach. We didn't make this trip lightly -- we know the udukiin value their privacy."

He made a weird motion with his head that Sigurdsson had trouble interpreting until the Matriarch gave her the answer: it was an udukiin nod of assent.

"I cannot take all of you in. Kaigor Kai Rii and one other."

"Two others," said Sigurdsson, quickly. "Aylarr understands your history and customs far better than I do. I don't want to... I don't want to fuck this up because I accidentally offend someone."

Udrach did the head movement again.

"And the other?"

"Jaeger," she said, nodding toward the dog who had sidled up beside her and stood staring up at Udrach, tongue lolling, tail wagging.

"A beast? You wish to take a beast into our most-"

"He is my kalthar."

She had no idea where the word had come from... or in fact, she knew exactly where the word had come from and why, and though never having heard it before, she knew exactly what it meant. And she agreed completely. Jaeger was indeed her kalthar, her talisman of strength.

Somehow, she also knew that Mirnas had gone to war with a kalthar at her side, though she had no idea what form it took.

Udrach stared at Jaeger for a moment.

"Welcome, kalthar of the Kaigor Kai Rii."

Jaeger cocked his head to the left and sat.

An odd sound came from Udrach, like a pair of rocks being ground together and Sigurdsson realised he was laughing. That was... *probably* a good sign...?

"Follow," he said finally, waving for two of the udukiin guards to open the green doors. "Do not move beyond the outer ring until I call for you."

Sigurdsson nodded as they stepped into the chamber and then almost immediately froze.

The room was enormous, its vaulted ceiling so high she could see small whisps of cloud forming. Entirely circular, there were tiers of seating around the circumference, all packed with udukiin. At the opposite side of the chamber, directly across from their entrance doors, was a raised platform, a head higher than the uppermost tiers of seats. Upon the platform sat three udukiin, the centre of whom was unmistakably the Priex Matriarch.

She wore very little in terms of finery -- few in the chamber did -- but Sigurdsson could see under the Matriarch's bright orange cloak the familiar glint of the armoured layer she herself now wore. The physical form of the Matriarch bonding.

She, Jaeger and Aylarr stayed where they were as Udrach marched to the centre of the chamber. All within had fallen silent.

"Udrach Kai Togru," said the Priex Matriarch, her voice carrying clearly despite its softness. She sounded and looked positively ancient. "The Priex Matriach welcomes and recognizes you. We sense your troubled mind. Speak of what troubles you."

Udrach remained silent for a moment, then rapped his staff on the floor twice.

"From out of the black, a great Matriarch shall arise," he said slowly. "Following in the footsteps of Ur she shall come, the blood of her enemies falling from her like rain."

"Kaigor Kai Rii," said every single udukiin in the chamber.

It took all of her willpower for Sigurdsson to stay where she was and not take a step backward.

The Priex Matriarch nodded in the odd, udukiin way.

"The prophesy is well-known to the Chamber," she said. "Why, Udrach Kai Togru, do you..."

As the Priex Matriarch trailed off, Sigurdsson felt tingling sensation in the back of her mind, almost like the white noise of a comm channel that wasn't precisely tuned.

"She has come," said the Priex Matriarch.

Turning back toward Sigurdsson, Udrach rapped his staff once more, then extended one hand, palm up, toward her.

"Freyja Sigurdsson of the Black, and her kalthar, Jaeger."

Taking that as her cue, Sigurdsson stepped forward, walking with a confidence she didn't quite feel, until she stood beside Udrach. Jaeger followed, as did Aylarr, one step behind.

A murmur rippled through the gathering of udukiin and Sigurdsson both heard it and felt it in her mind. It felt like a mixture of surprise and amazement but, thankfully, she didn't feel any anger. She took a quick glance at Jaeger and while he was standing alert, looking around the chamber, his tail was slowly wagging. He didn't sense any danger either, which was good -- at that point, Sigurdsson trusted his sense more than her own.

The Priex Matriarch held up two hands and the murmuring immediately ceased.

Udrach bowed and stepped to the side.

Jaeger sat.

Sigurdsson wondered what the living fuck she was doing there.

As the silence stretched on, Sigurdsson leaned back toward Aylarr.

"Do I talk now?" she whispered.

"Perhaps?"

"You're supposed to be the expert."

When Aylarr didn't respond, Sigurdsson looked up at the old Matriarch high above and tried to find some guidance from her passenger.

"Okay," she said quietly. "I need some help here. Show me what I need to do."

Almost immediately it was like a firecracker went off in her head. A flood of images and feelings and before she realised she was doing it, Sigurdsson was speaking loudly, confidently.

"I am Freyja Sigurdsson, of the Black. I thank you for allowing my friends and I to visit your beautiful world, in friendship, to return that which was stolen from you."

The udukiin listened, waited. She'd apparently said the right thing to get them to listen, but now she was being fed nothing more -- she was on her own again.

"We discovered this Matriarch," she said, running a hand down her armoured bicep. "A prisoner, having been tortured-"

There was an angry rumble from the assembled udukiin, but a calming sensation from her passenger told her to keep going.

"We freed her. Protected her. Brought her home to her people."

"Who would treat a Matriarch with such callousness?"

Sigurdsson didn't see which udukiin had asked. It didn't matter. The answer was the same.

"A group of humans who-"

"Like you!"

"Nothing like me!" she snarled. She didn't notice, but as she spoke, small spikes began to form on her armour. "I am many things, not all of them good, but I do what I do to protect people -- not for my own benefit."

"You will also note that she is not entirely human," said Aylar, with what seemed to Sigurdsson to be very careful wording. "She is human and she is icaran and she is bonded with an udukiin Matriarch."

The chamber fell silent for another moment.

"Of the three," said the assembled udukiin as one, and a chill went down Sigurdsson's spine.

And stayed there as she turned and spoke quietly to Aylarr.

"You said... Kaigor Kai Rii. It means the Matriach of the Three. That's what you said, right?"

"It is."

Staring down at her hands, Sigurdsson flexed her fingers, her icaran fingers, and looked at the semi-gloss of the armour the

Matriarch had formed around her arms when it had bonded. *Bonded*, not clung to, or hitched a ride on. Bonded.

A Matriarch would bond with someone suited to their task. A War Matriarch would bond with a warrior.

When the drop-ship had crashed on the Shattered World, they'd essentially fallen from space. She'd come out of the black.

"When we first found Freyja Sigurdsson," Udrach was saying. "She had crossed the Great Divide, through the Gateway of Ur."

"Following in the footsteps of Ur she shall come," said the rest of the udukiin, almost chanting.

Oh shit.

"Ril-galas blood, still wet, dripping from her hands," said Udrach.

"The blood of her enemies falling from her like rain," came the chanting response.

Oh shit.

The chamber fell silent as the Priex Matriarch stood and spoke.

"And as one shall the udukiin follow her."

"And so take their rightful place in the universe," chanted the udukiin, including Udrach.

"Oh, fuck me, fuck me, fuck me...," muttered Sigurdsson.

Jaeger stood and looked up at her, feeling her fear. The War Matriarch tried to send through calming impulses, but Sigurdsson shrugged them off -- she'd earned this feeling, deserved this feeling, and she wasn't about to let anyone take it from her. How long had her passenger known? How long had... it hadn't known until they crossed the Great Divide. The answer came as clearly as if it had been her own thought, but it clearly came from her passenger. The thought... *tasted* different. The wave of dizziness when they'd first encountered Udrach and his group. The jolt, like something had finally snapped into place.

That was when her passenger had known, but she -- her passenger -- had no frame of reference to be able to explain to a human what had happened.

A War Matriarch had been born.

A Matriarch of the Three.

Kaigor Kai Rii.

"Freyja Sigurdsson, of the Black," chanted the udukiin, causing Sigurdsson to actually jump slightly. "Kaigor Kai Rii."

Suddenly the Priex Matriarch was directly in front of her. Sigurdsson hadn't seen her come down from her platform or even seen a stairway or elevator that would have allowed her to get there so quickly.

"Why have you come?" said the old female, so quietly that Sigurdsson had barely heard.

"I thought I was returning a Matriarch. I had no idea... I didn't know the bonding would happen. I can... Can we reverse it? Let her bond with an udukiin?"

"Once fully bonded, a Matriarch cannot survive without its host."

"I didn't bring her here just so she could die," said Sigurdsson, running a hand through her hair. "What will happen to me?"

"If you remain a War Matriarch?"

"If I stay bonded. What will happen to *me*, to Freyja. I can feel the Matriarch in my mind, not all the time, but a lot."

"You will become one, over time."

"And what the fuck does that mean?" she said, not realising until after the words were out that she probably shouldn't be swearing at the leader of a species. She wasn't as good at the political stuff as Radko.

Radko. What the hell was he going to think about all this? What would he do in her situation?

He'd push forward with the plan. Try to get the udukiin on board with the war effort.

"You will not be... replaced, if that is your concern. I am as I ever was -- though significantly older," said the Priex Matriarch, her lips curling in a smile. "But I am much enhanced. I have lived beyond standard udukiin lifespan. I am stronger, my body repairs itself faster. I think more quickly, analyze more efficiently."

Before Sigurdsson could respond, an image popped into her head of food. A crust of bread and half-eaten bowl of oatmeal, sitting on the low table of her quarters back on Thor's Hammer.

"Your kalthar is hungry," said the Matriarch.

Sigurdsson looked down at Jaeger and he looked up at her, wagging his tail.

"So am I," she said with a chuckle, but it disappeared quickly as she returned her attention to the Priex Matriarch. "Look, Matriarch-"

"Yrtaan. Matriarchs do not address each other so formally. You may call me by my name title, Yrtaan Kai Foa."

"Okay. Yrtaan. I need some time. This is... I don't know what it is. I came here thinking I was -- I certainly had no idea I was about to fulfill a prophecy. And I don't know if I can, or should be this Kaigor Kai Rii. I don't like asking for favours of people I've just met..."

"We are Matriarchs, Freyja. We are family, not strangers."

Sigurdsson nodded, feigning agreement despite her discomfort.

"Sure. Do you have somewhere we could stay? My comrades and I? At least for the night, so I can try to clear my head and think this through."

"Of course. I will have lodging arranged."

"Thank you, Yrtaan."

As it turned out, the 'lodgings' were a suite of rooms that had been occupied by the last udukiin War Matriarch, long dead. The rooms had been kept in perfect condition while the udukiin waited patiently for her successor to emerge. By the time Sigurdsson, Jaeger, Elgraphaar, Aylarr and Frankenstein arrived, there was an impressive selection of hot and cold dishes and what looked to be fresh fruits and vegetables arrayed on the long table in the central room. A wide oval window looked out onto the flag-lined promenade.

Trying to distract herself, Sigurdsson picked over the fruit. She cracked open a reddish, spherical thing to find a soft, spongey white flesh. Pulling out a piece and popping it into her mouth, she was surprised to find it had the flavour of fresh, heavily buttered bread. She tossed it on the floor for Jaeger -- who happily set to work -- and picked out a small, green fruit.

"This is a lime."

Frankenstein stepped up beside her to examine the fruit. After a moment, he bobbed his mechanical head.

"It is indeed a lime," he said, surprise evident in his voice.

"I am unsure as to what this may be," said Elgraphaar, lifting the lid from a pot and sniffing the steam pouring out. "But based on the aroma, I will be eating some regardless."

Bowls had been set out on the table and Elraphaar ladled some of the thick soup into one, tasted it and ladled some more, the flavour clearly meeting his expectations. Setting out two more bowls, he filled them, then paused for a moment and filled a fourth bowl. He set one in front of Sigurdsson, one in front of Aylarr and one on the floor for Jaeger -- who wasted no time.

"Okay," said Sigurdsson, cracking open another of the bread-like fruit and dipping a piece in her soup. "Aylarr, can you give

Elgraphaar and Frankenstein the short version of what the living fuck we just walked into?"

After a few silent moments where Sigurdsson, the two icarans, and Jaeger ate their soup, Aylarr finally spoke.

"It would appear that in bonding with the Matriarch, Sigurdsson has fulfilled an udukiin prophecy."

"Kaigor Kai Rii, as the udukiin said?" asked Frankenstein.

"Yes. The Matriarch of the Three."

"Ah," said the brill. "Of course, the three: human, icaran and udukiin. Incredible."

"Yeah, fuckin great," said Sigurdsson. "They think I'm some kind of messiah, Frank."

"A leader, not a messiah," said Aylarr. "Despite the... religious overtones their prophecies sometimes contain, the udukiin are an entirely secular species. They believe -- fervently -- in their leaders and honour them in death, but there is none of the absurdity of blind faith in fictional deities that is the hallmark of religion."

"They said I was... they said that Kaigor Kai Rii was supposed to lead them to their rightful place in the universe. What does that even mean?"

"Perhaps," said Frankenstein. "That is for Kaigor Kai Rii to determine."

"What?"

"Based on the carvings we passed, perhaps the rightful place of the udukiin is that of defenders of the galaxy -- against the rilgalas."

"Let's just... fuck, can we back up for a second? You're all in agreement that this isn't some kind of mistake, that I am actually now War Matriarch of the udukiin?"

"It does seem that way," said Elgraphaar, the others nodding in agreement.

"The Priex Matriach thinks so," said Aylarr. "And I would be inclined to accept her appraisal of the situation over ours."

Sigurdsson pushed away her bowl. Suddenly she was no longer hungry.

Jaeger looked up at her and licked his chops, so she set her bowl down on the floor for him and he happily took over.

"So what do I do?"

"When you first decided to come the Shattered World," said Elgraphaar. "Your goal was to -- hopefully -- convince the udukiin to help us in the war."

"And now you are in an even greater position to make that happen," added Aylarr.

"You think I should..."

She trailed off, shot a look at the doorway to the suites. The Priex Matriarch was coming, she could sense it.

A handful of seconds later, the doors opened and Yrtaan entered.

"You no doubt have questions," she said, which Sigurdsson felt was an understatement.

"If...," she said, throwing a quick glance at Elgraphaar. "If I do this. If I accept that I'm Kaigor Kai Rii... what does it mean? What do I do?"

"You lead the udukiin to war."

"Against who, though? Whoever I want?"

Yrtaan smiled.

"We are guided by prophecy, but not blindly. We do not go to war frivolously, and Kaigor Kai Rii would not have come had war not been inevitable -- and indeed required. I believe you know already against which enemy war is now necessary for the udukiin."

"And everyone else."

"As you say."

Closing her eyes for a moment, Sigurdsson sighed.

"I don't know if I'm the right person for this, Yrtaan," she said, though it was a mild lie -- she was almost one hundred percent certain she was not the right person. "I'm not -- this won't mean anything to you, but I'm not Radko. I don't know if I can be what he is, I don't know if I can do what he does."

Elgraphaar cleared his throat.

"Radko has always believed in your abilities," he said. "And that the two of you are more alike than not."

Despite the situation, the words made Sigurdsson feel better -- significantly better. She felt a surge of feelings come over her and she knew they were her own, being amplified by her connection with her passenger.

"The Matriarch to whom you are bonded," said Yrtaan. "Would not have allowed the bonding to complete had you not been deemed worthy. In bonding, the Matriarch is in control as to whether to join or to reject."

"Perhaps why she was being tortured by ATC Castle," said Frankenstein. "They were, in all likelihood, trying to force or at least control a bonding in order to weaponize the Matriarch."

It was true. Sigurdsson knew it without having to consult her passenger and it occurred to her that was likely because of the now-complete bonding -- she knew what her passenger knew.

"You are Kaigor Kai Rii because of who you are," said Yrtaan. "Not by an accident or by a mistake. You are Freyja Sigurdsson, of the Black, and you were chosen."

There was dead silence for a full ten minutes, all eyes on Sigurdsson until she finally spoke.

"If I do this, how many soldiers could the udukiin bring to the war effort?"

"Four million."

Sigurdsson blinked. Yrtaan had clearly misunderstood the question -- four million was the majority of the population of the Shattered World.

"No, I mean how many actual trained soldiers," she said. "Warriors, ready to fight."

"Four million," repeated Yrtaan. "Udukiin are all trained as soldiers. Our entire population, save those too young or too old to be effective, would be at your disposal."

Not long after, Yrtaan had left, allowing them to discuss the situation amongst themselves.

"Four million soldiers would almost surely turn the tide of this war," said Aylarr. "But there are other things to consider."

"I can't take an entire species to war. I can't tell every fucking udukiin to pack up and fight on a world they've never seen let alone visited. I can't... if I do this and it goes bad, I can't risk putting the udukiin on the brink of extinction."

Sensing her unease, Jaeger sidled over and rested his head in her lap. As she scratched behind his ears, Sigurdsson felt herself calming. Somewhat.

"And," she said. "There's the fact that I'm not a particularly good person. I don't know if anyone should have the power to mobilize an entire species, but I'm fairly certain it's not the kind of power that should be in the hands of someone like me."

"I believe you are underestimating yourself," said Elgraphaar.

Standing, Sigurdsson shook her head. As much as she tried to put it behind her, the past had weighed heavily on her mind since she'd woken up on Thor's Hammer. Not just the hard line she'd had to take on Von Daniken's Landing, and the execution of Chanz, but everything, from the very beginning. She was being looked to as a leader, first of a colony and now potentially of a species, but she still felt like that teenage thug beating people up over drug money. Not all the time to be sure, but that thug, the pre-military Freyja, was always there in the back of her mind. The ghost of what she had been and the fear of what she might still be underneath the uniform. And now there wasn't even a uniform. No military rules and protocol to keep the thug in line.

"I don't think I can do this."

Though she didn't want to, she was about to say more when a commotion arose on the street below. Stepping up to the window, Sigurdsson and the icarans watched a pair of udukiin scouts, each astride some kind of two-legged reptilian mount, barrelling down the laneway. They were yelling something Sigurdsson couldn't make out, waving their naginata-type pikes. All through the streets, udukiin were disappearing into buildings.

When Udrach suddenly burst into the suites, everyone jumped. He held a crooked-ended staff in each of two of his hands.

"The ril-galas have crossed the Great Divide."

The three soldiers immediately scooped up their weapons and even Frankenstein slung his medical bag over his shoulder.

"Are they headed toward the city?" asked Sigurdsson.

"Yes. Priex Matriarch is leading a group of soldiers to prevent them from entering Her Vibrant Colours."

"What? Matriarch Yrtaan is leading the army?"

"In the absence of a War Matriarch, the Priex Matriarch acts as head of the udukiin military," said Udrach.

"Take me to her," said Sigurdsson.

"Take us to her," corrected Elgraphaar.

Bobbing his head in the strange udukiin equivalent of a nod, Udrach handed on of the staves to Sigurdsson. As she took it, she realised it wasn't at all what she had thought. Though it looked like ornately-carved black wood, it was actually some kind of metal, and warm to the touch. And, she assumed thanks to her passenger, she also now understood that it wasn't a simple staff to be used in melee combat -- though it certainly filled that role quite well. It was also an energy weapon, the crooked end serving as grip and stock.

Without another word, Udrach led them down and into the now-deserted streets, through Her Vibrant Colours and across the bridge. As they stepped off the bridge and onto solid ground, the icarans unslung their *aoran* rifles and Sigurdsson hefted her gunstaff. The weight was good, the balance was excellent. Though longer, it reminded her somewhat of her old sniper rifle Vidar. And since the udukiin also had two fingers and a thumb on each hand, the ergonomics were almost as perfectly suited to her new hands as the icaran-designed weapons.

When she looked to the line of defenders, she frowned. There was a cluster of udukiin near the centre and a thin line of soldiers beyond that -- too thin for the number of ril-galas Sigurdsson could see beyond. And the soldiers were just standing there. None were taking shots, trying to weaken the ranks of their attackers.

Something had gone wrong, and she said as much aloud.

They sprinted the rest of the way and looking at the approaching ril-galas, Sigurdsson couldn't help but feel a sense of déjà vu as she watched the heads of the oncoming foot-soldiers waving back and forth. But the front rank was new. The stalkers they'd encountered on the other side of the Shattered World. Dozens of them.

"She is injured," said one of the udukiin as Sigurdsson and her group approached the nearer cluster.

"Who is...," said Sigurdsson, trailing off as she looked down into the centre of the cluster.

Yrtaan looked up at her. Her torso was bloodied and one of her left arms hung limply at her side like it was made of jelly. She coughed up whitish blood.

"She invoked the name of Matriarch Mirnas," said one of the udukiin, quietly. "One of the ril-galas shot her before she had finished speaking."

"Which one?"

The udukiin looked up at her confused.

"Can you point out which one fired the shot?" snapped Sigurdsson.

"It was missing an eye."

Nodding, Sigurdsson waved over Frankenstein.

"See what you can do."

"Of course," said the brill.

Tapping her temple to activate her targeting optics, Sigurdsson stepped through the udukiin defense line and began scanning the attackers, looking for the one with the missing eye. Jaeger trotted up beside her, snarling at the ril-galas.

"Form up," she barked at the udukiin. "Shoulder to shoulder; weapons ready."

Several left the cluster around Yrtaan to join the line.

There.

The ril-galas foot soldier with the missing eye.

She raised her gunstaff, but she didn't get a chance to fire -- the stalkers charged.

And they were fast. Sigurdsson barely had time to swing her gunstaff outward in a defensive position before they were on her. She heard the snapping sound of their jaws as the stalkers attacked the line and heard the high-pitched thrum of gunstaves being fired and the whak of gunstaves being used as melee weapons. And she heard the cries of udukiin falling under tooth and claw.

Throwing off a stalker and hammering the butt of her gun-staff repeatedly into its chest cavity until it caved in, Sigurdsson glanced back to see another two-dozen udukiin soldiers had arrived to help. Then she turned back to the advancing ril-galas.

"The Priex Matriarch is dead," she heard someone say, and then others took up the chorus.

A brief thought flitted through Sigurdsson's mind that the udukiin, as a species, were now leaderless, but the thought never got beyond that. Out of the corner of her eye, she saw movement and turned just in time to see a stalker lunging toward her, claws raised, teeth bared.

And then a snarl from her left and Jaeger was there, leaping, locking his jaws around the stalker's throat in mid-air. The pair crashed to the ground together in a heap, but the stalker recovered more quickly. Sigurdsson watched in horror as with a single swipe of its clawed hand it sent a yelping Jaeger skidding ten feet across the ground.

She felt a drop of blood spatter on her cheek. Jaeger's blood.

As Sigurdsson watched Udrach and another udukiin take up positions protecting Jaeger, unmoving Jaeger, she felt an overwhelming despair come over her and she began to hear a cry of such pain and anguish that it took her a moment to realise where it was coming from.

It was coming from her.

But as she stared at Jaeger, saw him trying to lift his head as Frankenstein arrived at his side, and as she turned back to the ril-galas, the cry of anguish became a snarl and then a roar. A roar of burning anger and of absolute, unwavering defiance.

As she felt another click in her head, Sigurdsson knew that now her connection wasn't just to her passenger, but to all udukiin.

And they felt what she felt.

The udukiin began to take up the roar.

All of them.

The Shattered World roared its anger and its defiance.

Following in the footsteps of Ur she had come, the blood of her enemies falling from her like rain.

The udukiin were marching to war.

The ril-galas line took a step backward.

34

They had been expecting some kind of attack from the moment they'd sent out their signal, so, that it finally came was not the surprise -- the surprise was the form the attack took.

Once the signal had been sent, Hunter and her group -- if they could be called 'her' group anymore after the prior night's events -- hurriedly packed their belongings and whatever they thought they could use from Braemar. Leaving the members of the traitorous raiding party to fend for themselves, Hobson had slung the comm device onto his back and they'd set off again, following the river as planned.

It had taken the ril-galas almost six hours to find them.

Gritting her teeth against the pain, Hunter fired another pair of shots from her 33A1, putting both shots through the chest of an attacking ril-galas. Her damaged ribs had been painful while walking and had become borderline excruciating with the recoil from her assault rifle.

The attackers were of a type she'd not yet encountered. Clearly ril-galas, but sleek, with mouths full of sharp teeth, and hands ending in razor-sharp talons. Unlike the foot soldiers, who marched like an army, this new type stalked like predators.

Hobson double-tapped another of the aliens as he and his remaining Coldstream Guards closed tightly around the Prince.

An arrow from Ransom's bow skewered a stalker's eye and Hutch finished it off with his shotgun, the blast tearing a melon-sized hole in the thing's chest.

She should have felt the ambush ahead of time, sensed it just like she had back aboard the Vimy Ridge. It was the reason Radko let Hunter -- then Quon Li-Chen -- out of her prison and it was what had kept her and the people at Edinburgh Castle alive, but the strain of using her abilities to control another human, combined with the fog of pain from her injured ribs, had left her senses dulled, her mind unfocused.

She hoped it wouldn't cost them too many lives. Kaur was already dead and Wiggins was bleeding, though still fighting alongside Hobson. Grieve was nowhere to be seen, but that wasn't unusual in the slightest -- Hunter could still hear the snap of his rifle, so he'd no doubt managed to find a perch somewhere with a decent field of vision.

Her rifle clicked empty and Hunter swung the stock into the face of a lunging stalker, the jolt causing waves of pain to radiate from her ribs and she cried out, dropping to one knee.

The stalker shook off the impact and came at her again and Hunter quickly drew her recently-acquired T19 pistol and fired three shots in rapid succession into her attacker. It dropped to the ground, twitching as it tried to get up and Hunter fired three more shots into it before it stopped moving.

A moment passed before Hunter realised that the sounds of battle had ceased completely. No snarl of ril-galas stalkers, no bark of assault rifles, pop of pistols or roar of Hutch's trusty shotgun.

She looked around her. Her people were doing the same -- looking around, mildly shocked looks on their faces, slowly lowering their weapons.

They were still alive, somehow.

Hobson was the first to recover his senses, slinging his rifle and checking out the injury to Wiggins. The latter was still standing and Hobson was breaking out the bandages without much sense of urgency, so Hunter gathered that whatever Wiggins' wound, it was neither critical nor life-threatening.

Finding a nearby tree, Hunter leaned against it to catch her breath, close her eyes and try to compose herself. She needed some painkillers -- badly -- but the kind of painkillers that would help her in her current state were not the kind that would leave her with a clear head.

"You okay?"

She glanced up quickly, having not heard anyone approach.

Hutch stood there, giving her an odd look. Ransom was with him, slightly off to the side.

"More or less," she said, wincing at the ache in her side as she stood upright.

The pair just stared at her.

"What?"

"We've been calling for you for like ten minutes," said Ransom.

Looking past Ransom and Hutch, Hunter saw that not only was Wiggins bandaged up, but the gear Kaur had carried had already been redistributed and his body was being covered with river stone.

"Hutch," she said with a sigh. "You and Hobson need to be prepared to take over if I'm... not in a condition to lead."

In his eyes, she could see that he wasn't sure she had ever been in a condition to lead -- at least, not since the revelations of the night before. She didn't need to be a mind-reader to see it and probably couldn't have worked up the energy to get into his mind even if she'd wanted to. Somehow, he was able to keep the thoughts inside.

"That thing you did last night," he said. "It took a lot out of you."

It wasn't a question, so she didn't respond. Just looked at him expectantly until he continued with what he had to say.

"You knew how to do it. How to make that woman kill herself."

"No," she said. "I didn't actually know. I had what I felt was a sound theory. I was right, but I could just as well have driven her crazy."

She paused, shrugged, then winced because shrugging hurt.

"But yes, it took more out of me than I expected."

"So you won't be able to do it again for a while."

"I never want to do it again," she said quietly, flicking a glance to Ransom before returning her attention to Hutch. "You don't understand -- you wouldn't, you'd have no way of understanding. I had to be in for the whole thing. I couldn't leave or I would lose control."

"What? You mean leave the castle?"

"She means leave the woman's mind," Ransom said softly.

Nodding, Hunter swallowed heavily. Even talking about it was making her feel sick.

"If I let go of her mind before it was done, she might have freed herself. Shot another one of you," she said, closing her eyes.

It was as much -- or perhaps more -- of a shock to her than to Hutch and Ransom that a tear rolled down her cheek.

"I was there for everything. The realisation that death was coming. The abject terror, the absolute disgust at what I had... at what *she* had become. And the moment of death, that light winking out and then nothing. Nothing," she said, taking a deep, shaky breath. "Even if I *could* do it again -- which I'm not certain of -- that feeling... being inside her mind at the moment of death... it's not... something..."

Hunter suddenly lurched forward and vomited. Ransom was at her side in a moment, helping her into a sitting position, back against the tree. She handed her a canteen and Hunter took a small sip of water.

Nodding her thanks to Ransom, Hunter looked up at Hutch, who had looked away awkwardly.

"Wiggins is all right?" she asked.

Hutch nodded, still not looking her way.

"A lot of blood, but a minor wound. Kaur was our only casualty."

"How is His Royal Highness?"

Scratching at the stubble on his chin -- which had already begun the transformation from stubble to actual beard -- Hutch finally met Hunter's gaze.

"Physically? He's fine."

"And personality-wise he's a douchebag. Yes, I know," she said, taking another sip of water.

"It's worse than that," said Ransom, flicking a glance toward Arthur. The King-by-default sat in his standard sullen way, staring off into the water of the river.

"He said we should have just surrendered," said Hutch.

"What?"

"He's never going to be what you wanted him to be. That's not even an 'I told you so,' it's just a fact," he said, with a resigned sigh. "I didn't like this plan at the start, but you know what? It would have worked if the kid wasn't a self-centred little prick."

"Help me up."

They did, and led her over to the rest of the group -- letting her walk the last several metres on her own. Hobson and the Coldstream Guards were clustered around Arthur, of course, with Grieve perched on a rock off to one side, eying Hunter suspiciously. Ransom may have decided she didn't care about Hunter's old life, but it was clear that Grieve did.

"Hunter," said Hobson, breaking off a crust of bread and handing it to her. "If you're up to it, we should get moving."

She nodded, accepting the bread. He was right: staying in that spot, surrounded by ril-galas corpses was bound to attract attention. Scavengers at best, more ril-galas at worst.

"Once everyone has had something to eat and drink, we'll move on," she said. "We did well today. Getting out a message and fighting off this ambush. If we keep on this track, we'll absolutely take back Earth."

It was an overly optimistic statement and had only a marginal ring of truth to it. Certainly they had accomplished something important in getting out their broadcast, but the defeat of the ril-galas ambush had only bought them a little more time on the survival clock, it hadn't turned a tide by any stretch. The statement was designed to elicit a response. And it did.

Arthur snorted derisively.

"Something to add, Your Highness?"

"This is pointless."

"Our mission, or fighting back against the ril-galas?" asked Ransom.

He glanced up at her, then back down at his shoes. Hunter doubted anyone else would have been favoured with any acknowledgement at all, but she also knew how -- and how often -- Arthur thought of Ransom.

"All of it," he said. "We can't beat them -- we already lost."

Hobson gently cleared his throat.

"His Majesty is tired, we're all tired, and-"

"We don't have anything left," said Arthur, continuing as if Hobson hadn't spoken. "So our life is just going to be running from shelter to shelter and scrounging for supplies? Why the fuck are we bothering? It would have been better if they'd just killed us."

Hunter said nothing. There was nothing she could have said that would have mattered. Hutch was right -- Arthur would never and likely could never be what she'd hoped; he would never be a symbol worth following. She closed her eyes and silently cursed herself for falling so easily into a role she had no experience with: that of an optimist. Her background being what it was, she knew better than to trust people to do the right thing, to be strong in the face of adversity. Humans were selfish. Humans looked out for their own interests with little regard for others. Humans gave up hope. So why shouldn't she? She'd endangered her own people on a fool's errand to bring back a symbol around which humanity could rally. Instead, she'd rescued a spineless brat.

Looking up into the sky, a perfect blue sky now, she thought of what lay beyond. Of stars and spacecraft; of prison boxes and deals with naval officers and fighting through regardless of risk because there was a steadfast and borderline insane refusal to ever give up.

Everyone was watching her, she knew, watching her staring up into the sky. Watching a smile spread slowly across her face.

From the moment she left the Vimy Ridge, she'd second-guessed so many of her choices. But she knew that Radko had second-guessed his as well -- and Sigurdsson hers. The two of them had led people against all odds, making the hard decisions that had to be made in the name of the greater good. It hadn't all been sunshine and blue skies. Blood had been spilled, of both friend and foe, and of friend who became foe.

But they carried on.

They kept fighting.

Until that moment, it had never even occurred to Hunter that she was following in their footsteps.

"In the footsteps of giants," she whispered, mostly to herself.

Suddenly her mind felt clearer that it ever had.

"We stick to the plan," she said, turning back to her ragtag group. "We follow the river to the sea, then the coastline into Edinburgh."

Without another word, she slung her rifle over her should and began walking along the river edge, leaving Hutch and Ransom hurrying to catch up while Hobson got the King moving.

"What about Arthur?" said Hutch. "If he's going to start saying shit like that back in Edinburgh..."

"He'll destroy what little morale we have left."

"Yeah."

"I can try to talk to him?" said Ransom. "He seems to actually listen to me."

"You might have to do more than talk to get that little shit onside," said Hutch.

Ransom shrugged, but a blush crept into her cheeks.

"We do what we have to do, right?"

"You mean *who* we have to do?" said Hutch. He was smirking, which made Ransom turn a shade of red not far off from her hair.

"That's enough Hutch," said Hunter. "Take point with Grieve."

With a nod, Hutch quickened his pace and waved for the old rifleman to follow.

Hunter turned to Ransom, whose blush was fading.

"Talk to him," said Hunter. "See if you can get through."

"I'll do my best."

She slowed her pace to let Arthur catch up, leaving Hunter alone with her thoughts.

There was a near total silence aboard the Vimy Ridge. It had been that way since the call had come in from Mahoney.

Anna Cortez had been executed. No last-minute reprieve, no commuting of the sentence in acknowledgement of her service, or even on humanitarian grounds. To a one, the crew had clenched their teeth as they overheard Mahoney explaining it all to Radko. Khaifa's attempt to bring some common sense to the situation. Cortez's speech. The firing squad.

And they had all felt the surge of anger when he'd said that after it was done, they'd simply blown her body out of the air-lock.

They hadn't even kept her dogtags for any surviving family member.

To the crew of the Vimy Ridge, it was a miracle Radko hadn't ordered them right then and there to head back to Thor's Hammer, full speed, weapons free.

To Radko himself it was equally surprising.

His hands ached from having been clenched in tight fists and his vision kept blurring with tears that steadfastly refused to fall in the face of his incredible, burning anger.

He stood on the upper level of the command deck, staring through the observation dome. He'd had a holographic overlay pinpoint the position of Thor's Hammer and he stared out through the stars at the blinking orange triangle that repre-sented the station.

Perched on the railing behind him, heedless of the drop should she lose her balance, was Kestrel Cagliari. Though Cagliari hadn't been present when the news had first come through that Cortez had been tried and convicted, it hadn't taken long for word to spread through the ship and by the time Mahoney was calling back, Cagliari had already been on the bridge, hanging around the background. She had stayed with him the whole time, saying nothing, just being an unobtrusive, supportive presence.

Though he wasn't prepared to do so at that moment, Radko would have to remember to thank her for it later. As much as his exploits were portrayed as 'Radko did this' or 'Radko did that,' he would have been nowhere and accomplished nothing without his friends.

His friends.

The word caught him harder than usual.

He'd told Owens that he needed his friends and that was truer now than ever. But his other statement to Owens was also truer now than ever: he was running out of friends.

"Thank you," he said quietly, turning toward Cagliari. She was still wearing her flightsuit.

Smiling slightly, the pilot nodded and ran a hand through her short blue hair.

"You'll be okay," she said.

"Think so?"

"Know so."

Hopping off the rail, she stepped up beside him, taking a look at the pulsating triangle.

"You'll be okay because you *need* to be okay," she said. "Not because you're *actually* okay, but because if you're not okay, you can't do this. And if you don't do this, you think no one else will."

She looked up at him with a lopsided grin.

"How am I doing?"

"Pretty spot-on," he said, half-heartedly returning the smile.

Smile fading, Cagliari put a hand on his shoulder.

"I know this sucks. I know it. We've all lost people we care about, but not this way -- not to politics," she said. "My father used to have a saying, it was probably his favourite saying. Used it constantly, especially when his know-it-all daughter was being more rebellious than usual. He said you can't force people to change, you can only lead them to finding a better way."

She let her hand drop and looked back out toward Thor's Hammer, before turning toward and nodding to the Venn Shakara.

"Cortez was a great person and she believed in what you're doing. I'm really, really sorry that she's gone -- I'm not just saying that, I mean it -- but we need to make sure she died for something worthwhile."

"I know," he said, sighing. "You can't fight a war and expect not to lose anyone."

"Doesn't make it any easier when it happens."

"No, it doesn't."

They both fell silent, hearing someone coming up the ladder. Seeing it was el Bahari, Cagliari offered Radko a small smile.

"I'll be snuggling my fighters if you need me," she said, before hurrying down the ladder and off the command deck.

El Bahari watched her go before turning to Radko.

"I don't think she likes me," she said, arching a brow.

"You're an acquired taste."

The brow arched even further.

"I can't argue that," she said. "Perhaps the one thing you and I actually have in common?"

Before he could respond, she held up a hand.

"Our argument earlier, Commander. I was out of line and my criticism of your decisions became... somewhat personal in nature. No, not somewhat -- they were precisely personal in nature."

Pausing, she sighed and Radko took that to mean she wasn't finished.

He was correct.

"I stand by my statement about disagreeing with your methods. But I am also well aware of the fact that I am a bitch, and while I am usually able to maintain it at ice-queen levels -- yes, I know what the crew calls me -- you have a singular way of getting under my skin."

Though he tried to stop it, Radko started laughing, and el Bahari looked equal parts annoyed and perplexed.

"I'm sorry," he said. "Sorry, I just don't think I've ever heard such a blunt self-evaluation. For the record, you're not a bitch."

"Yes, I am."

"No, you're not."

"Why are we arguing this?"

"Look, Amira... sorry, I know you hate it when I call you that. Look, Commander, this isn't my first rodeo. I've served in the Commonwealth Navy since I was a teenager and I served with a great number of women. I went through the officer's program with a great number of women, several of whom became close friends. None of whom were ever given command of ship. No matter what kind of shiny veneer we like to put on our society, I saw first-hand how much harder those women had to work to be seen as being at the same level as those of us with testicles. Stop me if I'm wrong."

She said nothing, just crossing her arms.

"These women, they had to be driven to succeed. They had to prove they were *more* capable than their male classmates in order to been seen as being *equal*. So many of them -- if they intended to climb the ranks -- had to push aside things like having a love life. They would shoot down anyone who tried to hit on them, and so were branded bitches."

He paused, shaking his head.

"I'm sorry," he said. "I don't even know where the hell I was going with this story."

"I feel like you were trying to tell me I'm not a bitch."

"Or maybe I was trying to tell you that sometimes people take things they fear -- strong, capable, independent women, for example -- and try to diminish them by attaching insulting names to them."

"That may be a fair assessment. However, my apology stands. I feel I was out of line with some of my comments."

"Apology accepted."

"And...," she said, then paused, looking at her boots, then down in the command deck, then, finally, at the pulsating triangle indicating the position of Thor's Hammer. "No matter how different my views and yours may be, what Bianca Upshaw and her people did to your friend was reprehensible."

"Thank you. I-"

"If they'd had any courage at all," she said, turning to look him in the eye. "They'd have come after you directly."

"If they'd had any courage at all, Commander, they'd be right here with us, preparing to strike the ril-galas. Instead they play their political games and engage in continual marathons of verbal masturbation while the Earth burns."

"Do you think that everyone who disagrees with you is a coward?"

"No. People disagree with me all the time. I have no issue with it -- we've already had that discussion. We can't sit on our hands any longer and still survive this war. Not wanting to start a war isn't cowardice, it's admirable. Refusing to fight a war *you're already in* isn't just cowardice, it is certain death. Someone has to break this cycle and stand up and lead."

"And it has to be you, of course," she said sharply.

"Again, we've had this conversation already," he snapped. "No, it doesn't have to be me, except apparently it does. Who else do you see standing up to take the lead? Mahoney? I like him a lot, but he's been commanding a desk for over a decade. Can you name anyone -- anyone -- in the extant hierarchy of the Commonwealth Navy who you see as someone who would be willing and able to take the risk that I'm taking? To stand up and say if no one else is going to fight this war, I fucking will?"

As he stared expectantly into the Lieutenant Commander's eyes, her jaw muscles twitched several times and she clenched her teeth. Only a few moments had passed, but Radko could see something shift behind her eyes and knew before she spoke what her answer was going to be.

"No," she said, then paused for a long moment before continuing -- grudgingly, it seemed. "And even if there was someone else, they wouldn't be Finn Radko."

He tried not to notice the slight trace of derision when she said his name.

"No," continued el Bahari. "You are uniquely positioned to make this happen. Blind loyalty from your crew, friends in positions of power with our traditional enemies. One could imagine that you wouldn't be satisfied with stopping after the Hornet's Nest. With the little fleet you're assembling, taking Thor's Hammer would be a realistic possibility."

Much to his surprise, Radko found the statement more amusing than offensive, and he chuckled.

"El Bahari, I promise you I have no desire to install myself or anyone else as dictator."

"And yet you threatened to come after Upshaw."

"I might," he said lightly. "But if I do, it will have nothing to do with any desire on my part to rule."

His XO looked thoroughly unconvinced.

"You know what I want?" he asked, not waiting for her to attempt an answer. "I want Sigurdsson back safe. I want to hold a wake for Cortez. I want Earth free of ril-galas. I want to retire somewhere quiet, where I can watch a sunset and sip a cup of tea without getting fucking shot at. I want to stop living in a galaxy where humanity has become a passive participant, essentially waiting for extinction rather than fighting to live. I want to go to Thor's Hammer and look some of those kids in the eye without thinking that I have no idea if any of them have a future at all, let alone a future worth living for. I want to be able to say yes the next time a ten-year-old asks me if I think the ril-galas will be gone before she's my age -- and not feel like I'm lying."

"Then I hope for everyone's sake that this plan succeeds," said el Bahari.

Then she turned on her heel and headed down the ladder to the command deck. Radko watched her for a moment as she went directly to the sand table to review some data. It was only a moment later that Owens came up.

"Everything okay with you and el Bahari?"

"How would I tell?"

"Point taken. Is she going to cause problems?"

"Not really," said Radko, shaking his head. "Her issue is more with me, personally, than with what we're trying to do."

Owens nodded, then consulted his tablet.

"Ven Shakara reports repairs are complete. They can be ready to leave whenever we are."

Nodding, Radko rapped his knuckles on the railing.

"Then let's get underway."

It took longer than usual for her connection to Thor's Hammer to go through. One of her connections. It occurred to el Bahari that she might have been running more covert communications signals than Commonwealth Intelligence. While she didn't particularly like the secrecy, the figurative skulking in shadows, she had convinced herself of its necessity.

And now, at least, she knew where Radko's rendezvous would be.

Carncastle Gate was an immense gas giant just inside Commonwealth space. Once expected to be both the location of major mining operations and a point from which the Commonwealth could expand outward -- hence the "Gate" portion of its name -- the system had been entirely abandoned by civilized life. Recently it had served as a haven for several groups of pirates, including Captain Singh's group when away from their main base of operations on Casandra Hajek -- a habitable moon named for the explorer who had discovered it and died there.

She had to admit that Carncastle Gate was a near-perfect staging ground for Radko's assault on the Hornet's Nest. Positioned as it was, at the edge of Commonwealth space, it was less than a day's journey from Soviet space and directly across no man's land from icaran space. But more than that, it provided an almost direct approach to the Sol system while also using sensor-dulling natural phenomena like the Oort cloud and Kuiper belt to their fullest. Despite her feelings toward Radko, el Bahari had to admit that the plan was not just tactically sound, it was tactically brilliant. The assault would be timed so that the approach of the assault fleet -- Joint Task Force One, as Radko called it -- would put them behind the sun. By the time the Hornet's Nest saw them coming, JTF1 would be on their doorstep.

"Yes, what is it?"

El Bahari almost jumped as the voice of Upshaw came through her tablet.

"Bianca. I understand congratulations are in order," she said. "Deputy Prime Minister?"

"Yes. Do you have information for me?"

"I do, but first I need to know what's going on with Vossek. One of Radko's friends was with those pirates he went after -- I'm concerned if we don't hear from them soon, Radko might drop this rendezvous and go looking for her."

Upshaw snorted.

"Let him. We've already proven to him-"

"If he goes looking for Sigurdsson rather than proceeding with the rendezvous, you will have absolutely no evidence to use against him."

There was dead silence, as she expected there to be.

"I'm not an idiot, Bianca. I understood your plan as soon as you charged the young Lieutenant."

Another lengthy silence.

"Edward pursued the Azrael's Tear into the Udukiin Priex," said Upshaw finally, grudgingly. "The pirates launched an icaran shuttle, which the Adirondack shot down -- though Vossek reports he did see several icaran life pods make planetfall on the Shattered World."

El Bahari frowned to herself, running a finger over her lips. Why would the pirates head to the Priex? It made little sense given the open hostility shown by the udukiin to anyone entering their borders. She said as much to Upshaw.

"One of the items stolen from us," said the newly-minted Deputy PM. "Had at one time belonged to the udukiin."

"A weapon, I assume?"

"Not yet, but it would have been."

Eyes narrowing, a few items clicked into place for el Bahari.

Whatever this item was, Sigurdsson was *returning it*. Which meant it was important.

"The Adirondack shot down the icaran shuttle," she said slowly. "What of the Azrael's Tear?"

"Escaped. Vossek had to break off pursuit -- the udukiin presence became... difficult."

"Were they attacking the Tear as well?"

She could almost hear Upshaw frown at the question. It likely hadn't occurred to her to ask and she would be quickly re-reading Vossek's report to find out.

"Apparently not," she said finally. "Why does that matter? Pirates are lawless, they probably hand over stolen materiel to the udukiin all the time."

The udukiin had always been self-sufficient, thought el Bahari. They didn't need pirates any more than they needed trade agreements. If the udukiin didn't attack the Azrael's Tear, it was either because their visit was pre-planned -- which was unlikely, given that Radko seemed to have no idea where they were -- or the udukiin somehow knew they were returning an item of great value to...

Straightening her back, she stared at the wall for a moment, then at her tablet.

"Yes, that must be it," she said. "Where is Vossek now?"

"Irrelevant. I've given you the information you needed, now what do you have for me?"

"The location of the rendezvous."

"Let's have it."

The woman sounded positively predatory.

"You'll need to send your most loyal ships," said el Bahari. "Firepower aside, Radko has surrounded himself with true believers. Surrender will not come easy -- if it comes at all. Vossek should lead with the Adirondack. If that's to be our flagship, it should start out that way."

"Of course," said Upshaw, sharply. "And Prager will be there in the Lone Star."

"You'll need more. Radko is expecting to have four capitol ships -- I'd recommend the Monument Valley, the Galveston and the Marcus Keyes at the very least. A pair of missile boats couldn't hurt either."

"Yes, yes, I agree. The location?"

"The pirate base at Casandra Hajek."

36

The ril-galas could feel fear.

Even through the waves of anger crashing through her, Sigurdsson knew that's what their step backward had meant. And more, she knew they were afraid *of her*. Of what she now represented.

She was Kaigor Kai Rii, the great War Matriarch who had come from out of the black to lead the udukiin to their destiny.

Behind her, an army had gathered. Sigurdsson wasn't sure how many udukiin had taken up arms, she wasn't about to take her eyes off the ril-galas to check, but she could feel the buzzing of their minds as they gathered.

"Go back to where you came from," she said, biting off each word. "Or you will die."

The ril-galas line shifted again, but this time not to step backward. This time, it was to allow one of the stalkers to step forward, in front of the rest. It looked very much the same as the other stalkers, save for a splash of white across its otherwise black triangular head -- and its bearing. It carried itself differently, less animalistic.

A leader of some sort.

A second stalker with a similar white slash stood behind it, in line with the rest of the invaders.

"You won't get another warning," said Sigurdsson.

Tilting its head to one side, the stalker commander opened its toothy mouth impossibly wide and Sigurdsson could see the slimy musculature of its throat constricting in unnatural ways.

"Surrrrrenderrrr orrr we kk-kkilll all."

She simply stared for a moment. Though its lips weren't moving, the thing was somehow creating an approximation of human speech. And it clearly understood what it was saying.

"Surrrenderrr-kk," it said again.

For some reason, the creature's voice made Sigurdsson think of the rusty hulks of abandoned spacecraft. Dusty, creaking, flakes of oxidized metal cracking off in the wind.

There was a pause as Sigurdsson stared at the creature. And then she began to laugh.

It was not a kind laugh.

"I beat you on Von Daniken's Landing. I beat you on Good Hope. I beat you on New Madawaska," she said, taking a step toward the stalker commander. "I will not surrender. We will not surrender -- not here and now, not tomorrow, not ever."

With her left hand, Sigurdsson raised her gunstaff high above her head.

"I am Freyja Sigurdsson! I am Kaigor Kai Rii!"

"Kaigor Kai Rii!" murmured the gathered udukiin. It was perhaps more unsettling than if they had screamed it.

Sigurdsson's lip curled in a snarl.

"I am your end."

Dropping her left hand, she drew her *vayan* pistol with her right and blew the commander's head apart with her first shot and punched a fist-sized hole through its chest cavity -- and the ril-galas pilot within -- with her second.

The udukiin attack began before the stalker commander's corpse had hit the ground.

Holstering her pistol and raising her gunstaff, Sigurdsson sighted along the ornate barrel and picked her target -- a stalker moving quickly toward an udukiin already grappling with a ril-galas foot soldier. When she squeezed the trigger sensor the weapon fired its bolt of pure energy with barely a sound and no recoil at all. Excess energy flared from the six oval openings encircling the muzzle, creating a brief, bright halo of orange light around the gunstaff barrel.

The bolt slammed into the stalker and the creature erupted into a ball of flame as bright and as brief as the excess energy halo. When the flames disappeared, the stalker was down, a smoldering hole in its torso.

Ril-galas arm cannons boomed, udukiin gunstaves whispered and when the two forces were too close for firearms, the stalkers came to the fore and the udukiin drew their long, curved knives.

Sigurdsson used her fists.

Responding to her needs, her passenger shifted her organic armour to reinforce Sigurdsson's hands and wrists, her fists effectively becoming hammers.

A stalker leapt at her and Sigurdsson swatted it out of mid-air, an udukiin pouncing on it and impaling the creature with twin knives a scant second after it hit the ground. Another stalker charged and as she ducked under its slashing claws, Sigurdsson hammered a fist into its chest, then, grabbing it around the throat with her left hand, used her right to pummel it into a bloody pulp.

Dropping the remains to the ground, she stood straight, realising that the sounds of battle had gone.

The ril-galas had gone -- the few that had survived.

The battlefield was littered with corpses and though there were udukiin dead, Sigurdsson could see without a formal count that the ril-galas corpses far outnumbered those of her own people.

At first, she didn't even notice the change in how she saw things.

Her own people.

The udukiin.

Suddenly she was nearly overwhelmed with feelings of pain and hope and fear and longing and an image of herself sitting on her bunk back on Thor's Hammer, stroking Jaeger's head as he curled up against her thigh.

"Jaeger, oh fuck oh fuck," she whispered, Kaigor Kai Rii disappearing in an instant and being replaced with a terrified Freyja Sigurdsson.

Stumbling over corpses, she headed to where she'd last seen him, his body limp and bleeding -- fucking hell please let him be okay -- but the spot was empty. Empty save a bloodstain the size of an ATV tire.

Her hands began to shake as she frantically spun around, looking in all directions for some sign of Jaeger, her kalthar, her companion.

"Jaeger!" she yelled. "Please, buddy, please be okay please be okay please be okay..."

Another wave. More pain. A flash of her and Jaeger at the fort on New Madawaska. She'd just given him half of her peanut butter cookie. He'd barely chewed it, then licked her face.

Tears were stinging her eyes now. There was no doubt he was still alive, which gave her hope, but the amount of pain he was feeling... she couldn't finish the thought. Instead, she turned inward, closing her eyes and hoping like hell her passenger could help.

"I don't know how this works, but I know it's your psychic whatever that's allowing this connection," she said quietly. "I brought you home. I'm helping you fulfill your destiny. Please, I'm begging you, help me find him."

In that moment she knew that if Jaeger died, so would the entire ril-galas race. She would hunt them, wherever they went. She would mobilize every last udukiin into an army four million strong. She would march across the galaxy and she would kill every last one. She would find their home world and she would watch it burn.

The buzzing in her head intensified for a moment and then cleared, so much so that the world seemed to go completely quiet. And then she felt it. A sort of warmth in her mind and then a heartbeat and then the pain and confusion and she followed it like... like Jaeger, all those times he'd picked up a scent and felt a compulsion to investigate. Udukiin raised hands in salute as she passed and -- through her passenger's influence, no doubt -- Sigurdsson unthinkingly returned it as she headed through the battlefield toward a small building. It was no more than a hovel.

Udrach stood outside and opened the door for her as she approached.

Stepping inside, Sigurdsson opened her mouth to call out for Jaeger when she stopped.

He was there.

At the centre of the building's lone room stood a table. It was covered with a coarse blanket and laying on his side on the blanket was Jaeger. There was blood caked on his fur.

He lifted his head. His eyes met Sigurdsson's and she heard the thump of his tail against the tabletop as it began wagging and she felt a wave of such joy and love and that everything was okay now, and she began to cry as she knelt beside the table and gently stroked his head.

"It's okay, buddy. It's okay, everything will be okay," she whispered.

"Freyja."

Looking up, she realised for the first time there were others in the room. Frankenstein stood beside her. Elgraphaar stood off to one side, and Aylarr sat awkwardly on another blanket on the floor, her arms held tightly to her torso. Her armour sat beside her and she appeared hurt.

"Frankenstein," Sigurdsson said, standing, but not lifting her hand from Jaeger. "Is..."

She paused, taking a deep breath and collecting herself.

"Status report, please."

Frankenstein bobbed his metal head.

"Udukiin injuries are many, but their own medical practitioners appear quite skilled -- moreso than I with their physiology. The udukiin are very durable species -- most of the injuries I witnessed would be considered relatively minor."

Sigurdsson nodded, trying not to look too impatient.

It was good, the news about the udukiin, but it wasn't the information she was waiting for.

"Jaeger's injuries were quite serious," said the brill, reaching and stroking the dog's snout with surprising gentleness for a mechanical exo-suit. "His attacker's claw pierced his chest and caused damage to his heart."

Swallowing heavily, Sigurdsson said nothing.

Jaeger licked her hand.

A tear rolled down her cheek.

"I have largely immobilized him for now," said Frankenstein.

"Doc... is he," she said, stopping to take a shaky breath. "Will he be okay?"

"He requires time to heal, but I believe he will perhaps exceed the normal expected lifespan for his breed."

The relief was so palpable, so complete, then Sigurdsson felt a light-headedness that forced her to brace both hands on the table.

Jaeger would be okay. He would heal and he would live, maybe even longer than...

What the hell did that mean, 'exceed the normal lifespan of his breed'? She was about to ask, but then remembered Aylarr.

"What about Aylarr?" she asked, turning to the icaran woman. "What happened?"

"His heart was damaged."

"What? Yes, I got that, but what happened to you?"

"Jaeger's heart was damaged," said Elgraphaar.

"Icarans have primary and secondary eyes," said Aylarr, sounding very, very tired. "And we have primary and secondary hearts."

"A natural back-up system for the body," said Frankenstein, brightly. "Quite incredible. Though the icaran secondary heart is actually similar to the human appendix -- vestigial, not truly necessary to the operation of the body."

Her mouth slightly open, her eyes narrowed, Sigurdsson looked from Frankenstein, to Aylarr, to Elgraphaar and back to Aylarr.

"Jaeger's heart was damaged," said Aylarr. "And as you humans would say, I had a spare lying around."

Bursting into tears, Sigurdsson dropped to one knee beside Aylarr and spread her arms to go in for a hug.

"What are you doing?" said Aylarr quickly, making Sigurdsson pause.

"Humans squeeze each other to express gratitude," said Elgraphaar.

"I just underwent surgery, Sigurdsson. Please do not squeeze me."

"Okay," said Sigurdsson, laughing, wiping tears from her eyes. "No squeezing. But thank you, Aylarr. Thank you so much. You have no idea how much it means to me."

"He is your kalthar."

"And now you are both part icaran," said Frankenstein.

"Thanks to you, you magnificent bastard," said Sigurdsson, standing and embracing the brill. "You and your fucking genius science shit."

"*Medical* science shit," he corrected.

"As much as I am loathe to darken the mood," said Elgraphaar. "The Priex Matriarch is dead. Which leaves the udukiin leaderless."

"I don't believe they are," said Aylaar, looking to Sigurdsson.

Keeping her silence for a moment, Sigurdsson stroked Jaeger's flank. She figured it may have relaxed her more than it did him.

"We came here to hopefully get the udukiin to help in the war," she said, but it sounded hesitant even to her own ears. "And we now have a way to do that."

No one spoke, waiting for her to continue.

"If I do this... If I lead the udukiin to war, I need you to keep me grounded. I need to know you won't let me...," she paused and shook her head, trying to clear it. She was drained, physically and emotionally. "Emotionally, I can get blinded. Especially by anger. If I can potentially call an entire species to arms, I can't afford to let that happen -- I can't have udukiin dying because I got angry and marched them to their death to get revenge."

Feeling a cold nose against the palm of her hand, Sigurdsson had sudden flash image of the kindness she'd shown to Jaeger in the time they'd known each other, from sneaking him bits of her meals, to talking to him on the long cold nights as they awaited the next ril-galas assault. The sentiment was as clear as if he'd spoken the words: I believe in your goodness.

His endorsement meant more than anyone else's could have.

"I promise to stand with you," said Elgraphaar. "And advise you to the best of my ability."

"As will I," said Aylarr.

"My counsel is of course yours, at any time it may be required," said Frankenstein. "Though my skills would be perhaps more beneficial were I behind the lines rather than literally standing with you."

The brill turned his glowing blue 'eye' from Sigurdsson to Elgraphaar to Aylarr and back to Sigurdsson.

"I hope you do not think me a coward -- I only feel that is where I am able to of most benefit to our cause," he said.

Elgraphaar laughed.

"It's not your courage we question, Frankenstein, but your sanity."

When Sigurdsson had told Udrach she wanted to address the Chamber, it had seemed like such a simple thing. She would just talk. The udukiin would listen. They'd agree or they wouldn't, but all she had to do was talk.

As Udrach rapped his gunstaff on the floor at the centre of the room and announced that Kaigor Kai Rii would now address the Chamber, all eyes turned to her. The room was even more packed than it had been on her first visit and Sigurdsson wished she'd had the foresight to plan ahead -- maybe even write some notes -- on what she would say.

Complete and total silence fell over the chamber.

"I came here thinking I was returning something you lost," said Sigurdsson. She had no idea how she was going to say what she needed to say and she was trying desperately to channel

Finn Radko -- he seemed to be a natural at getting all speechy. "I didn't know anything about the prophecy of the Matriarch of the Three, I just knew what I had to do. I didn't know about the bonding, I didn't know a Matriarch could bond to a non-udukiin. I didn't know about your history with the ril-galas and I didn't know you as a people."

Holding her arms wide, she gave an exaggerated shrug.

"Apparently I knew shit all."

The stone-like rumble of udukiin laughter rolled through the chamber. Thankfully.

"But the things I do know are a lot clearer now. Clearer to me, for sure, and I expect much clearer to you as well. I am not udukiin," she said slowly. "And because of that, I can't say whether I am Kaigor Kai Rii. I can't be -- and shouldn't be -- the one to figure that out. That's for you to decide."

Turning, slowly, a full three hundred and sixty degrees, Sigurdsson tried to lock eyes with as many occupants of the chamber as possible.

"I'm not udukiin, but I'm also not fully human or icaran either -- I'm some impossible combination of the three. And if you decide that I am you War Matriarch -- *if* -- then I will lead you. I will lead the udukiin against the ril-galas and we will fight side-by-side with the humans and the icarans," she said, pausing briefly -- the next line was the only thing she'd really planned. "The udukiin taking their rightful place... as protectors of the black."

The chamber erupted. Udukiin pounded fists on whatever surface they could reach and Sigurdsson felt a panic rising in her and then suddenly understood that the hammering of fists was the udukiin equivalent of cheering.

An elder udukiin stood and the noise died. Sigurdsson recognized him as one of the advisers who had flanked Yrtaan at their first meeting.

"The udukiin people and the star fleet of the Priex will mobilize at your command," he said. "We will mobilize as a singular, unstoppable force under the command of Kaigor Kai Rii."

The chamber erupted in the pounding of fists again.

Sigurdsson raised a hand for silence and got it.

"No," she said.

The gathered masses exchanged looks with each other as Sigurdsson paused. It wasn't shock value she was going for with her pause, but she wanted to ensure she had their attention.

"We aren't looking at a war on a single front. There is no fort we can take to win the war, no one single planet that we can liberate to end this," she said. "Our enemy... they're everywhere. They have spread through star systems like a plague."

"Is that... not more reason for a single, massive force...?" asked one udukiin, clearly much younger than most of her peers.

"The ril-galas are already here, on the Shattered World," said Sigurdsson. "I will not leave the home world of the udukiin undefended or under-defended. If you are to become the protectors of the black, we have to be smarter about this, we have to think strategy not just throw wave after wave of soldiers at them and hope they breath their last before we do."

"This is contrary to thousands of years of udukiin military operation," said a gruff voice from somewhere in the chamber -- Sigurdsson had no idea where.

"And that," she said. "Is why it is the Kaigor Kai Rii who will lead you to your rightful place in the galaxy."

It was a bold statement and one Sigurdsson herself wasn't entirely sure of, but it had the desired effect.

The udukiin stood and hammered their fists on seats and walls and desktops and Kaigor Kai Rii was given unconditional command of the Priex's army and star fleet.

37

As the Vimy Ridge and the Venn Shakara approached Carncastle Gate, a debris cloud came into view. It wasn't big enough to have been a capital ship, but as Radko watched the look of concern crawl over Cagliari's face, he understood that it could be the right size for a hauler full of advanced starfighters.

"Outlaw Squadron, this is Cags on the HMCS Vimy Ridge," she said, having set up a dedicated channel with the same codes her fighters were all to be using. "We're arriving at Carncastle Gate -- I need a status report."

Several seconds of tense silence followed.

"Welcome to Carncastle Gate, Cags," came the response. "Glad you could join us. We were getting lonely out here."

Cagliari smiled in relief and so did Radko.

"Happy to be here," she said. "There's a debris field out here, though..."

"Yeah, we ran into some pirates who had a hard time understanding what we were doing. The icarans stepped in"

"Understood."

She looked up at Radko and he nodded. Rhekarr had confirmed that the Ven Vaar and the Vor Rokhar were holding position on the far side of the gas giant.

Radko locked eyes with Owens, who shook his head. There was no sign of the Leonid Gorshkov and no communication from Vladislav Kovalenko.

"Commander!" shouted Hamelin, the LiDAR tech. "I'm picking up a small ril-galas vessel entering the Carncastle Gate system.

"They probably picked up the explosion of the pirate ship," said el Bahari, appearing at Radko's side seemingly out of nowhere.

"We need to take it out before it sees us. Is it a battleship?"

"Negative, Commander -- it's less than half our size. Scout ship?"

"This would be a good test of our full fighter wing capabilities, Finn," said Cagliari, the hopeful note in her tone clear to everyone.

"Quickly," said Radko. "If that thing reports back..."

With a nod, she set off for the hangar at a full out run.

By the time Cagliari arrived in the Vimy Ridge hangar bay, the rest of her pilots were already doing their pre-flight checks. She knew those aboard the Ven Vaar would be doing the same -- she'd used her tablet to send launch orders to them all while she made her way to the hangar.

Locking her helmet into place, she settled into her seat and couldn't help but feel a shiver of thrill run up her spine as she was raised into the pitch black of the Argentavis. That split second of total darkness before the UHUD kicked in and revealed the entirety of her surroundings was one of the most calming moments Cagliari had ever experienced. Paradoxical, really; thrilling and calming at the same time.

As she docked her tablet, the fighter's holographic controls sprang up around her and Cagliari did her pre-flight checks as quickly as humanly possible, though she skipped over some steps. The advantage of having been the one to design the fighter, she figured, was that she could tell at a glance whether systems were performing the way they should.

"Outlaw One to Outlaw Squadron," she said, the Argentavis automatically connecting her to the entirety of Outlaw squadron -- those on the Vimy Ridge as well as those on the icaran carrier. "You know the drill: wingmen stick to your leaders and everyone watch each other's backs."

"Do we have confirmation of enemy fighters?"

"Negative, but that doesn't mean there aren't any."

Everyone acknowledged and Cagliari gave the order to launch, gunning the engine of her own fighter and rocketing out of the Vimy Ridge. On either side of her were her wingmen -- Dee and a male icaran pilot named Tennum. The other flights of three from the Vimy Ridge were led by Checkers and Daxma, while Wade, Bozon and Cervenka each led a flight from the Ven Vaar.

The ril-galas ship was of a type they had not seen before -- narrow and sleek, it was the smallest non-fighter the Vimy Ridge had encountered. And while was narrow, it was also tall. Cagliari was reminded of a marine creature, a fish she had been lucky enough to see up close while scuba diving as a child, back when the creature was classified as endangered. It would be reclassified as extinct only a few years prior to the ril-galas invasion. The fish was called a mola-mola -- an ocean sunfish.

The ril-galas sunfish did in fact have a fighter escort, four units. Neither the fighters nor the sunfish lasted very long under the combined assault of six flights of Argentavis fighters.

Cagliari couldn't help but smile as she looked at the scene being holographically duplicated around her. The stars, the gas giant of Carncastle Gate, the remaining fragments of the ril-galas ships. In the distance, the Vimy Ridge and Venn Shakara. Further out, the Ven Vaar and Vor Rokhar coming into view.

She was finally making a difference.

"Outlaw Squadron," she said, her voice unexpectedly thick with emotion. "Good work. Good work."

Radko and el Bahari had been watching the battle from the observation dome, looking back and forth between the actual scene as displayed by the magnification layer and the holographic representation of the battle displayed over the sand table.

When the ril-galas scout ship had winked out of existence on both, Radko turned to el Bahari and shook his head slightly.

"Those fighters are goddamned impressive."

"I can't disagree with that," she said, then frowned as Hamelin sent an urgent alert to the sand table. "We have another ship entering the system."

The Leonid Gorshkov, Radko assumed. He was about to order a comm line opened when he heard el Bahari swear. She pushed past him to move the mag layer over toward where the new ship was approaching and increased the magnification percentage.

Radko frowned, then swore himself.

The Leonid Gorshkov had a very distinct, basking shark-like look to its design. The approaching ship looked more like a great white.

"The Tianlong," said el Bahari, through clenched teeth.

Commanded by Admiral Zhang Jianjun, the Tianlong was not only the fastest ship in the Soviet Navy, but also the most notorious. Radko had lost count of the number of times its name or the name of its commander appeared in intelligence briefings over the years and there had even been a Bismarck-style hunt for the Tianlong close to five years prior. The Tianlong was fast and powerful, her commander cunning and dangerous.

And he was here at Carncastle Gate. El Bahari asked the question aloud that Radko had begun to form in his head.

"Why is the Tianlong here? You said we were meeting the Gorshkov."

"I don't know. Order Outlaw Squadron to get their birds back to the nest," he said, then opened a link to Rhekarr. "Admiral, if you could please ask the Ven Vaar and Vor Rokhar to hold position it would be appreciated."

"Of course," came the icaran's response. "Is there a problem?"

"The ship that just appeared is not the ship we're expecting. I don't want to spook them into doing something stupid."

"Understandable. The order will be given."

After thanking the Admiral, Radko closed the channel and turned to el Bahari.

"If we don't have the Leonid Gorshkov-"

"Then your plan is in serious trouble," she said, crossing her arms in what had become her default combative stance. "And you'll have put a lot of people in danger with nothing to show for it."

"Maybe you were right."

She raised a brow.

"About this being a mistake?"

"No, when you said you were kind of a bitch," he said. "Get me a comm line to the Tianlong -- I need to know what the hell is going on."

But Admiral Zhang, as his reputation would have implied, was one step ahead of them.

"Incoming from the Tianlong," said the young communications officer.

Radko signaled her to pipe it through. He stared at the approaching ship as he spoke.

"Tianlong, this is Commander Finn Radko of the HMCS Vimy Ridge. Welcome to Carncastle Gate," he said. It was all he could think of to say.

"It is a great honour to speak with such an illustrious naval officer as Commander Finn Radko," came the response. It was heavily accented, though easy enough to understand, and it dripped of sarcasm.

Radko thought he saw el Bahari smirk.

He was fairly certain the voice did not belong to Zhang. Whoever it was was employing one of the Admiral's favourite tactics -- insulting his enemy to provoke an emotional, rather than tactical response.

"I have no doubt it is," said Radko. "I would be happy to sign autographs if you'd like."

"Should we run into a shortage of toilet paper, we will no doubt take you up on that offer."

"You can also let me know when you're ready to speak naval officer to naval officer and drop the childish bullshit, Admiral."

And he killed the channel.

"You just embarrassed him over an open comm line," said el Bahari.

"That wasn't Zhang. All I did was make it clear I wasn't interested in trading insults with one of his underlings -- which is something someone like Zhang Jianjun will understand."

"You'd better be right."

"I'm right all the time, sixty percent of the time," he said.

Before el Bahari could respond -- and Radko could tell there was a stinging rebuttal forming on her lips -- another transmission came through from the Tianlong.

"Radko, you cannot small talk for shit."

The voice was again heavily-accented, but this time it was a Russian accent and Radko grinned.

"And you take too long to get to the point, Kovalenko," he said. "What the hell are you doing on the Tianlong?"

"Trying to drink baijiu," said Kovalenko. "Is utter shit. You need to come here now, Radko. We must talk."

"Vladislav... where is the Leonid Gorshkov."

"Gorshkov is reassigned to new captain," said the old Russian, the bitterness evident in his voice. "I do not command Tianlong, but Admiral Zhang he is interested in our plan."

Radko and el Bahari exchanged looks of surprise. The hardest of Soviet hardliners was on board with working with not only the Commonwealth Navy, but the icarans...?

"The Admiral wishes for you to join him for meal. And the commander of icaran vessel as well."

"Let the Admiral know I'd be happy to join him. We'll be over shortly."

Nearly an hour later, the icaran shuttle brought over by Admiral Rhekarr left the Vimy Ridge's hangar bay and headed toward the Tianlong. In addition to the two commanding officers, the shuttle also carried two icaran commandos as an honour guard, reminding Radko of his last trip to a Soviet vessel, and Cagliari -- at her own insistence. She really, really wanted to see the Tianlong first-hand.

As the group disembarked, they were met by a group of armed Soviet marines and Vladislav Kovalenko.

Radko couldn't hide his concern.

"Yes," said Kovalenko. "I look shit, I know. Is still good to see you, Radko."

"And you," said Radko as they shook hands.

Kovalenko did indeed look awful. Once a bear of a man with an impressively bushy beard, he'd lost a great deal of weight and his hair and beard were thinning. The Russian's eyes looked sunken and tired and he walked with the aid of a cane.

"Is illness," he said. "Doctors tell me is not terminal, but is serious, so Soviet Navy gives command of Leonid Gorshkov to young, healthy, virile man who is giant fucking moron."

"I feel they're underestimating Vladislav Kovalenko."

"As the Commonwealth does Finn Radko. Is curse of men like us, eh?"

"No argument here."

After Radko introduced the rest of the group, Kovalenko led them all into the officer's mess, where a simple meal of rice and what looked like seasoned beef had been laid out. At the head of the table, a man stood and smiled thinly. He was short, and probably just over sixty.

"Welcome to the Tianlong," he said.

His voice was smooth and he spoke English with only a slight accent.

"A pleasure to be here, Admiral," said Radko.

"And not be in chains," added Cagliari, unhelpfully. "But still under armed guard."

She nodded to the marines, who hadn't yet left their side.

"Shitty hospitality."

The thin smile remained in place, but it did not, Radko saw, reach Admiral Zhang's eyes. Those eyes shifted from Cagliari to Radko.

"You must be Commander Radko. I am pleased to have you aboard -- you have quite the reputation, even among Soviets. Helped, no doubt, by Captain Kovalenko's stories," said Zhang. "Which I suspect may be heavily embellished."

"Vladislav Kovalenko does not *need* to embellish his stories," said Kovalenko, dropping heavily into one of the chairs. "Admiral Zhang is just jealous of our exploits, Radko."

Radko smiled. At least his old friend's sense of humour remained intact.

Zhang indicated that they should sit and eat, and didn't speak again until they had and tea was served.

"Kovalenko came to me in the days after Naval Command reassigned the Leonid Gorshkov," said Zhang. "Your plan was already in motion and he had no way to contact you without -- as he put it -- letting the idiots know what you were doing."

"*Fucking* idiots," corrected Kovalenko.

"Yes, just so," agreed Zhang with a slight nod. "I must admit, Commander Radko, that your plan is daring. Surprising, even. But most impressive of all..."

He took a sip of tea, then set his cup down very carefully and his left eyebrow inched upward.

"It is tactically brilliant."

Whatever Radko had been expecting, such high praise from the scourge of the Commonwealth was not it. He said nothing, unsure of what, if anything, he should say.

Rhekarr saved him the trouble.

"We agree, which is why we have committed three warships to the cause," said the icaran.

Zhang's brow edged a little higher.

"Three? Our scanners picked up only your own ship, Admiral Rhekarr."

"A general who places all of his war assets in plain view of his enemy is not fit to command," said Radko. He was sure the translation was somewhat clunky, but the statement was lifted from one of Zhang Jianjun's many essays on the art of war. Radko had studied it and several others during his time in Intelligence.

"Indeed," said Zhang, chuckling lightly. "Indeed. And what other assets might you be hiding, Commander?"

"Admiral," said Radko, setting down his own tea and leaning forward. "That information is only available to *my allies*. I appreciate you having us over here for dinner -- it beat the hell out of the food we have on the Vimy Ridge -- but to this point, you haven't made it clear one way or another whether you're bringing the Tianlong into the fold for this mission or whether you're just humouring Kovalenko or just here for your own curiosity."

"I do not humour people, Commander."

"He is here to join," said Kovalenko, sipping his tea then spitting it back into his cup with a sour look. "Fucking tea. He is here to help, but Zhang is too proud to admit it."

"I am not too proud, Kovalenko. I would remind you that I outrank you-"

"I would remind you I am sick and don't give a shit. Your game is stupid, stop playing it."

Though Zhang glared at Kovalenko, it seemed to Radko that there wasn't any real malice behind it.

"Yes, Commander Radko. I will commit the Tianlong to the assault on the Hornets' Nest," he said finally. "Because whatever political differences we may have, none of them will matter if humanity dies."

Radko raised his cup of tea in a toast.

"If only our governments could think so clearly."

Zhang raised his own cup.

"If only."

The meal concluded with some small talk and then Zhang invited Radko to join him privately for another cup of tea and further discussion. When Radko agreed, the Admiral led him to an adjoining room -- an officer's lounge that was far more well-furnished than Radko would have expected from a Soviet vessel. A fresh pot of tea already waited for them and Zhang poured two cups.

"I appreciate your willingness to meet with me, Commander," he said. "I am aware that my reputation within the Commonwealth is not one that would... engender overtures of friendship."

"Frankly Admiral, I'm not sure mine is these days either."

Zhang raised a brow, but when Radko didn't elaborate, he continued.

"Kovalenko speaks highly of you. He and I have not always seen eye to eye, but I respect his opinion and his judgement. He feels that you are the one to lead humanity to victory."

Cringing, Radko set down his tea.

"I wish people would stop saying things like that," he said, rubbing his eyes. "Admiral, I'm nobody's saviour. I'm one guy with an idea. Yeah, I think it's a good idea, the right idea, but I'm not going to single-handedly save the world. I need people like Rhekarr and Cagliari and Kovalenko and Sigurdsson..."

He really needed Sigurdsson to be okay.

"...And people like you, Admiral. I need people who understand that none of our political differences matter at this moment in history -- that if we can't set them aside, this may be our *last* moment in history."

"The Commonwealth will always be my enemy," said Zhang.

"And my idealism will always be mine, but guess what? If we don't stand up and do something -- soon -- we won't have the luxury of being each other's enemy, because humanity will be on the brink of extinction."

"I have already committed my ship-"

"I know, and believe me I appreciate that. But now I want commitment from *you*."

Zhang simply sipped his tea, staring. Radko wasn't sure if that was a good thing or a bad thing.

"Kovalenko also told me that you were unbelievably stubborn and persuasive," said Zhang. "And he was right."

He set down his tea and stood, looking out the small porthole at the gas giant that loomed above them.

"Yes," he said. "Politics, for the time being, do not serve the greater good. You have my commitment."

"Thank you, Admiral."

"It remains, though, that we are but five capital ships against an extremely well-defended ril-galas installation."

Radko nodded.

"Five very capable capital ships," he said. "As well as your fighter squadron and a highly advanced fighter squadron from the Vimy Ridge."

"We still face near overwhelming odds," said Zhang. "And I have seen Commonwealth fighters, Commander. I would not call them highly advanced."

Unable to surpress it, Radko grinned.

"You haven't seen these yet. Neither has your LiDAR, but they're right there."

Stepping up beside Zhang, Radko pointed toward the blackness of space and watched with a mixture of amusement and pride as Zhang squinted, straining to see to what Radko was referring. And then his eyes widened and his left brow shot up as he saw the broad wingspans of three Argentavis fighters of his port bow.

"Invisible to LiDAR," said Radko. "And apparently all but invisible to whatever detection systems the ril-galas use. Cagliari designed them."

"Now I see why you put up with her."

Aboard the Vimy Ridge, el Bahari stalked the breadth of the observation dome catwalk like a tiger, muscles coiled and ready to strike. The crew clearly picked up on her mood and steered clear -- and she was fine with that. Radko had been gone much longer than sheds expected and while she wasn't overly concerned for his safety, el Bahari badly wanted to be free to disappear to her quarters. Minutes after Radko and his entourage had left for the Tianlong, she'd received a text-only message on one of her secret channels from Thor's Hammer. Ironhorse had wanted her to know that Doctor Khaifa was casting about for a constitutional law expert.

Though she wasn't certain what the doctor was up to, she knew she wanted to speak with Ironhorse as soon as possible to figure it out. And to figure out if Radko was playing any role in it. Requesting that the Ranger watch over Khaifa had been an almost knee-jerk reaction, but el Bahari was quickly beginning to see that the woman had been underestimated by almost everyone. Especially if Khaifa's new quest meant what el Bahari thought it meant.

"Commander."

Pulling herself out of her thoughts, el Bahari spun on her heel to face Owens, who had -- unnoticed by her -- joined her on the catwalk.

"Yes, Lieutenant Commander Owens, what can I do for you?" she said, trying to sound less combative than usual and failing at it.

Owens frowned and pursed his lips, looking at something on his tablet.

"We just received a transmission from the Azrael's Tear, sir," he said, still frowning at his tablet.

She shifted her posture slightly, unconsciously. Could Sigurdsson be alive? If so, it would certainly keep Radko from going off the deep end.

"Sigurdsson?"

"No, Commander, Captain Singh," said Owens and el Bahari was surprised at how disappointed she was.

The woman had rubbed her the wrong way from the moment they'd met and only part of that was because of Sigurdsson's closeness to Radko. She was an intimidating presence and el Bahari hated feeling intimidated.

"He's receiving reports from some of his... associates," continued Owens. "It appears as if there are a number of ATC Castle ships converging on a moon they use as a base of operations. A moon called Casandra Hajek."

"Singh's ship was no doubt identified by the Adirondack. ATC Castle must assume he's taken his plunder back to his hideout."

Owens just stared at her for a moment.

"What's the Adirondack?" he said finally.

"Pardon?"

Her heart skipped a beat.

She was keeping too many secrets from too many people for too many different reasons and it was a miracle she hadn't slipped up to this point. But she could still recover. She could still...

"The Adirondack is an ATC Castle ship, isn't it?" asked Owens.

Thankfully, he was speaking quietly -- no one on the bustling command deck below was paying them any mind.

"Yes, it is."

"How do you know what ship was pursuing the Azrael's Tear?"

A lightbulb went on and she lunged for it with both hands.

"Cagliari," she said. "I assume she was correct -- she may not be my kind of people, but she knows space ships."

Nodding, Owens chuckled.

"That she does."

El Bahari tried not to let her relief show.

She was spared any further questioning by a sudden burst of swearing from the LiDAR technician, Hamelin.

"Two ships... no, *four* ships incoming!" he shouted. "Two of them are very large!"

"Get them on the sand table," said el Bahari, already heading to the device. Owens was right behind her.

The hologram flared to life, positions marked for the Vimy Ridge, the Tianlong and the three icaran ships. The newcomers were also marked, and they were approaching quickly. They would be on them long before the Ven Vaar and Vor Rokhar could be in position to assist.

"Arm all batteries," said el Bahari. "Order Outlaw Squadron on standby."

There was an acknowledgement, and el Bahari vaguely heard the order being conveyed, but she was too focused on the sand table. A new blip had appeared between the Vimy Ridge and the Tianlong.

"Goddammit, is that Radko's shuttle?"

"Yessir. They launched before we spotted-"

"Who's flying CAP?"

"Daxma's flight, sir."

"Tell him he's now responsible for Radko's safety."

"Her."

She glared down at the crewman who'd spoken.

"What?"

"Daxma is female, Commander."

"I don't care, convey the order! And get me a mag window up here!"

They did, and she swung it around toward the position of the approaching ships.

"Weapon status?" she said.

"All batteries ready," said Owens.

"And Radko's shuttle?"

"Going as fast as it can..."

"But not fast enough."

"No."

It occurred to el Bahari, somewhere in the back of her mind, that if Radko died, she would have to assume command of the Vimy Ridge. She'd have her own ship again.

Almost immediately, the thought was pushed out by another, more pressing thought: they could be in mortal danger. The mag layer had kicked in and resolved the approaching ships. Two massive, almost x-shaped cruisers and two smaller, sleeker pursuit craft.

"Udukiin," she said quietly, feeling a chill run down her spine.

Several others on the command deck had recognized it as well -- she heard quiet swearing ripple through the crew.

The udukiin had not left their home system in centuries.

El Bahari was relatively certain there was no living human who had ever seen an udukiin capital cruiser with their own eyes and it crossed her mind that it was possible thirty minutes hence the statement may be true again.

"Gunnery teams are to target the nearest of the capital cruisers," she said. "Fire as soon as it's in range."

But...

What if she'd been right about all the things left unsaid by Upshaw? It had been clear that the ATC Castle facility that had been raided contained some kind of udukiin artefact, something Sigurdsson had risked her life and the lives of the Azrael's Tear crew and the icaran commandos to return to the Priex. There was only one thing the udukiin people valued enough to make such a trip anything more than a death sentence.

And now they were here. At a rendezvous location known by only a handful of people -- including Freyja Sigurdsson.

"All batteries stand down," said el Bahari.

Every single face on the command deck turned toward her, but no one spoke, no one confirmed the order. She slapped the ship-wide comms herself.

"This is Commander el Bahari. All batteries are to stand down immediately. I repeat: all batteries stand down."

As the confirmations flooded in, el Bahari felt equal parts relief and trepidation. If she'd made the wrong call, they were all dead. But if she'd made the right call...

"Commander...," said Owens, disbelief in his voice. "I have an incoming transmission from... from the udukiin flagship, identifying itself as Her Glorious Vengeance."

El Bahari stared at the approaching ships for a moment before joining Owens back at the sand table and nodding to open the line.

"This is Lieutenant Commander Amira el Bahari of the HMCS Vimy Ridge," she said, injecting as much authority into her voice as she could manage through the nerves. "I would request an explanation of your presence here."

There was a momentary pause before the response came.

"I am Gholl Kai Rendrek, steward of Her Glorious Vengeance. We have come to fulfill the destiny of Kaigor Kai Rii."

A look of confusion on her face, el Bahari turned to Owens, only to find him wearing the same look. As was nearly every other crew member within her field of vision.

"I... I'm sorry, Gholl Kai Rendrek -- we don't understand-"

"Kaigor Kai Rii will speak with Finn Radko now," said the udukiin steward -- which el Bahari assumed to be the udukiin equivalent of the ship's captain.

"Commander Radko is presently unavailable-"

"You may contact us again when he is."

With that, the connection closed.

"What the hell just happened?" said Owens.

"The udukiin want to talk to Radko."

"The udukiin don't want to talk to anyone, ever. They just blow everyone up."

"And yet they contacted us, looking for Radko," said el Bahari. "I suggest we try to avoid disappointing them."

38

All Hunter wanted was to sleep, preferably for three to four days. She'd never slept on a real bed, having just moved from one cot to another her entire life, but she thought she'd like to try one. A real meal would have been nice, too. Back when she'd been part of Nightwatch, they'd allowed her access to a magazine once in a while, heavily censored of course -- usually a third of the pages had been removed by the time she was allowed to have it -- but she had once removed a page on her own, stashing it under her pillow. The guards had found it eventually and taken it away, just like they'd taken away everything that gave her a chance to develop a feeling of self.

The page in question had been a full-page advertisement for a restaurant that probably no longer existed. It showed a beautiful blonde woman biting into a massive, fully loaded hamburger. The look on the woman's face was pure ecstasy and the hamburger looked like the most marvelous meal Hunter -- or Quon Li-Chen as she was at the time -- could imagine.

She took another mouthful of her cold, canned beans.

"I want a hamburger," she said around the mouthful as Hobson stepped up beside her.

He chuckled, looking up into the night sky. The stars were out, brighter than ever.

"Roast beef with mashed potatoes and gravy, and Yorkshire pudding for me," he said wistfully.

"I've never had a hamburger. Or roast beef or mashed pota-toes or Yorkie pudding."

"Yorkshire. Really? None of it?"

"I've only been *alive* for two years, really," she said. "And I haven't found any good restaurants in that time."

There was a long silence as Hobson continued to stare up at the stars and Hunter finished off her terrible beans.

"The sky was never this clear," said the Corporal. "Between pollution and the lights from all our cities, you could never see the stars like this."

"I have a friend who hopes that out of all of this, we can find some good. As terrible as this is..."

She looked toward Grieve and Hutch, who were cleaning their weapons together, chatting about something that caused them both to laugh. Wiggins stood guard. Ransom and Arthur sat huddled close together in quiet conversation -- Hunter hoped the girl was getting through.

"Would any of us even be speaking to each other in the world as it was?" she asked. "A retired Sergeant sharing a joke with a criminal? A member of the royal family spending time with an amateur archer from Canada? A member of the Coldstream Guards talking about the stars with a Soviet weapon?"

Like Hobson, she now looked to the stars.

"And up there, we had Commonwealth, Soviet and icaran forces working together."

"Out of the ashes rises the Phoenix?"

"One can hope."

"One can hope," he said, nodding then sighing. "I'm sorry for the behaviour of the Prince. He's young and he was never ex-pected to ever be in a position of responsibility."

"I was never exposed to young people," she said. "My whole life, I was surrounded by scientists and doctors. My whole frame of reference for how younger people think and act is a young woman from the Vimy Ridge named Cortez -- and now Harley Ransom. I should know that not everyone would be like them, but it didn't occur to me that a Prince would be so..."

"Not all Princes are the kind from fairy tales."

Hunter nodded as if she understood. Fairy tales were not something to which she'd been exposed and while she had a general idea of what they entailed, she wasn't sure what they had to do with royalty. But she understood enough to know that Hobson was, in an indirect way, acknowledging that Arthur had failed to live up to the expectations of many, including Hunter and her people. Including Hobson himself.

"Not everyone knows who they should be," she said, still staring into the stars. "Sometimes it takes a long time to discover who you are, and even longer to *decide* who you are. The Prince has a chance here that everyone deserves. He has a choice."

Though Hobson nodded, when he glanced back to Ransom and Arthur, Hunter was sure she saw disappointment in his eyes, as if he knew that Arthur had already made his choice.

"Get some sleep," she said, as gently as she could figure out how. "The morning will come quickly and we have a long day ahead."

The words still echoed in her head and no matter how Ransom tried to rationalize them, the truth wouldn't go away. Arthur had no desire to fight the invaders and actually felt surrender and even death were the better option.

A two hour march at dawn, softly talking with Arthur the whole way, had done nothing to change the Prince's outlook. So she'd tried another tack and she had no idea how it was working. If it was working.

Tugging off her toque, she stuffed it in her pocket and ran a hand through her unruly mass of red curls. Taking a deep breath, she closed her eyes momentarily, enjoying the crispness of the air, the warmth of the early morning sun on her face, the sound of the river passing by far below.

She stood in a small clearing at the edge of a steep cliff, far enough from the rest of the group that she could consider herself alone, but close enough to run back if they or she encountered any ril-galas. Or human traitors.

The encounter at the old castle still made her feel sick. Humans selling out humans. It was disgusting, but the more she thought about it, the less it should have surprised her. Humanity had been selling each other out for centuries or longer -- the only difference here was that they were selling each other out to a different species instead of each other. Hunter had spoken several times of a brighter future, but it was so hard to see most times.

And with Arthur, who they had wanted so badly to be a symbol of hope, now seeming to be the exact opposite...

Feeling tears well up in her eyes, she quickly wiped them away as she heard the crunch of footsteps approaching.

"I was wondering where you'd gotten to," said Arthur, his voice still sullen, but a slight smile pricking at one corner of his mouth.

"And here I am," she said in her near-perfect imitation of his voice.

He immediately scowled.

"I told you I don't like it when you do that."

"Sorry," she said, favouring him with her brightest smile. "I just wanted to see if it was good enough. Forgive me?"

After a moment, his scowl disappeared and he nodded.

"So...," he said slowly. "We're alone out here."

She smirked.

"And?"

"And... I know you like me, you made that clear."

She had, hadn't she? Her smile faltered, if only momentarily, and the Prince didn't seem to notice. Or if he did, interpreted it through his own lens. Of course he wouldn't consider that her interest in him was rooted in impressing upon him the importance of what they were trying to do -- that would have taken too much self-reflection. Arthur was too busy concentrating on her and specific parts of her rather than what she'd been saying.

Of course, she'd done nothing to discourage it and even gone so far as to pop a couple of the buttons on her shirt when going to speak with him. It had seemed at the time like the easiest way to get his attention and hopefully get him to start listening.

But he hadn't listened.

And so there they were.

"Are you saying, Your Highness, that we should...?"

"Yeah, I mean why not? We're probably going to be dead soon, may as well enjoy ourselves."

"So get naked then."

Dropping her jacket onto the ground, Ransom moved toward the edge of the cliff and began undressing, setting her clothes gently on a large boulder at her side. She could hear Arthur behind her, taking off his clothes with almost manic speed. Coming up behind her, the Prince pressed himself against her and she turned to face him, pushing him away gently. He looked her up and down twice.

"Don't get ahead of yourself," she said. "Turn around."

Reluctant to give up the view, he hesitated for a moment before following her instruction. Once he had, she stepped up and pressed herself into his back in much the same way he had done to her. They were nearly the same height, her mouth brushing against the back of his neck. Reaching around, she laid her right hand flat against his belly and slowly slid it upward to his chest, feeling his breath quicken, and then up to his neck and then over his mouth.

And then reached around with her left hand a slid the knife between his ribs, angled upward, the tip of the blade piercing Prince Arthur's heart.

He twitched, but she held him tightly, silently, as he died. When she felt his body begin to go slack, Ransom withdrew the knife and shoved, and the last surviving member of the British Monarchy tumbled forward over the cliff. When his body hit the rocks below with a crunch, Ransom flung the knife away, over the cliff and as far down the river as she could manage, wiped the blood from her hand and quickly dressed.

Running back through the woods, she stumbled out where the rest of the party was resting and rehydrating, and she put on a mask of shock and horror.

"He jumped."

Everyone turned toward her. Hobson shot to his feet.

"What?"

"He jumped," she said breathlessly. "Arthur, he... he just jumped."

When they all ran through the trees and toward the cliff, Ransom ran with them, though a slight step behind.

When they arrived at the edge and looked down and saw Arthur's broken body, she didn't stand with them. She sunk to the ground, her back against the boulder.

When they asked her what had happened, she told them.

"He wanted us to... He came and found me and took off all his clothes. I told him no. That I wasn't interested. And he... took it badly," she said, drawing a shaky breath. "So he said fine, but he said it like it was an insult -- *'fine.'* And he said we're all dead anyway and he just fucking *jumped*."

Some people were sad, some were angry, some were both. But under a lot of it, Ransom could sense a current of guilty relief -- or she thought she could. Hutch had been right all along, that Arthur was never going to be what they needed him to be. Now they wouldn't have to go back to Edinburgh with that disappointment. Now someone else could step up and be the symbol they needed. Be the leader they needed.

Ransom looked up at Hunter, who had stepped over to her and squatted at her side.

"Are you all right?"

"More or less," said Ransom, shrugging.

"He didn't... do anything?"

"To me? No," she said, shaking her head. "It wasn't like that. He just..."

Trailing off, Ransom rubbed both hands over her face. There was a faint smell of blood on her left hand.

"I guess it's like we said the other night," she said quickly as Hobson joined them. "Some people can't handle the new normal. Those people who attacked us couldn't. Maybe... I dunno, maybe he -- Arthur -- maybe knowing his old life, which was pretty fucking cushy, was never coming back... maybe it broke him?"

Hobson nodded, sadly. He looked older than he had an hour ago.

"Arthur...," he said, pausing and clearing his throat. "Arthur was the youngest of the Royal Family and the most sheltered. His brother went to the Commonwealth Military College in Dover, but Arthur had no desire to do anything like that."

The Corporal seemed very uncomfortable speaking of the recently-deceased in negative terms.

"He wasn't cut out to be a leader," he said.

"Or a survivor," added Hunter.

Hobson shot her a disapproving look and she shrugged.

"He wasn't," she said. "I wish it were otherwise, but it's the truth -- he said himself several times that we'd be better off dead. That he decided to make that decision for himself shouldn't have surprised any of us."

"I just... I have a lot of guilt," said Hobson.

The way he said it made Ransom's heart break a little.

"This isn't your fault," she said emphatically.

"I know. My guilt isn't... It's because all along, ever since I took up the lead in protecting Arthur, I kept wishing, kept thinking how much better things would have been if it had been Edward -- his brother -- who had survived rather than him."

Hunter smiled sympathetically. To Ransom, though, it looked more like someone faking an emotion she didn't quite feel. Not that she thought Hunter uncaring, but knowing -- now -- the woman's background, there were other things that made sense. Her stand-offish nature, her awkwardness in more delicate conversation. Hunter probably didn't feel things in quite the same way as those with a 'normal' upbringing, whatever that might have been. And Ransom certainly couldn't be one to judge another for putting on a mask for people.

"Never feel guilty for thinking of the bigger picture," said the psychic weapon.

"I'm sorry he couldn't be what you... what we all hoped he would be."

"What matters now is how we move forward," said Hunter, standing.

Ransom stood as well and a second later Hobson followed suit, wincing as one of his knees made a popping sound.

"I'd like to retrieve the body," he said.

Feeling a wave of panic rise in her gut, it was only through sheer willpower that Ransom kept her face neutral. The odds that the fall had broken Arthur enough to disguise a stab wound were astronomical. If they retrieved the body, someone would surely notice... but Hunter was shaking her head.

"We don't have the equipment to climb down, nor do we have the luxury of time to find another way to the bottom," she said. "I'm sorry, we have to leave him."

There was a pause where Ransom was sure Hobson was going to protest, but instead he just nodded.

Ransom tried not to breathe a sigh of relief.

"Do we have anyone on board who knows *anything* about the udukiin?" asked Radko, hurrying off the shuttle and into the nearby crew lounge that had, once again, been drafted into serving as a makeshift briefing room for command.

El Bahari slowly shook her head.

"Nothing beyond the basic species introduction classes we all took at the Military College."

"What about the Tianlong?"

"Zhang claims to know as little as we do," said Owens.

"But he agreed not to engage them until we know what's going on?"

"Yes," said Owens, nodding. "His exact words were 'I'm not an idiot.'"

Running a hand through his hair, Radko turned to Cagliari.

"Kestrel? Anything?"

She shook her head.

"We steered clear of the Shattered World just like everyone else."

"Everyone except ATC Castle," said el Bahari.

"Yeah, that's what I was about to say -- we know ATC Castle went in, *and*," she said, pausing for emphasis. "We know Sigurdsson went in to return that Matriarch."

It was the first time Cagliari had mentioned the Matriarch aspect of Sigurdsson's side adventure, keeping it quiet at Radko's request, and he watched el Bahari's reaction. It was slight surprise, but not shock -- more like surprise that a suspicion had been proven correct.

"So," he said. "Do we think they're friendly?"

El Bahari actually laughed at that. Radko was fairly certain it was the first time he'd ever heard her laugh and it was a much lighter sound than he'd expected.

"They haven't tried to attack yet -- that's about as far as I'm willing to go. And," she conceded. "They want to talk, which means your friend may have made a good impression."

A few moments of silence passed before Radko spoke again.

"Then I guess we have a chat with whatever the hell a Kaigor Kai Rii is."

"You," said el Bahari.

"Me what?"

"The Kaigor Kai Rii wants to speak with you not us. The udukiin have been very specific in that."

Leaning against the bulkhead, Radko rubbed his eyes and sighed.

"They want me to go over to their ship, don't they?"

It was barely a question and everyone knew he didn't need them to answer.

"Alone," he said.

"Yeah," said Owens.

"Well, tell them I'm on my way, but I'm bringing a pilot," said Radko, nodding to Cagliari, who nodded back. "It's been a long time since I logged any flight time."

"Understood," said el Bahari. "I'll let them know."

"This is fucking creepy, Finn," said Cagliari as the shuttle glided toward the gaping maw that was the udukiin flagship's landing bay.

She was entirely correct -- it looked like they were flying into the mouth of some immense space predator. Everything about the ship, from its hull to its weapon emplacements to the landing bay deck plates and bulkheads was a shade of red. Some a deep, blood red and some a bright, vibrant red that reminded Radko of the lipstick an ex-girlfriend of his had worn almost constantly. Her name had been Yvette, she was from France and she was very likely dead now, he realised.

He sighed. Exhaustion was turning him morbid.

Cagliari heard the sigh and interpreted it as something it wasn't.

"Sorry, I'll stop."

"No, no, I'm just tired. You're right, it's fucking creepy."

As they fully entered the bay, Cagliari whistled softly, looking at several large fighter craft racked along the walls. They were big -- bigger than any fighters the Commonwealth had ever had -- but they were clearly fighters. However, unlike the Argentavis, they appeared built for raw power. The Argentavis was a superiority fighter. These were large hammers.

A glowing ring suddenly flared to life just below the surface of the deck plates and began pulsing.

"I'm assuming that's where I land," said Cagliari, almost to herself.

She gently set down and confirmed breathable air outside, then cycled the shuttle's airlock. When she popped open the exterior door, she took an involuntary step backward.

Right outside stood four udukiin, armed with tall staves and looking less friendly than one would expect of a welcome party for an invited guest.

"You are Radko?" asked one of the udukiin, jabbing a finger toward Cagliari's chest.

She shoved the finger aside before it made contact with her breast.

"Hands to yourself, you-"

A knife was at her throat. One of the other udukiin had drawn the sharp curved blade from a sheath affixed to its armoured vest.

And suddenly that udukiin had a REV-2 pistol in its face as Radko stepped down from the shuttle and into the hangar.

"I'm Radko," he said. "And I'm fucking tired of being invited onto people's ships and having weapons pointed at me."

He looked each of the four udukiin in the eye. He hoped he was looking them in the correct set of eyes.

"Your Kaigor Kai Rii invited me here," he said. "And I'm pretty sure it wasn't so my friend and I could be threatened by you."

"Very true."

Looking up to the source of the gravelly voice, Radko and Cagliari saw a fifth udukiin standing about three meters away, carrying a similar, but more elaborately carved staff.

"I am Udrach Kai Togru," said the new udukiin. "I welcome you aboard Her Glorious Vengeance."

At an elaborate hand signal from Udrach, the four udukiin guards backed off and so Radko holstered his sidearm.

"Do you want me to stay with the ship?" asked Cagliari.

Radko shook his head and she hopped down with him.

"Kaigor Kai Rii awaits," said Udrach, motioning for them to follow.

It unsettled Radko that the four guards fell in behind them, but he supposed it was understandable. He and Cagliari were, after all, humans who had been invited onto an udukiin cruiser. It was far from a normal or comfortable situation for either side. They were led through the impressively arched red corridors of the cruiser -- Her Glorious Vengeance, as the udukiin called it. Radko had to admit the name had a certain ring to it and one could certainly never mistake the purpose for which the ship was designed.

They were led in silence, neither Udrach nor the other udukiin saying a word as they traveled deep into the heart of Her Glorious Vengeance and it wasn't until they were led into a large chamber, the walls lined with armed udukiin soldiers that Cagliari spoke up -- and even then it was a whisper.

"I kind of expected we'd have seen Sigurdsson by now," she said.

"Silence!"

One of the udukiin guards swung the butt of his staff hard into the small of Cagliari's back, sending her sprawling onto the deck plates with a yelp of pain. Teeth clenched, hand on his pistol, Radko spun to face the offending guard but before he could react there was a snarl and a bark and Jaeger was there. The dog had placed himself between Cagliari and her attacker and the udukiin immediately backed up two steps and... and knelt. Head bowed.

And every udukiin in the room tapped their staff on the floor three times.

"Welcome to Her Glorious Vengeance," said a very familiar voice.

"Kaigor Kai Rii," chanted the udukiin.

Radko saw Frankenstein -- Frankenstein was there? -- helping Cagliari to her feet and then he looked to the other side of the long chamber where a pair of massive doors had parted and where the Kaigor Kai Rii now stood.

Hands on hips.

Smirking.

Fucking beautiful.

"Freyja..?"

Her smile broadened and they walked toward each other, both trying very very hard not to just break decorum and run. When they finally met, after what seemed like ages, the pair just stood awkwardly for a moment, staring at each other.

"For a while there," said Sigurdsson. "I wasn't sure I'd see you again."

"For a while there, I was feeling the same way."

And then she reached out, grabbed him by the front of his uniform and pulled him into a kiss.

Several moments later they separated, feeling dozens of eyes upon them.

"So, uh," said Radko, clearing his throat. "You're, what, a guest of this Kaigor Kai Rii? I take it you got the Matriarch back safely?"

"Uh... we need to talk."

He frowned. She stepped back and spread her arms and for the first time he really noticed what she was wearing. It was one of the armoured vests like the udukiin wore - though sized perfectly for Sigurdsson -- and some kind of armour on her...

His frown deepened and then his eyes widened as he locked eyes with Sigurdsson. Her smile had faded slightly and appeared to now be more hopeful than the joy that had brought it forth previously.

"Is that...?"

"Yeah, the Matriarch. I'm not a guest of Kaigor Kai Rii, Finn. I *am* Kaigor Kai Rii," she said, and it almost sounded like an apology. "Like I said, we need to talk."

For a moment, Radko didn't know what to say, and by the time he had begun to form a response in his mind, Sigrudsson was nodding to one of the udukiin.

"Udrach, get Cags something to eat," she said, then smiled slightly at Cagliari. "Elgraphaar can fill you in on what's been going on."

"Um. Okay."

Kaigor Kai Rii nudged Radko with her elbow.

"Follow me."

So he did. Back through the large doors by which she'd entered, down a short, blood-red hallway and into a surprisingly small room. A pair of udukiin guards had followed them, but stayed in the hallway and Sigurdsson closed the door as she and Radko entered. He was relieved it would be just the two of them.

"Might want to sit down," said Sigurdsson, a very faint nervous tremble in her voice. She nodded toward a table set in the centre of the room, four chairs around it.

As Radko sat down at the small table, Sigurdsson picked up an oddly-shaped bottle and two equally oddly-shaped glasses from a nearby shelf. Uncorking the bottle, she poured a translucent, greenish liquid into each glass until they were half full. Radko wondered if there was some intent to that -- optimist versus pessimist kind of thing -- but as Sigurdsson recorked the bottle, set it aside and settled in across from him, he looked into her blue eyes and didn't care about metaphors.

Sigurdsson picked up her glass and swirled the liquid.

"It's better than it looks," she said.

"I should hope so."

Lifting his glass, Radko could detect several different aromas from the liquid. Freshly cut grass. Cinnamon. Ginger. Lime. Locomotive. Though he didn't make any assumptions that any of those things were actually in the drink -- it was one of the most absurd things about humanity, our innate ability to smell, taste or see the familiar in the unfamiliar. Ask any human what any strange type of meat tasted like and almost invariably the answer would be chicken.

He took a sip. The taste was strange, but not unpleasantly so, and it left a nice warmth behind when he swallowed.

"How potent is this stuff? And what's it called?"

"It's called *baze* and it's barely alcoholic. I'd guess maybe three percent? Hard to say for sure -- the udukiin don't label shit like we do -- but I had four glasses the other night and was barely buzzed. One glass won't do you in, I promise."

Chuckling, he took another sip.

"So," he said. "What the fuck?"

She laughed and it made him smile.

"Yeah, it's been an eventful few days," she said.

Giving him the short version of her adventure -- the crash landing on the Shattered World, the ril-galas presence, the first encounter with the udukiin, her embarrassingly slow realisation that she wasn't so much returning a War Matriarch as becoming one. Her final acceptance of the fact and her decision to use it to do some good.

"And you accepted the title of Kaigor Kai Rii?" asked Radko.

"It's not that simple, Finn. It's not... it's not a job you apply for," she said, slowly spreading her three-fingered hand on the tabletop. "It's an ancient udukiin term. It means Matriarch of the Three."

She smiled a little as she saw the understanding in his eyes.

"I wish I'd been that quick to catch on," she said.

"And now you're leading the udukiin to war?"

Her smile faltered.

"Yeah. I am. I don't want to -- I mean I want us to win this war, but I don't like the idea of thousands of udukiin living or dying at my whim," she said. "But what I like even less is the idea of this war continuing indefinitely. More friends dying. Maybe you dying."

Glancing away, she wiped her eyes quickly and Radko pretended not to notice.

"I didn't want to be Kaigor Kai Rii," she said. "Maybe that's why it took me so long to figure it out -- I was in denial or something. But then I realised what I could do. What I could accomplish with the udukiin marching behind me."

There was another long moment where they just held each other's gaze before Sigurdsson again spoke.

"Do you trust me to do this?"

Reaching across the table, he took her blue hand in his own.

"Without question."

They just sat there like that, hand in hand, for a long time until Sigurdsson -- so reluctantly it seemed to cause her physical discomfort -- broke the spell.

"We can't do this right now," she said quietly, lowering her head into her palm. "I want to, believe me..."

"But time is not on our side," said Radko, finishing her thought.

"Yeah."

Looking up at him again, Sigurdsson smiled sadly.

"Even when this is all over," she said. "Even if it ends the way we want it to... I'm a goddamned udukiin War Matriarch. You're a Commonwealth Naval officer. How do we even...?"

"We live in the moment, Freyja. We take whatever happy moments we can find and we hold onto them like our lives depend on it. We're fighting for the people who can't fight for themselves," said Radko. "But we're also fighting for ourselves. To give us a chance to have a life again."

"To go to a cottage and have some steaks," she said.

"Exactly. So let's solve one problem before we start on another."

"And by 'solve one problem' you mean just win a war," she said with a grin.

"Yep."

"No problem."

"So," he said, turning serious again. "Just how large is the udukiin force you can lead?"

"That I *can* lead? Fucking huge. Four million," she said, quickly holding up a hand when his eyes widened. "That's basically every adult udukiin -- they're all trained to fight, but there's no way I'm leading an entire species into battle. I accepted this Kaigor Kai Rii thing, but I'm putting limits on it. They want to march -- all of them -- but I've laid out some ground rules."

Radko leaned forward, listening. It didn't even occur to him that sitting there with Sigurdsson, talking about their future, the future of the war, even the weird green drink, was the most comfortable and relaxed he'd been... well, since the last time he'd sat down and talked with Sigurdsson.

"I brought a hundred thousand soldiers," she said, surprisingly nonchalant about a number that would more than double what the Commonwealth could deploy. "Half here and half on Her Divine Retribution. I left two more capital ships back in the Priex -- Her Righteous Fury and Her Graceful Violence -- along with the rest of the soldiers. They're defending the Priex and are in reserve as reinforcements if we need them. On Earth or anywhere else."

"Shit," he said. "That's impressive. And side note: those are some serious ship names."

Sigurdsson grinned broadly.

"I know, I fucking love it. Ask me the name of my ship."

"What the name of your ship?"

Narrowing her eyes, Sigurdsson scowled.

"Her Glorious Vengeance," she said in a low, near-snarl. And then laughed.

"Bloody hell I missed you."

"Same here, Finn," she said, taking the last sip from her cup.

"But seriously," he said. "This udukiin thing. I mean, that prophecy sounds ominous, no?"

"What, about leading the udukiin to their rightful place in the universe? I guess," said Sigurdsson. "Aylarr says everyone interpreted that as meaning conquering or ruling or just fighting wars, but here's the thing, Finn."

She leaned in closer.

"No one bothered to ask the udukiin what *they* thought it meant. No one. And honestly the udukiin don't give a shit about conquering, they just don't think like that. They're happy with their Shattered World and their Priex."

"So..."

"So, what if their rightful place in the galaxy *is as its protectors*? Everyone acts like the udukiin are some scary war-loving psychos, but fuck Finn, they're like an entire society of Radkos. They're all true believers in doing what's right. They fought and beat the ril-galas the last time they tried to invade, for fucks sake."

"An entire society of Radkos?"

Sigurdsson grinned.

"You get the point. We've always needed allies, no matter what the dipshits in charge think. You brought in the Soviets and the icarans and now I've brought the udukiin. This could be the turning point we've been looking for."

Radko nodded. She was right -- having the udukiin on board changed the playing field in a dramatic way. He was hesitant to say it tipped the scales in their favour -- the ril-galas presence was too strong and too entrenched to think of Joint Task Force One as anything other than underdogs -- but the udukiin presence made the odds of success and survival at the Hornet's Nest that much greater.

"Speaking of the dipshits in charge," said Sigurdsson. "How are things on the home-ish front at Thor's Hammer?"

His entire demeanour changed, he knew it. And he knew Sigurdsson saw it immediately and the look of concern that came over her face both touched him and made him angry at himself for allowing his feelings to show so...

No, he thought. Sigurdsson was the last person from whom he needed to be hiding his feelings. So he told her the whole story, with as much detail as he could without losing his composure. He watched as Sigurdsson's jaw muscles clenched and unclenched and clenched again as she heard about what had happened to Cortez and the scowl she wore was one that would cause enemies to rethink their life choices.

"Freyja," he said gently. "I know what you're thinking -- believe me, I do -- but we can't let ourselves be blinded by this."

"What they did was state-sanctioned murder-"

"You don't think I'm aware of what they did? You don't think I spent every minute thinking up ways to get her out of there?" Radko said gently despite the firmness of the words. "Anna was executed because of her friendship with me. But I have to keep reminding myself that my mission -- our mission, the mission Anna died protecting -- is exponentially more important than my personal need for revenge."

Standing, Sigurdsson paced the room twice, then stopped, her back to Radko.

"Jesus fuck I'm scared, Finn," she said quietly.

Radko blinked and stared at the back of her head.

"What?"

"I'm scared," she repeated. "I'm scared of me."

"What do you mean?" he asked, standing and quietly pushing in his chair before approaching and placing a hand on Sigurdsson's shoulder. She immediately and unconsciously reached up and put her hand over his.

"Back on the Shattered World," she said slowly. "Jaeger was hurt. Badly. And I lost it, I went absolutely apeshit and, see, the Matriarch thing, it's not just me that's affected. She's got this psychic bond to the udukiin. And Finn I could feel my rage through them -- all of them. I could feel it reflecting back in waves. They flew into a rage because I did, and I used it. I used *them* like I was taking a swing with my own fist."

"Against the ril-galas."

She nodded, conceding the point, but it was a side-point to what she was trying to say.

"But it was still because I let my emotions get the better of me. I reacted. And I do that all the time, I react. Just now I was ready to fly straight to Thor's Hammer and lead a boarding party to drag DeFreitas and Upshaw to the nearest airlock and blow them into space."

"Freyja..."

"No, Finn, this is a big deal. I know I've been responsible for other peoples' lives before, but at Fort Hathaway it was like a hundred people. Now, with basically every udukiin ready to follow me into battle, I could have the lives of the entire species in my hands. With one wrong, rage-fueled decision, I could be responsible for their extinction."

"The fact that you're aware of it," Radko said, touching her cheek to make her look at him. "Means the chances of it happening are slim. And for the first time since we first spoke over that shitty comm line between the Vimy Ridge and Fort Hathaway, you and I are fighting on the same front. We're together now and we stay that way -- we help each other, we support each other and we stop each other from fucking things up. Right?"

"Yeah."

She didn't sound convinced.

"But?"

"But," said Sigurdsson. "I don't know how much the udukiin would question the decisions of Kaigor Kai Rii. You have el Bahari to question-"

"Every goddamned thing I do."

"Pretty much," said Sigurdsson, a smile briefly flickering to life. "Believe me, I trust myself with you here more than I do otherwise, but you're not *here* here. You're on the Vimy Ridge and I really -- really fucking *really* -- need a voice of reason at my side."

"Freyja, what's the one thing that even people who hate me would admit I'm really good at?"

"Resources. Finding what you have available and using it to its max potential."

"I'm glad you came up with that so quickly or it could have gotten awkward," he said with a smirk. "But yes, you're right. When the world ended, I had my ship and crew, I had a team of Rangers and I had a psychic. Then I got some icaran commandos and a Soviet carrier. You have Elgraphaar, Aylarr and Frankenstein. And Jaeger. I don't know Aylarr or Frankenstein very well, but I know Elgraphaar and Jaeger and they're both stubborn and not afraid to tell you when they disagree."

Sigurdsson chuckled. It was true, all of it.

"Use what you have at your disposal," said Radko. "Back then, I had input from Owens and Grey and Locaris and Quon. Now I have Owens and el Bahari and Rhekarr and Cagliari and you. I once read a paper by some Commonwealth Admiral who said commanding a ship was a lonely post; that the captain stood apart from his crew. I think that's bullshit. I think that a commander -- Naval or otherwise -- who stands apart from those he commands is a weak commander."

"And not a commander that people will follow when shit hits the fan," said Sigurdsson, nodding at first, then laughing and shaking her head. "Fucking hell Finn, how do you do that?"

"Do what?"

"Make people feel better about themselves. Make them feel like everything will be okay."

"Because, in spite of everything we're going through, I believe everything *will* be okay. We will fight. It will be bloody and brutal and," he said, his eyes flashing. "We will win because I won't allow any other outcome."

Sigurdsson smiled.

"*We* won't allow any other outcome."

"So sayeth the Kaigor Kai Rii and so shall it be done," he said, with overwrought seriousness. But it made her laugh and he was yet again struck by how much he loved the sound.

"You're an ass."

"I am indeed."

"The Constitution states that should the position of Deputy Prime Minister become vacant during the term of the sitting Prime Minister," said Khaifa. "An election to fill the vacancy shall be held at the earliest practical opportunity."

Ironhorse, sitting opposite the doctor's desk, opened his mouth to speak, but Khaifa held up her hand for him to wait. They were in her office in a hastily-called meeting after she had spent a long time in discussions with Amadou Babacar, a lawyer who had served the Commonwealth for many years prior to the ril-galas invasion. Babacar sat with Khaifa and Ironhorse, as did a middle-aged woman named Truus Van Der Berg.

Babacar had been expected -- after all, Ironhorse had helped Khaifa track him down. But Van Der Berg had been a surprise to him and one about which he wasn't sure what to think. Her sharp features reminded him of a bird of prey and her grey eyes seemed to see through everything, which was understandable given that she had served in the CSID -- the Commonwealth Security and Intelligence Division -- for years. CSID was the Commonwealth's civilian law enforcement and intelligence agency. Van Der Berg had been a spyhunter.

"In the event elections are not practical," continued Khaifa. "There are clear directions as to who can be appointed to the role on an interim basis."

She nodded to Babacar, who picked up where she left off.

"Essentially, you go through the list of extant elected officials -- excluding those assigned to defense and security portfolios --

and appoint the highest ranking. If that person is unable to assume the role, you proceed to the next highest and so on until the role has been filled."

"Do we think DeFreitas is aware of this?" asked Van Der Berg. It was the first time she'd spoken and to Ironhorse, her voice had an undercurrent of ice. Or of cold steel. It made him uncomfortable, which was a feeling to which he was unaccustomed.

"DeFreitas seemed to be under the impression that the current state of the Commonwealth gives him these kind of emergency powers," said Khaifa.

"Which it does not," said Babacar. "Not without an official vote in the House of Commons."

Khaifa nodded.

"But the bigger question is do we think DeFreitas is still the one making the decisions? Ironhorse?"

The request for his opinion was unexpected and it took him a moment to respond.

"I think he's still making the decisions," he said carefully. "But I'm not sure he's making them based on all available information."

Looking into him with those creepy eyes, Van Der Berg nodded, then turned back to Khaifa.

"As we all know, Upshaw has essentially become a firewall between the remaining government of the Commonwealth and its citizens," she said. "All information flows through her and it only makes sense that some of what comes to her does not get passed along."

"However," said Babacar. "The Prime Minister knows full well the extent of what he can and cannot do. I have worked with him in the past -- he was too well-versed in the Constitution then for me to believe he is being led along the garden path by Upshaw now."

Leaning back in her chair, Khaifa began slowly drumming her fingers on her desk.

"So potentially we have a Prime Minister knowingly violating the Constitution, appointing an ATC Castle exec to the second most powerful position in our government."

"And there's the matter of the execution," added Van Der Berg.

"Yes," agreed Babacar. "At the very least, the quick trial and summary judgement were gross violations of Anna Cortez's Charter Rights."

Leaning forward, resting his forearms on his knees, Ironhorse frowned.

"Sorry, maybe I'm missing something -- I'm just a soldier, not a law expert -- but what's the plan here? I mean, yeah, it seems DeFreitas is doing stuff he shouldn't and I'm in total agreement about the Cortez shit... but what are you going to do about it?"

"That's the problem, Captain," said Khaifa. "I just don't know yet."

But the somewhat uncomfortable look in her eye and the way her fingers, drumming on the tabletop suddenly froze, told him that she did know what she was going to do. Or, at least, what she thought she was going to do

And, he realised, he was pretty sure he knew as well.

There was only one thing he could think of that would require a spymaster, a constitutional law expert and a special forces soldier all in the same meeting.

41

Another text-only message had come in from Ironhorse and el Bahari, despite standing on the command deck of the Vimy Ridge, had taken the risk of reading it. The message had been short and simple:

Khaifa meeting with expert in constitutional law (Babacar, Amadou) and ex-CSID investigator (Van Der Berg, Truus). Upshaw appointed Deputy PM, appears unconstitutional. Unsure of next step, but suspect potential leadership challenge.

Though el Bahari had done her best to maintain her calm, she hadn't been entirely successful.

"Everything all right, Commander," asked Owens.

He was starting to be a little too perceptive for her own good.

Was everything all right? Of course it wasn't. Everything was precisely the opposite of all right and, if Ironhorse was correct -- and she trusted his judgement without hesitation -- things were about to get significantly more complicated. And dangerous.

"We're currently surrounded by three icaran warships, an infamous Soviet destroyer and a pair of udukiin cruisers, Owens," she said instead. "Two years ago this would have been the makings of an absolute slaughter. Old ways of thinking die hard."

"That was a long time ago," he said. "They're allies now."

"Now," she said with a derisive snort. "But for how long?"

Owens frowned.

"Have you always been such a pessimist?"

"I'm not a pessimist, Owens -- I'm a realist. Someone on this ship of fools has to be," she said. She was angry now, and too tightly wound to hold it back. "Two years is not 'a long time ago.' Do you know what was *actually* a long time ago? Slavery. World War II and the Holocaust. The Terror Wars. And we, as a species, are still grappling with the same fear and racism and bigotry that brought us all those things. Now we have outside forces to aim them at instead of just each other."

She pointed toward the sand table, where holographic representations of all the ships hovered around the Carncastle Gate gas giant.

"Do you honestly believe that this will continue? That if we manage to defeat the ril-galas and drive them from Earth, we will all be one big, happy family? Because, Mister Owens, I would point out that humanity's track record for keeping peace with each other, let alone keeping peace with alien governments, is exceptionally poor."

"People can change, Commander."

"Some people can change," she corrected. "Not all. Not most. Even now we're working against each other."

"What do you mean?" he asked, eyes narrowing slightly.

"Oh, don't be naïve. Radko is doing this all on his own authority, isn't he? Against orders to have no communication with the Soviets and icarans? And what happened with Lieutenant Cortez is, I would say, humans working against each other. ATC Castle chased and shot down the shuttle carrying Sigurdsson to the Shattered World and, as you yourself told me, they're now making a major move against Hajek."

"Radko is also bringing people together."

"Of course he is. But it remains that he is -- rightly or wrongly -- creating a faction within humanity that is and will continue to be at odds with other factions. I want to be clear, Owens, I don't doubt the Commander's motives," she said, putting extra care into her enunciation. "But I feel the game he's really playing is far more dangerous than the game he thinks he's playing."

"And what game do you think he's really playing?"

"I don't think he's aware of it, I believe him when he says what he's trying to accomplish," she said. "But I fear that he's inadvertently laying the groundwork for civil war."

"Radko does not want civil war, Commander."

Taking a deep breath, she willed herself not to snap at him.

"You aren't listening," el Bahari said, with a level of patience that surprised even her. "I don't believe he wants it, but he is creating the conditions under which a civil war could arise and no one on this ship is willing to admit it or question it. Loyalty is admirable, Owens -- blind loyalty is simply stupidity under another name."

She was saved from any continuation of the debate by an announcement that Radko's shuttle had returned -- and by an urgent ping from her tablet. Given the content of the last message, el Bahari couldn't help but open the message, and when she did, she swore.

"The Adirondack has broken off from the group at Casandra Hajek and is pursuing the Azrael's Tear," she said, looking back up at Owens. "Singh is supposed to be part of this rendezvous, is he not?"

"He is," said Owens, but he was looking at el Bahari with open suspicion. "How do you know what the Adirondack is doing?"

"Oh grow up Owens -- do you think Finn Radko is the only person who can have friends in interesting places? I would think the greater concern should be that Singh is leading an ATC Castle ship right to us."

"The Azrael's Tear has LiDAR-masking-"

"Yes, LiDAR masking armour plating. And as per Cagliari's report, the Adirondack still seemed able to track it."

They both turned as Radko and Cagliari walked onto the command deck.

"Commander," said el Bahari. "You're still alive, so I take it the meeting went well?"

"It did," he said. "As it turns out, Kaigor Kai Rii is Freyja Sigurdsson."

She stared at him. Blinked twice. Owens looked equally shocked.

"What?" they said, almost in perfect unison.

"Long story. The short version is that those two udukiin ships and the soldiers they carry are now part of our task force. Owens, please let the Tianlong and the icaran ships know."

With a nod, Owens set off to do just that.

"Commander, we have a problem," said el Bahari. "An additional problem. It seems the Azrael's Tear attempted to return to its base on Casandra Hajek, but ATC Castle had several ships there in a blockade of sorts."

"Why would they blockade the pirate moon?"

"My guess? They thought you were there or they think you'll be headed there. But the important issue here is that the Azrael's Tear fled and is being pursued by the Adirondack."

"And Singh is supposed to be joining us here."

"Which will lead the Adirondack here."

"Because the Adirondack can somehow track the Azrael's Tear despite the armour plating."

"So we need to intercept the Adirondack," said Cagliari. "Stop them before they get here and blow the operation."

"Agreed," said el Bahari. "As much as I'm loathe to attack another human vessel, the Adirondack must be either destroyed or disabled before it reaches Carncastle Gate."

"I can take Outlaw Squadron," said Cagliari. "Our armour is more advanced than the stuff on the Azrael's Tear -- the Adirondack couldn't see us at all."

"We'll go. The Vimy Ridge, I mean," said Radko. "We can get to the Tear faster than your fighters can under their own power. You can launch Outlaw once we're in range."

"With all due respect, Commander, we need to be here, at Carncastle Gate," said el Bahari. "We -- more specifically you -- are the lynchpin to this whole operation. You can't leave now, you need to coordinate things with our recently-acquired allies."

Cagliari nodded.

"She's right, you need to stay here. But you're right about us getting this done quicker if we launch on-site. Maybe one of the icaran ships?"

"No," said el Bahari, shaking her head. "The second an icaran ship showed up on their LiDAR, Vossek would report back about an incursion into Commonwealth space and it would be flagged as an act of war."

Sighing, she glanced at the small translucent ships floating above the sand table. There was really only one solution that made sense to el Bahari, and she didn't much care for it.

"Sigurdsson," she said finally. "Ask her to transport Outlaw Squadron on Her Glorious Vengeance. The Adirondack violated udukkin space and took aggressive action within the Priex -- they can't claim innocence and they can't classify it an act of war when the confrontation, as far as anyone will know, was provoked by ATC Castle."

It struck el Bahari not for the first time that she was becoming quite good at that type of subterfuge, at twisting things just enough that they remained technically true but became enough of a deception to increase the odds of a favourable outcome. She was, she realised, playing her own game, apart from the games being played by Radko and Upshaw.

Radko, much to el Bahari's relief, nodded his agreement.

"I'll contact Freyja. Cags, get your fighters ready."

42

The mood of the group was understandably sombre, and though no one dared admit it even to themselves, there was also a mild sense of relief. Arthur was dead. The whole reason for undertaking the mission was gone and yet they would also now not have to return to Edinburgh Castle and present the heir to the throne, a symbol of Britain, as a spineless wretch with a death-wish.

In the end, Arthur had gotten what he'd wanted, Hunter supposed. He felt they'd all be better off dead and now he was. Hunter didn't feel she'd be better off dead. Despite all she'd been through, the thought of ending her life had never crossed her mind. She did, however, feel she was better off with Arthur dead.

The thought should have come with some guilt, she knew, but she didn't feel any.

Perhaps one of the advantages of not having a normal mind or the emotional responses of a normal person.

Ransom had been more subdued than usual since Arthur's death, but so had most of the others -- excluding Hutch, who didn't appear to give a damn -- especially Hobson, whose entire post-invasion life had been dedicated to protecting the Prince. Hobson was a good man, a good soldier and the kind of person humanity was going to need if it was to survive the ril-galas, and survive itself afterward. It occurred to Hunter quite by surprise that getting Hobson out of Balmoral and into the fold had become the mission's success story. Arthur had been largely irrelevant from the moment she understood his personality, but Hobson could actually make a difference.

And she'd begun to see a different side of Ransom as well.

Despite her skill with a bow, everyone -- Hunter included -- had a tendency to discount Ransom due to her young age. Hunter should have known better, having seen everyone but Radko make the same mistake with Anna Cortez. There was a leader in the young redhead. The question was whether she was willing to let it out.

She watched Ransom rubbing at her left forearm. She'd been doing it quite a bit since Arthur's death, as if alleviating the itch of a healing cut that wasn't actually there.

"Are you going to be all right?" asked Hunter.

The question seemed to startle Ransom.

"What? Yeah. Yeah, I'll be okay. You know, just... not really how I was expecting things to go."

"Me either. But we've always worked with what we have, so we just have to keep doing that."

Ransom nodded.

"I guess keeping this a secret -- going to Balmoral for Arthur, I mean -- was a pretty good idea after all," she said.

"Unfortunately."

"I'm sorry, Hunter. I'm really sorry. For what it's worth, I think you're right," said Ransom. "The people do need someone to look to as a symbol."

"I'm not sure we're going to find one."

Ransom glanced back at Hobson, then back to Hunter.

"I didn't know what he looked like before we met him. Arthur, I mean."

Hunter didn't respond. She didn't think she was supposed to -- this was Ransom thinking out loud.

"Makes me wonder if anyone would have recognized him when we got back to Edinburgh. If he'd survived, I mean. Could we have brought, like, anyone back and told them it was the heir to the throne?"

A frown began to crease Hunter's brow. She was usually quite good at figuring out what people were talking around when they started half-conversations of the kind Ransom was currently engaged in... but this time she was having a hard time following the meandering trail of thoughts.

"What if...," said Ransom, chewing her lower lip. "Someone could replace him?"

Hunter stopped walking for a moment, then hurried to catch up to Ransom once more.

"What do you mean?"

"Well, I mean we'd have to ask Hobson whether or not Arthur was too famous to pull it off -- I don't think he was, but Hobson would know for sure. And if it's something that's at least possible, we... replace him. We give the people what they need, but what we couldn't get from the real guy: a symbol who can give them hope. Wave a fucking sword at the top of the battlements. Tell everyone to never give up, never surrender -- all the Churchill stuff."

The water burbled by as they walked along the river, getting ever closer to the sea. Hunter watched the water -- water had always fascinated her for some reason -- and rolled Ransom's statement over in her head several times.

"Just temporarily," said the girl, possibly taking Hunter's silence as disapproval. "Get the people inspired, then maybe the fake Arthur dies in battle or something."

"And becomes a true symbol," said Hunter. "An incorruptible memory."

"Yeah, pretty much."

There was a great deal of hope, almost desperate hope, in Ransom's voice.

"Who?

"What?"

"Who would we find to be the replacement Prince, assuming Hobson and the others are willing to proceed?"

Ransom looked at the water. The trees. The sky. She swallowed heavily. Hunter noticed Ransom's hands were shaking and the urge to look inside the girl's mind was strong. But she resisted.

"Me," said Ransom.

Hunter stared, knowing she'd heard the response correctly, but her brain refusing to process it fully.

"You?"

"Do you see another option?" said Ransom, in her near-perfect vocal impression of Arthur.

"But you're... not male."

"I have the body of an athlete," said Ransom in her own voice, shrugging. "I've got broad shoulders from my years with the bow. My boobs aren't very big -- we can hide them by, like, wrapping my chest tightly with fabric. Maybe get me a leather jacket to wear or something. And this..."

She flicked a hand through her unruly mass of curls.

"This can be cut. Shaved even, if we need to."

"You would do that? Give up your identity and become someone else?"

Ransom gave her a sidelong glance and a raised brow in response.

Of course. That was exactly what Hunter had done. She'd given up Quon Li-Chen and become Hunter -- she'd chosen who she wanted to be. And while Ransom's plan was somewhat different in that there had already been a Prince Arthur where

Hunter had never existed previously, there were similarities in the situation and motivations.

Hunter couldn't argue that the people needed a symbol around which to rally and she herself was never going to be that symbol -- aside from her lack of ties to Earth and her lack of history there, she had little doubt that now, once their group returned to Edinburgh, she would also have rumours about her abilities floating around. Her position as a leader in the resistance movement would likely be in jeopardy once they returned, but there was still a chance to give the people what they needed.

All she needed to do was convince Hobson to go along with it, then convince the rest of the team to go along with it, then turn Ransom into a convincing male and make sure no one ever found out the truth.

Easy.

Briefly, she flirted with the idea of trying to use her powers to create a kind of blind spot in people's minds, where they would just accept Ransom-Arthur at face value and not question too much. Ultimately, even if she could figure out how to accomplish it, Hunter doubted she'd have been able to withstand the strain of trying to affect so many minds for so many hours a day -- for who knew how many days. Or months. Hopefully not years, but there was the possibility.

Hunter wasn't certain if Ransom had considered the possible length of her... performance.

"You could be masquerading as Arthur for months," she said.

"I know, I thought of that," said Ransom. "Let's be honest, Hunter, I've been masquerading as a normal person for most of my life. Hiding what I really am. Hiding what I do. This won't be as much of a challenge for me as you think."

"I'm sorry."

"It's fine, it's good to think of the problems we might run into."

"Not for that. I'm sorry that you've had to hide yourself for so long. I know how hard it is. I didn't hide myself, but I didn't know who I was. I suspect they're very similar feelings."

"Yeah, I expect."

"I don't know if your plan will work," said Hunter after a lengthy silence. "It will be a huge risk to even try it. Some people are bound to recognize you."

At that, Ransom actually laughed.

"No they won't. You know how many people at Edinburgh Castle even know my name? Not counting the people here with us now, I can probably count them on one hand. I'm a kid, who the fuck is going to pay me any mind? The only thing they recognize is my hair," she said, twirling a lock around her finger. "And I always wear it down. Half the time you can't even see my face."

The girl shrugged.

"No one will miss Harley Ransom. And hopefully King Arthur can inspire them."

It certainly wasn't ethical and Hunter shouldn't even have been considering it... and yet she was. And considering it very seriously.

Doing the wrong thing for the right reason. It was how Radko had classified his raid on the ATC Castle training facility to resupply the Vimy Ridge and though she thought she'd understood what he'd meant at the time, she realized she hadn't truly understood until that moment. That was also when she realized she'd already made her decision.

"I'll talk with Hobson," she said.

Hobson, as it turned out, was surprisingly amenable to the idea. Hunter had expected it to be a long, drawn out debate, with Hobson steadfastly refusing to budge. Instead, he'd been more concerned with logistics than anything. When Hunter asked him about it, his answer had been very simple.

"I have guarded the Royals for nearly twenty years, Hunter. I don't want everyone's last memory of them to be a boy who refused to face what his subjects faced. The Crown means something to us. It's hard to explain to someone who isn't from the Commonwealth generally, but Britain specifically."

He paused, rubbing the back of his neck and looking like he felt guilty about what he was saying.

"I don't want hundreds of years of history to end with 'and then the last of British Royals jumped off a cliff.'"

Hunter just nodded.

"Do you think she can pull it off?" asked the Corporal.

"You've heard her do the voice."

"I have," he said, nodding. "She'll have to give up the bow. Or at least look like she's worse than she is for a while. The Prince had taken archery lessons, but she's exceptionally good."

"She was a competitor at the Commonwealth Games," said Hunter, surprising herself with the amount of pride evident in her voice, pride on Ransom's behalf at her achievement.

But it was happening. Ransom was going to become Arthur... or at least it could be happening. Hobson had been the first hurdle, but Hunter reminded herself there were still several to overcome.

For the remainder of their daylight trekking, she stayed to herself, planning, plotting, trying to bring forth every objection she could think of and then find a rational response. They were in a desperate situation, everyone knew it, and in some ways that made her job a little easier. She wouldn't necessarily need to completely negate objections -- all she'd need to do was inject some doubt about those objections and show people that the plan could work. The survivors of the human race badly wanted to believe that not only was there a plan, but it was a plan that just might have a chance of succeeding.

Hope could be a powerful thing.

They sat huddled around the small fire, the tight copse of trees hopefully concealing the light from their enemy, the spindly branches and their fall leaves hopefully dissipating the smoke enough to avoid notice. Everyone was silent, all eyes darting back and forth between Hunter and Ransom, who stood at her side. The girl stood straight, met every gaze and didn't project any nervousness or unease at all.

Hunter realised that Ransom, whether any of the group realised it or not, was *auditioning*.

"You've got to be fucking kidding me," said Hutch.

Right on queue.

"We need someone to inspire our people," said Hunter. "We all know it was never going to be Arthur himself, but we have a second chance to make this work."

"But she's a girl," said Hutch. "And we all know what she goddamned well looks like."

He was playing his part exceptionally well. When Hunter had first told Hutch about Ransom's plan, he'd laughed not because he thought it was absurd, but because he'd thought it was fantastic and wanted to help them pull it off. Hutch had never thought much of the actual Prince, but, he had to admit, Ransom was someone who had earned his respect. She was someone whose words and deeds he could trust. Having her in the role of symbolic hero or whatever they wanted to call her was probably the only way their original plan could have succeeded anyway.

But Hunter had asked him to be skeptical in public. Rather pointedly, she had explained that given his history of dissent --

with essentially everything, all the time -- the rest of the group would be more comfortable moving forward if he disagreed at first and was seen to come around, as opposed to if he simply agreed at the outset.

She was about to see if she was right.

Ransom quickly and clearly addressed his two points, saying more or less what she had said privately to Hunter.

"Show of hands," said Ransom. "Who here knew my name before we got on that helicopter?"

Grieve was the only one to raise a hand. Hunter should have, but didn't.

"Now how many knew what I looked like?"

A couple of others raised their hands.

"And how many of those could have identified my face if wasn't framed by this?" she asked, using her hands to flip her hair into the hair.

Everyone but Grieve lowered their hands.

Ransom cleared her throat and when she spoke, she did so in the voice of the dead Prince.

"So out of our entire group," said Ransom-Arthur. "Exactly one of you would have been able to positively identify me without my wild mane of fiery locks? I believe your concern should now be allayed, Mister Hutchings."

No one was looking at Hunter at all any more and more than one mouth was agape.

Hutch just laughed.

"You've got to be fucking kidding me," he said again, but this time more out of amusement.

"Arthur's death doesn't change what we need," said Ransom, in her own voice. "We need a symbol to give people hope."

"So since the one we wanted didn't work out, we just get a fake?" asked Grieve.

"Aren't they all?" said Hobson.

Everyone turned to him.

"How many symbols we've fought for over the years have been everything we thought they were? Our leaders have always been deeply flawed human beings, sometimes worse than the leaders of the people we fought against. Our countries are just social constructs and we fought and died over a thin red line someone drew on a map. Our flags are just pieces of coloured cloth stitched together in a particular way and have over the years stood for subjugation and slavery and intolerance, yet people revere them. Christ knows the Royal family have never been perfect -- I can tell you that the rumours about Arthur's uncle, Prince Gerald, were entirely true -- but they are a powerful symbol nonetheless. Most of them that I knew were not the people they presented themselves to be in public, but those public personas could do marvelous things."

He paused to sip his tea. No one spoke, knowing he had more to say.

"I saw normally stingy people donate to a children's hospital because of a speech by the Queen. I was there when the King convinced the Commonwealth and the Soviets to sit down and draw up the last peace agreement when it seemed neither side would even talk about it let alone put anything in writing. Now, I know I have a greater respect for the Monarchy than most of you. I know that. But regardless of how you feel about the people who have occupied Buckingham Palace over the years, the symbol of the Crown, the symbol of the Monarchy is powerful."

"King George VI and Queen Elizabeth during World War II," said Grieve quietly.

"Walking through London after the Blitz," Hobson said, nodding and taking another sip of tea.

"Defiant. Proud."

"The embodiment of the British resolve."

"Gloriana reborn," said Grieve, holding up his tin cup in Ransom's direction. "The King is dead. Long live the King."

And one by one, the others agreed to the plan.

Now they just had to make it work.

43

Being aboard the udukiin cruiser was uncomfortable for all the pilots, but less so for Cagliari. The rest of Outlaw Squadron -- or the three flights of three she'd brought with her -- had remained in the hangar with their fighters, but Cagliari had joined Sigurdsson on what passed for the command deck on Her Glorious Vengeance. She was still uncomfortable being surrounded by udukiin, but at least she had one friendly face.

Jaeger looked up at her and wagged his tail.

Make that two friendly faces.

Sigurdsson, despite all appearances and her fearsome reputation, was nervous.

"I've never fought a space battle before," she said quietly. "This is Radko's thing, not mine."

"You're not fighting it," said Cagliari, nodding toward the ship's captain.

His name, she was fairly certain, was Gholl and the way he paced the command deck, checking in on every station, Cagliari doubted anyone could possibly be more prepared for a battle.

"Your crew seems to know what they're doing."

Sigurdsson turned toward her, half-smiling.

"I know. I just don't like being out of my element."

"Imagine being sidelined completely. Knowing you can help, but having the one thing you need in order to help being locked away."

"I'm glad we could get them back for you."

"Fuck, so am I!" she said, laughing. "Have you heard of the Royal Sovereign?"

Sigurdsson nodded.

"Radko mentioned it a couple times. Big battleship, right?"

"That's the one," said Cagliari. "My father's company designed it, seriously so far ahead of any other designs that had been proposed it was mind-blowing. But after the shit hit the fan and the Commonwealth asked ATC Castle to finish it, I was shut out. I designed a good quarter of its systems, but I wasn't good enough to help finish the damn thing."

She shook her head as much to clear away the anger as to express her disbelief.

"I need to stop getting so worked up about it, I know. It's just really frustrating."

"You are such a walking contradiction, you know that?"

"What?" said Cagliari, genuinely confused.

"Cags, you're a rich kid, a trust fund kid, a legendary party girl... who also designed some of the most sophisticated star-fighters ever seen. And designed advanced systems on the most sophisticated warship ever built. And," said Sigurdsson, with a shake of her head. "You're only twenty six."

"Well... I'll be twenty seven in a couple of months."

"Still."

"Yeah, but it doesn't change the fact that it seems like I wasted a lot of time on drinking, fucking and getting stoned. Like I wonder what we could have done... I wonder what the Commonwealth's defenses would have looked like if I'd taken all of that energy and put it into projects at the company, rather than pissing it away clubbing," she said, running both hands through her short, blue hair. "Would we have been better prepared for this? Would we have been able to prevent them from taking Earth if we'd gotten the Argentavis into production sooner? If I'd started working on the Royal Sovereign systems sooner or put more time into it earlier?"

Gently, Sigurdsson placed a hand on the shorter woman's shoulder and offered her a sympathetic smile.

"Congratulations, you've made it to the guilt phase of your leadership role," she said. "Here's the thing: no one person was ever going to prevent this clusterfuck. Honestly, we're an insanely fractured species. We hate each other over the smallest differences, we fight wars over whose invisible friend is the one true invisible friend -- hell, we fight over who is worshipping the same invisible friend in the right way. The point is, we're so goddamned factional and so goddamned stubborn about it that we're an easy mark for invasion. I'm surprised it didn't happen sooner."

She could see in Cagliari's face there was an argument forming, so Sigurdsson held up a blue finger. It still sometimes surprised her that she had icaran hands.

"Unless your fighters or computers or other crazy inventions were going to change human nature and make us all come together and sing around the fucking campfire, you were not going to change what happened."

"I guess," said Cagliari, crossing her arms in what seemed a very teenager way to disagree without verbally disagreeing.

"Don't sulk. We don't allow sulking here," said Sigurdsson. "The ship is called Her Glorious Vengeance, not Her Unshakable Moodiness."

Thankfully, Cagliari laughed.

An alert began to sound and suddenly Gholl was at their side.

"The enemy ship approaches," he said.

With a nod, Cagliari headed off toward the hangar, calling back to Sigurdsson over her shoulder.

"I'll be back before you know it."

Regardless of the situation she faced, Cagliari always felt so relaxed the moment she was raised into the pitch black of the Argentavis. That moment of calm blackness and then the UHUD kicked in and she smiled. That moment was better than any opiod she'd ever tried, and she'd tried most.

"Okay. Time to fly."

She tapped on the holographic display to go through her quick pre-flight check and then cycled up her engines.

"Outlaw One to Outlaw Squadron -- all wings check in."

"Outlaw Ten, Eleven and Twelve confirm ready," said Bozon, checking in for his flight.

"Outlaw Seven, Eight and Nine confirm same," said Daxma.

Glancing at the UHUD, Cagliari saw her own wingmen, Outlaw Two -- Tverdovsky -- and Outlaw Three -- whose name was Jacobs, but whom everyone referred to as Snake -- checking in with their readiness.

"All right," she said. "This is a hit and run, the goal is to disable. They can't see us on LiDAR, but don't get complacent -- we need to get this done before Her Glorious Vengeance takes too much fire."

With that, she gave the launch command and her fighter, with her two wingmen at her side, rocketed out of the udukiin ship and into space. The black wings of her Argentavis spread wide as she accelerated toward the target

"This is what I was born to do," she murmured.

"Attack ATC Castle vessels?" asked the tinny, disembodied voice of Daxma.

"Fly," said Cagliari, chuckling. "Fly, Daxma."

"Understood."

"Adirondack weapon emplacements are active, Outlaw Squadron."

It was Sigurdsson, her voice piped through the direct line from Her Glorious Vengeance to the whole squadron.

As Cagliari watched, the Adirondack launched two missiles, both at Her Glorious Vengeance. A warning shot, no doubt hoping to scare off the udukiin -- an absurd hope, as far as Cags was concerned, but she wasn't going to complain about Vossek using up his ammunition. Besides, it meant that however they'd tracked the Azrael's Tear, the same methods were ineffective against the Argentavis fighter. With the udukiin warship appearing, the ATC Castle ship had given up its pursuit of the Azrael's Tear and Captain Singh was taking full advantage, his pilot steering the pirate ship over and behind Her Glorious Vengeance before rocketing off away from the engagement.

"Mission at least part-way accomplished," murmured Cags.

In Cagliari's estimation, the Adirondack was an ugly ship. It simply had no style. A rounded wedge-shape, the craft had three conical engines positioned at the end of three short, articulated arms. It was almost painfully typical in design, a real-world counterpart of the "rocket ship" look popularized in early science fiction.

But it did have teeth, she had to admit.

She and her flight wheeled to avoid a rail gun round that whizzed safely past its real target -- the udukiin cruiser.

"Outlaw Squadron," she said, the built-in systems of the Argentavis automatically connecting her through to the whole group. "Priority targets as follows -- Blue Flight rail guns; Orange Flight engines; Black Flight, comm relays."

Orange was the flight led by Daxma, while Black belonged to Bozon. Blue, of course, was Cagliari.

"Priority target confirmed Outlaw One," said Daxma.

"Confirmed," said Bozon. "Comm relays targeted."

The three flights split off, each wheeling and diving and swooping toward their targets.

Bozon's group was the first to open fire and Cags could only imagine the confusion aboard the Adirondack as they began to take damage without having seen anyone fire at them. A second later, Cags had a rail gun emplacement in her sights and unloaded a barrage of her own. The hull around the rail gun ruptured and bloomed in a brief fireball and then the Adirondack began listing to one side -- an engine had just been knocked offline thanks to Daxma's flight.

Aboard Her Glorious Vengeance, Sigurdsson stood nervously beside Gholl, hands clasped behind her back and Jaeger, as always, standing stock still and alert at her side. His tail was straight up, the dog clearly sensing her anxiety.

A small shudder ran through the ship.

"Missile impact," said one of the udukiin.

"Negligible damage," said another.

"Enemy ship has taken damage," chimed in a third.

Gholl simply nodded at each update, never taking his eyes from the large, pentagonal viewport in front of which he and Sigurdsson stood, watching the battle unfold.

"She's lost an engine," said Sigurdsson, her fingers twitching nervously. Being an observer rather than a participant in the battle was more difficult than she'd imagined.

"And weaponry," said Gholl, calmly inclining his head.

He was right. Plumes of debris and vented gas erupted from several points on the Adirondack and their rate of fire had dropped to less than half.

Sigurdsson tapped the device on the bulkhead that connected her to the fighters.

"Outlaw One, status report."

"Doing just fine, Freyja," came Cagliari's reply. She sounded like she was smiling. "Looks like we have another engine out and no fire being taken by any Outlaws to this point."

Sigurdsson nodded to herself and hoped it would stay that way.

"Enemy ship has lost a second engine," said an udukiin.

"And have now lost propulsion," said Gholl as the third and final engine on the Adirondack flared in a bright flash and tore itself apart. "I would recommend we have the fighters withdraw, Kaigor Kai Rii. Her Glorious Vengeance can finish this."

"Disable only," she said firmly.

"As you wish."

"Outlaw Squadron," she said, activating the link once more. "Bring the birds back to the nest -- we're about to show ATC Castle how this ship gets its name."

"Understood, Freyja."

After a few moments, Sigurdsson saw the flash of light on black wings as the Outlaws returned to the hangar almost directly below the command deck. She nodded to Gholl, who rubbed his chin and stared at the Adirondack a moment before issuing his order.

"Preliminary barrage," he said. "Fifty percent capacity."

There was no acknowledgement of the order, it was simply and efficiently carried out. The weapon emplacements along the upper parts of Her Glorious Vengeance's X-shaped hull erupted and hundreds of projectiles slammed into the Adirondack. Pieces broke off its hull and something exploded in its nose cone, but the ship remained intact and Sigurdsson couldn't see any venting oxygen.

"Do you wish to speak with them, Kaigor Kai Rii?" asked Gholl.

She thought about it for a moment before shaking her head. Vossek might recognize her voice, which would connect this whole encounter to Radko, which would defeat the purpose of her bringing the udukiin ship out as the interceptor.

"You can speak on my behalf, Gholl."

At a snap of his fingers a channel was opened.

"Human vessel, this is Gholl Kai Rendrek, steward of Her Glorious Vengeance. Respond."

When the reply came, it was Vossek. His voice was tight, but Sigurdsson couldn't tell if it was fear or fury or both.

"Rendrek," he said, making the typical human mistake with udukiin names. "You have launched an unprovoked attack on-"

"Cease speaking, shithead," said Gholl, and Sigurdsson could see the twinkle in his eyes as he said it -- she'd taught him the term specifically for this purpose and the normally stoic Gholl had seemed delighted to employ it. "You violated the Udukiin Priex. You brought violence to the Shattered World. This will be your only warning -- should your vessel approach the Priex again, you will be destroyed."

There was a pause and Sigurdsson had little doubt that Vossek was consulting with someone.

"Rendrek, we were in pursuit of a fugitive, a traitor who-"

"You were in pursuit of the one who returned our Matriarch," said Gholl and it seemed the temperature on the command deck dropped several degrees. "You represent those who stole her from us. That you are not currently being tortured to death is but for the grace and compassion of the Kaigor Kai Rii. Do not waste her compassion."

Gholl glanced up at Sigurdsson.

"For I do not believe it to be limitless."

And he immediately closed the channel.

"Fire again," he said. "Ten percent capacity."

The udukiin cannons peppered the Adirondack again, an exclamation point of sorts on Gholl's statement to Vossek.

"All fighters have returned," said one of the crew.

"Enemy ship is disabled. No activity in engine systems or weapon systems," announced another.

Sigurdsson nodded, staring for a moment at the drifting Adirondack. As long as people like Vossek were around to put their own interests first, humanity would always be an easy mark for invaders. She sighed, then turned to Gholl.

"Take us back to Carncastle Gate, Captain."

The trip was quick and had been quick all around -- intercepting the Adirondack, dealing with it and getting back -- but it still felt like too long. Sigurdsson had paced the deck the entire time and once they'd arrived back at the rendezvous and Outlaw Squadron had returned to the Vimy Ridge, Sigurdsson herself took the first available shuttle over. The udukiin weren't pleased about it, but she took a pair of guards, which allayed their fears somewhat.

"How are we going to do this?" she asked, once she'd dismissed her guards and she and Radko were alone in the crew lounge.

He poured two cups of tea and handed one of them to her.

"Do what?"

"Keep it all together. I was thinking about it while we were disabling the Adirondack," said Sigurdsson, blowing on her tea to cool it. "People like Vossek are never going to be on board with the kind of cooperation we're trying to build here. And there are a lot more people like Vossek than I think either of us wants to admit."

"And some of them are really highly placed," said Radko, nodding and sipping. "But we did get Zhang on board and he's one of the last people I'd have expected to be allied with."

"True. Still, we're so entrenched in our factionalism... holy fuck Finn, I'm starting to talk like you."

"Is that a bad thing?" he asked with a chuckle.

"No, it's just I'm supposed to be the blunt instrument of this arrangement and you're the philosopher."

"Philosopher, huh?"

"You know what I mean. You're the one who's all about setting aside differences for the greater good. I guess you're rubbing off on me more than I thought."

"Or maybe being Kaigor Kai Rii is bringing out your sense of purpose?"

Sigurdsson paused mid-sip and looked at him over the rim of her mug. The thought hadn't occurred to her that by taking on this role with the udukiin, her perspective on the war would change. She had always been responsible for the lives of others, but always in small, manageable groups and usually, aside from a handful of soldiers directly under her command, her responsibility was for the protection of the group. Now she wielded the kind of power and influence she'd never even dreamed of. She could send an entire species to war.

Their lives were in her hands.

Their future was in her hands.

Maybe Radko was right and she'd subconsciously adapted to her new role. She briefly wondered if her passenger was altering her thought processes at all, but she immediately felt -- both on her own and through a feeling that came from the Matriarch -- that such alteration of minds was beyond her capabilities even if it had been within her desires. Which Sigurdsson felt fairly strongly it was not.

"I do feel the weight of responsibility, that's for sure," she said finally. "Seriously Finn, on a scale of one to ten how fucking crazy are we?"

"I'd say a solid thirteen."

"That's about what I was thinking," she said, downing the rest of her tea in a single gulp, then leaning on the bulkhead beside Radko. "We've talked a lot about me, given... given I'm now an alien warlord. What about you? How are you holding up with all this shit?"

"I'm fine," Radko said, taking another sip of tea.

"Yeah, my bullshit detector is going haywire."

He forced a smile and set his mug on the nearby table and when he leaned back against the bulkhead, he shifted over slightly so his shoulder pressed against hers.

"I don't know. That's the honest truth, Freyja -- I don't know. I haven't had time to be anything but Finn Radko, CO of the Vimy Ridge. I haven't had time. And I just lied to you, because I know I'm not holding up well."

Frowning, Sigurdsson rested her head against his, but didn't speak.

"I'm terrified this isn't going to work. That I'm just going to lead all these ships, all these resources -- all these amazing, courageous people -- into oblivion and in doing so kneecap any future defense against the enemy," he said. "I'm worried about what's happening on Thor's Hammer. Are those assholes going to just keep picking off my friends one by one with these sham trials? And if they run out of friends are they just going to start rounding up people who I had lunch with once, or talked to at a party?"

He felt her fingers intertwine with his and he smiled slightly, squeezing gently.

"And there's Cortez. Anna Cortez who deserved a nice, long, happy life. I was already blaming myself for her cancer and now she's been executed for no other reason than that she supported me. How do I even start to process that?"

"I wish I had some answers for you. All I really have for you is that I believe in this mission. I believe that this is our best shot at breaking the ril-galas hold on us. And I believe in you," she said, squeezing his hand. "Not just Commander Radko the Invincible, but Finn. The guy. The guy who was there for me at Fort Hathaway when I needed a friendly voice. The guy who, when he couldn't come help me himself, sent me enough troops and gear to get us through. The guy who barely missed a beat when I showed up with alien arms."

They both chuckled at that.

"That guy?" she said. "Fuck, man. That's the guy I'm following, not this Commander Radko asshole people treat like a superhero."

"You're such a sweet-talker," he said, laughing.

"I'm a leader now, I need to be all speechy and shit," she said. "But I'm also being serious. No one is here at Carncastle Gate out of boredom, we're all here because we know your plan and recognize it as a good plan. And all of you -- the Vimy Ridge, Outlaw Squadron, the three icaran ships, the Tianlong -- thought you had a good enough chance at victory to justify the risk before you added two udukiin cruisers to the team."

She stood up straight, stretched, then turned to face Radko, putting a hand on each shoulder.

"And while I may be biased," she said. "I think we're a pretty major addition."

"You'll get no argument from me," he said. "And thank you. Really. It's just... it's nice to have someone I can talk to. Someone I can talk to as Finn, not as that asshole superhero guy."

DAVID WHALE

"I'm here for whatever you need."

The clothes were slightly baggy, but not overly so. The shoes had been a problem, but since Ransom had worn combat boots anyway, she just kept her own footwear. Her old shirt had become the fabric Hunter had used to bind the girl's chest to help hide her true identity and a sharp hunting knife owned by Grieve had made short work of Ransom's hair.

What had once been a mass of red curls was now short and boyish and, if Hunter allowed herself to admit it, far more even and stylish than any of them had expected.

She held out a small mirror for Ransom to see her new look and the girl smiled at her reflection.

"I should have cut my hair a long time ago," she said. "This looks really good. Maybe you should open a salon when this is all over?"

"Maybe," said Hunter.

Presenting her to the rest of the group, they were suitably impressed -- even more so when they watched how she'd changed her walk. All of it combined with her uncanny ability to mimic the late Prince's voice made even the most skeptical among them feel that the plan had a solid chance of working.

It was still a reckless plan with so many potential pitfalls, but the truth was they didn't have anything better. The people needed a symbol and with a symbol not presenting itself, they needed to manufacture one. Lie to the people for their own benefit. Governments had been employing that technique for centuries, even when nothing terribly important was on the line -- who could possibly blame Hunter for trying it when there was so much at stake?

As the group set out, the others gave Ransom and Hobson a wide berth as the soldier gave the pretend Prince information on the background of the boy she would be replacing, information she could use to improve her mimicry.

Hunter found Grieve, mostly concealed by bushes, calling for a halt. She silently passed along the hand signal for the others to stop and take cover and she and Hobson were up with Grieve in a flash.

"What do you see?" asked Hobson.

"There," said the old soldier, pointing through a stand of trees to where the remains of a burned out village stood.

On the far side of the ruined village stood the now-familiar tumorous, purple-tinged mass that was a stage one processing plant for the ril-galas. The structure in which their human victims were herded, executed and skinned before being sent off to the larger plants for rendering. It looked like a scab on the landscape, standing between the village and the coast. Going around it would cost them travel time, but...

Grieve, looking through his binoculars, made a low growling sound in his throat.

"Bastards," he said, then handed the glasses roughly to Hunter.

It took her a moment to focus them properly and another to find what Grieve had been seeing.

Four ril-galas foot soldiers. At least two stalkers.

And a group of around thirty humans, sitting sullenly in a makeshift pen, under guard.

As she watched, two of the ril-galas forced ten of the prisoners to stand and marched them into the structure.

"We can stop this," she said, handing the binoculars to Hobson, who looked and swore under his breath.

"We certainly have to try," he said.

Hunter waived the rest of the group forward and explained the situation. They all took turns viewing the situation.

"There's only eight of us left," said Wiggins. "How much of a chance do we stand?"

"Does it matter?" asked Hunter.

"What does that mean? Of course it matters."

"I think what she means," said Hutch. "Is if we just walk away to save our own skins, are we really any better than those shits who tried to sell us out?"

The question was met with silence and several members of the group staring at their shoes.

"I was an anarchist," he said. "Before all this happened -- that's what I was. I made car bombs. Pipe bombs. Honestly thought I still was an anarchist up until the other day, when I saw what real anarchy does to people. Turns them on each other. Makes them sell out their species to save their own hides. Now I don't know what the fuck I believe."

He paused, popped the magazine out of his shotgun and began replenishing its shells from the pouch on his belt.

"Except that I'm not letting these alien twats get away with turning those folks into meat."

"So we're just going to run into a ril-galas base and what? Start shooting?"

"Stay here if you're scared."

"That's enough, both of you," said Ransom, quietly but firmly. "I agree with Hutch, we can't just walk away from this."

"I have no intention of doing so," said Hunter. "Those of you who don't want to be part of this, you'll need to find a path around. We will, hopefully, see you back at Edinburgh Castle."

Hunter was relieved that in the end, only Wiggins and Fairbairn left. Her preference would have been to have all members of the group involved, but she could accept losing two -- it was better than the alternative. Though Pradesh seemed to be equal parts furious and embarrassed that her long-time partner Fairbairn would leave at such a time.

Grieve and Ransom were the forward scouts as usual, though at first Hunter had been hesitant to put Ransom out there. She was, for all intents and purposes, now the heir to the throne of Britain and they had invested quite a bit in the charade. However, having their best scouts in play would increase the odds of their survival, so Hunter had relented. They had split into two groups: one led by Corporal Hobson, with Grieve acting as scout and sniper; one led by Hunter, with Ransom as scout and quasi-sniper with her bow.

Darting forward at the sound of one of Ransom's eerily accurate birdcalls, Hunter took cover behind a four foot tall section of blackened brick wall. A sign, twisted and equally blackened, lay on the ground by her feet. It was advertising some kind of twelve year old whiskey and she briefly wondered if it was the brand that Radko liked.

"Two foot soldiers just came out," said Hutch as he slid in beside her, his shotgun at the ready. "Not sure if it's the same two we saw go in or if there are more inside."

Nodding, Hunter double-checked her ammunition situation. It was the same as it had been when she'd last checked, thirty seconds prior. Bringing the 33A1 rifle to her shoulder, she peeked around the edge of the wall. From their position, she could just see the edge of the pen and a handful of people sitting on the grass within, and part of one of the alien guards.

"No sign of the stalkers from this side," she said quietly.

There had been no sign of the stalkers since Hunter and her group had begun their slow creep toward the plant and the fact was gnawing at her. It didn't make sense for the stalkers, the most nimble ril-galas they'd seen to date, to stay inside the plant, so she had to assume they were out on patrol. The question was where?

"I can see Grieve up ahead," said Hutch, pointing toward the far side of town.

She could see him too, carefully picking his way through the rubble. And she saw him signal the all-clear to his half of the group just as Ransom popped up at her side.

"The stalkers are moving around, all through the town," said Ransom. "Like a search grid."

"Do they know we're here?"

Ransom shook her head.

"I saw them go through their captives, like they were doing a count. I think someone made a run for it when the ril-galas weren't looking."

"Good for them," said Hutch.

"Potentially good for us, too," said Hunter. "With the stalkers drawn away, it could make our job significantly easier."

"What about you?" said Hutch, turning to Hunter. "You said you could feel these things."

"Not always. Right now, the panic and terror of those people... it's drowning out everything."

She saw Grieve slowly getting into firing position. His first shot -- and ideally, first kill -- was to be their signal to attack. Rifle pressed firmly to her shoulder, Hunter rocked on the balls of her feet and rested her shoulder against the wall, only a few inches from the corner. She was ready to pounce and she knew from the silence behind her, Hutch was as well. She heard the slight swish as Ransom drew an arrow from her quiver and

Hunter realised that this was probably the last time for a while that Ransom would be herself and not the Prince. If they succeeded in rescuing the prisoners here, this is where the act would begin.

The shot rang out.

One of the ril-galas foot soldiers fell.

Hunter swung out from behind the wall and fired a burst from her assault rifle and Hutch stood up, firing a pair of booming shots from his shotgun.

Gunfire sounded from across the town as Hobson's group opened fire.

Loping out of a ruined church, claws outstretched, a stalker launched itself toward Hutch, but there was a soft twang of a bowstring and the creature was suddenly skidding across the ground, one of Ransom's arrows protruding from its chest.

Ducking back behind the ruined wall, Hunter gritted her teeth as bolts from ril-galas cannons hammered into the broken pavement to her right, fragments showering over her. As she swung out to return fire, her eyes widened. The foot soldier was less than a metre in front of her. Too close to use its arm cannons as anything but a blunt instrument, the creature swung, catching Hunter under the chin and sending her sailing through the air.

She landed, heavily, nearly four metres away, brick fragments biting into her back and no breath in her lungs. She rolled onto her side, gasping without taking in any air. Spat out a mouthful of blood. Saw her attacker approaching, saw its arm cannons begin to glow.

Rifle. Her rifle.

Gone. She'd dropped it when the thing had hit her. Fumbling with her sidearm, she watched the ril-galas soldier point both gun pods directly at her head. She saw the air distort around their barrels -- the telltale sign they were about to fire.

It was okay, she decided. This was fine. She had decided who she was.

She was Hunter, and she was very happy to have found Hunter. Hunter had saved Quon Li Chen, probably even more than Radko had.

And then, suddenly, there was something between her and the ril-galas.

"Not on my watch," said Hutch, punctuating the statement with three quick blasts from his shotgun.

The alien hit the ground, a puff of dust and crushed mortar briefly obscuring it from view while Hutch helped Hunter to her feet.

"You okay?"

"I'm fine," she said, spitting another gobbet of blood onto the ground.

The others had already begun closing in on the plant, and Hunter -- scooping up her lost, and thankfully undamaged, rifle -- followed Hutch to take up position with them.

Two more foot soldiers had come charging out from the plant, but Hobson was well-positioned to take out the first with a double-tap and Hutch, using his powerful shotgun to carve chunks off the other, had it down and dead within seconds.

Ransom, already in character as Arthur, was making her way through the prisoners. A word of encouragement here, a pat on the shoulder there. Letting them know this was real, that they really were now safe. Or as safe as any of them could be in the circumstances. The reality was slow to sink in and as Hunter saw it slowly dawn on people, it almost made her smile.

Almost, but not quite.

"We have to go in," she said, turning toward the plant.

Hutch and Hobson, who were standing with her, both turned in the same direction.

"There may still be some survivors in there," Hobson said, nodding, then popping a fresh magazine into his rifle.

They let Hobson take point, being the only one of the three actually trained in close-quarters combat. Despite the vile exterior, the interior of the plant seemed almost utilitarian and straightforward. Hallways, doors, but little else. It reminded Hunter of the Nightwatch labs on the night she'd escaped. It was quiet and there seemed little security -- after all, who would be crazy enough to try to get inside a place like that? The quasi-peaceful feeling didn't last long.

"There's something up ahead," she whispered. "Not human."

Hobson nodded, the barrel of his rifle never wavering, and Hutch took up better positioning to the left and behind the Corporal. Whatever was ahead of them, one if not both would have shots. Hunter hung back slightly, ready to step in if either faltered, but more than willing to let the two of them, the more experienced firearms users, handle it if possible.

Hobson saw it first and swore, immediately opening fire. A second later, Hutch did the same. By the time Hunter caught site of the enemy, it was already dead, twitching on the floor in a puddle of fluids. Hutch fired another shot into its chest for good measure.

"The fuck is this thing?" he asked.

No one had an answer. If Hunter had to describe it, she'd say it looked like a smaller ril-galas stalker had been cut off at the waist and grafted onto the body of an absurdly large tick and covered in armour. A ril-galas centaur tick. Its semi-translucent abdomen was partially engorged, sticking out from under a dorsal shield. There appeared to be something solid within the abdomen and when Hobson shone his light on it, all three took a step backward.

It showed the shadowy form of a partially-digested human arm.

There was a scuttling sound down the hallway to their left.

"Hunter...," said Hutch, nervousness evident in his voice. "Are you sensing any humans alive in this place?"

Closing her eyes, she reached out, opened her mind like she rarely did. She quickly filtered out Hutch and Hobson and she found other minds. She flinched and her eyes snapped open.

"Yes," she said, a shiver running up her spine. "But not in a state where they'd prefer rescue over death."

The scuttling was now to their right as well. The ticks were trying to surround them.

"We should go," she said quietly. "And quickly."

"Yeah, I agree one hundred per... cent..."

Hutch faltered, his jaw clenching as they all realised at the same moment that the scuttling they'd just heard was directly above them.

Hunter looked up into the eyes of a ril-galas centick, its six legs somehow allowing it to hang from the ceiling above. She tried to raise her rifle, but the thing lashed out with one clawed hand and knocked her 33A1 bouncing and skidding down the corridor. As the creature reached out for her, she heard a boom and its head dissolved in a cloud and with a second boom its torso caved in. It fell to the ground, knocking Hunter over and then Hutch hauled her to her feet, the barrel of his shotgun still smoking.

She looked toward her rifle, but she could see the shadow of another tick down the corridor, so instead she drew her pistol.

"Wait," said Hutch, unslinging his backpack.

"Wait? We don't have time to wait, Hutchings," said Hobson.

"We have time to blow the shit out of this place," Hutch said, pulling out his bomb-making materials. "I'm not leaving here with it still standing. Just keep them off me for sixty seconds."

Raising her pistol, Hunter stood back-to-back with Hobson, each covering one of the two corridors that fed into theirs. She knew from experience that Hutch could assemble an explosive device with remarkable speed, but she still wished they had more people with them, more guns to point at the enemy.

Hobson's rifle barked twice and it was all Hunter could do not to turn around and look, but she kept her eyes on her corridor. Scuttling. A shadow.

An arachnoid leg.

A shoulder and... a torso.

She fired four shots in rapid succession, one catching the thing in the shoulder, the other three slamming square into its chest. It occurred to her that these tick things might not keep their 'pilot' -- the real ril-galas -- in the same place as the others, but they had neither the time nor the opportunity to check. They just needed to put enough bullets into them to make the question irrelevant.

As her target fell, she heard Hobson fire again and again heard scuttling from further down the corridor.

"Hutch...?"

"Almost, Hunter. Almost."

She was about to respond when she felt the wave of his emotions a second before she heard his voice.

"Fuck!"

"What?" asked Hobson, both startled and worried. "What is it, what's wrong?"

"I've got enough teramite here to turn this place into a dust cloud," said Hutch. "But my detonator is damaged. I can't trigger the explosion."

He paused.

"At least not remotely."

"Explain," said Hunter, not taking her eyes off the corridor. There was another shadow there. No, two shadows.

Three.

"Teramite is unstable. I can detonate it with a powerful enough impact. Like a shotgun blast."

"Does your shotgun have enough range to detonate the explosives without taking us with it?"

"Nope."

"What about Grieve's sniper rifle?" asked Hobson.

"We're in a maze of corridors," said Hunter, adjusting her grip on the pistol. "There's no way to do this from a safe distance, is there Hutch?"

"No. There's not."

"All right then," she said, feeling remarkably calm. "Hutch, take my position. Give me the shotgun. I'll bring this place down once you're both clear."

Again, she knew the response before it was said aloud.

"No," said Hutch. "You got us this far, you need to take us the rest of the way. This is where I get off the crazy train."

Hobson tried to say something, but Hutch cut him off.

"This isn't a debate," he said calmly, almost kindly. Almost. Hutch was still Hutch, after all. "I've done some bad shit in my life and I've done some good shit. Most of the good shit has been since these assholes came to Earth and I'm not proud of that fact. Of the fact that it took this to make me into something I could be proud of. So fuck these aliens. I'm going out, but they're coming with me. I can stop this place right here from taking any more lives and all I have to do is die. Not a bad trade."

The feeling struck close to home for Hunter and she felt a lump in her throat.

Hutch was a pain in the ass and they had only seen eye to eye about a third of time, but they had managed to forge a mutual respect and work together for the common good. It was more than many people could say and it was all one could ask for in the times they faced. It had saved many lives, many times over, including their own.

Except for today.

Not trusting herself to speak, Hunter simply nodded and extended her hand to Hutch.

He understood. He said nothing as he shook her hand, just nodded and smiled slightly.

Then Hunter raised her gun toward the corridor again and unclipped one of the flash-bang grenades from her vest.

"On three," said Hobson, his own grenade in hand. "One. Two. Three."

They lobbed their flash-bangs down opposite corridors, fired two quick bursts after them then ran toward the exit. They heard the grenades go off and they heard the squeal of the ril-galas ticks as the grenades blinded and deafened them and then they were outside in the shining sun, stumbling as their eyes adjusted.

"Back!" yelled Hobson. "Everyone back!"

Hunter heard the boom of Hutch's shotgun and then the louder, near-deafening boom of the teramite detonating and then she was flying forward, carried on a concussion wave of hot air as the plant erupted in flames. Landing heavily on her chest, the wind forced from her lungs again, Hunter rolled over to see the mushroom cloud rising from the burning skeleton that was once the tumorous blight of the ril-galas rendering plant. It was gone now, nothing but flame and debris, and so was everything that had been inside it.

Including Hutchings.

Hunter realised she didn't know the man's first name. Or even if Hutchings was his real name.

Pushing herself up to her knees, she sucked in air and tried to get her breathing under control. She could hear voices, but they were indistinct and nonsensical until she heard one right in front of her.

"Hunter," said Ransom-Arthur. "Are you all right? Where's Hutch?"

"He stayed." It was all she could say.

Hands grabbed her under the arms and helped her to her feet -- Hobson, who had recovered much more quickly than she had. Turning back to Ransom, Hunter was about to tell her -- tell everyone -- about Hutch's sacrifice when suddenly a large black blur hammered into Ransom's back, knocking her to the ground.

A ril-galas tick stood over her, raising its claw for the killing blow and Hunter reacted. She didn't think, she didn't plan, she just reacted.

All of her hate, all of her anger, all of her pure, unadulterated rage at the universe, from her time as a test subject of Nightwatch to how she was treated by the Rangers on the Vimy Ridge to her loathing of those humans who would sell out their own species. Her fresh pain at the loss of Hutch. And of course, her abhorrence of the ril-galas themselves. All of it was fired like a missile directly into the alien's mind and it staggered backward as if shot and then collapsed to the ground, twitching, until someone lunged forward and put four bullets into it.

Hunter dropped to her knees again and fell forward, catching herself with one hand while the other cradled her pounding head.

She watched as if in slow motion as a drop of blood splattered on the dirt beside her thumb. And then another. And a third and fourth.

There was sound inside her like rushing water and all she could smell was the coppery scent of her own blood. Through her left eye, the world seemed almost greyscale and a hollow itch formed at the base of her skull.

She'd broken something inside herself, she knew.

Looking up, she saw Ransom rushing to her side and the girl helped her to her feet.

She was broken, but she'd saved Ransom.

Long live the King.

45

On her fourth coffee in three hours, Khaifa was too wired to sleep even though she knew she should. To be fair, she wasn't sure she'd have been able to sleep even if she hadn't been pumped full of caffeine -- the documents spread out before her had her mind spinning. Her meeting with Babacar and Van Der Berg had ended hours ago, but aside from a quick trip to get something to eat, the doctor hadn't left her office. In some twisted way, she didn't want to ever leave her office again -- instead, she just wanted to curl up into a ball under her desk and wait for it all to be over. Wait for the ril-galas to leave, wait for normalcy and sanity to return to humanity.

Of course she knew that was absurd. The ril-galas weren't going to just leave of their own accord, just like normalcy wouldn't miraculously return to the human race.

And neither of those items would be encouraged to happen under the watchful eye of DeFreitas and Upshaw.

It had taken her far longer to realise it than she cared to admit, just how completely the two of them were...

She didn't even know what they were. Power hungry? Probably. Insular? Definitely. But what shocked her the most was how okay they seemed with maintaining the Commonwealth's current status quo. Just maintaining what the Commonwealth had and, of course, strengthening their own grip on it.

Holding up the one particular set of papers that caused her head to spin the most, Khaifa sighed heavily and leaned back in her chair. She noticed as she held the papers that her hand was shaking and tried to blame it on the caffeine, but she had always been a horrible liar.

Khaifa barely glanced up as Ironhorse entered the room.

"Captain," she said.

"Doctor. I brought cookies."

At that, she did look up.

"What?"

"Cookies," he said, setting a small paper bag on her desk. "Just sugar cookies, but they're fresh. There's a woman at the market-place who makes them."

The marketplace was a former storage bay that had, out of necessity, been converted into the bastard love child of an open-air market and a shopping mall.

She opened the bag and the smell that wafted out almost made her mouth water. Pulling out a still-warm cookie, she took a bite and closed her eyes, savouring the sweetness.

"These are amazing," she said around a second bite.

"I know, I ate a whole bag on the way up here," said Ironhorse, without a trace of guilt. "I ran into Van Der Berg while I was down there."

Khaifa finished her cookie and took a sip of coffee to wash it down before looking up at the Captain, raising a brow. No one just 'ran into' Truus Van Der Berg, especially now.

"She did consulting for ATC Castle," he said.

"Yes, I know. She left CSID for the private sector, then came back about a year before the invasion."

He nodded.

"Just seemed odd, you meeting with a former PMC. Given the situation."

"How does the military feel about ATC Castle, Captain Iron-horse?"

The question appeared to catch him off guard and he stared for a moment as she took another cookie.

"I don't understand the question," he said finally. It was a stalling tactic of course and she knew it.

"Yes you do."

"There are some members of the Commonwealth Armed Forces who would prefer a more... distinct separation between our military and a private military contractor," he said carefully. "And there are others who look to ATC Castle as the future."

"The future of the Commonwealth?" she asked, her brow creased in a frown.

"Yeah, but more specifically the military. They have better pay," he admitted. "Better benefits. Gear developed by the company for their operators -- top of the line stuff."

"You almost sound envious, Captain."

The right side of his mouth twitched upward in a half smile.

"I used to talk about Ciara Raze the same way, but it doesn't mean I was going to leave my wife for her."

Khaifa chuckled. Once upon a time, Ciara Raze had been the biggest music star in the Commonwealth and companies had stumbled over each other to hire her for their ad campaigns. She was also an incredible beauty and notorious party girl -- and, if Khaifa remembered correctly, had partied quite a bit with one Kestrel Cagliari. Whether or not the celebrity was still alive, she had no idea. Though she assumed that if she was, someone, somewhere would have gotten word out.

"I didn't know you were married," said Khaifa. "I'd love to talk to your wife sometime."

"So would I. She was a flight attendant aboard the Astral Navigator."

"I'm sorry," said Kaifa, closing her eyes briefly and leaning forward to rest her elbows on her desk.

A luxury starliner, the Astral Navigator was the civilian equivalent of what the HMS Royal Sovereign was to the Commonwealth Navy -- the biggest, most advanced ship in existence. It had also been lost with all hands, the last ship to be destroyed before the ril-galas had set up their blockade around Thor's Hammer. Between passengers and crew, nearly seven thousand lives had been lost.

"It seems like a long time ago," he said.

"It does indeed," she said quietly. "I lost my husband shortly after you lost your wife. He was... killed in action helping Radko."

It was a lie, but a reasonable one, one that wouldn't tarnish Harlan's memory. Wouldn't paint him as the villain, which is something that Radko had been adamant about despite the circumstances of her estranged husband's death.

Ironhorse just nodded.

"Why do you ask?"

"Pardon?"

"About the military. Their feelings toward ATC Castle."

Taking a deep breath, Khaifa shuffled some of the papers on her desk.

"Captain, do you know my official title here?"

"Minister of Health?"

"Director of the Ministry of Health, actually," she said. "It's an important distinction, because to be a Minister I would have had to be elected."

"But as Director, you were appointed," he said nodding. "Something that can't be done with a Deputy PM?"

"Yes. There's also this..."

She held up a paper that had several sections highlighted and she noticed again that her hand was shaking.

"This is a page from the Commonwealth Constitution," she said. "Section four, subsection G, clause seventeen. Constitutional scholars call it the 'Questionable Health' clause."

Clearing her throat, she began to read the highlighted excerpt.

"Should it be determined that the Prime Minister of the Commonwealth, due to physical or mental malady or disorder, be no longer fit to carry out the duties of his or her office, the office of the Director of the Ministry of Health shall serve notice and, with documentation of their findings, apply this clause to effect the temporary removal of the Prime Minister from office. The duration of said removal shall be for no less than thirty days and shall continue for as long as is medically required."

Ironhorse simply stared at her as she set down the papers and looked him in the eye.

"If the Prime Minister is removed, the Deputy Prime Minister would assume the role of PM for the duration of his removal."

"But we've already established that the appointment of Upshaw is unconstitutional," said the Captain.

"And so legally, we don't have a Deputy PM," she said, nodding slowly.

"So... who takes over...?

"The most senior member of the Royal family, believe it or not."

Frowning, Ironhorse shook his head.

"Well we don't exactly have a Royal hanging around, so is there a next best thing clause?"

Khaifa inhaled deeply and breathed out slowly. She was no longer meeting Ironhorse's gaze, instead focusing intently on the pages in front of her. When she spoke, reading again from the pages, her voice was unusually quiet, unusually devoid of emotion. Or perhaps it wasn't devoid of emotion -- perhaps it showed nervousness? Fear?

"If no member of the Royal family is able to assume the role, the role of Prime Minister of the Commonwealth shall be filled by the Director of the Ministry of Health. The Director shall assume the duties of Prime Minister only until such time as the Prime Minister, Deputy Prime Minister or a member of the Royal family is able to assume the role."

Though el Bahari had been expecting another update on the Thor's Hammer situation, she had not expected it to be so detailed. Or so shocking.

"And she was reading directly from the Constitution?"

"Yes," said Ironhorse. "I got a copy and confirmed for myself. Section four, subsection G, clause seventeen, if you want to see for yourself."

"No, it's fine," she said, leaning her head against the bulkhead. "I believe you."

Taking a deep breath, el Bahari suddenly found her quarters far too small, the Vimy Ridge much too far away from Thor's Hammer.

"What do you want to do?" asked Ironhorse after a few moments of silence.

"We knew this was a possibility and we planned for it," she said, closing her eyes.

She didn't say that they hadn't planned for it so soon, but she didn't have to.

"We planned for it, yeah," said Ironhorse. "But we aren't fully prepared for it. Not everything is in place to deal with this right now, Amira."

A soft beep came from her tablet, another connection request on her encrypted channels. Upshaw.

"Upshaw is requesting a connection."

"What will you tell her?"

"Nothing," said el Bahari. "She's unstable. If she finds out Khaifa is thinking about invoking the QH clause, she'll round up Khaifa, Babacar and Ven Der Berg and there will be more show trials and executions and then it will be outright civil war."

"You don't think we're headed in that direction already?"

"Not if things can be handled... properly."

"Meaning your way."

"Meaning logically," she said, more sharply than was likely required. "As opposed to being based on paranoia or a need for revenge. I have to go."

She didn't wait for an acknowledgement before terminating the connection and accepting Upshaw's.

"What took you so long?" demanded the Deputy Prime Minister.

"Don't be so fucking stupid," snapped el Bahari. "I'm the XO of a naval vessel, I'm not at your beck and call. That's what you have Vossek for. What do you want?"

There was silence for a moment and it made el Bahari feel good to imagine Upshaw stewing at her comments, looking for a way to dispute them and realising that the naval officer was correct.

"Vossek has reported back from the moon of Casandra Hajek," said Upshaw, her voice tight. "You're not there."

"We've been delayed. We ran into a ril-galas ship, a type we'd never seen before. One of our engines was damaged," she said, making it up as she went. "Repairs have only just now been completed -- we've been back on course for less than twenty minutes."

Every so often, it amazed el Bahari how fluid her lies had become. How well one could flow into the other and how she somehow managed to keep them all straight.

"We've now lost contact with the Adirondack," said Upshaw. "They were in pursuit of the pirate ship that raided Duster's Range, the Azathoth's Tongue-"

"Azrael's Tear."

"Its name is inconsequential."

"It successfully raided one of your most secure R&D facilities. I'd hardly call that inconsequential."

She shouldn't have said it, but she found she rather enjoyed baiting the woman.

"Vossek pursued them as they left Hajek," said Upshaw, biting off each word as if the conversation were now causing her physical pain. "He reported an udukiin vessel entering the area and we have had no contact since."

"Then he's probably dead."

"Your flippancy is becoming-"

"It is not flippancy, Bianca -- it is realism. Vossek ordered the Adirondack into the Udukiin Priex, knowing full well how they react to such incursions. Not only that, but he began firing his weapons in close proximity to the udukiin home world. The only surprising thing, if the udukiin have tracked down and destroyed the Adirondack, would be that it took them this long to do it. What Vossek did was at best fatally irresponsible and at worst an act of war."

Again, el Bahari closed the connection without waiting for a response. If Upshaw complained, she could realistically claim that she had been called away to tend to her duties. It was partially true -- Radko had arranged a substantial strategy meeting to incorporate their newly acquired assets into the attack plan against the Hornet's Nest.

As was expected, Admiral Zhang was the last to arrive. His security team had had a difficult time understanding that the

Vimy Ridge was not, in fact, a hostile ship anymore and that when Radko personally guaranteed Zhang's safety, he'd meant it. But the Admiral did finally arrive, two armed marines at his side, and took his place among the rest of the senior officers clustered around the sand table.

To Radko's immediate right stood Sigurdsson, Gholl Kai Rendrek and Jaeger at her side, the Admiral Rhekarr from the Ven Shakara and the commanding officers from the other two icaran ships, Captains Jerynaar and Locavara. Singh stood on his own, glaring at the sand table. El Bahari was next, directly across from Radko and positioned between the icarans and the trio from the Tianlong. Owens stood with her, and Cagliari, as the commander of the air group -- or CAG -- stood to Radko's left.

Hovering above the sand table was a holographic version of the Hornet's Nest.

Radko took a sip of tea as he mentally prepared himself. He couldn't remember what the tea was called -- it was something Zhang had brought over from the Tianlong and had had his assistant prepare for the meeting -- but he was glad to have it. What was it about having a cup of tea that just seemed to make everything easier? Looking around the table, he noticed that he wasn't the only one holding a steaming cup. Sigurdsson and Gholl each had one, as did Captain Locavara of the Ven Vaar, and Lieutenant Commander el Bahari.

"First off," said Radko. "I'd like to thank you all for being here. Every single one of you has taken great risks to stand where you are now and you've put aside many years' worth of hostility. The species and political factions represented around this table have given each other a lot of reasons for dislike and mistrust."

He paused and sipped his tea.

"However, that you are all willing to set that aside for the greater good gives me no small measure of hope for the future.

A future in which maybe, just maybe, we can continue to work together instead of creating more reasons to stay apart."

There were a few nods around the table, but no one spoke.

"The Hornet's Nest," said Radko, nodding to the hologram. "We've all agreed that this installation is critical to the ril-galas presence here. It's a base of operations, a deployment centre, a supply depot, and based on our intel reports, it also appears to be a repair facility."

"And as such would be well-defended," said Gholl.

"Very much so," agreed el Bahari. She tapped a command into her tablet and a second group of holograms appeared with the Hornet's Nest, representing ril-galas armada deployment as of the latest reports from Commonwealth Intelligence. "As you can see, there is a substantial ril-galas military presence around the installation."

"But what you can also see," said Radko. "Is that they're as stupid as we are."

There was more than one confused frown at the table.

"Look at their deployment and tell me what you see."

They did and Cagliari was the first to clue in. He had assumed she would be, being a fighter pilot.

"Above and below," she said quietly.

"Exactly. When we fight our naval battles, either human on human or human on icaran, both sides approach the same way. We come in more or less level with each other and start hammering away with our cannons."

"The ril-galas are deploying as if they are ships on a sea," said Gholl.

It was a succinct way of putting it. The enemy ships were deploying from the midsection of the Hornet's Nest and staying largely within that same plane, choking up a straight-on approach but leaving the Hornet's Nest's uppermost and lowermost sections largely undefended -- or, at least, seriously underdefended.

"A rapid approach, either from above or from below may catch them off-guard," said Zhang.

"Both," said Gholl.

"Half of our force attacks from above," said Rhekarr, stroking his chin. "And half from below."

Sigurdsson nodded.

"Make them divide their defense force," she said. "Do we think we'll get any help at all from Thor's Hammer? I mean, if they see us attacking, are they likely to launch any ships to help us, or at least distract some of the enemy?"

El Bahari pursed her lips and let out a small, dissatisfied grunt.

"From the Commonwealth forces, it's possible, but I wouldn't count on it. I feel confident in saying Admiral Mahoney would want to, but there is considerable resistance within the government to -- and forgive me for using the term -- kick the Hornet's Nest," El Bahari said then turned to Zhang. "What of the Soviets?"

"I cannot say," said Zhang. "I no longer have confidence in our leadership's ability to recognize an opportunity."

"The pirates will help," said Singh, slowly. "We are nothing if not acutely aware of when an opportunity to strike has presented itself. Though our firepower certainly cannot match that of the Commonwealth or Soviet navies."

"It's better than nothing," said Radko.

"Regardless of additional help," said Zhang. "The plan, I assume, is to hit with separate forces, one from above and one from below?"

Radko nodded.

"Exactly right, Admiral. The original plan was that Admiral Rhekarr and the Ven Shakara would lead the Leonid Gorshkov and the Azrael's Tear in one prong of the attack and the Vimy Ridge would lead the Ven Vaar and the Vor Rokhaar in the other. Obviously the plan has had to be adjusted a bit."

He entered some data on his tablet which translated to small holographic versions of all their ships popping up above the sand table.

"With our new assets, the groups will be as follows... Admiral Rhekarr will still lead Alpha Group from the Ven Shakara and the Vimy Ridge still leads Beta Group," said Radko. As he continued to lay out the roster of the two group, each ship hologram slid under its commander as he read off the name. "Under Rhekarr, Alpha Group will be comprised of the Vor Rokhaar, the Ven Vaar, and the Tianlong. With the Vimy Ridge will be the Azrael's Tear, Her Glorious Vengeance, and Her Divine Retribution. Outlaw Squadron will be split equally between the Vimy Ridge, Her Glorious Vengeance, the Ven Shakara and the Ven Vaar."

The sand table display abruptly shifted to show the attack plan.

"In the initial attack run, all vessels will drive through to the Hornet's Nest," he said, the sand table displaying the attack in real time as he spoke. "Fighters will launch immediately upon engaging the enemy, but all capital ships will focus on the Hornet's Nest for first and second volley. We need this strike to be immediate and devastating. After that, Admiral Zhang I would like you to redirect the Tianlong to target the ril-galas vessels that will no doubt be trying to take us apart by that point. You're our most maneuverable capital ship, so it makes the most sense. Gholl, with the firepower you have, I would request that Her Glorious Vengeance do the same."

The Soviet and the udukiin both indicated their agreement.

"And what of the Azrael's Tear?" asked Singh.

The question was expected. The Tear was, after all, not sufficiently armoured to withstand sustained conventional weapon barrages from capital ships, let alone the energy beam weapons carried by ril-galas capital ships. But it had other advantages over their enemy.

"The Tear's agility is going to be her greatest asset, Captain," said Radko. "You will be our surgical strike missile boat. Get in, pick your target, fire off some missiles and get out. Repeat as often as you can, do as much damage as you can. The munitions stores of the Vimy Ridge can supply you with as many missiles as you can reasonably carry."

Singh nodded and as he did, Radko noticed el Bahari rubbing her chin deep in thought, her brow more creased than usual by a deep frown.

"Lieutenant Commander el Bahari, if you have a question, now would be the time."

She seemed almost surprised to be asked.

"Yes, Commander," she said, dropping her hand to her side and clearing her scowl. "Not all of us will survive this attack."

No one spoke. They didn't need to -- they all knew this could be their last mission.

"As much as I'm loathe to bring this up... at what point do we retreat, should this go badly?"

"We don't."

El Bahari blinked and stared at him for a moment. Many others did as well, though Radko did notice that Rhekarr and Zhang simply nodded.

"I beg your pardon, Sir?" said Owens.

Radko sighed.

"This is the battle. It's this or it's nothing," he said shrugging. "I'm not trying to be dramatic, but we fight to the bitter end, win or lose, because we have to win."

"What about living to fight another day?" asked el Bahari.

By the way she asked it, Radko knew she already knew the answer. More importantly, he could tell she already agreed with the answer.

"Another day won't happen if we lose here. If we don't take out the Hornet's Nest, we will never be able to break the ril-galas. We will never free Earth. We are a food source to the ril-galas -- how long do you think before they turn their focus from harvesting Earth to finding the last pockets of free humans?"

"And after that, how long before they increase their push into other areas?" said Rhekarr. "They already kill humans and icarans by the thousands every day. It is time to stop this."

"Should any of us reach the point where destruction of our ship is inevitable," said Singh. "That ship itself becomes a powerful weapon."

The assembled commanders nodded.

"Can I make a request?" said Sigurdsson.

Radko turned to her, a small smile on his face.

"Of course."

"I'd like for Her Glorious Vengeance to be our vanguard," she said, with Gholl beside her, nodding. "The udukiin have history with the ril-galas and when our battle group shows up, I want those fuckers to understand the shitstorm that's about to hit them."

"Psychological warfare," said Rhekarr approvingly. "They will very suddenly and very clearly realise that they are no longer fighting the war they thought they were fighting."

Placing a hand on Sigurdsson's shoulder, Radko nodded.

"Request granted. Let's make them shit their pants."

47

Edinburgh Castle loomed up from the horizon like the fortress it was and it was more beautiful than Hunter had ever imagined it could be.

It was safety, it was success, it was food and dry beds and it was medical supplies she felt she probably needed fairly badly. Her nose had stopped bleeding after half an hour, but between her mouth and her nose she'd lost enough blood to feel light-headed. Her eyes were still taking too long to focus on things and it seemed like one was almost seeing in greyscale.

But worse was what was happening in her mind. Under normal circumstances -- normal for Hunter or Quon Li-Chen, at least -- there was always a low-level buzz in the back of her brain, the everyday thoughts of those around her, kept to a minor annoyance by the fences and walls and locked gates she'd built in her mind, the only way to retain her sanity. Now it seemed the fences had been thrown down, the locked gates left open and the walls crumbling. The dull buzz was now a continual roar as random spikes of thought drove through her mind, from everywhere and everyone.

Exhaustion from everyone.

Relief and hope from those they'd rescued.

Nervousness from Ransom.

A feeling of failure from Hobson about which she badly wanted to tell him to fucking stop, but she could barely think through the driving rain of everyone else's thoughts.

And there was fear and hostility from those manning the walls of the Castle, seeing a group approaching but not yet knowing who or why.

But the worst, by far, was the staggering number of suicidal thoughts that pounded into her like bullets from every direction. She was crying before she realised it, dropping to her knees sobbing before she understood why.

So many with so little hope. So many who felt it was better to die by their own hand than to face an uncertain future.

Hunter, who had as a defense mechanism safely locked away her emotions in childhood, was now feeling the emotions of every human around her.

"Hunter," said Ransom, quietly and in her own voice. "You have to get up. You're the one everyone will recognize."

Hunter nodded, but that was all she could manage. Ransom hooked her arm around Hunter's waist and helped her to her feet, supporting her as they began to walk again.

"Thank you," said Hunter, roughly wiping her eyes. It didn't make a difference, the tears wouldn't stop.

"What's going on?" asked Ransom, her voice barely a whisper.

"I can't... block anything," said Hunter, tapping herself on the forehead. "I'm feeling it all. From everyone."

"Oh my god, Hunter... okay. Okay, we can fix this. We can fix this."

She paused, glancing around. Waving over Hobson and Grieve, when Ransom spoke again it was loud and clear and as Prince Arthur.

"I need to help Hunter with something, something that can't wait. Hobson, I need you to make sure everyone gives us space. Grieve, I need you to go on ahead to the Castle gates, let them know who we are and that we'd greatly appreciate them not shooting at us when we get closer."

Grieve and Hobson both nodded, but both also looked at Hunter with doubt and concern.

Though Hunter was staring intently at the ground, she felt their concern as clear as day. It both touched her and made her feel sick.

"My abilities," she said slowly, knowing the soldiers wanted and deserved an explanation. "I can't filter out the noise anymore. I'm feeling it all, hearing it all -- it's like a tornado of thought and emotion inside my head and I can't control it."

Grieve nodded and headed off. Hobson paused for a moment, seeming like he was about to speak, but instead nodded to Hunter and followed Grieve.

"Okay, sit down," said Ransom, leading Hunter to the remains of a car. It had been stripped near bare, but the seats remained. "Look at me."

She did, with some difficulty. Not because she didn't want to, but because her eyes seemed dead set on making their own decisions.

"Can you hear me?" asked Ransom.

"Yes."

"I mean in your head. Can you hear my thoughts, feel what I'm feeling?"

"I can hear everyone and feel everyone."

"Look at me, Hunter," snapped the young woman and Hunter immediately obeyed, not even having realised her attention had drifted.

"I'm looking at you."

"Keep looking into my eyes. What colour are they?"

"What?"

"My eyes. What colour are they?"

Hunter squinted and tried to focus.

"Blue. With... flecks. Flecks of gold? I think gold."

"How am I feeling?"

"...what?"

"Jesus fuck, Hunter, focus! How am I feeling! Tell me how the fuck I'm feeling!"

It was like wading through quicksand, pushing aside all the noise, all the waves of terror and despair, to find one, single person. One grain of sand in a desert. But she did it.

"You're scared. You're scared about taking over the Prince's identity," said Hunter, then paused and felt a tear roll down her cheek. "You're scared for me. For my well-being."

"Yes. What else?"

"What else?"

"Tell me what else I'm feeling."

Closing her eyes for a moment, Hunter swallowed heavily, then again locked eyes with Ransom.

"You're... hopeful. That you can inspire people now, like you couldn't before. And you're... disappointed? In yourself for some reason...," she said, screwing up her face in concentration. "Because you weren't willing to stand up like this before. To lead. But there's also... I don't know..."

"Go on," said Ransom, softly.

Hunter noticed Ransom's eyes welling up.

"I think it's disgust," said Hunter. "At the things you've done. The people you've killed? But not... not disgust for having done it."

The young woman nodded.

"Disgust at how I don't feel the slightest bit of remorse," she said. "Hunter, every time you start to feel overwhelmed, like the dam isn't going to hold back the river any more, I want you to focus on me. Just me."

Hunter shook her head.

"I'm not sure how much control I have any more, Harley. I don't know if... once I get inside your head, I don't know if I can control what I see."

"I don't care," said Ransom. "I don't care what you see. You focus on me, do you understand? No matter where you are, no matter where I am, you reach out and you find me and you focus on my mind until yours is calm. Jesus, Hunter, I'm not asking you, I'm begging you to please do this for me."

They were both crying now.

"Why would you do that for me?"

Unable to restrain herself, Ransom reached out and grabbed Hunter in a fierce hug.

"You believed in me, Hunter, when no one else did. You have no idea how much that means."

In a flash, Hunter was back on the Vimy Ridge. She was Quon Li-Chen again and she was being given a chance at freedom by the ship's frustrating, brave, possibly insane commanding officer. He had believed in her. When no one else did.

She squeezed Ransom a little tighter.

By the time they walked through the Portcullis Gates, the whispers had already started.

Hunter did her best to focus on Ransom, but the waves of emotion hitting her still leaked through. The curiosity, the old feelings of pride in the Monarchy that had been thought extinguished. The hope.

There was hope, just thinking that one of the Royal family had survived.

Hunter had, thankfully, been able to walk into the castle under her own power. Standing tall, confident, head held high,

Ransom walked two paces ahead of her. All eyes were on Ransom.

No, she corrected herself. All eyes were on Prince Arthur.

She watched as Ransom nodded to people, smiled at others, shook the outstretched hands of still others.

Gratitude and hope.

It cascaded through the crowd like dominoes, tumbling one after the other.

Hope.

Hope for the future.

A chant of 'long live the King' started somewhere off to the left and was soon taken up by nearly every voice in the crowd.

Ransom -- no, *Arthur* -- turned back to Hunter and their eyes met.

The chanting grew louder and morphed into something else, another phrase: Pen Draig.

Pendragon.

The once and future King had returned in Britain's hour of greatest need.

Britain could be saved.

The world could be saved.

There was hope.

48

"You need to get back to your ship," said Radko. "We launch the operation in sixty minutes."

They were sitting -- he and Sigurdsson -- on a chesterfield in the rarely used officer's lounge of the Vimy Ridge. The lounge was now little more than additional storage, as the much larger enlisted crew lounge had become the catch-all meeting spot aboard ship. It seemed very few cared for the division between officer and enlisted anymore, which was fine with Radko. It was also fine with Radko that it left the officer's lounge to him and Sigurdsson.

Well, him and Sigurdsson and Jaeger.

The big German Shepherd was curled up on the carpet, snoring softly.

"I know," said Sigurdsson, staring out at the stars and making no move to get up. "I just want to stay here like this forever. I know we can't, I just... I'm ready to stop."

"Me too," he said. "I'd love for us to just curl up in bed and sleep."

"We have something we need to do before we sleep, Finn," she said with a grin.

He laughed.

"Yeah, and we have something else we need to do before we can do either of those things."

Slowly, Sigurdsson stood. As she did so, Jaeger raised his head and Radko marvelled again at how in-tune the dog was to its master. No, he corrected himself, not master. Friend. Companion. Comrade.

"Finn..."

He looked up at her. The tone was... it was the kind that had in the past been used for the stereotypical 'it's not you it's me' conversation.

"About the future. I really don't know what all this means," Sigurdsson said, spreading her arms to indicate her passenger and thus her role with the udukiin. "Long-term, I mean."

Standing, he nodded and put an arm around her as they looked out onto the imposing hull of Her Divine Retribution. He knew exactly what she meant and had thought about it himself. With the death of the Priex Matriarch, Kaigor Kai Rii was the ranking figure in udukiin society. She was for all intents and purposes the empress of the Priex and neither knew for how long. There was a very real possibility that Sigurdsson would be leading the udukiin well beyond this mission to the Hornet's Nest and even beyond -- dare he even consider the possibility -- victory in the war.

"One step at a time," he said gently. "Let's make sure there is a future before we start complicating ours."

She smiled, but there seemed a sadness behind it. Maybe she was doubting there was a future for them, maybe she was thinking it was just too far away -- he didn't know for certain. He wasn't sure what he himself thought, he just knew they had other bridges to cross to make any of it even a possibility.

"You take care of yourself," she said.

She gave him a quick kiss and then left, Jaeger at her heels.

Watching her go, Radko felt something twist in his gut.

That had sounded like a goodbye.

By the time he made his way to the command deck, Radko was in a foul mood and determined to take it out on the ril-galas.

El Bahari's first statement upon his arrival didn't improve his disposition.

"I can guarantee no official assistance from Thor's Hammer," she said.

"Explain."

"My brother-in-law is aboard the station. He's... well-placed to see and hear things about the current disposition of the government. DeFreitas is paranoid, Upshaw is feeding it and neither seems to have plans for any military action beyond further fortification of Thor's Hammer."

"We assumed as much," said Radko, sighing. "I'd hoped for more, but I can't say I'm surprised."

"Sir," she said, lowering her voice. "Are you planning to make good on your threat against ATC Castle?"

"Amira, if we take out the Hornet's Nest and liberate Earth, I won't have to -- they'll implode. Their reputation will be destroyed. Everyone will know them as the people who put corporate interests in the way of saving humanity," he said. "I will be the least of their worries."

Though she seemed like she wanted to say more, el Bahari nodded instead and returned her attention to the sand table.

"Her Glorious Vengeance confirms safe return of Kaigor Kai Rii," said Owens. "Gholl advises they are prepared to depart at your order."

"All three icaran vessels and the Tianlong confirm likewise," added el Bahari.

"And Singh?"

Owens looked up at Radko with a half-smile.

"He's been confirming readiness for about half an hour, asking us what's taking so long."

"Advise the Captain that if my ship were as small as his, I'd have been ready half an hour ago too."

"Yessir, Commander," said Owens, chuckling. Several other command deck crew members stifled laughter or chuckled.

When Radko looked over to el Bahari, she was scowling in his direction.

"Do you really think this is the time for humour?"

To her credit, she said it quietly enough that none of the crew would overhear. No matter what anyone might say about the woman, el Bahari was incredibly aware of what the disposition of command staff could mean for the crew -- and what a devastating effect open dissent between CO and XO could do to morale.

"I can't think of a better time for humour," he said. "Nothing relaxes people like laughter. And we haven't really had much to laugh about lately."

"I can't argue with that."

Stepping up to the sand table, Radko stared at the holograms hovering above it. The display was of their current position -- the gas giant of Carncastle Gate, the Ven Shakara flanked by the Ven Vaar and the Vor Rokhaar. The Tianlong was above the group and the Vimy Ridge was alongside Her Glorious Vengeance and Her Divine Retribution, with the Azrael's Tear directly ahead. The eight ships that represented the entire strength of their little group, this Frankenstein's Monster of a fleet, this resurrection of his dream to create Joint Task Force One. When Radko and Cortez had first begun laying the groundwork for what would morph into the current mission, he had the Vimy Ridge and he had an aging but still formidable Leonid Gorshkov. He'd felt relatively confident that the icarans would contribute a ship, but it wasn't until Admiral Rhekarr had contacted him out of the blue one day that he knew he had the Ven Shakara to add to the task force. That Rhekarr had then convinced two other ICA naval ships to join had been an incredible coup, and having added Cagliari's Starfighters and even Captain Singh and the Azrael's Tear had made JTF1 stronger than Radko had allowed himself to hope. Even Kovalenko, now in such poor health , admitted that the mission was better off with the Tialong than it would have been with the Leonid Gorshkov.

Add to all of that the sudden and unexpected addition of not one but two udukiin dreadnoughts, as he'd learned they called them. His mind still reeled when he thought too long about what had transpired between Sigurdsson and the udukiin, and he badly wanted to sit down with her and hear the long version of the story. But for now, he was just happy to have them as allies and to have their dreadnoughts join the task force.

Joint Task Force One, after nearly two years of talking about it, of trying to convince the Commonwealth that it was necessary, of eventually going behind everyone's back to try to get it done... it was finally a reality.

And it was ready.

"Let's get underway," he said.

As the order was relayed, he felt the thrum of the deck plates change and he dismissed the sand table display, replacing it with the strategic display of the Hornet's Nest.

The two groups stayed together until they reached the Kuiper Belt.

"Alpha Group, this is Vimy Ridge. Good hunting," said Radko.

"And you," said Rhekarr, his disembodied voice floating back over the comm lines.

As the two groups separated, Radko's group -- Beta Group -- reconfigured, with Her Glorious Vengeance taking the lead.

Cagliari, who had been watching tensely from the sidelines, approached the sand table. Outlaw Squadron had already done all of its pre-flight checks and so she had come up to the command deck rather than sit in the hangar and wait.

"I just wanted to thank you again," she said.

"I should be thanking you, Cags," he said, smiling a little. "Outlaw Squadron has already been a tremendous asset. So have you."

She smiled and might even have blushed.

"It's nice to be appreciated. It's also nice to be able to make a difference for a change."

"I understand," he said.

"I know you do."

There was a slightly awkward pause before Cagliari spoke again.

"Don't let shit get in the way."

"Of what?"

"You and Freyja," she said, holding up a hand to stop the response forming on his lips. "I'm serious. We're fighting this war so things like that can happen. So people can stop just surviving and actually live. So when all this is done, you just fucking do it, all right?"

She waited until Radko nodded, then she headed off the command deck toward the hangar.

"She's right," said el Bahari.

"I know she is," said Radko, not caring that the XO had been eavesdropping. "But it's complicated."

"Of course it is. It always is, even when it's two normal people."

"Are you calling us abnormal?"

"She's an udukiin messiah and you're you."

"Commander," called Owens. "Pair of sunfish ahead -- they don't appear to have spotted us yet."

"Pop everything up top," said Radko as he hurried up to the observation dome. A moment later, the secondary sand table flared to life and a mag window appeared on the dome, centred over the two ril-galas scout ships -- the sunfish.

As planned, Her Glorious Vengeance moved out ahead of the Vimy Ridge, and slightly above, making sure it wasn't obstructing the Commonwealth vessel's line of fire.

There was no preamble, no warning shots. The second Her Glorious Vengeance was in weapons range, it unloaded on the sunfish and Her Divine Retribution joined in only seconds later. Super-accelerated flechettes tore into both ril-galas vessels, shredding their hulls and causing ruptures throughout their complicated power distribution systems. Flares, alternating between bright blue and angry orange, briefly burst through the cracks before first one ship then the other blossomed into a spherical fireball.

The Vimy Ridge hadn't needed to fire a single shot.

"A fine reintroduction," said Gholl.

He stood as usual, feet planted, one set of hands clasped behind his back, the other set of arms folded over his barrel chest. Sigurdsson, beside him, found herself nodding.

"A good warm-up for our gunners," she said.

Seeing the dreadnought in action against the Adirondack had been one thing -- it had been a relatively safe target, not powerful enough to really take on Her Glorious Vengeance, and not a target they had any intention of destroying -- but seeing it unleash its full power was incredible. For the first time in a very long time, Sigurdsson felt a little butterfly of hope fluttering in her chest. Hope that there might actually be a future for her after this war; that it might be possible for this war to be won.

"Thank you," she said.

Gholl turned to her, all of his left eyes squinting while his right eyes remained fully open. It was, she had learned, the udukiin equivalent of a raised brow.

"For doing this. For following me. For following Radko."

"You are Kaigor-"

"Yes, I'm Kaigor Kai Rii. I may not have known you very long, Gholl, but you don't strike me as the type to blindly follow," she said.

"Freyja Sigurdsson..."

He'd said it slowly, awkwardly, like the name felt wrong on his tongue.

"What you have done for my people simply by existing as Kaigor Kai Rii is immeasurable. You have given us purpose. You have reminded us of our past and what made the udukiin people great. You need not thank me for anything, Kaigor Kai Rii. Ever."

"It's not a matter of need, Gholl Kai Rendrek. It's a matter of wanting you to know I appreciate it."

He nodded and then a moment later, shook his head and barked out a short laugh.

"I feel I must apologise," he said. "I had always thought humans to be bumbling fools."

"Not all of us," said Sigurdsson. "Just quite a few. But it's okay, I always thought udukiin were psychopaths."

"Not all of us. Just quite a few."

49

Cryptic messages had, from what Khaifa could gather, always been a forte of Truus Van Der Berg.

Something is happening. Charge of the Light Brigade.

She read it again, scribbled as it was on a scrap of napkin.

"What the hell does this mean?"

"She didn't say anything," said Ironhorse. "She just somehow got it into my pocket. Spies, right?"

Frowning, Admiral Mahoney -- who, Khaifa realised, was probably courting disaster by simply being in her office -- took the note and read it again. Slowly, his expression changed, eyes narrowing slightly and high jaw muscles tightening.

"Admiral...?"

"Into the mouth of hell rode the six hundred," he said. "Flashed all their sabres bare, flashed as they turned in air... Charging an army, while all the world wondered."

"I beg your pardon?"

"A poem, Doctor, about a near-hopeless military offensive."

Carefully, Mahoney folded the message and handed it back to Khaifa.

"You'll have to excuse me Doctor," he said as he turned to leave.

"Where are you going, sir?" asked Ironhorse.

The old man smiled slightly.

"I'm not going to sit and wonder."

50

"Hornet's Nest dead ahead!"

Radko just nodded. The statement from Owens had been for everyone else, everyone hunched over their stations or over tablets. Radko was watching with his own eyes as the ril-galas station loomed ever-larger. He glanced at the sand table, which displayed current enemy deployment thanks to information being fed in from Hamelin at the LiDAR network control and supplemented by the other ships in the task force.

The ril-galas had taken notice. The invader armada was redeploying to face the sudden appearance of a Commonwealth frigate and, more alarmingly he was sure, two udukiin dreadnoughts in their midst. The redeployment was bad for Beta Group as it meant they'd be facing stiffer opposition, but it would be a major benefit to Alpha Group.

"Alpha Group starting their attack run," said el Bahari, glancing up at Radko. "The ril-galas were so focused on us that Alpha is nearly on their doorstep."

"Scramble Outlaw Squadron," he said. "And let's try to clear them a path. All batteries forward fire. Relay to the dreadnoughts."

"Forward fire, aye," she said. "Relaying."

"Outlaw Squadron away," said Owens. "Getting damage reports -- nothing major at present."

"Outlaw One to Vimy Ridge."

Cagliari's voice came through crystal clear and Radko made a mental note to ask her, once they had time, to upgrade the older comm systems on the Vimy Ridge with ones like her Argentavis fighters.

"Go ahead, Outlaw One."

"Keep an eye out on your starboard stern, you've got an admirer."

The lack of concern in her voice surprised Radko.

"Confirmed," shouted Hamelin. "But Commander, I'm getting clear readings."

That meant an actual ship, not the semi-organic kind of vessel created by the ril-galas. In the early days, they'd hardly been able to track the invaders on LiDAR at all. It was only through Hamelin's near-obsessive attention and the assistance of a psychic that they'd been able to do it, and though their methods of detection had improved since then, readings for ril-galas vessels were still indistinct.

"Show me," said Radko, heading to the rear of the observation dome.

A mag window popped up for him and he centred it on the approaching ship.

It was large, the size of the Vimy Ridge at least twice over. Taller than it was wide, its hull gleamed white and the six massive rear-mounted engines blazed as it powered through space to catch up to Radko's fleet.

"I'll be damned."

El Bahari was suddenly beside him.

"Radko, isn't that-"

The comm line crackled to life, cutting her off.

"HMS Royal Sovereign to HMCS Vimy Ridge, this is Admiral Phillip Mahoney."

"Admiral," said Radko. "Lovely day for a shakedown cruise."

"Yes, quite. Tell me where you need us, Commander."

Muting the channel for a moment, Radko turned to el Bahari.

"No formal help?"

She just shrugged and he unmuted the comm line.

"Form up with the Vimy Ridge, Admiral," he said. "I'm glad the government came to its senses."

Mahoney snorted.

"You give them too much credit, Commander. You and I may be sharing a cell after this."

"Then let's make sure this is worth it," said Radko.

A glance from el Bahari and it was Radko's turn to shrug. Something was happening on the station, something that went beyond the Cortez situation -- something that would lead Mahoney, ever conservative in his action plans, to launch the Royal Sovereign on his own authority. The help was welcome, but the unknown impetus behind it put an uncomfortable feeling in Radko's gut.

"Something wrong, Commander?"

El Bahari was looking at him with a frown. Not quite concern, but orbiting the same star.

"I don't know," he said, nodding toward the Hornet's Nest, looming ever larger ahead. "Let's cross this bridge before we worry about the next one."

She nodded, then undid the top button of her uniform jacket and withdrew the command chip that hung on a chain around her neck. Her half of the code to activate the Vimy Ridge's nuclear arsenal.

"I believe it's time."

Withdrawing his own key, Radko followed the XO to the sand table console. In unison, they inserted their keys and confirmed the command via retinal scan.

A loud ping sounded throughout the ship, followed by the hollow, automated announcement 'nuclear warheads armed.'

"Prepare for nuclear deployment," said Radko, hearing the order echoed on down the chain of command.

The Hornet's Nest filled his vision now, the mag window rendered unnecessary. Flashes of light bloomed near its crown, where Alpha Group had begun hammering home their assault.

Directly in front of him, the station was untouched.

His own group had been bogged down by the enemy redeployment.

As the whole ship shuddered under a barrage of enemy fire, Radko swore and slammed his fist down on the railing.

"We need to break through," he said through gritted teeth.

"Ramming speed," said el Bahari, looking over to him from where she remained at the sand table.

"What?"

"I read your report on the blockade at Thor's Hammer," she said. "You rammed the ril-galas battleship, using the ERA armour as an offensive weapon. The Royal Sovereign has the same armour, which gives us two very larger battering rams."

He nodded once.

"Do it. Relay to Mahoney."

After waiting for her acknowledgement and confirmation from the Royal Sovereign, Radko opened a fleet-wide channel.

"JTF1, this is Radko. Alpha Group, keep pressing the attack. Beta Group, the Vimy Ridge and Royal Sovereign are about to punch a hole through the enemy line. Take advantage, it won't last long."

He flicked off the main channel and opened a direct line to the Sovereign.

"Ready, Admiral?"

"Yes, but Radko, I want to apologise-"

"You can apologise if we survive, Sir. For now, just fight."

"Understood."

"Ramming speed on my mark. Three... two... one... mark!"

Deckplates thrummed as the ship's engines fired at full power, the Royal Sovereign keeping pace directly to port and slightly above the Vimy Ridge.

"Prepare forward missile batteries. Prepare dual broadsides."

Confirmation of readiness came almost immediately.

"Forward batteries fire at will."

In perfect unison, dozens of missiles silently rocketed outward from both Commonwealth ships, slamming into the ril-galas line, creating a sudden, brief fireball. And just as suddenly, the Commonwealth vessels were there, into the debris, full speed ahead.

Impact.

The entire ship shook and Radko was thrown to the deck, leading heavily on his left knee. The Vimy Ridge echoed with the screaming of stressed metal and the holographic Vimy Ridge on the sand table flashed as the impact activated dozens of ERA plates, sending electrical pulses through whatever they had just hit.

Radko had no idea what type of enemy ship they'd rammed, and he didn't care. He hauled himself to his feet, glanced up to make sure the Sovereign was holding formation and then looked directly to port and smiled.

They were dead centre of the ril-galas line.

"Full broadsides, port and starboard. Now!"

Along the flanks of both the Vimy Ridge and the Royal Sovereign, cannons and rail guns erupted. A first ril-galas battleship blossomed into a short-lived fireball, then a second. An entire wing of enemy fighters flared and disappeared. A sunfish took heavy fire and lost control, plowing into another of the same, and both exploded.

"Another broadside!" said Radko. "Forward batteries, deploy nuclear warheads. Concentrate all fire on the Hornet's Nest!"

The broadsides hammered into the reeling enemy line and as the vibration of the cannons faded and Radko watched the nuclear warheads streak toward the ril-galas station, a dozen black, birdlike shapes shot past the Vimy Ridge, then arced back to begin attacking the enemy fleet's undefended rear.

"Sir," said el Bahari, pointing to the sand table.

The display had shifted to show the Hornet's Nest, the ril-galas deployment, and the positions of all JTF1 vessels.

Nuclear strikes had been registered by both the Vimy Ridge and the Royal Sovereign. And Her Divine Retribution had followed directly behind the Vimy Ridge and was now unloading into the station with its own weaponry while Her Glorious Vengeance tore into the ril-galas line.

"Alpha Group reports the Vor Rokhaar has lost propulsion control," said Owens.

A pair of ril-galas fighters strafed the Vimy Ridge, causing a minor shudder to run through the ship, followed by a sudden jolt. Several crew members staggered.

"Owens?"

"We just lost one of our positional thrusters, Commander," said Owens as the corresponding component on the holographic display blinked red.

"We need to reduce thrust," said el Bahari, tucking an unusual stray lock of hair behind her ear. "We can't maneuver well at this speed without a full set of thrusters."

"The Vor Rokhaar's engine core has ruptured!" said Owens, looking up sharply. "She's gone."

From the very beginning, they had known that some would not survive the mission, that they might lose entire ships, but the reality still hit hard. Radko had led them into battle. The icaran crew had given their lives to his cause. To the liberation of Earth.

"How many nukes do we have left, Amira?"

She quickly scanned the continual stream of data on her tablet.

"Sixteen."

"I want them all fired into that thing," he said, jabbing a finger toward the Hornet's Nest. "And I want all nuclear-capable vessels to do the same."

Nodding once, el Bahari relayed the command, then, suddenly Owens cried out.

"Brace for impact!"

A ril-galas fighter, spinning out of control, slammed into the Vimy Ridge.

An explosion. Fire.

Thrown against the rail, Radko felt a burning pain on the left side of his face and saw flames and heard yelling. The sounds were all muffled.

The hiss as the fire suppression systems kicked in.

Someone, probably Owens, read off status reports. A hull breach directly below the command deck.

Blinking, trying to focus, Radko realised he couldn't see out of his left eye. Putting his hand against the spot, it came away slick with blood. He was dizzy. His vision darkened and he fell to the deck.

"Medic!"

It was el Bahari and she sounded very far away.

"Commander," she said. "Can you hear me?"

"Yes, I can."

Something cold and hot at the same time was pressed against his face and the pain subsided. He felt something else pressed against his left eye and then the medic injected him with something and the pain was almost entirely gone.

He was helped to his feet and he touched the patch over his eye and looked down into the command deck to see el Bahari barking orders to execute his order to launch all remaining nuclear warheads.

"Commander," the medic was saying. "You need to sit down. The damage to your eye-"

"I still have one eye," he heard himself say, but it sounded like it was coming from somewhere else. "I'll be fine."

"You need surgery."

"And do we have a fucking ophthalmologist on this ship?"

"No, sir."

"Exactly. Help me get down from here."

In the minute and a half it had taken for Radko, with the medic's assistance, to get to the main sand table, the warheads from the Vimy Ridge had already found their mark, and volleys from elsewhere among JTF1 were doing the same.

Through his remaining good eye -- possibly his remaining eye period, thought Radko -- he watched the sand table as bright circles bloomed for every hit the Hornet's Nest took.

"It is enough?" he asked quietly.

El Bahari turned to him. The look on her face gave him his answer.

"All missile batteries are to continue targeting the Hornet's Nest," he said, his voice sounding weak even to himself. "All other gunners are to select targets of opportunity."

"Yes, Commander."

"Sir," said a communication technician, whose name Radko was struggling to recall. "Private communication for you from the Tianlong."

"During a battle?" said el Bahari.

Radko tried to shrug. Wasn't sure he succeeded.

"Send it to my tablet," he said, gently making his way to one of the few unmanned stations on the command deck. "Go ahead, Tianlong."

"Radko," said the disembodied voice of Zhang. His voice was tight, his words even more clipped than usual. There was some sort of klaxon sounding in the background. "The Tianlong has been badly damaged. My crew is preparing to abandon ship."

A numbness began to creep over him, and Radko was fairly certain it wasn't just his injury.

"Admiral..."

"Commander, I would request that you divert the Azrael's Tear to pick up our lifeboats."

"Consider it done. We'll make sure you get home safely."

"Not me, Commander. The captain, as they say, goes down with the ship."

Though he probably should have, just out of politeness, Radko didn't argue. He knew, should it come to that, he wouldn't leave the Vimy Ridge.

"Understood."

"Radko... your plan was well-conceived and well-executed. It was our best chance. There is no shame in having taken it, and there is honour in this defeat," said Zhang. "We simply did not have enough firepower. We ran out of nuclear warheads; it's that simple."

Lowering his head, Radko closed his eye. He knew Zhang was right, but that didn't fill the emptiness he now felt. Didn't make this any less of a defeat.

And all because they just ran out of...

He opened his eye. Checked the status of Tianlong.

"Admiral."

"I am still here, for the moment."

"Your ship still has engines online."

There was a slight pause and somehow Radko knew that Zhang had immediately caught his meaning.

"Our reactor," said the Admiral.

"I can't ask you to-."

"You do not need to. It is our best tactical decision -- the Tianlong is no longer a factor in this battle in any other capacity," said Zhang. "So we will become Joint Task Force One's final nuclear warhead."

For a moment, neither man said a word.

"Radko," said Zhang. "Do not let this be wasted. You have... dare I say, opened my eyes to what we need of the future. Old prejudices die hard, my friend. But I pray they die with our generation."

The transmission was closed on Zhang's end before Radko could reply.

He stood, unsteadily, and made his way back to the sand table just as Owens was announcing that the Tianlong's reactor was beginning to overheat.

"And...," he said, glancing up at Radko. "They're repositioning themselves."

"To point toward the Nest," finished Radko. "Owens, order the Azrael's Tear to become Search and Rescue -- the Tianlong has launched lifeboats. And have Cags give them and Zhang cover."

"Zhang is going to ram the station and detonate his reactor," said el Bahari. "Isn't he?"

Radko was fading. He was still bleeding and the loss of blood was starting to get to him. He needed surgery, which he could only get at Thor's Hammer. He managed to nod as he leaned heavily against the sand table.

"Have everyone pull back. And someone help me back up top," he said, pointing to the observation deck.

"Commander, you can't-."

"Help him up there," snapped el Bahari.

He wasn't even sure who it was that followed the order, but he made it up, where there was still a slight smell of smoke and burned plastic. The ugly blob of the Hornet's Nest still filled the space in front of him, explosions still ripping across its surface from the sustained attack of JTF1. The alien station was in bad shape, but not bad enough. All of his task force had been forced to divide their fire between the station and the enemy fleet, if only to keep themselves alive long enough to push through more damage.

Above the Nest, something glinted in the sunlight.

The sleek form of the Tianlong, pointing straight down at the crown of the station.

Hanging in space.

Waiting.

The sword of Damocles.

And then its engines fired, an angry red that could only mean every single safety measure for the ship's reactor had been disengaged. The reactor core was destabilizing; the ship likely already flooded with radiation, its captain either dead or dying as a result.

For a second, the ship simply hung there, and then, like sprinter hearing a starting pistol, it shot forward. The Tianlong's sharp bow drove deep into the Hornet's Nest, the stations quasi-organic hull splintering and fracturing, small explosions rippling outward in a mesmerizing geometric pattern. But the Soviet ship kept going, boring right into the enemy installation until Radko could see nothing of the ship but its engine glow and then-

And then the world went white as the Tianlong's reactor exploded.

When the world returned, the Hornet's Nest had cracked open like an egg straight through from top to bottom. Its top half was a mangled mess, torn open by the explosion.

A vibration rolled through the whole of the Vimy Ridge as the shockwave from the detonation hit. Radko, already slumped against the glass of the dome, felt it through to his bones.

He watched as the two udukiin dreadnaughts -- both still flying, much to his relief -- swooped in and began unleashing their fury on the reeling ril-galas defense fleet.

He watched the Royal Sovereign unleash a broadside.

Saw some of Outlaw Squadron outmaneuver a wing of ril-galas fighters.

Watched secondary explosions tear through what remained of the Hornet's Nest.

Slowly, unsteadily, Radko stood. Made his way to ladder that would take him down to the main command deck, Made it most of the way down, too, before stumbling on the last three rungs and falling to the deck with a thud.

El Bahari, of all people was at his side in a flash.

"What the hell is wrong with you," she said sharply, but quietly.

"That's a very long conversation," he said as she helped him up and then none-too-gently dropped him into a chair with full view of the sand table.

The sand table showing a holographic likeness of the mangled Hornet's Nest.

He looked up and el Bahari was doing something with her face. It wasn't something he'd seen before, it was...

"You're smiling."

"It happens sometimes. You're bleeding. Badly."

"That also happens sometimes."

Holy shit he was light-headed.

"Owens," he said, as clearly as he could. "Due to my injuries, I am placing Lieutenant Commander El Bahari in command of the HMCS Vimy Ridge."

"Understood, Sir," said Owens, who took a moment away from damage reports to smile and wink at Radko.

Narrowing his eye, Radko beckoned el Bahari in closer. With a frown, she did so.

"I'm going to want it back, though."

She smiled again and headed back to the sand table. Back to work.

A tablet sat beside him. He didn't know whose and he didn't care. Picking it up, Radko blinked away the fuzziness creeping into his vision long enough to stab his finger into the right sequence of commands to open a channel to Her Glorious Vengeance.

"Freyja."

"Finn," she said. He could hear the smile in her voice. "Are you okay?"

"Essentially."

"You're a bad liar."

"I'm a great liar. But Freyja," he said, breaking into a smile. "Guess what?"

"We did it. Finn... We did it."

"Yeah," said Radko, his gaze slowly settling on the glowing holographic Hornet's Nest, slowly tearing itself apart.

He raised his fist, palm upward, and slowly extended his middle finger toward it.

"Yeah, we did it."

COMING SOON...

CRY HAVOC

RADKO'S WAR, BOOK THREE

www.ingramcontent.com/pod-product-compliance
Lightning Source LLC
Chambersburg PA
CBHW030646120726
47905CB00001B/84